Queen's Lane

I. Christie

ISBN   0-9744037-9-2

Second Printing 2003

Cover photo by Catherine de Souza
Cover design by Anne M. Clarkson

Published by:
Dare 2 Dream Publishing
A Division of Limitless Corporation
Lexington, South Carolina 29073

Find us on the World Wide Web
http://www.limitlessd2d.net

Printed in the United States of America

IV

Acknowledgments:

Thank you Martha for the many years you've been beta reading my stories and teaching me that too much description loses the reader.

Thank you Frances for checking out the 'wet' scenes to certify them as authentic.

Thank you to one of the most supportive Web-hosts I have ever had the pleasure to exchange work with: Webwarrior on the Athenaeum.

www.xenafiction.net

There are many authors on the Internet who write very good sexual situations that fit. One that stands out, and that is relevant to this particular style, is the woman who writes under the name of penumbra. Thank you for your *Kink Series* that really inspired this story.

J.A. Bard aka I. Christie

VI

This is dedicated to the one person (more if you're lucky) that comes into our lives and inspires us to be and feel sensual. It does not have to be someone we're married to or devoted to, just someone who inspires us to open to the experience.

Chapter 1

Tires squealed, the engine downshifted and the steering wheel pulled powerfully to the right as Susan Nikolas pushed her BMW roaster's speed higher to take the corner into the business parking lot. As expected, her four wheels clung to the slight curve of the drive; **sliding** negligible. The convertible top was down regardless of the frosty morning with the driver's reddened cheeks and the tips of her ears attesting to the fact that driving at high speeds on the freeway in the cold morning air was a nippy experience. She could hear her leather coat squeak as she shifted in her seat. Her gloved hands gripped harder on the steering wheel as her red Beemer leaped forward at the last stretch of the straight road. Small curses were whispered as she angled the car to the center of the road to avoid the recent tree clippings along the corporate building's landscaped entrance. She had a time to beat...her brother's, and tree clippings were not going to...

"Shit!" she hollered as she pumped her breaks at the unexpected detour roadblock. "Whooo," she groaned happily. The detour was to the front entrance which had an even better approach. She made another right turn, and the roadster hugged the driveway as it began its twist, running past the front of the building to the back where the employee's entrance was. Collins, the head of security, was as usual, standing in his knife sharp pleated uniform on the

1

bottom step of the glassed entrance, giving her his best intimidating glare about her driving in too fast. He did it to everyone, including her father, president of Nikolas Corporation.

She rolled Betty Boop, her roadster, into the underground parking lot alongside of the silver jaguar, her father's secretary's car. Cathy's boyfriend knew where to get a deal for 'his' friends. Stepping into the elevator from the parking area, she was immediately engulfed by someone's cologne. If the door had not closed, Susan would have walked back out and used the stairs. When the door opened into the lobby area, she was sure her face was turning colors from holding her breath.

The security and information desk sat right smack dab in the center of the building's lobby and to this area, she headed.

"Morning, Elaine. Someone should air that damn elevator out. Is my father in yet?"

"Good morning, Susan...ahh, Ms. Nikolas. No, Mr. Nikolas isn't here. There was a big snag in the contract with that eastern electronics firm he's trying to buy-out, so he flew out late last night. I've been getting all sorts of complaints about the elevator. If the odor is still there at lunch I think Eduardo is going to go on a search and destroy mission for the culprit. It's his favorite cologne...until now."

Susan made a face at the Ms. Nikolas her father insisted the staff use when addressing her. All family members were to be addressed formally. He did not want a lax environment in the head quarters' office, thinking work would also become lax. It was not as if she was permanent staff or anything. But, that was Daddy.

"Is noon still a good time?" Susan pushed her bag strap back up on her shoulder.

"Yeah. We lost Cindy, but Melody and June from the third floor will join us." She suddenly giggled. "Eric got a new outfit. It shows off both his nice ass-sets," she stressed. "He looks good when he does those punches and kicks. Oh...and Jimmy called in sick," she grinned at Susan. It was a standing bet between some of their friends at whether Jimmy would come into work the day after he returned from a business trip or stay at home.

Elaine paused as she looked at the switchboard. "Jimmy's line. This must be that woman again. She called yesterday after Agnes left. I gave her this time to call back. I thought he would be in."

"Another woman he jilted? I thought he stopped giving out his number here?"

"Not that type of a woman. It's a rancher in Arizona. Jimmy bought a horse for Amy."

"Hmmmhmm. Let me take the call. Jimmy and horses? And here I thought he wouldn't know a foot from a hoof, or thought a horse and stud refers either to a man's sexual proclivities or drugs. Give me a few minutes, and then transfer her to my line."

"Okay, Susan. I'll call Agnes and tell her you're on your way up and get you a cup of java ...strong. You look like you need it!" Elaine's voice called after her as Susan moved to take advantage of the elevator that chose that moment to open.

"John, Mark, Lori, morning to ya all," Susan greeted them as they all traded places. "Don't take the left elevator down unless you want to see how long you can hold your breath," she advised the sales representatives.

"Ohh, gawds. They still haven't aired it?" Mark groaned.

True to Elaine's word, the cup of coffee was sitting on the edge of her desk with a sliced bagel smothered in cream cheese on both halves...and she knew it was also toasted. Just the way she preferred it.

Agnes, if you weren't already Jimmy's secretary, I would hire ya, she hummed as she munched a bite and gulped a mouthful of 'just right' coffee.

Since Susan's father paid her as a contractor, Susan did not have the nice amenities as her brother did, but he shared what he could, including the projects he could not or did not want to do. Susan was hoping by her dependable work ethic and contribution of ideas to the business that was still largely family controlled, her father would relent and waive his steadfast rule that he would no longer hire his daughters as permanent employees.

"Hello, this is Susan Nikolas; whom am I speaking with?

[Walker, from Queen's Lane. We've been trying to get in touch with Jimmy Nikolas for the last week. Perhaps you can relay a message to him. We've been boarding a mare he purchased from the auction up here, and he needs to pick her up. Boarding her indefinitely was not part of the purchase price.]

"Well, Mrs. or Ms. Walker, I'll..."

[If you're going to use a title, it's Doc. He's got two days to move the mare.] Her voice sounded firm and final, though not unfriendly.

"Right. I'll...or what will you do?" It was not out of arrogance she asked, but rather out of an automatic response to the challenge, the tone of her voice. *What can she do, turn it lose? I mean then the humane society steps in, right?*

[Wait a few days and find out, if you're that curious.]

She was curious. "I'll tell him. Does he have your number?"

The woman gave it to her and then hung up. In the background of their conversation Susan could hear the buzzing sound that portable phones gave when the user was moving around or pacing. Susan found it annoying.

Susan called her brother and left a message. Next on her list of to dos was to call the number her Saturday evening date had given her as a contact to a WEB designer. Quickly she tapped out the number while taking another quick sip of her coffee.

4

[Ready, Right and to the Point. Cobley's fencing school.] A brisk voice answered the phone.

The unexpected and familiar voice startled her. *Damnmotherfuckinasshole he gave me his number! Damn asshole.* "Cobley, how unexpected," her voice oozed with sarcasm.

[Susan! Hey, Saturday night was wonderful! Will you marry me?] The voice seemed to have missed her tone of voice.

Susan blinked for a moment. *Marriage? A reputed two nights of bedroom gymnastics and he wants to marry me? Jeeze, get a life Junior.*

"I'm too young, Cobbie. Ask me when I'm in my forties." Now that was a painful thing for her to admit because she had just turned thirty-five, and at one time she had used thirty-five as her time line for marriage.

[No, no. Susan, I'm really serious!]

Was that a whine? "Cobbie, I am too. We have only known each other for less than a month, bonked two times, of which I only remember one, and you want to marry me?! Think about that! Damn-it-to-hell, Cobbie! You also lied to me twice, you fuckin' asshole!" Remembering those two important points had her temper rising. So far, all her past boyfriends and previous dates had that annoying quality of finding it necessary to lie to her, and she had not been able to fathom why. Her girlfriends told her they did not have the same problem. What were the odds for her to be getting them all?

There was silence on the other line. [When can I see ya again?]

"You're not hearing me! You lied to me! There was no group meeting at the bar, was there? And that shit about the phone number – you lied about that too!"

[When are we going out again?] His breath was heavy sounding and each word was enunciated, giving Susan bad feelings about this.

"You lied to me! That's not something to be basing any kind of relationship on, Cobbie, no more than basing it on a fuck! And marriage?! Hell, I don't even know you!"

The phone on the other end was slammed down before she had a chance to do the same.

"Asshole!" She punched in another extension and listened to her associate's voice answer. Damn, she went out with another loser. Her odds were pretty bad, enough to maybe stop while she still had some faith in – what? Her taste in boyfriends was down right horrible – period. Hell, even in high school she ended up with idiots. What was wrong with her?

"Marilyn, this is Susan."

[Hi, babe. So, how did it go with Junior?]

Marilyn was at the bar with her husband and some of his cronies and their wives/girlfriends when Susan came in Saturday night. Susan had mistakenly believed Junior was part of Marilyn's group. That was enough for Marilyn and her husband, a very gallant man reflecting his military school upbringing, to strongly advise Susan not to go anywhere outside of the bar with Junior, but true to the Nikolas' stubborn streak, she had told them since everyone knew who she was going out with, there should be no problem.

"He wants to marry me," Susan told her dejectedly.

[Jeeze, what did you do to him?]

"Listen, I got a favor to ask you," she hopped Marilyn would not ask anymore about the date. Steve, Marilyn's husband had told her that he thought junior was just stringing her along, which she suspected but did not see any harm in going along with it. After all, in a small town where most everyone knows everyone, how much trouble can a girl get into?

"Do you think you can find out the number of whoever designed the WEB page for Cobbley's Electronics?"

[The Maverick they call him. He's on one of the chat rooms every night, giving out advice on WEB stuff. He's their geekazoid, Hon. Steve and he got into geek talk before we left that party about three weeks ago.]

"Shit! Junior bragged that it was Nielson, the one I'm trying to get his phone number to."

[That's the supervisor. That was the bald guy tryin' to goose every bottom near him. Is that what this is all about? You're trying to snag their geek? You should have told me last night. I would have saved you a wasted night. Junior is trouble, Hon. I talked to Helen, my friend that works at the Stop-and-Shop mart. She and her boyfriend, Bobby, stopped in for a few beers and a game of pool 'bout fifteen minutes after you two left. She said he has been away for about ten years. Do you know what that means?]

"Well, that explains why I haven't seen him around. Because he's been away doesn't mean he's been somewhere bad."

[Now you're defending him? Susan honey, you aren't bad looking, you've got money behind you, and you really have promise in the business, but you have the worst luck in picking men to date.]

"Yeah, it seems so. I think for the next Lenten season, I'll give them up."

[You Catholic?]

"Nope. But if my odds don't improve...I'll have to do something."

[Hire one of those dating agencies.]

"Oh, I can just see Daddy's face when he hears of that."

[Honey, if he wanted you married he would have done that for you long ago. You know him, whether you like it or not. I think he hopes you'll stick around just out of bull dog stubbornness to prove him wrong.]

"Ha! He keeps telling me he expects me to leave and get married, or, married and leave."

[Reverse psychology. You are so damn predictably stubborn, if he tells you you can't get something done, he can depend on the fact that you will. It's in your genes, Honey. Just like your Daddy. You might want to try some of that yourself when you want something from him.]

"I don't see that," she returned tight lipped.

[Have you told your father yet about this idea of yours to improve our WEB services?]

"I was going to today. I wanted first to get the names of people that would make it happen, show samples of their work, and then ask for a good employment package to offer them."

[Hmm. You better do it before someone else steals your idea and puts his name on it. Well, let me do instant messaging and see if I can get him.]

For the rest of the morning Susan worked on the presentation, adding the necessary stats and examples, and then E-mailed a copy to her father and cc'd one to Marilyn, whose name she had added as one of the contributors of putting the project together.

After her noon kickboxing session, she headed out to her once-a-week volunteer work at the local shelter. It was her contribution to the community in the name of Nikolas Corporation and unconsciously a connection to her alcoholic cousin that would sometimes stumble in for food and a bed. As children, they had been best friends…in high school they drifted apart…he choosing the wilder bunch of kids to hang out with.

*****

Chapter 2

Three days later Susan emerged from the large meeting room. She was dressed in a silk suit, matching low heels, a minimum of jewelry, and had her short hair fluffed up, compliments of Marilyn's last minute pep talk. She even put on more makeup than she usually wore. Her father had liked the WEB idea and gave her the opportunity to present it to his cronies on the board, who also liked it. However, her father wanted someone else to head it up, someone with more experience, which she was given the task to find.

With mixed emotions, Susan followed her father into his office.

"Yesterday you said I could handle it. It's my idea!" she started when the door closed behind her.

"I was tired and wasn't thinking clearly. Susan, you don't have any skills in setting up WEB sites. Your talent lies in ideas and getting the right people together. Stick with what you do best."

"What if I want to branch out, and change my job description? Daddy! I'm tired of doing the same thing over and over again. I want to grow and explore other things in the business. Why can't I play a bigger part in what I helped put together? I can be an assistant and learn the ropes."

"You want me to be real blunt?"

Susan prepared herself for the worst. When he asked that question, it meant he was tired of arguing and was going to say something painful to end the discussion.

"What?"

"You're at the marriage age. As soon as you get married, you'll have a kid because your biological clock is running out, and then you will quit because I won't hire your husband who is too lazy to find a job on his own, and even if I hired him he wouldn't be worth anywhere near what he's paid. Then I'm stuck with a department you know like the back of your hand and no one else does."

Anger started to shake her frame. This excuse had not been used for a few years...but it did not lessen the hurt. To be compared with her sisters was an affront to her dignity and pride, especially since she took her responsibilities seriously and put in an honest days work. Susan's blue eyes closed to slits as she bit back her reply. Turning on her heel, she left his room, slamming the door behind her. For some obtuse reason, this was her emotional detonation button with her father.

Grabbing her keys and purse, she left her office, resisting the impulse to slam her office door closed. Rather than taking the elevator, she took the stairs down to the basement parking lot, getting some satisfaction from the energy it expended as she tore down the stairs.

*****

Betty Boop's engine was gunned as the shiny red chasse roared around the curling drive, leaving tire marks, and headed recklessly down the road. As the speed built up once on the freeway Susan's anger at her father and his personal insecurities that he kept throwing in her face in one way or another, also built up. She added a few curse words in the direction of her two older siblings that were more than ten years her senior and from her father's first marriage. Her father obviously liked to hold onto grudges.

*****

Sam, her younger brother, found her in the dark, sitting low in her car with her head back,. She was either staring up at the stars or passed out. He didn't know until he saw her light blue lantern like eyes tracking him with her head still tipped back on the seat. She was in the usual place she drove to when she was upset and wanted to think. Earlier she had stopped by to borrow Mutt to stand guard while she listened to the wind blow through the trees in the park without being mugged.

As he neared the car he could smell the strong odor of alcohol. "Little Bop...damn. Come on. Let me drive you home."

"Hmmhmmm. Not leaving Betty Boop here." She tried to shake her head but the movement threatened to send her sore stomach into dry heaves again.

"Okay, right. Hold on," he muttered.

Susan laid her head back on Betty Boop's upholstery and could hear the uneven drum beat of Mutt's tail against the car seat as he stood to greet his beloved master. Susan turned her head to watch the dog dance on the seat as Sam unconsciously stroked his best friend's back.

"Hi, Connie...Yeah, it's Sam. Can you do me a favor?... No, no. I need someone to drive Betty Boop back to Susan's...Yeah. I thought you'd jump at the chance." The loud noise in the background made hearing difficult for Sam.

"And don't you put any bruises on her virgin body!" Susan hollered.

"Hmm...Yeah...Bombed out of her mind." He laughed at whatever was said. "Okay. We'll wait for you at the park."

"Sam, remember when you found Mutt, near the school yard?" She studied her younger brother's profile recognizing their father's mark on the shape of head and firm jaw. His coloring was their mother's.

"I didn't find her near the school yard," he told her leaning against the car and looking up at the night sky.

"Oh. I thought that's what…"

"I only said that because if I told Dad I took it from this guy whose father was beating it up, Dad would have told me to take it to the pound."

"He was only a baby…a little puppy!" she warbled.

"Hmm." Sam leaned down to get nose to nose with his pet and cooed to him. "Yeah, baby. You are just a mutt, but you're my Mutt. Uh, baby?"

"Hmmm. Do you use that tone of voice with your boyfriends, Sam?" she teased.

"I'm the master all right, and I tell them to get on all fours and let's get social," he shot back. "Come on. Hand me your keys. Here they come now. He was just around the corner at Jake's Place."

The jeep rolled into the parking lot and out hopped Connie, rubbing his hands. "Thanks, Tony!" He waved to his ride and turned back to the two figures near the car. "Hi, ya cuz! You don't look so good, Little Bop." Then he grinned and took the keys from Sam. "Betty Boop and I will be fine. Mind if I take her for a spin?"

Connie treated Betty Boop as reverently as any proud and protective owner of a red roadster would, so Susan did not mind him driving it. Though Connie's social life was spent in his favorite bar, he abstained from alcohol, using his father and brother as examples of why he chose nonalcoholic drinks.

"Make sure it's not in a bar parking lot. Those jokers may just throw up all over her in their adoration of her bod."

Sam grinned looking over at Susan who was glumly holding onto her head.

"Leave the keys in Susan's apartment. You're not going home, Susan," he told her firmly, when she looked at him as if to give a feeble argument. "All you'll do is drink some more or wallow in wasted grief. Why do you let Dad get to ya?"

Her cousin Connie shook his head, hearing it many times before, and hopped into the driver's seat without opening the car door. "Later, gators. Oh, hey cuz. Have you heard from Jimmy? The dude was supposed to call me about the horse he bought Amy and I haven't heard from him."

Susan leaned out the car door of Sam's Silver Mercedes. "No. When did he leave?"

"Two days ago. He flew out to Flagstaff. That weenie said he would call when he reached the farm and let me know the ETA of the mare. Amy is so damned excited she's driving her Mom crazy."

"Hmm," Susan put a hand to her head that was spinning. "Okay. Well, let me get my shit together, and I'll go chase him down."

Susan leaned back into the leather upholstery of Sam's car. She knew she was not going to throw up anymore. She had heaved everything up before Sam arrived. Poor Mutt was not cut out to be nursemaid for stupid humans that drank their hurt and anger away.

The ride to Sam's place was quiet. He usually did not play music when he was deep in thought.

"All right, deep thinker, what's on your mind?" Susan asked him as they pulled into his parking spot. His condo was about five or seven minutes down a winding pathway through a miniature park with a stream that could be seen from his front room window. She swung the car door open and slid out. "Whooooa, what happened?" Susan leaned against the side of the car as her world took a sideways tilt.

13

"You're drunk, that's what happened. Come on. The walk will do you good. Come on, Mutt. Get over here. Heel."

Sam guided her to the front room couch, tossed her a pillow to hug, and then went to the bar and fixed something strong that Susan knew was going to sober her up real fast. She shuddered at the remembrance of how awful it tasted.

There was nothing wrong with her memory…it still tasted awful. Susan gagged a few times but finished the concoction managing not to curse.

"All right. Now that that's done, let's find out what's going on with Jimmy." He pulled over his phone and dialed Jimmy's cell number. It rang a few times then an unfamiliar voice answered with some expletives.

Sam had the phone on speaker, and both siblings looked at each other surprised. Whoever it was hung up when they did not respond.

Sam cleared his throat. "Who was that?"

"Some guy."

"I know that!" Sam retorted in an exasperated tone. "Jimmy does not go out with guys. He's afraid someone might think it runs in the family."

Susan knew what he was referring to. In fact, Susan suspected it was one of the reasons Jimmy was so sexually active with women, anxious to prove he was not gay. It was also the reason why their father did not give a job to Sam in the family business. Sam lived on interest he earned on his shares from the company business, his dealing with stocks on the Internet, and the trust payments from their mother who had set up accounts for each of her children before she had succumbed to cancer – or rather killed herself in a one car accident rather than wither away in agony.

"He could have just picked up the phone…but, why would someone else pick up Jimmy's phone? What time is it?"

"Ten forty five." Sam glanced at his Queen Anne's Clock, an antique he had picked up at an online auction.

From memory, Susan dialed Queen's Lane. It rang a few times before it was picked up.

[Queen's Lane Ranch.]

The voice was husky and breathless, distracting Susan for a few moments. Blinking a few times, to refocus, Susan then took a deep breath.

"This is Susan Nikolas, I'm sorry about calling so late, but I was wondering if you can tell me when my brother, Jimmy Nikolas, left your place?"

There was a pause for a moment, and Susan thought she could hear a page being turned. [He hasn't been here for over three weeks.] This was not the same voice as the one she had spoken with earlier in the week, but it had the same clipped tone. This woman was more cautious in her speech. She wondered why.

"Really? He left here two days ago on a flight to Flagstaff." Susan's voice was unsteady as all sorts of thoughts crossed her mind.

[Really,]" the voice returned, indicating that point was no longer of interest to her. [I have not heard from him,] was added when Susan did not say anything as she was trying to think of where else she could go to gather more information.

"What about Doctor Walker?"

[Doc is out of town for a few weeks, but she would have told me if someone contacted her about the pickup of the mare.]

"Did she tell you she talked to me?"

There was a moment of silence. [No. She did not.]

"Well, then. You missed something. Is there a number I can reach her at?" Susan's voice was edgy and impatient.

[She's on a business trip. When she calls in...I'll ask.] The voice was firm.

"Can you write my cell phone number down?"

[Hold on…. go ahead.]

Susan gave her the number and then Sam interrupted and added his number.

[Who are you?] the voice demanded.

"I'm his brother, Sam. Look, we would really appreciate it if you can call us as soon as you can with any information that can lead us to his whereabouts. We really are worried about him.

[When he arrives to pick up the mare…I'll give him your numbers.]

Suddenly it dawned on Susan the woman did not like being on a speakerphone.

"We didn't get your name," she hinted.

[No, you didn't. Good night.]

"How rude!" Sam responded when they heard the click.

"Yeah. Wonder what that was about. Let's try the Internet for available flights to Flagstaff, huh?"

Sam deftly moved through his favorite site for securing airfares. They both cursed at the last flight that would be leaving in forty-five minutes.

"Get a ticket!"

Sam clicked away while Susan made a quick use of the toilet, grabbed her purse and coat near the door, pulling the door open.

"Hey! I'll drive ya! You aren't going to make it on time on foot, Little Bop. Remember you don't have your car."

"Well hurry it up!"

"Let me get this paid…. Okay. Come on, Mutt!"

*****

"You're not going to be all that fresh and nice when you reach your destination," he commented as he wrinkled up his nose while speeding towards the local airfield where she would grab a short flight to the main airport in San Diego.

Susan did not want to think of the booze and throw-up smell that must be clinging to her. Maybe in the plane toilet she could freshen up...or something. She cursed silently to herself, remembering there were no toilet facilities in the small the puddle jumpers.

"Well, if I face dragon lady, maybe it will keep her at bay."

"When you arrive there are always places to buy some cloths, toiletries and the likes."

"Yes, Sam. Like I don't travel enough to know that?" She laid a hand on his arm when she realized she snapped at him. "Sorry. I'm just..."

Sam patted her hand and for the rest of the ride an uneasiness settled between them, both worrying about their missing brother.

He drove around the winding airport driveway and stopped in front of the curb where she jumped out, slamming the door behind her.

"Call me when you arrive. No excuses, Susan!"

Susan nodded.

As she waited to pick up her ticket she checked the times of her connecting flights. From San Diego it was about a two hour flight to Phoenix, giving her fifty-seven minutes to get to her next flight to Flagstaff, making the entire trip about three hours long... provided she was not held up with security...but then, she had nothing but a purse to carry, and she already knew there was nothing sharp in it. It was too small for anything but a wallet stuffed with credit cards.

The small puddle jumper to the main airport was bumpy and thankfully not very long. The rough landing had her eyes opening startled and looking around her disorientated. For some reason her dozing mind was trying to picture what the owner of the husky voice from Queen's Lane looked like. Stretching in the cramped space, she tried to get her blood moving, hoping it would help her brain get focused.

Okay, I need some cloths, toiletries, and something to eat.

As she moved along the walkway to her connecting flight, she weaved past tired passengers that were slowed down with their baggage dragging behind them on wheeled carts.

Once she had her seat she promptly fell asleep not waking until the wheels hit the runway. The shops in Phoenix that she needed were closed, so she found a seat in the area of her last connection and wearily watched passengers until it was her time to board. She was determined that she would not break down and buy a tourist T-shirt.

She had less disembarking travelers to weave through at Flagstaff, but most of them had ski equipment bags and ski board carriers, making her passage more challenging. The only place open was a bar that also served coffee and some snacks. She paid for her coffee and warmed bagel, carrying it to a table near the corridor. Susan liked to people watch, and at this early morning hour there were few people to watch and they all looked too weary to be interesting…except… Her eyes rested momentarily on a tall dark red haired woman who was being handed a dozing child from an equally tall dark haired woman who grabbed a bag and made a dash up the small ramp that led to the waiting planes.

Susan took a third bite of her dry bagel and then washed it down with hazelnut coffee.

All right. Next on my 'to do' list is to call Sam and let him know I'm here.

She tapped in the number rather than locate it in her address book on the cell phone.

[Who's this?]

"Hey, Sam. It's me. Susan...your sister, the last I heard. What's wrong with you?"

[Listen, Susan, Connie's had an accident.]

Susan's heart stopped. She knew it could not be in Betty Boop because Connie was too careful a driver.

"What happened?" Her voice rose slightly, worrying someone hurt him while carjacking Betty Boop.

[About two hours ago, I got a call from Aunt Bea. She said Connie is in the hospital. Someone attacked him inside your apartment.]

"He got attacked in **my** apartment? What was he doing in there?"

[Dropping off your keys, remember? Anyway, he's unconscious, but stable. I don't think anything was stolen but your place has been trashed. The cops won't let me straighten it up until they get more pictures, the insurance company wants to take a look and, jeeze, and so does your asshole apartment manager. What the hell is wrong with him?]

There was a long pregnant pause.

Susan breathed in slowly then exhaled. "He is a real dickhead. If I could, I would change locks and not give him a copy of the key. Listen Sam...I don't have any steady boyfriends ...and I don't take boyfriends home."

Both were thinking of one of Sam's ex-boyfriends that stalked him and trashed his place whenever Sam did something he did not like, like go out with others.

"It's gotta just be some kids in the complex doing some crazy stuff...I...damn! How's Aunt Bea taking it?"

[Not good. She's there at the hospital holding his hand until he comes to...] There was another pause. [Think this has anything to do with Jimmy's disappearance?]

"Sam! You read too many conspiracy books. No I don't! You were better off on the theory of the jealous boyfriend...which there isn't one! Shit! Shit! Shit! The way things are going I wonder if we have some sort of hex on the family."

[Okay, okay. Just a thought. You know, from the peek I got over the cops shoulder...it did look just like what a jealous lover would do, Little Bop. The good news is, your Dragon Lady called back.]

"**My** Dragon Lady? Oh, the voice from Queen's Lane. What did she have to say?" Susan noted a hum started in her body at the memory of the voice that had followed her in her dreams.

[Yep, that's the one. She apologized and she gave me her name, Caitlin McKenzie. Does the name ring a bell, ding-ding?]

"No, who is Caitlin McKenzie?"

A shadow fell over her table and she looked up distracted. The tall redhead wrapped in a warm coat stood near her table. In her arms was a tired child, maybe about four-years old who was also dressed in a thick coat, and who was rubbing her eyes with one hand and clinging onto a ragged bunny in the other.

"That would be me," a familiar low husky voice replied.

[That's...hey. What's going on at your end?] Sam could barely hear the other conversation.

"I...ahh. Can I get back to you, Sam?" Susan decided the voice sounded much better in person. For some reason it sent little chills up her spine changing the earlier sensation the humming had.

[Can it wait for later? I need to get some sleep. I have a business meeting this morning.]

"Right. I'll keep in touch."

Without taking her eyes off the steady dark green ones that were studying her just as thoroughly, Susan slowly folded up her phone and laid it on the table.

"Tauntie?" The tired voice called looking up at the woman in question.

"Yes, honey. We're going home in a minute." Long fingers soothingly stroked the child's back. "It's nice to see you take deadlines seriously, Ms. Nikolas."

Good guess at who I am, Ms. Caitlin McKenzie. "Actually, I'm here to look for my brother, Jimmy, Ms. McKenzie. But, I'll arrange for the mare to be moved. Just give me the necessary information and I'll have her moved as soon as I can."

"As soon as you can...must be a favorite family phrase. So, where are you planning on staying...just in case the mare needs to find her owner?"

"I don't know yet. I thought I would catch up on one of my missed meals of the day, and then I was going to hit the yellow pages. You have any suggestions?"

The redhead continued to study her while the child in her arms lifted a hand to touch the woman's face. "We have lots of room, Tauntie," her little voice piped up helpfully.

Ms. McKenzie shifted the child's weight again. "We do have room. It's probably going to be difficult to find anything this early in the morning or get a ride."

Though Susan could not hear an audible sigh, she thought by the expression on the impassive face, a mental one was made.

Caitlin looked down at the sleepy child then back up at Susan. "You're welcome to spend the night."

Susan nodded. It would take care of some of her problems. And she was tired.

"I would appreciate it." There was a decidedly nice feeling of accomplishment when she accepted the offer; however, she was too tired to pursue the why of it.

"How many bags do you have on the carousel?" The tall redhead nodded toward the exit while moving that way.

"Ahh. None. I left without...picking anything up. I was at my brother's place when I made the reservations and it was one of those now or wait until late tomorrow type of situations." Susan was talking to a retreating back and

21

wondered if the owner of the broad back had heard anything she said.

So, she now had a face with the voice as well as other attributes. Caitlin McKenzie wore her dark red hair long, which was now pulled back into a braid and tucked into her hooded coat. She had malachite eyes that went well with her coloring and freckles...she was tall, and did not hold lengthy conversations.

Susan was not a short woman, but Ms. McKenzie's strides gave her a good idea what it was like to have short legs as she hurried after the woman who moved quickly down the airport's corridors, escalator and out into the cold air. The child's weight did not seem to affect her pace.

"Jeeze!" Susan tried to snuggle further into the coat she was wearing; however, her leather coat stopped above her waist, leaving a lot of her uncovered. Her scant covering made her feel as if she were wearing only a windbreaker. Silently she was cursing herself for not finding out about the weather before leaving. But then, she still would have no luggage. *Damn, I'm going to literally freeze my butt off.*

"The truck isn't far." A white cloud of vapor dispersed from the figure in front of her.

After about ten minutes of the heater and fan in the truck going at top speed Susan could finally feel her fingertips warming up and her toes...they were still there. She looked over at the profile of her hostess. "Nice coincidence for you bein' at the airport. Dropping a friend off?"

The response was the barest of nods.

All right, not a real talker. You already figured that.

Susan looked out the window where it was black with the exception of a few lights from passing vehicles and homes. Her reflection stared back at her. The rumbling of her stomach reminded her that most of her breakfast was left in the park's bushes where she upchucked it along with the booze, and that the snack at the airport did not make up for her missing meals. She sighed and wrapped her arms around her tighter, staring out the passenger's window at nothing. The child's seat that separated her and the driver held a sleeping child whose clutch on her faded pink rabbit was loosening. Susan reached over and gently moved it to the child's chest where sleep deadened arms instinctively twitched around it, reclaiming it and pulling it closer.

*****

A shake from a hand on her shoulder had her waking up startled. A small Spanish looking man nodded to her and gestured to the house. The lights around the compound gave the place the appearance of an old three-storied Victorian house, but she was not up on architecture to know if that was the real style.

At the front door the redhead stood, handing off the sleeping child to a woman who did not look related to the child. Susan blinked and tried to remember what the child had called Caitlin McKenzie.

Susan walked up the steps looking around her and thinking how comfortable the enclosed porch would be during the warmer seasons.

"Ms. Nikolas, the cold is getting in," Ms. McKenzie's voice prodded Susan as she stumbled up the stairs while looking around. In the entrance hall, a firm hand guided her along a long hallway.

"I can walk," she mumbled.

"Good. Let me show you to a room. Our day on the ranch starts early. You are not expected to join us. I have a T-shirt you can sleep in. If you want, Tothito will take your clothes and return them later in the day cleaned. I suggest you take the offer," Ms. McKenzie rattled off briskly.

The woman she mentioned was an older woman who nodded politely at Susan then tilted her wrinkled face toward the redhead.

"You have a message. It's an ASAP."

The redhead nodded and raised an eyebrow at Tothito.

"I will assist her. Go, go." She waved her wrinkled hand. "Come with me." Tothito nodded to Susan and then gestured toward the stairs where she was intending on leading her. Susan was directed to the second room in the hall. Pushing open the door Tothito turned on the light, then dimmed it. Quickly and efficiently the covers to the bed were pulled down.

"The shower and bath tub are in there. Towels are clean. I will bring you something to sleep in."

While peeling off her cloths she decided a shower was in order or she would not want to sleep with herself. The bathroom that adjoined the room was small, and it shared itself with another room. It had fresh towels and a robe hanging on the back of the door.

When Susan had finished her shower she felt in a better frame of mood, but bone tired. Padding into her guest room she spotted a nightgown neatly folded, lying on a pillow. Her cloths were gone.

*****

"So, what did you find, Jose?" Caitlin listened quietly, as her caller gave her a report.

"And he hasn't picked it up? ...Try the slopes; maybe he's a snow enthusiast. ...Yeah. I owe you now." She laughed at the response she got. "Right. I'll tie you up all right; only if your wife takes advantage of you while you're all tied up, don't complain to me." She laughed again. "Pansy. Okay, bye."

She dropped the phone on its antiqued cradle and sighed.

Doc leaves for only three days and trouble raises its ugly head. Maybe Doc read in her tealeaves there was trouble so she took off with the excuse to check on some horses and called **her** to clean up the mess. This was not the season for horse sales, Caitlin grumbled to herself. Mares were usually pregnant, and winter meant poor farms willing to sell some of their precious stock before the winter snows killed them off, Caitlin reminded herself. Doc hated this time of year for that reason and kept in touch with the animal protection societies.

Right. At least she didn't ask me to make the buying trip. Caitlin, you goddamn well know, if she sent you, you'd buy the whole starving herd, or buy feed for the winter. You damn softie.

Caitlin leaned back in the chair and closed her eyes. A soft knock roused her.

"Caitlin, we start feedin' them four leggeds in a bit. Best to dress for it," Tothito warned her.

"Yeah. Did you get our unexpected guest settled?"

"Not unexpected," she corrected her. "She cleaned up and is now walking in dreamtime."

"She smelled like she had a rotten bar night," Caitlin muttered. She shook her head and turned off the light in the study. "Next time you see in those dreams of yours that we're having a visitor let me know. I don't want to have to hear a conversation about me in an airport coming from a perfect stranger," she continued to grumble as she followed Tothito up the stairs to change into work cloths. She did not want to add that she recognized Ms. Susan Nikolas at the airport from a photo and was slow in leaving the airport until she knew where Susan was going to stay.

"Not perfect stranger," Tothito corrected her again.

"I never met her in my life. Believe me, I would have remembered."

"You talked to her," Tothito pointed out, "and ran a background check on her and her family. Doc didn't."

"I like to know who I'm doing business with…and, she's still a stranger in my book," Caitlin returned defensively.

Tothito merely nodded her head. Caitlin knew she did not change her mind on the subject, and if she pursued it, Tothito would tell her a lot of other things on the subject that would be more than what Caitlin wanted to know. Where Doc liked to read tealeaves, Tothito read the stones. And with both women, there was no arguing with them about what they thought they saw in their respective 'do-dads' as Caitlin referred to them when she was disgusted.

*****

Chapter 3

The annoying buzzing of a cell phone had Susan opening one blood shot eye, and then the other. The unfamiliarity of the room had her sitting up struggling to figure out how she ended up in an old style bedroom, in an old-fashioned nightgown, buried under a thick comforter. She did not do nightgowns.

The continued buzzing had her struggling out from under the heavy covers to grab her purse. She unclipped the phone from her handbag strap.

"Yeah," she croaked in her best half-asleep voice, and then cleared her throat.

[Susan?]

For a moment, Susan's mind went blank and then a burn in the pit of her stomach started, which turned into anger. "Junior, how the hell, did you get my cell number?"

[Where are you Susan?] the voice continued, sounding menacing.

She shook her head not believing what she was hearing...or was she imaging it? No. There was something about the voice and it made her nervous. "Junior, I asked you how you got my cell phone number," she repeated firmly, determined not to let this get out of hand.

[You didn't return home last night,] he accused.

"What business is that of yours?" she asked incredulously, and then hung up on him. "Shit!" She did not believe her hanging up on him or her refusals to be taken in by his game would stop him. *Damn, damn, damn. What is it with Sam and me that we attract the real strange ones!?*

Quickly she dialed Sam's number. His answering machine came on. "Sam, you're right about the boyfriend. Only he's not a boyfriend. I think its John Cobley, Jr. Damn...I hope this is not going to be another one of those stalker things. Not a good family trend to continue." She hung up and slammed the phone down on the bed. Picking it back up she dialed her aunt's number and got her older cousin.

"Hi, Kay, this is Susan....Yeah, I heard about Connie. How is he doing? ...Awake? ...Great! Kay it makes me feel real bad because he was attacked in my apartment. It's supposed to be a secured apartment complex ...Yeah...Dad is taking care of it? That's a new one. Why is he interested in me all of a sudden?......"

Susan listened with impatience. Kay was in on all the family gossip. Therefore, she had to listen to how her father loved her, and he was upset that someone had broken into her apartment when the security was supposed to be high quality.

Yada, yada, yada. So if I'm so special, why doesn't he hire me as salaried instead of a contractor, and instead of giving me excuses as to why I should be happy with my present status?

She closed her eyes and decided when she got back, if the weird apartment manager did not throw her out, she would start looking for another place. The owner of the apartments hated scandals as much as her father. When her father got involved in her personal life, she usually was screwed...and it was not a pleasant experience.

"Do you have the number to the hospital? ...No, I don't want to send flowers. I want to talk to Connie...Hold on, let me get something to write on." She rummaged in her purse and then resettled on the bed. "Okay, go."

As soon as she hung up from Kay, her cell phone rang. At this rate, her battery was going to run too low to vibrate.

She hesitated then picked it up. "Hello? ...Junior? Listen you little asshole, if you are responsible for hurting my cousin...Yes, he's my cousin....I don't care if you don't believe me! You damn motherfucker. You hurt my cousin!" *Shit! He doesn't even have the brains to deny it.*

Susan hit the disconnect button and furiously tapped in the number to the hospital. Her light to the battery was telling her it was low. "Room two-twenty-two, please... Auntie Bea!...Hello.....Yeah...I'm really sorry. Is...can I talk to him?...oh....Well, tell him I called....No, I'm out of town. Hey, my phone is dying on me. I'll call later...bye." The phone died somewhere in her conversation. Well, at least she did not have to worry about Junior's calls.

For a moment, she sat thinking. She should have recognized the warning signals ...she had seen them with her brother's former lover. Lying to get what he wanted, possessiveness, and they were not even a couple, jealousy over petty things, and control outside of the bedroom. Her problem was, she had been too drunk and wanted to be fucked ...and she did in more ways than one...again. Damn she could not pick boyfriends! A sudden fear that maybe he passed on some disease had her picking up her cell to dial her doctor for an appointment.

"Damn." She tossed the useless phone on top of her bag and decided another shower would benefit her greatly, and then she needed to find her clothes.

After stepping out of the bathroom towel drying her hair, she found the bed neatly made, and her clothes, including underwear neatly folded on the covers. Grateful she slid into them, liking the fresh smell of laundered cloths.

A disappearing maid, huh? Maybe this is a magical place. Yeah, right. Okay, my stomach says food first. I hope the stories of farm breakfasts being big and hearty are true.

Susan left her purse in her room pulling out her ID and sliding it in her back pocket and then what cash she had in the other. No sense in lugging the purse around.

After wandering around lost, she finally found the kitchen. It was warm and had a nice odor of prepared food. There was a plate of food covered on the table with a note to her.

Before reading the note she flipped the napkin off the plate, already her visions of a large breakfast dimming with the small size of the plate. There were two muffins and that was all. Disappointed Susan read the note.

Ms. Nikolas,
On the table is something light to eat. If that is not enough, there is food in the refrigerator. Help yourself. Coffee is premixed just turn it on.
When chores are done, we'll be back.
C

"Hmmm. Trusting me with the food, huh? I'm so damn hungry if ya got a cow in there I'll eat it all, Ms. Caitlin McKenzie."

A tiny giggle from behind her had her spinning around. The child from the airport was standing in the kitchen doorway with her ragged bunny dangling from her small fist, and dressed in long pants and matching shirt, with the declaration on the front of 'I run the show'.

"Hi. My name's Susan. What's yours?"

"Tiffie."

"Have you eaten yet?"

The child nodded her head.

"Well, I haven't." Susan walked over to the refrigerator and looked back at Tiffie. "Do you think there is a cow in here?"

The little girl giggled again. The refrigerator had lots of food but Susan somehow did not feel right about fixing herself a large breakfast in someone else's place, even if the note told her to. Sighing, she instead focused on the coffee pot that had only to be turned on. After turning it on under the watchful eyes of Tiffie she then shared one of the muffins while she waited for the coffee to finish. She looked at the clock which showed it was almost noon.

"Do you eat lunch here?"

The little head nodded solemnly.

"Have they left you alone?"

The little head shook no.

"You gave someone the slip?"

"Sslp?"

"Never mind." Voices from outside distracted her. When she looked back toward the doorway, the child was gone.

Four bundled up bodies tramped into the kitchen.

"Boy does that coffee smell good!" One of the shorter women groaned, turning into a small room nearby to wash her hands, by the sounds.

The other two bundled figures started to unpeel their coverings back in the small entranceway to the kitchen while the tallest of the group walked by her removing her wrap and coat.

"Did you sleep well, Ms. Nikolas?"

"Yeah. Thanks. I…so can we drop the Ms. Nikolas and try Susan? After all, I've slept under your roof. What name do you go by?" *Oh, bother. That was clumsy. It was just short of a bar come-on.*

Green eyes tracked to hers as her hand continued to move toward the coat rack, which seemed to know exactly where to drop her coat. "Ms. McKenzie will do. We were going to sit down to lunch, would you like to stay or would you like me to drive you back into town now?"

Susan's belly rumbled her choice before she could say anything. Embarrassed she cleared her throat. "I would like to stay for lunch, since you offered…Ms. McKenzie."

"Linda, add another plate, Ms. Nikolas is joining us. I'll be back."

*****

Lunch was a quiet affair, as if they all took their meal seriously, unless it was Susan's presence that caused it. Tiffie did not join them for lunch nor did Tothito.

The drive back into Flagstaff was quiet as well. Ordinarily it would have bothered Susan but she had a lot on her mind. She had two problems but the most important one was trying to locate the whereabouts of her brother.

Ms. McKenzie was kind enough to drop her off at a car rental place. As she was about to step out of the truck she suddenly remembered the horse, another problem. Closing the door against the chill, she turned back to her driver.

"I forgot all about the horse! Look..."

"Two days. If you need a driver, I'll find you one. And Ms. Nikolas, you might want to think about hiring a private investigator to look for your brother."

"Thanks for the extra time. I really appreciate it. And...thanks for letting me spend the night."

The redhead gave a curt nod, taking note that Susan chose to ignore the suggestion of hiring a detective. Some people just did not have the common sense to know when they were out of their element...and by the way Ms. Nikolas was dressed...she was in for a cold if not rude awakening.

Susan ran to the small office that she was hoping had a heater going full blast. Her next stop was going to be a clothing store.

"You sure aren't dressed for the weather," the kid behind the desk remarked as he tore off her copy of a contract, stapled it to her credit card receipt, and then handed her that and the keys.

"Yeah, well, I forgot to check the weather before booking my flight." A thought occurred to her. She pulled out her wallet and flipped to a picture of Jimmy. "I'm looking for my brother, Jimmy Nikolas." She showed him the picture. "He would be looking to rent a horse trailer and truck."

The kid shook his head. "We don't rent the heavy stuff. You should try the yellow pages."

"Thanks, I'll do that...." *after I get some warmer clothes.*

It took her too long to her way of thinking to find her car, when actually it was a few very cold minutes. The car started up after a few turns, and she had the heat switch under her white tipped finger ready to slide it up as soon as the needle registered the car's engine was ready to pump out warmth instead of cold air.

Two hours later she had four days worth of warm clothes, with gloves, underwear, warm boots and a duffel bag to carry them. Now she needed a place to stay so she could get situated and call Sam with a number to reach her. Her cell phone was dead but her pager, which she kept for times like this, was constantly going off. The phone numbers she did not recognize so she did not bother to look for a phone.

Most of the nice hotels were full with skiers, but Marriott's Inn had an opening. It was a small room but the right size for the short amount of time she planned to be there. As she dropped the overnight bag on the baggage chair in her room, her beeper went off again. Glancing at the displayed message she cursed under her breath.

Daddy! Shit. Gotta call home, ET.

She picked up her room phone and could hear the line humming as it reached out to touch someone....

"Hi, Dad....Yeah, I'm in Flagstaff....No, I haven't found him yet. I'm going to start with the yellow pages and look for whoever handles horse trailers. You called missing persons yet?....It's been more than two days, Daddy." *Honestly, his trepidation of a scandal is too much.* "It's not his habit to disappear for over two days without even telling Agnes." *Shit, who else would cover for him...*"How's Connie?" she asked, changing the subject.

Oh, joy. Shit hit the fan.

After the problem with Sam's ex-boyfriend, her father had no patience with his offspring making bad choices of who they associated with and most of all had sexual relations with. Susan got the idea that Daddy's kids were not his favorite people right now.

I think I need to start my own business. She sighed again, holding the phone away from her ear as his voice grew louder. Daddy and John Cobley, Sr. were not golfing buddies, nor any sort of buddy. Secrets in the family were hard to keep. By now, everyone in the family knew Cobley Junior was responsible for Connie being in the hospital and most likely there would be an unofficial posse from the clan looking for him.

Right, right, Daddy. Okay, yada, yada, yada...I wonder what the nightlife is like here. Lots of college kids. Hm. Not nice Susan. Leave those young boys alone. Shit, you better hope the bar cards them.

Finally, her father rang off.

*****

Caitlin held the phone away from her ear as Doc ranted about 'how could so much shit happen', when she had only been gone for four days.

"Well...shit happens...as the sayin' goes," Caitlin drawled, ready to bail and head for her nice quiet woods or a sail out on the ocean...alone.

[This is somebody missing and it's a rich man's somebody.]

"Sooo?"

[Police will be knocking on the damn door! What do you mean so? Hells bells, Caitlin. Well, I found a few nice prospects to add to our brood mares and safe homes for the other horses. Better these people recognize they can't care for their horses before it freezes out here, and it's too late to save them.]

"Right. You're all heart. So, when are ya coming back?"

[I guess I can be back by tomorrow. I'm going to have these mares sent over to the ranch in Tuscy. Until Tendra gets back with her lover, we're too short handed to take on two more horses. How's Tiffany taking her mother's absence?]

"Fine. But she also misses her grandmother. The sooner **you** get back the better. I damn near froze to death throwing out food for the herd. Moreover, mucking stalls is not the type of exercise I would chose for warm ups...besides breathing in horse waste is not healthy. Mother, how can you still like doing this?"

[Hmm. It's in my blood, Lass. So, what did you do with the young woman from Colina?]

"Dropped her off at a car rental place in town."

[Are you sure Tothito heard it right, she has a stalker back home?]

"Tothito does not carry tales." Caitlin pursed her lips. She was not going to mention what she had overheard at the airport when she dropped Tendra off because then Doc will try to get her involved. She was on vacation. She just wanted to get back to her place to take advantage of it.

[Well...Do you think that might have to do with her brother's disappearance?]

"No."

[So, what are you going to do?]

"Let the police handle it, Walker. Mother..." she took a deep breath trying not to let her mother push her buttons, "can you just get your butt back here so when they

35

are knocking on the door I don't have to say you're out of state buyin' horses! Everyone knows this is not the season for horse tradin'."

[They know what I'm doing. Hell, I've purchased horses for most of them over the years. All right, all right. You know...]

"No."

[But...]

"NO!"

There was a heavy sigh on the line. [I don't believe you.]

"I'm not getting involved. This is not my business!"

[Of course it is! They're customers of ours...in a sense. Your father would have already done a background check on the whole family, and had people out checking on the last known whereabouts of the missing kid!]

"Walker, come home, damn it! I want to go to sleep in my own damn bed," Caitlin growled and hung up on her mother. Walker knew her too well, and never missed an opportunity to point out the similarities she and her father had, down to the gestures and verbal pauses. She hated being an easy read to her mother who used it when it fitted with her needs.

******

Chapter 4

Susan was sitting in the bar watching the young kids play their pick-up games and wondering when she had tired of it. Her three times a week at the bar scene had been scaled down gradually to weekly, and then monthly, accompanied by safe and boring sex. It was what she called a mutual masturbation session where two people are horny, and rather than doin' oneself, one has another do it. Still the same feeling. Sore the next day because she had fucked her brains out, but empty inside. She shook her head when the bartender asked if she wanted another.

Not drunk and not really sober, Susan walked unsteadily to her car, more from being tired with an empty stomach than from alcohol. Leaning against the dark car rental and breathing in the cold refreshingly clean night air, she decided a cab would be better. She did not know how to drive in snow, and there was snow and slush everywhere. Looking around carefully in the pitch darkness, she tried to see what was giving her a creepy crawly feeling. This Junior thing was definitely making her edgy.

Shit.

Taking a deep breath, she focused on the silhouettes of the two buildings in the direction she had walked from, with their bright lights declaring they had the best beer and women around. She forgot which one she had stepped out of.

Does it really matter? They all have pay phones and both will have bouncers.

After being carded and paying a cover charge, she stepped into the bar she knew for sure she had not been in. The two phones were taken and there was a line of three people waiting for each so she moved to a table where she could watch the phones. Her eyes rested on two people that were wrapped around each other standing in a line to either the phones or the restrooms. Susan's alcohol slowed brain did not register their genders, only that one wore very little clothing and the other was dressed in black leather pants with a black silk shirt unbuttoned to a sparkling belly button. Her eyes lifted to a young woman that angled towards her table. The woman wore combat boots with a lot of skin showing for the weather outside, and with enough piercings on her body to be a walking advertisement for the business. Once she was close, Susan nearly whistled at the tattoos.

The well decorated woman stopped at her table. "Can I get you something?" she hollered over the music.

"Seven up!" When the woman left, Susan sent a happy note to herself that she had stopped at the three she had set her limit to. Of course, it would help if her stomach was not empty. Worrying about her brother gave her little appetite.

While waiting for a phone to become available and for her drink she turned her attention to the dance floor. The dancers on the floor were dancing a lot more provocative than from where she had just come from.

Oh mmm. This is...oh...boy. Dancing like that can really get a girl in trouble.

*****

"Caitlin, going out?"

"What gave you that clue?"

Linda smiled. "She trying to rope you into something you don't want to do? Let me guess. It's the Nikolas woman and her brother."

"Sometimes Linda, I wish Walker would let people clean up their own messes without askin' me to get involved."

The tall redhead stalked out of her room, down the stairs, and out into the cold night. Linda shook her head as the door closed quietly behind the otherwise noisy Caitlin. The baby was sleeping with her favorite bunny and a big smile on her face from the story she read her, and there was a nice warm bed waiting for her.

****

Caitlin found a parking place in front of HobbsnNobbs and slid out into the cold air. She knew one of the owners, Jonnie, and was hoping she was in. Bracing herself mentally for the meat market scene, she stepped up to the guard at the door. The face was familiar and she received a big grin with a wave at the money and driver's license she was presenting to get in.

Jonnie was at her favorite place, holding court, as Caitlin described it. Jonnie liked the description and coined it. Some of the kids were dressed with little clothing on, however warm socks stuck out of their combat boots, which, if she thought about the weather outside, it made her cold.

"Caitlin!" Jonnie turned to look at the passing barmaid, gave her an order and then turned back to her old friend. "Eleanor said you were back in town. Sit down. Shelly, honey, let Caitlin sit there."

"No, that's okay, Shelly. I can drag another chair over."

Jonnie inspected her friend and decided she was here to talk. Caitlin did not talk much, so it must be a real humdinger. She would give her about four stiff drinks and then ask the kids to give them some privacy. Four should loosen her up just enough so she did not have to listen to her insisting that nothing was wrong, and then get down to what was bugging her. She did not have the patience to wheedle out of Caitlin information if she was not ready. Caitlin was a professional Dom, and Jonnie had never seen anyone get away with manipulating her…except Doc Walker.

By the time Caitlin finished her fourth, Jonnie was busy settling an argument at the pool table. It was as Caitlin was fixin' to down the fifth that she spotted one of her problems stumble into the bar. This was a surprise to her. She had the impression Susan Nikolas was straight…maybe she was bi…or maybe she was lost. A smirk appeared on her face as she watched the woman sit at a table and then stare at two women intertwined in the line to the 'can' before nervously shifting her eyes to the phones.

The line to the phones was not as long as the women's restroom line, but Ms. Nikolas made no motion to move to either. Her blue eyes were like bright lights in the dim lighting of the bar, and they restlessly moved around the room, and then stopped when they caught sight of the dancers. Caitlin glanced towards the dance floor and watched a couple put on a show. Their sensuous dance sent a pleasant tightness to her belly and then to her wet spot that had not been given much attention lately. Clearing her throat, she looked back at Ms. Nikolas. The woman definitely was turned on. Others obviously thought so too, because one of the braver women got up from her table of friends and approached Susan Nicolas' table. After the tenth woman was turned away, Caitlin decided to see what was going on. Ms. Nikolas looked like she really wanted to dance.

Goddess have mercy! What is wrong with you Caitlin? The woman is trouble! Obviously you've had one too many and you've lost your senses.

Caitlin stood in front of Ms. Nikolas' table and while waiting for her to notice her she took that time to watch the woman's eyes devour another couple that was doing more than dirty dancing. From where she was, she could see pants unzipped and an arm half buried in the pants as the two women moved to another rhythm that blended in with the drums.

Drums. Dangerous things, she thought hazily.

Susan felt she was being studied and lifted her gaze to the tall redhead who was silently standing next to her table, looking down at her.

"Oh...hi," she gulped, hoping her flushed face from the thoughts she was having while watching the dancers was not readable in the dim lighting. Susan took a deep breath as she saw whom the towering woman was and what she was wearing. Caitlin McKenzie's hair was pulled back, probably tied behind her head. Her top consisted of a black woven leather vest, which showed off her nice muscular tanned arms and shoulders and probably offered a good view of her cleavage if she should get eye level with her. Susan's eyes got stuck at the v shape of the vest, and then resumed their journey, down black jeans that snugly outlined long legs and ended over a pair of black silver tipped western boots. Half boot, Susan thought. No way to get full boot tops over those jean bottoms.

Ms. Nikolas' voice woke Caitlin out of her haze and she watched the light blue lantern eyes slowly move over her body, liking the feel the gaze did to her stomach.

"Ms. Nikolas. Having a relaxing night?" *That is a hungry look I did not expect to see from her...or for that matter, see her in a place like this. Probably the booze.*

The pale blue eyes returned to Caitlin's for a moment and both women held their breaths as they disengaged their thoughts that threatened to manifest into something incredibly stupid.

41

"Can you call me, Susan?" Susan leaned back in her chair with an abrupt movement, breaking the spell for both, but the rush Susan received from the view seemed to heighten the effect of the three drinks.

"Susan..." Caitlin corrected, "you look like you've had quite a few."

Susan smiled and held up her fingers showing three. "I just came in here to use the phone but...you know, I've never seen a phone line so long before, have you?"

Caitlin sighed and pulled out a chair. Should she tell her the long line was to the restroom?

"What do you need the phone for?"

"I need a ride home."

Caitlin's eyebrow rose. "California?"

"Oh, no! To the hotel." She giggled at the thought of asking Caitlin for a lift that far and her saying yes.

What a ride that would be, two thoughts marveled.

Susan leaned forward, her elbows thumping on the table. Caitlin leaned forward also, wondering what Susan had to say.

"You see that couple over there?"

Caitlin did not have to look, but she did.

"Yeah."

"She's getting finger fucked on the floor. Are they allowed to do that?" *Say yes and I'll ask you for a dance neither of us will forget, Ms. McKenzie.*

Caitlin suddenly had the urge to laugh but instead looked down at her hands to hide the big grin. The desire in the blue eyes was giving Caitlin a hot rush. Something she had not felt in a long time. The barmaid came over, placed Caitlin's flavor near her hand, and asked Susan if she wanted another of the same.

Susan leaned forward again, and Caitlin leaned forward too. "Can you give me a lift back to my hotel?"

"Right now?"

"Ohhh, no. It's startin' to get interestin'. That other bar I was at didn't have this type of dancing going on." *And you are not yet primed, Ms. Caitlin McKenzie. Give me another thirty minutes.*

"Sure, why not?" *Why not? Caitlin McKenzie, you know why not! You just described her as trouble...surely you don't want to get into that? Ouch. Was that a Freudian slip? Okay, so I'm tempted by those damn eyes...but, I'm not that crazy...yet.*

"Get me a Southern Comfort on the rocks." Susan smiled at the booted barmaid and let her eyes rest on her bottom as she turned to walk away.

"That's your preference?" Caitlin asked surprised.

"Don't have a preference. I'm still...testin' and tastin'." Susan had a crooked grin on her face as she thought about the woman's bottom. *And what were you referring to Ms. McKenzie?*

Caitlin thought she had referred to the drink, but the way Susan's eyes rested on Jan's bottom she wondered if she meant that about other things in her life. Silently she groaned; however, she was curious.

Susan's eyes returned to the dance floor watching only the dirty dancers and by her breathing, Caitlin could tell she was aroused. Caitlin's eyes wandered over the figure before her, stopping at the curve of the breasts that pushed out from the soft silk blouse. She was not wearing a bra. Caitlin could see the nipples were hard and...she tilted her head a little sideways. It looked like Ms. Nikolas was wearing nipple rings. Caitlin closed her eyes and said a little prayer to get her safely through this evening.

The music changed and the dancers on the floor changed. Caitlin could see also a change in Susan's expression. The tip of a pink tongue was drawn across her pinker lips which Caitlin thought must be numb by this time as she sipped half her drink that Jan had served in a larger glass than usual. The blue eyes blinked a few times and a small sigh escaped her lips as she gazed after the couple she had been watching. They were putting on their coats to leave.

Susan returned her attention back to Caitlin. She leaned over the table and Caitlin did her thing and leaned towards her.

"Hey..." she tried to keep her voice down in the noisy atmosphere.

Caitlin could see what the next comment was going to be and she imaged in her head the room becoming dramatically quiet just as she shouted her realization that she was in a women's bar.

"Wanna dance?"

Caitlin's mouth dropped. She thought for sure....

Susan smiled and with a finger extended, she lifted Caitlin's jaw back in place.

"Didn't think I would ask, huh?"

Caitlin stood up, not wishing to be outdone, extending her hand to the smirking woman. As they stepped onto the dance floor Caitlin turned to face Susan, who pressed her body against hers, lifting her mesmerizing eyes to gaze into hers.

"You want to lead?" her lips asked.

She's definitely bi. "That's the only way I dance," her lips returned.

"Good. I'm tooo drunk to lead anyone anywhere."

"Uh huh." *Good. I won't have to fight on the direction we're going in.* Caitlin could feel Susan's heartbeat thumping at a fast pace against her leathered chest. She had this bizarre feeling Susan was form fitting her body to hers, as she glided around with her over the floor to a slow song. Her hips were glued to hers and... Caitlin's eyes opened wide. "No dirty dancing," she told her with mock seriousness.

"I'm not; it's more of holding on so I don't fall over,"
Susan protested, not lessening her pressure as Caitlin guided
her around the dance floor.

Caitlin's eyes rose to the ceiling as her hips of their
own volition, stayed glued to the body that was feeling too
good under her hands. Caitlin slid the hand she had on her
partner's back a little further down, liking the feel of the
muscles. If she were more daring…or not worried about
getting too involved with Doc's customer, she would have
let both her hands slide down to cup the buttocks and press
them both together more firmly, doing some dancing that she
had not done for a long time. However, Caitlin was not that
drunk.

Caitlin! You need to get laid! But not by this one.

Caitlin did not know if she was imagining it or if it
was real but she could swear she could feel the Nikolas
woman's hard nipples pressed against her. Ideas of a bed,
plenty of lubricant and some real intimate getting to know
her seducer were lowering her resistance to getting involved
with Ms. Nikolas.

When the song mercifully ended, Caitlin pulled at
Susan's hand. "Come on. You have reached your limit."
And so have I.

"Hey! I don't do well with people telling me what I
should do. It's a power thing, ya know?" But she offered no
further resistance.

"Uh huh. Even with the boys?" Caitlin meant to
remind Susan that she was into men, but found she also
wanted to know. Silently she cursed herself for drinking too
much so that she was allowing herself to become too forward
with this woman…who she **really** felt was trouble.

"Brrr. This weather can sober you up quick," Susan
commented burrowing deeper into her new coat as Caitlin
quickly ushered her out into the cold.

Once they were in the truck and the heater was going full blast Susan turned to her. "So, you really want to know, or were you just commenting?"

"First, tell me where you are staying."

Susan pulled the cardkey out of her zippered coat pocket and dangled it in front of Caitlin, who grabbed the hand and steadied it, turning on the cab's interior light so she could read it.

"Okay." Recognizing card and to which motel it belonged to, she turned the truck around and headed back towards the other side of town. "So, tell me." Caitlin groaned inwardly at herself. She was going to drive herself crazy if she kept up this game because she knew they were both going to end up returning to their own beds...alone. *Caitlin Ann why on earth are you letting this woman get to ya? She is trouble! She's bi...for one...*glancing quickly over to her passenger's dark profile she winced. *And I will bet anyone that she's never been to bed with another woman ...outside of sleeping.*

"With guys...I like being in control...with the girls...well, sometimes I don't mind being out of control...It's all about getting a good fuck, pure and simple. But, ya know, I don't think women do it as well as men. Must have to do with practice." Susan hiccupped, "S'cuse me." *Well, Ms. McKenzie, will ya take the challenge?* Susan took a deep breath and regretted drinking half of the Southern Comfort. Normally she was the aggressor and here she was too woozy to stay focused on her goal...what is her goal anyway?

Bed a cowgirl? Oh, joy. This is going to be a first...and I may not even remember it with what I drank...Oh, no, Little Bop...you bed this woman and you'll remember! Wonder if she'll leave her boots on and bring out her riding crop...and we'll have to do some saddle work too.

Caitlin was shaking her head. Caitlin suspected the drunken Nikolas woman was hoping to try her first woman

46

tonight and she was her test subject. Nuhhhuuhhh. Not her. She did not want to be anyone's experiment.

But then, if she's willing to give out personal information...if it's interesting...I can't see any harm in listening. I mean, what can I get into that I can't handle from just listening?

"So, are you saying when you fuck the girls you are not as good as a guy, or are you saying when a girl fucks you, they aren't as good as a guy?"

Susan was sitting sideways, resting her back on the locked door so she could study this woman she was attempting to...*this is the strangest conversation I can ever remember having with another woman...what am I doing here? Shit, telling fish stories is all.* "I've never had anything but compliments about **my** performance behind the stick," Susan boasted, not bothering to tell her she has only been with men and was referring to those experiences.

"Uh huh. I see." *So, Ms. Nikolas, do I ask for details or let you go on with your innuendos? Think I'll just drop her off at her hotel, and let her pass out in her bed with her hand between her legs, dreamin' of what she isn't going to get.*

Caitlin drove the truck past the front of the hotel and then around the back until she was near enough to Susan's room number.

"Are you sure you don't want to come in for tea or something?" *Damn. What lights your fire, Ms. Caitlin McKenzie?*

"Yeah." Caitlin's eye caught a shadow moving around the rooms and groaned inside at her cautious nature. "Let me park the truck and at least make sure you get inside safely."

The card slid in the slot, the door pushed open, and the light switch flipped on, while Caitlin's eyes sought out what was in the shadows that gave her an uneasy feeling, waiting for Susan to check out her room.

"Oh, shit!" came from the interior.

Caitlin moved into the room quickly, pushing the door closed behind her. In the sitting area a chair sat in the center of the room with pillows piled up in the chair and bound in place with brand new 3/8th inch cotton rope. The knot ties were typical bondage knots, half hitches and a square knot at the chair legs. Caitlin pursed her lips at the sight and quickly continued with her visual inspection; already knowing no one was in the room.

Ms. Nikolas, you have an interesting following.

"Damn! This is something new," she muttered tugging at the pillows.

"Don't move anything." Caitlin dared to put two hands on upset Nicolas woman's shoulders to pull her back. She could feel Susan's body shaking. She was not sure if it was from anger or fear.

The large bed had the linen pulled back and her few bits of clothing placed on the bed in suggestive poses. Two pairs of very sexy panties were tacked to the wall with a note attached to one of the panties crotch. It had no worded message just a picture of a penis. There was definitely a message here.

Caitlin went out to get the hotel security and while she was gone Susan pulled her underwear down and the note. When Caitlin returned she had to remove from a tight fist the paper that Susan looked like she may tear up as her next step.

"You're tampering with evidence," Caitlin told the furious woman. However, after getting a look at the hotel security guard that showed up, Caitlin kept the paper. He had enough to talk about. His eyes kept moving from Susan to the clothes on the bed and then to the chair that she had not moved.

By the time someone from the police department dropped by, it was early morning. Caitlin groaned as she thought about the horses that had to be fed in a few hours. She had planned to leave as soon as Doc Walker arrived, which would be sometime midmorning. That did not give her any time for a nap before she hit the road.

The police finally left and not in a good mood.

"I gotta go."

"But...I mean..."

"Horses have to be fed, stalls cleaned, the chores need to get done."

"Well, can't the others do it?"

Caitlin sighed. *Ms. Nikolas, surely you did not expect me to spend the night or any other time with you, did you?*

"Everyone is needed."

By then Caitlin was irritated and she knew why. The hotel security officer overstepped his official capacity when he started on a too obvious line of personal questions, which ended abruptly when Caitlin finally threw him out with threats to report him to his supervisor. Caitlin was sure he was ready to pull out his dick and beat himself off with the inappropriate questions he was asking.

Shit, where the hell did they dig up this scumbag to act as security officer? I sure as hell hope no one gave him a master key to the rooms.

It did not help when the two equally witless cops that appeared an hour later continued with the inappropriate questions ripe with innuendoes. She suspected the three were buddies and had a conference at the front desk before the two officers made it to Ms. Nikolas' room. Caitlin put a stop to the officers' attitude by using her cell phone in front of them to call their supervisor, who was a childhood friend. The two were new young kids on the force and did not take kindly to having their leashes yanked, which further irritated Caitlin because it meant she would have to be careful so they did not find a cause for hassling her, though she knew their watch commander, Rogers would yank them back hard. Yet, they were young and looked stupid enough to want to try taking her down a peg or two on their own. *Damn, Rogers.*

Can't you people hire some decent meat that doesn't have ego problems? She was so irritated she had already made up her mind to report the security guard but wanted to wait until Ms. Nikolas left town. No sense in her suffering the repercussions.

"Okay, okay! Excuse me!" Susan held her hands up in exasperation. At the moment she was rather dejected about the problems she kept having in her personal life.

Caitlin turned abruptly to leave.

"Ms. McKenzie?"

She paused at the door but did not turn around.

"Thanks for driving me back. I really do appreciate it…and for hanging around while they took the reports."

"You need to hire someone to find your brother, and you need to get a bodyguard to protect you from… whoever did this."

She turned to face Susan who had moved close behind her. "I assume you know who did this?"

Susan shook her head. "No. I don't know anyone out here.

Caitlin pressed her lips together tightly. Either Susan was acting very dumb or she was clueless about stalkers. Since she was not about to explain the basics of stalkers and how she concluded that it was a stalker, she hesitated. She was already too close to being involved in something she did not want to mess with. It would mean she would have to prolong her stay in Flagstaff, and she did not want to remain any longer than she had to. She had her own businesses to run, as well as favorite retreat and haven and that is where she wanted to be…right now. This was supposed to be a two-week vacation…and she ended up babysitting horses instead of enjoying her own version of rest.

"Well, see if you can get some sleep. You have one more day, and then you have to really get the mare moved."

"If it's the cost…"

"It's the room. We have a working ranch; we need the stall she's in for the winter storms that will be hitting soon. You have reported him missing, right?"

"Daddy said he did."

Caitlin studied her for a moment more. *Caitlin, don't get involved! Just ignore those gorgeous eyes.* "Have a nice nap." She turned and left, hearing the door close behind her accompanied by a chain sliding along a bar.

"Right. Like I can sleep after this," Susan mumbled to herself. Susan made a mental note to call the manager of the hotel and speak to him about his guard. *What's going to happen if a woman seriously gets injured here? That asshole and the night cops are not the people I would want to report anything to. I think I'll add the police chief to my list of people to call. Daddy said they golf together. All that male bonding over clubbing those small white balls over green turf and into small dark holes should be put to some good use besides making Freudian jokes.*

Susan dropped on the remade bed and closed her eyes, not expecting to fall asleep immediately, but she did.

*****

Chapter 5

Doc Walker arrived midmorning and took over the chores, which Caitlin hated. She grew up on the horse ranch and was happy she left it for something that did not demand a rigid morning ritual of feeding others that could not wait for you to recover from a hangover or just getting in late and then there was all the other maintenance they required that could not wait. What happened to the good old days when horses wandered over the wide-open plains and took care of themselves?

We had to herd them together into small areas and give them small stalls to live in, and now...hell, now we gotta worry about diseases from over crowding and clean up after them so they don't fall in their waste!

"You're leaving already!" Doc objected as she watched her daughter toss her overnight bag into the trunk of her borrowed silver Toyota MR2 Spyder. Caitlin had a wardrobe at the farm so she usually only brought bare necessities for her mercifully short trips. Her hand rested on the hardtop to the convertible.

"Yes. It's too busy here."

"You don't look like you slept much."

"There are places to pull over."

"How about that Nikolas' mare?"

"I gave her until tomorrow. Her brother put a deposit on a truck and trailer at Hank's place."

"Good. It's the one I recommended to him. Something to say for that one; that makes one out of three things I told him. So, I can expect someone here today?"

Caitlin slid into the car and rolled the window down. She was not going to start a lengthy conversation with Jenny Walker on whether or not Ms. Nikolas was going to be by today or tomorrow. She usually lost arguments with her mother because she did not argue logically.

"Bye." Then quickly rolled the window back up as she picked up speed out of the forest. She made a short stop for gas, a nice hot cup of strong coffee and a small sandwich that tasted awful, and then she was back on the highway, heading for home, about a fourteen-hour drive. She was happily headed out of Flagstaff gingerly sipping her hot cup of coffee when her cell phone rang.

"Oh, hell!" She glared at the phone resting in the cradle on the car console. She leaned over and accurately jabbed the talk button when it rang again.

"This had better be good news."

[Caitlin! My but you are cranky. You need some sleep, grouch.] Walkers' voice came through the speaker.

"What do you want?" Caitlin demanded, admitting to herself that she was grouchy and needed more than a sip or two of her coffee.

[We got a visit from someone asking about the Nikolas woman. Elaine told him nothing and he looked real pissed. He gave the name of John Smith.]

"Sooo?"

[John Smith? Ya got ta be kidding, Caitlin!]

"There's the police...call them. After last night, they'll remember her. Though...why would he ask about her if...damn, Walker! I'm not getting involved!"

[Caitlin Ann McKenzie! I'm just askin' ya to make sure she's okay. Damn. What are we going to do with the mare? It'll be here another how many months before someone picks her up. I need that stall for Molley's Love. She's due in the spring and needs her space back before it gets too cold!]

"Damn, Walker!" Exasperated Caitlin leaned forward and punched the disconnect button then looked both ways before making an illegal U-turn, carefully balancing the hot drink. The car bounced as it crossed over the wide swatch of land that separated the two directional highways. *Shit, Miles is going to be real upset if I hurt his baby.* She had traded Miles, an employee and nephew, of her security firm, the use of her Harley in exchange for the use of his more sensible vehicle for the long cold weather travel, since her new SUV was in the shop being customized. Compliments of her last job.

After her morning conversation with Rogers, she did not expect trouble from his two officers or from anyone else that may retaliate for her citizen's complaint. Caitlin grew up with too many of the older officers on the force to fear about that; it was someone taking it out on Ms. Nikolas, she had told Rogers. He had assured her everyone would be cool...that's when she learned Mr. Nikolas had called the police chief and reported his son missing and wanted to make sure his daughter did not meet up with the same fate.

Shit! Both were groaning. The police chief knew Mr. Nikolas and his son from a golf tournament they yearly attended in Palm Springs. He was the one that recommended Doc's place to Jimmy Nikolas to pick up a well-behaved mare for his cousin Amy for her fifteenth birthday.

Caitlin found the rental car still parked in the bar's parking lot, so she sat and waited, finishing her coffee and sandwich. The dozing Caitlin heard the taxi pull up an hour later, depositing the dark haired women with her duffel bag in the gray slush next to the parked Ford.

Caitlin followed the dark blue Ford Taurus to the trailer lot and continued up a hill, stopping at a distance.

Through binoculars, she studied the area. From there she spotted the police car arrive, and as it pulled in, another car from an empty lot across the street, pulled out and drove some distance, made a U-turn and then reparked, but by the fumes from the exhaust, the motor was still running. She picked out the license number and called it on her cell phone.

"Hey, Kinney, this is Caitlin....Yeah, still here. Can you run this license through for me?...No, he's tailing your princess....Yeah, Ms. Susan Nikolas. Call me back on my cell."

When Ms. Nikolas pulled out of the trailer lot she shot her car into the traffic and headed for, what Caitlin presumed, was Pulliam Airport. The other car followed her, nearly causing an accident while trying to get onto the road.

"Hells bells, Walker. Why do you have to be right?" she muttered as she shifted gears.

Caitlin punched the on button to her cell to stop it's buzzing, as she was making a turn onto the freeway to the airport. "Yeah!"

[Caitlin, that license is to a rental from the airport. It was checked out to a John Cobley, Junior. Know who that is?]

"Yeah. My guess is it's the one who trashed Ms. Nikolas' room last night."

[Could be. He's from Colina, California, the same hometown as her. She's leaving on the one o'clock flight to Phoenix and then to San Diego. Jerid and Mac said she just about called Hank on them because they were giving her a hassle. They seemed to see it as their duty to give her the business because those two dickheads that took the call this morning are on the white board for inappropriate behavior with a citizen. She called in a complaint. Know anything about that?] He made a sound close to a grunt, when Caitlin snickered.

"I was there and called a complaint of my own in but I went directly to Rogers."

[When they get back from duty, I'll read them their beads and tack their names up there with their pals. Those two shit heads aren't worth getting one's ass in trouble for. Hell, what is the force coming to?]

"With you and Rogers leadin' the troops, I'm sure you'll get the young bucks in line." *So, she isn't afraid to report misconduct...well, Ms. Nikolas, do you take prisoners? Do you prefer handcuffs or leather? And, more importantly, just what do you do with prisoners?*

[Mistress Caitlin, save the bullshit for someone that believes in that crap. I'm too old for it.]

"Oh, please. You're the same age as me and you love it just like you loved the scout leader's role. You'll always be that role model the guys look up to. Jeeze, Kinney. Go on a vacation and get out of that maudlin mood."

[I think you're right. Hawaii sounds good at this time.]

"Just remember to take the right board with you. I'm at the airport, Kinney. I'll let you know if I need backup."

[Just make sure she gets on the damn plane, please. Hell, the worst type of male bonding besides getting drunk watching weekend sports is golfing. The Chief is breathing down my damn neck to keep her safe.]

"Bye, Kinney." Caitlin ended the call in a droll tone. Kinney hated golf. He was a frustrated surfer too far from the ocean and had to substitute his surfboard passion for a snowboard to remain sane. His other problem was that he loved Flagstaff and could not bear moving.

*****

Chapter 6

Susan's dreams were about how she would have liked the night to progress. Long ago she had decided that in fantasies anything was a go...well, almost. Since her father was paranoid about homosexuality among his children, Susan's dreams and fantasies lived out her desires to experiment with her urges to be with women. Therefore, dreams of her and Caitlin were not shocking but rather sensuous and erotic. She had a series of dreams, but the one she remembered on waking was of Caitlin taking her on a picnic in a grassy forest, and from the contents of the picnic basket, pulled out a jar of jelly and peanut butter and proceeded to serve lunch on Susan's body. The strawberry jam was dabbed on one nipple and peanut butter on the other. It was odd because it was Caitlin that was wearing the nipple rings and a clit ring, not her. Naturally in fantasies anything and everything is possible. When she woke up, she was horny.

She had slept for four hours, but was too wound up to go back to sleep, and then she had things to do. By one the flight her father had booked her on was leaving so she needed to hire a detective and to arrange for someone to deliver Amy's horse to a stall that had been rebuilt and waiting for it's occupant for weeks now. Their fifteen-year-old cousin was going to be flying over here herself if Susan did not make the arrangements today…or so Sam told her yesterday when she called him with an update. First things first. With a firm resolve not to let another woman suffer under what she understood to be misconduct of an officer…she called the Police Chief and then the Hotel Manager. Being financially independent tended to make her more pro-active when she ran into men or women who tended to be abusive in their authoritarian positions. She was being noble, to her disgust.

By ten, a large carafe of coffee from the kitchen was sitting at one end of the table, and a bouquet of flowers sat at the other end, sent as an apology from the management to the behavior of the night security guard. In the center of the desk was the phone book, opened to the yellow pages on horse trailers. Yesterday she had started to call around, and today she had two more to go. Lifting the receiver as she found her place where she left off a heavy knock on her door startled her, causing her to drop the receiver back into the cradle. Moving quickly to stand in the bathroom that was next to the door, she pulled her clothes into place. She was wistfully imagining it was Ms. Caitlin McKenzie returning to apologize, though she knew it would not be her…she really had not done anything to apologize about.

"Yes? Who is it?"

"Police, Ms. Nikolas. We're investigating Jimmy Nikolas' disappearance. Can you open up the door?"

"What's your name and badge number?"

Daddy did not raise a fool… entirely. She thought with a smirk. This was going to be her revenge for the hotel dick and the two cops from earlier in the morning. She wrote the officers badge numbers and names down and called the police number that was plastered on the phone. Yes, they worked for the police department. No, dispatch could not say exactly where they were. Susan supplied the voice of the dispatcher with her name and their whereabouts.

The voice at the police desk then admitted that, indeed, that was where they were.

Their interview was an attempt to grill her on exactly everywhere she had been since she arrived in town. She was beginning to wonder if they were related to the two that had questioned her earlier....being a brotherhood and all.

"Why do you want to know about my where-bouts these last few days? I know where I've been, and I'm not the one missing. Is this some sort of warm up to getting around to the real problem? If you can't figure out how to do a missing persons investigation I'll talk to your supervisor who can send someone out who can do it. I've a plane to catch by this afternoon and would like to get my business here finished by then." *Shit, I hope getting butch here doesn't get my ass arrested. I'm not as intimidating as Ms. McKenzie and these two do not look as green.*

"Ms. Nikolas, calm down. We're just trying to..."

"Asking me where I've been is not going to find my brother anytime soon," she told them firmly.

After they left, Susan returned to the yellow pages. When she started something, she liked to finish it. The very last listing was a jackpot. He remembered a Mr. Nikolas. He put a deposit down for a horse trailer and truck. *Damn, Jimmy. Why did you pick the last place in the phone directory?*

All she needed to do now was pay the difference on the bill and call Queen's Lane. Now that brought a big smile to her face.

The buzz of the hotel phone had her picking it up curious...though not hopeful for the voice she would like to hear from. "Hello?"

[Susan. You don't need to stay any longer. I hired a local detective to look for Jimmy. Be on the noon plane, and back here. You have a desk of work to clean up.] Susan's father's voice was clipped and he sounded a bit peeved about something.

Shit! Probably wants me to either pick up some of Jimmy's workload or to clear my desk and drop my company badge off. Damn you Junior! Why can't Daddy just take our side sometimes? All he's doing is making us easy targets every time he gives in to someone who whispers something bad about us. You'd think he had a past or something he's trying to hide.

Susan then called Queen's Lane. The voice from the first time she called the farm answered the phone.

[Walker, here.]

"Doctor Walker, this is Susan Nikolas. I just wanted to let you know, I located the place my brother rented a trailer and truck. So, ah..." she took a deep breath. "Ms. McKenzie had mentioned that when I'm ready to pick up the horse she would help me find a driver."

[She did?] *Ms. McKenzie? That imp. She did not tell the Nikolas woman that her brother contacted Hank. She let her find out for herself. Ahh, Caitlin. You're not that sneaky unless you're interested.* [Well, she's already headed home, but I know whom she was thinking of. Where is the trailer located?]

"Reading's Horse Trailers and Supplies."

[Yeah, I know which one.] *Hanks place, all right. Caitlin Ann McKenzie...you are one to talk.* [I'll need an address of the stable where you want her delivered and you'll need to pay the driver cash in advance for the rental and gas for both ways. The rental place can estimate the mileage.]

"Right. Okay. Let me get back to you."

After six calls back home, she finally reached Sam so he could call Queen's Lane and tie up the loose ends.

Susan packed her bag while she called the airlines to verify her seat. She had one hour. She paid her bill and then grabbed a cab to where she had left her rental, hoping it was where she remembered, and then drove to the trailer place to pay the bill. She stepped out of the car, pulling her new coat tightly around her. She again made a mental note to never live where it snows.

"Hi. My name's Susan Nikolas. I called you about..."

"Yeah, yeah, right. Doc from Queen's Lane just called and said she was sending the Lotha kid to pick up the truck and trailer. You going to pay up on the bill...both ways?"

"Yeah." Susan looked at the gas mileage and total bill then signed it. "I was wondering if you could tell me something. When my brother came over here to make the arrangements did he come alone?"

"He didn't come here at all. He called it in and paid the deposit by credit card."

Shit!

"He was over at Rosa's Cantina. I could hear their music going in the background. They got the worst music ya ever wanta hear."

A little alarm went off in her head and she thought about it for a brief second. Her brother did not drink. He was borderline diabetic.

"Where is Rosa's?"

"Up the road about fifteen minutes to the right. I hope you're not planning on going there."

"Why?"

"It's rough and a woman alone means you're looking to be picked up. Those guys there, they don't take it kindly when a single gal shows up and doesn't put out. If you know what I mean."

Great! Damn, Jimmy! What were you doing there? A thought occurred to her that maybe Jimmy was not there per se but rather needed the phone because he was going somewhere else up that way.

"What else is up that way?"

"Rider's Ranch, Peanut Creek, and some great snowboarding slopes 'bout thirty minutes further up."

Snowboarding! Now we're talking. That SOB better not have taken off snowboarding without even...no, that's not like him. He would have called.

A hand touched her shoulder and she turned to find that it was the same two police officers that had talked to her about her brother's disappearance.

"I thought you had a flight out of here in an hour?" the younger one asked.

"Keeping tabs on my time? That's interesting." Susan was annoyed. "I'm finishing up **my** business...nice to see you're doing your job." *Assholes. I'm surprised they aren't escorting me to the airport. What bug got up their arses? Can't have anything to do with a phone call I made earlier, now could it?*

After nodding to everyone, she returned to her chilly car. Gunning the engine, she darted into the traffic and headed toward the airport. She turned the car in and lugged her bag to the check-in counter. As she was waiting for her turn, she spotted someone that looked very much like John Cobley, Junior dressed in a funny outfit with a hat pulled over his face. As if that would hide him.

Oh, shit. How the hell did he know I was here? Damn! Where's a cop when you need them...but then what would I say? I think this is the guy that trashed the hotel room because he may have done it to my apartment? No proof, just my word.

When he saw her look at him he quickly turned his back toward her but she did not need to see any more. She left the line, ran into another plane's ticket area, and looked for a place to use the phone. Not finding one available, she moved back into the crowds. She decided hiding was not going to work. Instead, she returned to the line and when it was her turn, she turned her ticket in, or actually, sold it to the first person that had the cash so she would not lose all her money. She sold the first class ticket for the regular price. She then proceeded to the waiting area trying to figure out how she could get him on the plane. While she sat in the lounge area seat numbers in groups of ten were being read off. She got up and lined up behind the others, not looking at Junior who was hiding behind a pillar.

Well, he does have a blind spot. Alleluia.

With her heart pounding in her ears she slid between the line and the open door. She moved between the people that were looking out at the planes and slid behind her own pillar, sitting in a chair that had a view onto the plane ramp, just to make sure he moved onto the plane.

Once he walked down the ramp to the plane's body, she was up and flying out of the airport. Breathless she looked around her.

Well, it's rent another car and drive home. I sure as hell hope he doesn't rent a helicopter.

She went back into the airport and found long lines for car rentals.

Damn, by now he knows I'm not on that plane. Maybe a shuttle.

Susan was walking through the snow sludge trying not to slide in her hurry when she looked up at the windows to the terminal.

Shit, Junior. Give it up!

He was watching her and not looking friendly. His face disappeared.

A silver Toyota Spyder sports car pulled in front of her nearly running her over. Panicked she looked over her shoulder then turned in surprise when the passenger door swung open.

"Get in!" A low husky voice commanded.

Peering in, she grinned, shoved her bag in the small space in the back, and hopped in. The car slid through the snow.

"Close the damn door, you're letting the cold in," grumbled Caitlin.

Susan grunted as she struggled to pull the door closed as they turned a corner sharply. Gravity was working against her. A dark gloved hand reached out to her collar and pulled her back into her seat and the door came with her.

"Strap in."

The small car was expertly moved through the slippery slush and traffic until they were heading back into Flagstaff then past the city and into the forest peppered with farms.

"So you make regular visits to the airport?"

Silence.

"Mind if I ask you, where we are going?" Susan tried again.

"Walnut Creek."

"Oh. Why not just drive me home?" she gave her a bright smile.

"You're probably bugged."

Susan's eyes opened wide. "You think so? And just where?" *She has got to be kidding!*

"Get anything from him that you're keeping in that purse?"

"Nope and the purse is new, so are the cloths. How do you know I even know him or that it's him I'm running from or that I'm running?"

"Jewelry...?" she ignored Susan's questions as being moot at this point.

Other than her nipple rings that Caitlin had seen in the bar, Susan was not wearing any jewelry that she could see, but she just thought she would ask to see what Ms. Nikolas would say.

Susan cleared her throat. "Ahh. Well..." *All right, let's hear you tell her that he gave you a clit ring. Go on. I mean...that would sort of tell her what she already guessed.*

"He gave me a ring," she mumbled.

"Are you wearing it?"

66

"Yeah   You're not going to tell me a little itty bitty ring is a homing device. I mean really...that's spy thriller stuff...make believe!"

The car was descending a winding road with views that normally Susan would be ooooing and ahhhing.

"Take it off," Caitlin ordered briskly. Susan was right, the nipple rings most certainly did not pose a threat, but she was pissed off and this seemed to be a harmless way to vent it on the dark haired woman whose blue eyes captivated her.

"What?"

"Are you hard of hearing? Take it off!"

"Well, can you pull over somewhere?"

"No."

Susan was quiet for a while.

Caitlin was laughing to herself, a little puzzled why she was finding it so difficult to remove the nipple rings and why she needed her to stop. She thought she would give the suddenly shy Ms. Nikolas a nudge.

"So, where is this ring?"

There was more silence.

"Damn it, Ms. Nikolas, just take if off and hand it to me."

Susan cleared her throat. "Ahhhm. It's a clit ring."

Caitlin nearly took her eyes off the slippery road. Again, Ms. Nikolas surprised her.

"Well, pull your damn pants down and remove it." *Oh, yeah. I get ten big juicy points for this one.* "We don't have much time." *Just don't ask me 'time for what?'*

Since Susan was not refusing her out-right to remove something that was just part of her excuse to harass her, she did not see any reason not to continue with the game. It had to do with power...something Susan had said she was familiar with. Caitlin was curious how Susan would react to a woman taking control over her...and her imagination supplied her with a few suggestions on how to test out her curiosity.

"Okay, okay. Just...don't look."

Caitlin burst out laughing while she tried to keep them from running off the winding road.

"I'm serious!"

"Okay, just hurry it up!" Caitlin bit her lip to stop the undignified giggles that threatened to bubble out. The peripheral view was great. Her eyebrows rose at the sight of a shaved pubic area that stood out sharply against the dark jeans. She nearly turned her head for a better view, but the car was sliding on a patch of wet snow. However, when the woman's hands reached between her legs to remove the ring Caitlin almost sent them into the snow embankment. They both managed to survive the ordeal, but Caitlin was creaming her pants.

"Here."

Caitlin automatically held out her gloved hand and only realized what was dropped in it and where it had been moments later as she curled her fingers around it. She swore she could feel wetness on the warm object through her leather glove... which caused her to nearly moan out loud just thinking where it had been.

Hell, woman, ya need to get some legal candy. But stay away from this one, she is so sweet she is poison.

Caitlin pulled up to a cabin hanging over a river, looking none too safe. Sliding out of the driver's seat, she disappeared for a moment and then was back, tucking her tall frame behind the wheel, and quickly pulling back onto the road. The ring rested in her pocket.

"Now, you're sure that was all he has given you?"

"Well..." *do a few good fucks count, one of which I have no recollection of?*

"I'm not asking for intimate details..."

Susan looked over at Caitlin suspiciously. *Does she read minds? Naww. Or she would have known about the clit ring.* A smirk appeared on Susan's face.

"So...kinda surprised ya, huh?"

"He and you must have been quite a hot item." Caitlin noted she did not answer her question. *Not entirely a Dom and not entirely a sub. Let's see what you're made of Ms. Nikolas.*

Susan frowned. "No. Not really. We..." she cocked her head to one side thinking how it all started, "we met at a party. Mutual friends and all...you know parties...the conversations get pretty wild. I mentioned I had nipple rings and it somehow got to a dare for me to get a clit ring." She sighed heavily. "Shit...I don't even remember getting it done...or how the hell I ended up in bed with him...shaved." Susan looked out the window, her hand unconsciously going to her throat, as a small suspicion started to grow. She shook her head wondering if she was jumping to conclusions just to have an excuse for her drinking too much that may have caused her to have a black out.

"So, all this from one night with him?" The car slowed as it lined up behind a long line of other cars carefully negotiating the curves and resisting a glance at the snowy crevices of the red cliff rocks to both sides of them.

"No. I...actually went out with him two weeks later. I...it was going to just be a group of us...but it was just him that showed."

"And you didn't figure it was a set-up?"

"We are talking about a small town... besides, I was also going because he said he had a phone number for me to a WEB designer I was trying to track down. Fuckin' dickhead gave me **his** phone number. The only difference was this time I remembered being fucked."

"Uh huh. So, is all this worth the one fuck you remember?"

Susan glanced back out the window. "That asshole is going to get his when I get home," she replied softly, not really knowing what she was going to do, but she had enough cousins to consult with and come up with something.

Caitlin slowed her speed further as they drove through the busy streets of Sedona.

"I always wanted to visit Sedona. I hear it's a great mystical place." Susan's eyes looked back and forth at the shops and tourist buses that lined both sides of the small town.

"Not on this trip."

"Where are we going now?"

"You live in Southern California, right?"

"Yeah. But what if he's waiting for me…?"

"I'm sure your father has enough money to hire you a bodyguard."

Susan was silent as she watched the boring landscape slide by them. Pretty soon her head was resting against the window as she slept.

Caitlin looked toward the woman then shook her head. Glancing at her again, she raised the gloved hand that the clit ring had been deposited on and she sniffed it. Smiling she licked the spot and purred.

By the time they hit Phoenix Caitlin was too tired to drive, so after pulling out a map and having Susan study their route, Caitlin exchanged places after a visit to the restrooms and snack machines. Neither mentioned that Caitlin could have dropped her off at the Phoenix airport to grab a flight home.

Susan did not realize how long Caitlin's legs were until she tried to reach the pedals.

"Damn woman, you have giraffe legs."

Caitlin held back the caustic remark deciding it was best not to get too familiar with Ms. Nikolas. Why, was something she did not want to get in to, just like why she was driving her instead of making sure she was on a plane to Phoenix.

After a long tedious hour of driving in silence, Susan spoke up. "Caitlin, talk to me to keep me awake."

"You want to change places?" A napping Caitlin mumbled.

"No, I want you to talk to me."

"I don't do chatty Cathy."

There was a long moment of silence and then Caitlin could feel the car slow down and then stop. Without a word, Susan climbed out of the car walked around to the passenger side and tapped on the passenger window.

"All right. You win," Susan told her when Caitlin rolled down her window.

"I win what?"

"The stubborn award."

Caitlin got out and walked around to the driver's side imagining what it would look like for Susan to have crawled over the...*Caitlin! You have a long ride ahead of you with this woman. And this is a small car...best to keep it real formal.*

Caitlin put the car into gear and pulled out onto the roadway.

Susan looked out at the boring scenery. They were still traveling through desert, which was tiring to her eyes. She leaned her head against the car window and fell asleep, while her busy mind figured out a way to get the recalcitrant Caitlin to talk...about herself.

Susan found Caitlin did not like to eat while she drove, so she figured on one of the long drives between stops she would use a snack to tease her. At the next stop, Susan caught Caitlin's eyes resting on a bag of Cheetos as she was getting her coffee. Susan decided that would be her bait to draw Caitlin out.

After forty-five minutes into another long drive through a landscape that did not capture Susan's attention as much as her plan, she opened her bag of Cheetos and made a show of sucking and licking the orange colored dust left on her fingers.

"What one? Hmmm. These are yummy to suck on. Nice and cheesy…don't ya think?"

"No." Caitlin gave a glance at the bag that Susan was holding loosely and suggestively between her legs. Inwardly Caitlin was giving herself high fives. *This one is easy to train. Let's see what she does with frustration.*

After Susan finished half the bag, she again asked Caitlin if she wanted a bite.

"Yeah. I'll have one."

Susan's eyes widened. "Oh…great." *Oh, shit.*

Susan leaned over and put the long cheesy tidbit in front of the red lips.

Caitlin's gloved hand curled around Susan's wrist pulling it toward her so the Cheetos tidbit was in front of her mouth. She bit off enough so her lips touched Susan's fingers.

Take that you big tease!

Susan pulled her hand back quickly. Her body's reaction was not at all what she was expecting. In fact, she did not know what to expect. *Jeeze! Who is this suppose to drive crazy?*

"What's wrong?" Caitlin did a quick glance her way, trying not to grin. *Points for me, minus points for you. Except, I will give you two points for thinking of it.*

"You haven't had much experience in feeding people while one is driving, huh?" Caitlin put as many innuendos in the question as she could, not expecting Susan consciously to register them.

Susan looked at her, and then ate some more of the Cheetos, again making a show of licking the orange stuff that was clinging to her fingers. *Hey, Ms. McKenzie, this is my game. I lost the first one, but…not this one.*

Ohhhhh, Caitlin. You have met your match. This drive is going to be real interesting, Caitlin purred to herself.

"I usually drive...." Susan paused and then decided just to leave it at that.

"Drive many places?"

"Not any great distances. I get drowsy. And you?" *I sure would like to know what your mind is conjuring up with that answer.*

Caitlin's eyes remained on the road. *Come on Ms. Nikolas, surely you can do better than that.*

"Want another...Cheetos?" Susan asked trying to tease another answer from her.

"Hmm."

Susan took that for a yes and leaned over, this time carefully placing the tidbit close to her lips. Lips touched her fingertips and a stronger jolt of hot fire hit her groin area and sent her brain into loop-backs, as a tongue touched her fingertips. In her mind, Susan was picturing Caitlin's mouth covering her fingers and sucking the cheesy dust off.

"Arizona is the furthest...alone." Caitlin decided she deserved one point for the second try in the form of a short answer. She could see Susan was getting distracted.

After the tongue on her fingers, her senses went into over load. Susan decided the game was too rich for her blood and settled for watching the freeway mileage signs pass by.

Well, Ms. Nikolas...I can smell when a mare is in season and baby cakes, you are in season. Caitlin smiled behind her dark glasses.

****

73

Queen's Lane

Chapter 7

Susan was dropped off at her brother's condominium because it was Sunday and she knew he would be home. Caitlin waited for her brother, Sam, to show at the condominium's security gates, gave Susan the name of a security firm that specialized in bodyguard assignments, and then took off without even a backward glance.

Sunday was a mixed day of emotions for Susan. Watching Caitlin take off...probably never to see her again left her really wondering what she was going to do with the rest of her life. She had a brief conversation with her father...not an especially good one. He was not saying anything, just listening, and that meant trouble. She was depressed so she slept the rest of the day safely ensconced in her brother's guest bedroom.

Monday was a nightmare and it got worse for the next six months. Both father's sued the other with their children becoming the plaintiff and defendant, confusing the judge until he heard both sides...though it was Susan presenting hers and John Sr. presenting his son's. Junior never showed up for the trial, which was understandable since he had a warrant out for his arrest for attacking Connie and answering questions about the destruction of her apartment. Junior's father blamed it all on her and her temptress ways, and if it were heard in a predominately-

75

religious right town, he would have gotten away with it. However, Junior had attacked an individual, her cousin Connie, who ID'd him, so the ruling was against Junior. Her father's lawyer, her father's because this court battle was not her doing, found information that Junior had been in a mental institution for about four years due to his stalking tendencies. That was just great to hear. Susan's opinion of her luck with men had just taken a nosedive, though since her meeting of Caitlin McKenzie, that did not seem to matter any more.

Stanton Nikolas was not happy with the publicity the court battle was generating. It was a small town so it was THE news. Therefore, Susan was a scandal and could not work for the business. She became instead another wealthy unemployed child who received large chunks of money from a trust and from dividends from owning a good percentage of the family's business in stocks. She managed to occupy a portion of her time with visiting the gym in the condominium complex when she knew most of the residents were at work, and getting in some real workouts with her bodyguards that taught her a thing or two in self-defense. Then there were those people that all of a sudden started to appear while she was working out, which made having bodyguards handy. Some of the residents wanted to get pictures of her to sell to the local news.

She also spent a lot of time on the Internet, doing research to help Sam get his small business venture launched, and reading lots of Internet stories. Her social life was dead though her dream world more than made up for it. Just when she had thought she had made love to Caitlin McKenzie in every known position, her imagination provided more, fertilized by Internet slash stories on various Lesbian WEB sites...however, Susan was not ready to admit just what the attraction was implying. She had finally became comfortable with admitting only to herself that she was Bi-sexual but had never gotten the nerve to act on her sexual fantasies with women, since homosexuality with her father was a sore point.

The good news was that her brother, Jimmy was found. He had been beaten, robbed and left for dead along a well-traveled part of the highway outside of Tucson. A truck driver's dog found him in the desert. He had been unconscious in a small hospital for about a week before the detective located him. The truck driver was happy with his reward, a brand new stereo system for his truck while his dog experienced the trickle down effect and got a bone.

The reunited family was happy on that score, and Amy finally got her horse.

*****

Queen's Lane

Chapter 8

"Susan, sweetie, I love ya like a brother....but ya gotta give me back my privacy. Because your bedroom life is dead does not mean mine has to be," Sam implored her as she sat staring out the big bay window, her habit for the last three weeks.

Susan gave an internal sigh as her eyes watched the small stream in the landscaped garden trickle into a spout that dropped the water down to another level of the garden. Her hand resting draped over the chair back, twitched. He was right. The hearing as to whether there was enough evidence that Cobley, Junior was responsible for the attack on Connie and breaking in and vandalizing Susan's apartment finished three weeks ago, and she had not left his condo since. It surprised everyone that the ruling had been in her favor, since the local news had nothing nice to say about her and said little about Junior's past and present. His father's excuse of why Junior was not present was that he was touring the wilds of Europe and did not have any type of long distance communication device with him. This, discounted as unbelievable by the Judge, ordered Cobley Senior to produce his son for arrest and trial on the last day of the hearing...for which Junior did not show. The personal attacks against her character went onto the Internet, accompanied with photos from their sexual encounters, including a collection of which she had no recollection. The world-wide WEB humiliation was something she had to adjust to, and there was no one to reach out to, so she had been doing a lot of soul searching the last two weeks…but now, it was time for her to go back to her own place. The condo association was getting on Sam's case about the lack of privacy her presence was causing in the small-gated community.

"You're right; it's time to get on with life." She surprised herself and her brother by actually getting up from her seat and walking into the guestroom/office to begin gathering her things. She pulled blouses off hangers, carefully folding them and stacking them on the guest bed.

All right, I got this figured out. It's just depression from the trial and the Internet shit. Like the therapist said, it's normal and just takes time to recover from…hell, might as well go back to my own place if I'm going to hibernate, or maybe plan a trip somewhere where they don't have Internet.

Susan shook her head as she started folding her pants and stacking them neatly next to the blouses. Two weeks ago, when she thought she was going absolutely mad, she hired a detective to find Caitlin McKenzie. It was really a crazy thing to do in the midst of all the mess that was going on in her life…but the only time she seemed to feel safe was in her dreams…which were of the tall redhead. Sometimes they were erotic, sometimes of mundane things….but they were of Caitlin McKenzie….and she just wanted to see her again. All she knew was that she lived somewhere in California.

Lucky I remembered her license plate was from California and the strange acronym it reminded me of. So, she was borrowing someone's sports car…and a guys? Her boyfriend? Naw…

Smiling she tried to think of just what type of vehicle Ms. McKenzie would own or why she would borrow someone else's. A few racy models came to mind but she dismissed them as not friendly to her long legs which would get claustrophobic on long drives.

I wish I knew what she really told the detective I hired. He sure was in a hurry to end our contract, and giving me the excuse that he had voided the contract by breaking the number one rule by telling her who his client was. She forced him, he said. What did it matter? Of course I don't mind if he told her. You'd think she tied him up and tortured him...maybe with a feather. What did he say she told him? Ah, yeah, 'Don't send anyone else to find me.'

That message gave her a nice feeling.

So, does that mean for me to come instead? Oh, Susan...you are just stretching that message. Hmm. Maybe...maybe not. It certainly is something to think about...

The last two days of looking at her life, she examined her motive for looking for this person she could not get out of her mind. She decided it was not just because she had rescued her once before, and she associated her with the lifeline out of this nightmarish life she was living.

Oooohh, yes, Ms. McKenzie. You just reach out and touch someone ...that someone being me.

No, she decided that it was something more, and she wanted to explore that something more. Susan picked up the pile of jeans and put them into the box her brother had miraculously produced, chuckling at the image of Caitlin touching her.

"All right, that about does it." Sam looked up from the second box he was helping her toss her things into. "I'll see about getting whatever you may have left to your place sometime this week."

Susan closed the top of the box. "That's okay Sam. I'll come by for the ..."

"No, no. No problem."

"Sam, you're too busy to come by. I feel like..." she stopped from adding, *an unwelcome relative. Like you're tossing me out on my butt and changing the locks behind me.*

Sam would tell her she was using the guilt trip on him. Their normally good relationship was shot after six months of living together and under the microscope eye of the public. It had not been fun for either of them.

"Whenever..." she finally told him as she carried one of the boxes down to Betty Boop. She slid onto the driver's seat, as her brother settled the second box on top of the other and drew the seat belt over them to stabilize them.

"Drive safe. See ya Saturday at Dad's. Don't forget to bring a gift!" He hollered after her as she drove toward the guard gate waving.

She caught sight of some of the condo owners stopping to watch as she drove by.

Damn. There is no fun becoming an overnight celebrity with nowhere to hide in this town. Asshole, Junior disappears and all that the newshounds have is me...and that's a pile of crap! How come they don't pound on his father's door and ask about his son's last four years that he spent in a mental institution for stalking and drugging women on the college campus? Huh, huh? How can he be so damn lucky? That rotten dickhead. He thinks he had the last word by posting pictures of me naked on the damn WEB, but this isn't over by a long shot! Fucker! If I get hold of that dickhead, I'm going to cut his balls off and send them to his papa via the Internet, with zoom pictures demonstrating the technique!

Her car tires squealed as she took a corner aggressively and ignored the glare of the passengers in a car she passed by. She stopped abruptly at the next light that was red. Waiting for the light to change Susan's eyes surveyed her surroundings, something she learned from her bodyguards...hyper vigilance with a purpose.

82

Realizing her bodyguards would not be protecting her forever and wanting to take care of herself reasonably well, she had watched them and asked questions, appreciative that they were not put off with her relentless questions that sometimes took on hysterical tones.

Susan smiled, thinking about the people that came to her assistance during the hearing and afterwards, and from places she had not expected help from; like one of the new hires in her father's company, the Maverick. Sam and Maverick, the geek she had recommended her father hire, spent two tireless days tracking the origin of who was sending to employees of Nikolas Corp and some of their customer's pictures of her in all sorts of sexual situations. A WEB page was also posted, named after her, with personal information posted both truthful and made up, with vindictive intentions. The duo had located the origins, and sent a nice virus its way. The Geek had found that the originator liked to create E-Mail addresses with his initials embedded in the script. They then attached a virus to the pics that were maliciously contrived or were not particularly complimentary, and anyone that opened up the attachments to view any of the pictures had a crashed system to contend with. It was some consolation. At that point, she was too depressed to care and did not want to hear any more.

The light turned green and a honk from behind her reminded her she was not the only one on the road.

She flashed her ID to the new security guard at the apartment complex's gates, and as she was driving in she noticed he quickly went to the phone after she moved on.

Jeeze, I forgot all about them. That damn church Cobley goes to owns this place now. Hell! Now what?

Parking in her marked space, she looked around noticing for a Sunday night there were many empty parking stalls.

What are they attending, some sort of church rally? Naw, they couldn't have recruited the whole apartment complex to their bullshit! Gawds what is this place coming to?

Susan grunted a little as she slid one box with her foot toward the elevator and carried the other. Out of the elevator, she peeked, looking for trouble. She spotted a new camera focused on the elevator and another looking down the hall.

Shit! Now we get electronic surveillance. Is this because of the break-in to my apartment?

As she was fiddling with her keys, she could see the manager with two guards at his side, approaching from down the hall. At one time it would have looked rather intimidating, but after her six months of living in hell it just looked like more trouble.

Susan pushed the door opened and took a cautious look in before using her foot to push in one box while she carried the other.

"Ms. Nikolas, might I have a word with you?"

Not even in the door...Hell, what happened to civility?

"Well, I have my hands full at the moment. Can it wait until I at least get a cup of coffee, Mr. Bellings?" *Damn, creepizoid. Probably used my place while I was gone.*

"This won't take long." He dropped a letter that looked official on the box she was balancing in her hands, and then left with his two bodyguards. She noticed he held it up dramatically to the camera in the hall before dropping it on her box.

Bodyguards. Cameras...Empty parking places...and Eric moved out...unless they asked him to remove his 'Day Sleeper. Do Not Disturb.' sign. What's been going on while I've been away?

Dropping the box near the kitchen counter she ran her finger over the counter. *Well, at least Kim's kept up with the cleaning. Now that probably gets their goat.*

Her housekeeper, Kim, lived in the women's shelter for the homeless. Susan liked her, though she did not understand her with her heavy accent. John, the director of the shelter, had told her Kim needed extra work, asking her if she could help her out. Until she spoke better English, Susan could only think of offering her a job she hated the most, cleaning her apartment. After a few weeks, she encouraged Jimmy, her brother, also to hire her since he was a disaster when it came to cleaning up after himself. If Kim did not like cleaning other people's messes until she could get a job that was more to her liking, Susan wasn't aware of it. Kim was a very private person.

Kim was a legitimate immigrant, but had fled from her own family that wished to enslave her to a life that was not of her own choosing. She certainly picked up the American spirit fast enough. John Gonzales, the manager of the shelter had a sister that was a nun in New York that Kim had sought refuge with when she tried to leave her family's control. Sister Angela in turn contacted her brother and here she was in this small town with few prospects but at least away from her family's manipulation.

If she can survive...so can I.

Susan looked around her apartment seeing it for the first time since junior had trashed the place. Too much had happened since her trip to Flagstaff and returning...she just did not feel safe enough to return to what should have been her safe haven in the storm. There were many new things, never been used stuff, shining on cleaned surfaces. Sam had taken care of the repairs and replacing what was broken, like the nice guy he is.

To make herself feel better, she knew that Cobley Sr. had to pay the bill for the entire refurbishing and cleaning within a week of the judge's order or he, not his son, would face a contempt of court and spend a weekend or two in jail. Though his son was absent from the court hearing, his father was there everyday, unlike her father, staring at her with his stable of supporters from that weird church that was buying up property like it was on sale.

Stretching her legs out while relaxing on her couch she idly glanced at the new painting on the wall, horses against a stormy sky.

Fuck! The damn coffee is over six months old and I don't have any milk.

Further dejected, she opened the letter she suspected was an eviction notice. Her eyes opened wide. The philosophy of the owners, Girard, Inc., does not agree with her type of behavior nor did they feel threats of a lawsuit for not properly protecting her apartment from an outside resident was called for, the letter informed her. They had no problems with other residents with break-ins, and personally believed Ms. Nikolas gave her boyfriend…Susan's blue eyes narrowed to slits, giving them an eerie light…a copy of her key which was strictly forbidden in the rules of being a resident on their property.

"Boyfriend! You dickheads! You sons of stupid fuckin' dickheads!"

For the next five to ten minutes Susan pounded the sofa pillows picturing fat Henry Girard and his religious followers who had been hounding her with biblical misquotes…and with spelling errors during the trial as she pummeled the pillow.

Shit, shit and shit!

Susan stood back sweating and breathing heavily while glaring at the pillow that had taken on the image of Girard. It had miraculously survived her beatings.

Okay…I got a handle on this…shit…okay. Well, great. I haven't felt comfortable here since they bought the place anyway. It's been like living in a community of eyes and now with the damn cameras, I'm not even gonna be able to pick my nose without getting some sort of note from the damn manager. Next thing they're going to say we can't even do doggie style in our apartments, and then we can only have sex in the bedroom...on the bed in missionary. Shit. I need to get out of here anyway.

Like most of the residents, Susan was uncomfortable with the new manager who delivered proclamations and for a while was stuffing everyone's mailbox with religious flyers until the residents in mass, visited his office/apartment. It had been wearing her down.

She picked up her phone and called Eric her neighbor to see what was going on.

[I'm sorry. This number is no longer in service. Please check your number and dial again.]

Eric moved! A grin appeared on her face as she hoped that the rest of the empty parking spaces meant that others had moved too. *Hmm. So, if they move everyone out of here, what can they turn this place into? A religious community? They gotta be kidding. This town doesn't have anything to sell. The land is too dry for farming, and there isn't enough money to attract industry anymore...not even one of those sweat shops like over the border. Even Daddy is saying the reason for him to have his headquarters here is gone. The tax breaks don't even out on the location anymore.*

*****

A Month Later

"All right, let's go over my list again. Check apartment for anything left, uh huh," *if I could I would have people dump their used condoms in the bathroom...* "got that, apartment cleaned, everything shut off, bills paid, storage paid a year in advance, delivered what I don't need over to Kim in her new place, got my two small suitcases and laptop, and next...deliver Betty Boop to Connie. Oh, plane tickets....where ....okay. Well...."

Susan looked around her now empty apartment that had been cleaned, witnessed by a camera that Sam brought over, since neither trusted the manager who seemed reluctant to give up her deposit. The past month had been both a difficult time and a relief. For three weeks she had looked for another place but by the stares and leers she received she decided to leave town and do what her heart...or maybe just curiosity...was pulling her to do...look for Caitlin McKenzie. She found a lot of the other fellow residents in the apartment complex were leaving due to the over-zealousness of the new manager's keeping a peeping eye on everything.

Over the Internet, by playing with the acronym that was on the license plate of the sports car Caitlin had driven, Susan found a word match to a security firm in the San Francisco Bay Area...that had been founded by a C. A. McKenzie. It had taken her two days of elation to come back to earth but ...now she knew what she was going to do...travel until she found Caitlin Ann McKenzie. The woman was a semi-retired recluse, according to month old newspaper stories. She had made the headlines, though information on her had been sparse while the person she was protecting made it big. She should have told the PI she hired to do some work on the Internet before charging her for all his meals, travel and motel services.

So that's why she knew what company to recommend for a bodyguard. Okay... Ms. Caitlin Ann McKenzie, I'll find you yet. It was difficult to leave the grin off her face as she pulled in front of Connie's condo and did not even have to wait. Connie was on the curb waiting to take possession of Betty Boop.

"Cuz, this is the greatest! I don't wish on anyone what happened to you for me to get this lovely lady...but..."

"You're getting her because I want to travel...and I know you love her as much as I do...that's it." Susan looked over at her dark haired cousin that she readily admitted to anyone that asked that he was her favorite relative, besides her brothers. He recovered well from his beating and did not seem to have any apparent scars, but Connie was a brawler during most of his youth. His brother's leaving home for the streets like their father had Connie taking another look at his life and becoming a responsible family member of the Nikolas Corporation.

"I'll toast to that then, to your wandering urge. Oh, boy!"

"You don't mind if I drive to the airport, do you?"

"Oh, no, no. You gotta say bye to the Boop. Listen Little Bop, you be real careful now, huh? Single women in big cities..."

"I'll be just fine. Dad's secretary said to call regularly, Sam wants me to call regularly ...hell, I'll be keeping the long distance phone company's income in the green for a long time. I think I'll feel a lot better in a hotel then that apartment. Since I got back I've been getting creepy feelings I've been watched."

"Cuz, you should have said something! Linda knows this guy that sets up security software and stuff like that for companies. We could have had him over..."

"Wasn't that her last boyfriend?"

"Well...yeah."

"Connie, didn't she dump him for you?"

"Well, of course...but we're friends."

"I think you need to check her place, not mine... I'm gone. Besides, I looked everywhere I could think of and didn't find anything. I think it's just left over feelings from that damn court shit ....oh! Here's a good place!"

Susan pulled over to the airport curb and hopped out with Connie pulling the suitcase and laptop out, putting them on the cart, and hopping back into the car when someone honked that they wanted their place.

"Stay safe, Cuz!"

Susan waved and rolled the cart to the check in counter. She pulled out a book as she waited in the long security check line.

Her plane arrived in San Francisco on time and with no problems. Hotels were packed with a business conference in town. After overhearing a conversation from two women that were having the same problem mention *La Maison* having some rooms still available she ran her finger down the yellow pages and found the number. They had a single occupancy room left.

****

Chapter 9

The taxi dropped her off in front of the steps to *La Maison*. Bellhops were busy elsewhere so she pulled her belongings up the stairs into the hotel's lobby and up to the front desk. As she picked up her keycard to her room, she decided she was too restless to sleep right away.

"Do you know of any good bars around here?" she asked the impeccably dressed man behind the night desk, right down to the manicured nails.

"What kind of bar did you have in mind?"

"I'm a tourist. What kind would you recommend?" *Well that should tell him I have time on my hands and no business meetings to wake up for.*

"Uh huh. You interested in the tame or the wild, straight or narrow, church crowd, the leather crowd, gay, Lesbian, BDSM…what'll it be?"

"BDSM? Haven't been to one of those. What's the dress code?" *And what the hell is it?*

The guy behind the desk shook his head looking at her closer. "You're too vanilla for that group, Ms. Nikolas. You'll need a warm up before you go jumping into that crowd," he nodded knowingly. "You'll also need a chaperone. A woman alone, no matter what bar, is candy in front of a sugar starved crowd."

Susan regarded the guy in front of her. He had a nice body and was probably gay. Sam should be here with her.

91

"You have such a person in mind?" *What the hell is vanilla? Does he mean I'm too white? Ahhh...socially challenged or too much of a prude, maybe. Hmmm. Obviously he didn't view junior's shots of me. Thank the gawds.*

He laughed and shook his head. "I might. So, you want to start out with the leather crowd first?"

"Sure. Do I need my own leathers?" Dressing up like the great warrior princess crossed her mind, though leaving the sword and round thingie at home would be a good idea.

"Borrowing is not recommended. Not everyone cleans their leathers very well." The easy smile revealed a perfect set of white teeth. The kind a movie star wears.

Leathers. A tingle that she had not felt in a long time had her more than interested. The image of a black leather glove wrapped around her wrist came to mind.

"Okay. Where's the local cow shop?"

He wrote down the address of a place. "Ask for Tom. Give him this card and he'll get ya outfitted. It's expensive, so let him know your limit so he doesn't get carried away."

"Great!"

He grinned and then added, "A tame bar for tonight is the liquor bar in your room. You really don't want to go bar hopping alone," he advised again.

Susan looked at the back of the hotel card where in neat writing was the address of the leather shop and turned it around and read the name of the night manger of *La Maison* on the other side. "You're Jack?"

"That's me."

"Okay. Thanks for the tips."

She rolled her belongings up to her small room and nearly flung herself onto the bed in glee. It was high off the ground and had a nice bounce to it. After unpacking she picked up the yellow pages to see what kind of businesses

San Francisco and cities surrounding it had going. She had not finished the A's before falling asleep.

*****

"Hanna, this is Jack. I can't believe it but…yeah, it's her all right."

Within ten minutes, Jack was reaching for his cell phone. "Yeah?...Hey, Mistress M. Haven't heard from you for a long time. Feeling better?... Yeah, your number is in town…..Naww. She looks a little worn out but — could be the traveling, though she wanted to go bar hopping right away….No, no. I recommended she not go out without a chaperone ….Yeah, she actually took my advice without an argument, but like I said, she looks a bit strung out…no, no, not on drugs! No, she's not drunk either….Right, we'll keep an eye on her. Think there will be trouble?...Okay."

******

Caitlin put her phone down and sat back in the richly padded leather chair. She had been thinking about the dark haired blue-eyed woman since she dropped her off at her brother's condo …well, if she was really truthful with herself it was since she heard her voice over the phone demanding information about her brother. As if her mother kept detailed reports on everyone she sold a horse to… which in some cases she did.

When word got to her that there was a detective snooping around for her whereabouts in San Francisco at her old haunts, she personally dropped by to see who was looking for her and did a bondage routine on him to make sure he stopped. After her last job going sour she was not in the mood to play stalking games.

Caitlin's face broke out in a big smile. She dressed just for him in tight black motorcycle leathers, a low cut leather vest with enough cleavage showing as to leave little for the imagination, and with her thick cycle boots instead of stiletto heels. She kept her helmet on with the thickly shaded visor down. The still fresh scar on her shaved scalp would be easily recognizable until her hair grew back in. She certainly made an impression on him, but when a naked man is tied up with his legs spread-eagled in a chair and a big thick boot is resting between his legs, and the black soles touching his precious body part, it tends to be an attention getter.

She got a chill of pleasure when he spoke the name of his employer. So, Ms. Nikolas wanted to find her. She had worded the warning carefully, hoping Susan Nikolas would figure it out and come out and find her herself. She had followed the hearing via the Internet and being the voyeur she was, downloaded the pictures the Cobley kid had posted before they were tampered with, and then herself went hunting for the person that had wiped Susan Nikolas' chances of getting a job with any reputable firm out.

The early morning that she had seen her at the airport took her by surprise. Her own business, dropping off Tendra, her younger sister, distracted her for a few moments as mother and daughter, Tiffie, did their good-byes. Tiffie did not like her mother disappearing while she was asleep.

Later when she had returned home, curious about Susan's stalker, she did a background check on Junior. She worried about Susan Nikolas who seemed to be too naïve to defend herself. Her worry was justified. Junior was a real techie genius that got into trouble even while he was in the mental institution he was sent to for observation due to his stalking tendencies. She guessed he would be keeping tabs on Susan via cameras in her apartment since his family owned an electronics store that dealt in high tech surveillance equipment.

Without spending too much time thinking about her motives, she did exactly what she had told Walker she was not going to do. She booked herself a flight to San Diego, California and rented a car to take a small trip to Susan's hometown.

Entering Susan's apartment was too easy, with none of the advertised alarms going off which was a big tip-off to Caitlin that someone had entered previously, and that someone had disengaged her security system so even if Susan set it, it would not go off. She had also found small cameras throughout the apartment, even in the bathroom. She left them. From what she could gather, Susan had not been to her apartment since her return from Flagstaff. The news had said she was holed up with her homosexual brother, hiding. The local news found Susan Nikolas good for their sales and hounded her more than reporting on the perpetrator whom they could not locate.

Back in her rented car, Caitlin pulled off her sniper mask and cursed to herself silently.

Caitlin, you got yourself involved in a mess. Make this one promise to yourself...don't do anything more until she comes to you.

A few days after her return to San Francisco she had a new customer that wanted to speak with her personally about setting up his place for protection. She and his small band of bodyguards were looking over what he had in place when a big explosion knocked them all down. She and one of his surviving bodyguards managed to drag him out of the burning building. She had not heard from him after her release from the hospital, and she did not really want to. She had a monster of a headache, no hair, and a new scar that scared the hell out of her and her family. It was enough that she took some time off to reconsider her policy on who to take as clients. She lost track of Susan, but her company was still supplying the bodyguards, and if she wanted to know anything...all she needed to do was ask.

*****

Caitlin smiled as she turned her chair to look at the painting over her desk. She had been feeling sorry for herself until the detective had showed up looking for her. And now...the bait had been taken.

She's here. So, let's see just what she is interested in.

The image of Susan's hands reaching down in her pants to remove the clit ring came back to her. Unconsciously she curled her hand that had taken the wet ring from the embarrassed woman. Now she had it hanging above her desk in the console room. After all...she had won it.

Caitlin rose from her comfortable leather chair. A few days off visiting some old haunts in San Francisco sounded nice, besides she had a doctor's appointment to keep in three days.

It's time to educate Ms. Susan Nikolas to another side of life...my version of the erotica world.

*****

Chapter 10

In the morning, showered and fed, Susan started her exploration of San Francisco, stopping in at the *Ole Leather Shop* just before noon. Since she had nowhere to put anything she bought she limited herself to window-shopping until she got to the leather shop.

"So, you're the tourist." Tom was bulky with well-defined muscles, sported a tattoo of feathers around his each bicep, and wore black leather with no frills.

He began with a tour of the shop, starting with an assortment of collars from plane to those encrusted with spikes and or studs. Susan shuddered at the collection and quickly moved on. For some reason she got panicky looking at the collars.

At the nipple display case, where everything that can pinch and titillate the nipple was displayed, the two struck up a conversation and Susan found herself laughing at the stories Tom had about leather bars, the dos, don'ts and gaffs newbies made. Tom offered to escort her to her first leather bar that night with his lover, which Susan without any qualms, accepted.

She learned that Jack and Tom were a couple, and Jack was the bottom. She learned what a bottom is and that the leather bar they would take her to that night is not their usual spot, but one that both men and women attended. Their favorite place was an all male leather bar a few blocks from where they would be visiting. She also learned how to dress properly in her new power outfit.

*****

By ten thirty after the sun went down and nightlife began to wander, Susan was geared-up in her leather outfit, and her ride was tapping on her door. She knew it was Jack because she looked out the peephole. He was dressed in a black leather vest, and a leather armband encircling his right bicep. He also was wearing two earrings, and from the profile, which revealed his hairy chest, a nipple ring on his exposed nipple.

"Hi, Jack! You're right on time. You time yourself?" she joked, as she swung the door open.

"Hi, Susan. Yep. Mister perfection. Let me look at you. This is your début so you have to be just right."

Susan stepped back into the room, taking off her coat and waited as Jack walked around her. "Good, good. How do you feel?"

"Like my butt and tits are going to catch cold. This puts a new slant on the phrase 'hanging out.'"

"It will be warm in the bar, and you're wearing more than most. You don't want to show everything on your first visit." He smiled. *Believe me, you'll be kept warm with all the men and women hittin' on you, girlfriend. Very nice bod.*

The black leather long pants form fitted over her with the exception of her butt cheeks, which were exposed. There were other pants on the rack that left the butt and crotch exposed…chaps Tom called them…but she decided to not over-do it for her first purchase and Tom had agreed, saying the same thing as Jack about first impressions.

Her black leather bra barely covered her nipples. Tom had suggested some leather collars but the thought of it gave Susan a chilling shiver that crawled up her spine and instead suggested a leather band for her arm. Tom explained it would be sending mixed messages and she should wait until she knew what she wanted, however, to keep the more aggressive people away, he told her to wear a leather wrist band on her left hand. Susan did not pursue the meaning since her attention was sidetracked as an interesting couple walked in the shop and Tom excused himself to personally wait on them.

While she waited for Tom, she watched the couple shop in the battery operated dildo section with Tom giving them pointers on the advantage of each selection that gyrated, vibrated, pulsed and moved in different directions, with some ejecting whatever liquid it was filled with. Susan laughed when the more feminine of the two waved a two-headed dildo at her and winked.

Before Jack arrived for their date, Susan had been walking about, feeling the sensuousness of the leather against her bare skin and especially against her freshly shaved mons. She sat on various pieces of furniture, savoring the feel of her bottom being exposed as the skin on her buttocks took on a hypersensitive feel to each fabric she sat on. It was quite erotic and while waiting, she kept her imagination busy with possibilities.

Jack helped her on with her new leather coat and as it moved over her bare buttocks, Susan's stomach did flip-flops with from the sensation. This was going to be an interesting night of discovery, she thought. She patted her small leather pouch that carried her money and ID, just as Tom recommended.

***

"We'll sit up there along the balcony railing. I reserved a table!" Jack yelled in Susan's ear.

She nodded looking up at Jack, and then returned her eyes to the packed candy store. Tom's hand on her elbow guided her through the crowd. Eyes hungrily raked over her while Tom exchanged quick greetings with various people, pushing his way forward.

"Why don't you sit there? You'll have a sumptuous view of the show," Jack told her as Tom went off somewhere. He helped her off with her coat; draping it over the seat back with enough to cover the area she was going to be resting her bare posterior on.

Jack took off his leather coat, giving Susan a good view of his bare chest and ringed nipples. He also had a tattoo from the military on one muscular arm. He was not as buffed as Tom, but she could tell he took care of himself.

Susan leaned forward toward Jack. "Hey, this is the most assorted type of crowd I've ever seen!"

Jack nodded. "See that guy over there in the suit!?"

Susan turned her head in the direction he was pointing. The figure was dressed in a tuxedo but...

"It's made of rubber...he's into the BDSM scene. It's also his birthday so that's where the mixture of the crowd comes in. Friends from his job probably are curious and this is a good way for them to get a free look. Lots of eye candy....no?"

Susan glanced at him and wiggled her brows then returned her eyes to the scene around the birthday boy.

"Oh, my!" Susan's eyes nearly popped out. "Is that all of him?"

The birthday boy had a large erect codpiece on that was decorated with all sorts of glittery stuff.

"Yeah. That's what he's known for....but he's a sub. Tonight he's master, but at the stroke of midnight...his master will yank him back in place."

"Sub?"

"Submissive." From there Jack yelled to her the descriptions of roles and what the rules were, and Tom, who returned with drinks, added his comments.

Susan had examples of all kinds of bodies dancing before her eyes and doing all sorts of things that her imagination had not thought of even during her horniest times of the month. She also had a lot of offers and was happy when Jack and Tom politely declined offers that were stronger than she was used to. Her one unchaperoned excursion was to the women's restroom which gave her an appreciation of Jack's suggestion she not go out alone until she had an idea at what was out there. The atmosphere was more aggressive than what she was accustomed to in her small town. Her bare bottom was treated like a cross between Aladdin's Lamp and a squeeze ball as she moved to and from the restroom, and during her time in line.

Jack leaned over to her, "I noticed you wear nipple rings. You wear a clit ring too?"

Susan shook her head. The reminder had her picturing the tall redhead closing her long fingers over it. This brought a pleasant shiver to her body. "I'm thinking of getting one though." The smile that made its way to her face had the two men looking at each other with smirks.

"Wait until you're with someone," Tom yelled in her ear. "Trust me when I say, it is the most erotic and emotional bonding you can have with your lover to do it for her or him." *Message delivered, Mistress M.*

Susan grimaced remembering the last time it was done and who gave her the ring.

*****

On the drive home the guys quizzed her.

"So do you feel you're a top or bottom?" Jack asked with a smirk.

"Top...well...with a guy anyway, I've been a top." *Regardless of the film footage Junior showed over the Internet. Asshole!*

"Whooo. A dominatrix in training," Tom teased. He glanced her way and noticed a dark look in the woman whose slitted pale blue eyes were reflected in the taxi's window that she was glaring out of.

"And with a girl you like being the bottom?" Jack prodded.

"Well...I've never been with a woman...but I would like to try it."

"Really?" Tom chuckled. *Uh huh. Mistress M will undoubtedly like to hear that. No bad habits to break...but then again, I'm sure she would have fun breaking them.* "Well, the way you were watching Karen and Jessie, you are ready."

"One of these days I would like to try a three-way. It's a fantasy I have." *Susan, you are admitting this in front of two men you have only known for less than two days and you aren't even drunk!*

"Well, we know a couple that likes to do that." *Oh, boy! Small town girl, are you ever in for an education! And are you ever lucky that the schoolmistress is lookin' out for ya.*

"Do what?"

"Introduce women into three-ways. That's where they get their kicks." Tom had a big grin on his face, thinking that their friend had pegged this woman very well. He was hoping she was right in thinking she was her type...because if not, there was going to be two very disappointed women.

"Want us to set up a meetin' for you?" Jack asked leaning a little forward to see her. *Girlfriend, someone knows you betterin' your own mother.*

Susan cleared her throat nervously. "Sure." *That's what this is all about...finding out who I am and what I want to do with my life with no Daddy or small town minds to worry about.*

"They're going to ask for a certificate of health from a doctor. There's a clinic on 9th and Haven. They have their own lab right on site." *Mistress M. likes her women certifiably clean.*

"Uh huh. Right. Safe sex and all that." Susan was thinking it would ease some of her own fears of what Junior may have passed onto her.

The rest of the drive Tom gave Susan pointers in where to go and where not to go if she wanted to do the night scene and the warning, never go alone or without telling someone where she was going; after all, she was a single woman alone in the big city. Her first night out-on-the-town came to an end as the taxi pulled up in front of the hotel.

"See ya later. May your erotic dreams, Susan, keep you in the flow of good things to cum."

"Hey, you were listen' to that skinny woman with the...the...well, with those thingies on her tits. Thanks for the wish, though. It's been really fun tonight, guys. I'd like to do it again soon. Good night and the same to both of yas."

Susan ran up the stairs to the hotel and while waiting for the elevator, she thought about the provocative exhibition of the human body in leather and other strange body clinging types of fabrics. It was a definite turn-on and watching the action on the floor and all around her was verrrry stimulating. Maybe, she found her sexual nitch.

Before falling asleep, she masturbated while imagining she was with the tall redhead, Caitlin, who continued to haunt her in erotic dreams.

If these dreams keep on, and I don't get laid soon, I'm going to have to get a dildo. Something I should have gotten a long time ago. This shit with junior may not have happened if I had one of those things that did all those moves and the only thing I had to worry about was the battery going dead.

*****

The next day she again looked through the yellow pages trying to figure out what she wanted to do with herself, career wise, and then went for a walk to look around at the types of businesses and how they appeared in real life. She stopped at the clinic the 'boys' recommended and within an hour was happy to hear her blood work showed clean. They also gave her the new litmus HIV test that was still in the testing phases. Since she already had a physical before she left home she was not expecting anything surprising.

In the late afternoon as she was returning from lunch, she got a message from a Lunette Haley. Calling her back she found that she was the woman Jack and Tom had said liked to introduce women to three-ways.

[Dinner tonight? We can talk about it and you can meet Larry. If we all feel comfortable with each other, we can go from there. Nothing has to be done tonight, and anytime you feel uncomfortable, let me know.] Lunette's voice was ordinary and soft, which surprised Susan. She admonished herself that she thought it was going to sound like one of those ads for men to call and chitchat with a sexy woman. After last night's bar visit she wondered how many of those deep husky voices on the other side of those phone-for-sex were really women.

"All right. Where do you want to meet? I'm not that familiar with the San Francisco area."

[Ask the cab driver where La Rue is.]

"Okay. Is there a dress code or anything I have to follow?"

Lunette's throaty laugh had Susan picturing a woman with her head thrown back and neck exposed for her lips to suck on. For someone that had never been with a woman in flesh, only in dreams, Susan was surprising herself.

[You are a good student already, Susan.] Her voice went lower and seductive. [Do you have something that covers your body, but reveals certain aspects?]
"I'll see what I got."
[Good. Five o'clock sharp. The reservation will be under Haley]

*****

"Mistress, M. You read her right. We begin lessons tonight. Any instructions? ....Okay."

*****

Susan flipped through the yellow pages and found the store she wanted and the hours. Hurriedly she left her room for a quick shopping spree.

To get to the restaurant at five sharp required her to synchronize her watch with the hotel time, which she hoped was set correctly, have the cab be on time, and then walk around the block until her watch read a minute before. She remembered Jack's advice about first impressions.

Susan stood a moment in the restaurant's foyer, letting her eyes adjust from the contrast of the outside brightness to the low lighting in the interior. A hostess in a bright red tight fitting latex suit and corset, which left little to the imagination, was standing next to the podium looking rather preoccupied with taking a phone reservation. While Susan waited, she tried to see what was on the other side of the arched doorway without appearing to do so.

"Yes, can I help you?" the woman turned her undivided attention to Susan.

"Yes. I have a luncheon meeting with Haley."

"Yes. They are in booth twelve. Ms. Nikolas?"

"Yes."

"Follow me, please." The woman picked up three menus and led the way through the arched doorway.

As Susan followed her hostess, her eyes traveled to the bottom that the red dress snugly wrapped around, and then guiltily moved her eyes to study the dinning room. There were a scattering of tables in the center of the room, some occupied, and against the two walls were curtained booths. Most of the booths had their curtains pulled closed.

The hostess stopped at booth twelve whose curtains had not been closed, placing three menus on the table. She extended her hand to take Susan's coat.

Susan slipped her new leather coat off, showing a blue lace blouse that revealed her braless breasts with the gold nipple rings catching the reflection of the low lights. Her skirt, a black leather short piece, was two inches below her crotch. She wore no panties, which would easily be noticed when she sat down.

A small trim muscular woman, dressed in a very revealing shinny red latex dress was sitting on the inside of the booth and next to her was a masculine looking woman with nice biceps that Susan was sure would burst out of the tight latex shirt she was wearing if she flexed.

She nodded to the couple and waited for Lunette's inspection to finish. It was slow and seductive. She gracefully waved Susan to the bench seat opposite of them.

"Nice outfit," Lunette hummed. "This is Larry."

Larry nodded her head smiling. Her raven black hair was slicked back, lying flat against her shapely skull. "I understand you want to know what it's like to be with a woman," she stated in a deep and husky voice.

It was very Greta Garbo to Susan's ears. *Oh, yeah, baby,* Susan's brain buzzed, *this is different.* Susan cleared her throat and smiled giving her best seductive look. "Yes. Are you interested in showing me?"

The couple smiled. Now the basics needed to be decided.

"Well, let's order. During dinner, we can get acquainted." Lunette picked up her menu.

The drapes had been pulled across their booth, giving the small area a very cozy feeling with the light over the table giving off enough light to see what they would be eating. Their dinner table was made of thick glass without a tablecloth. There was a string of lights that ran along the bottom of the booths so just as the couple got a good view of Susan's naked white crotch she also could see Lunette's dark curly hairs peeking out from the red dress, and she definitely had a ring on as something was sparkling from between her clipped curly hairs.

While they waited for their lunch, the conversation served as an introduction and relaxed Susan. Lunette's strange sense of humor, Larry's droll remarks on Lunette and Susan's comments had the three laughing, and by the time the food arrived Susan felt comfortable with the couple.

However, dinner was not like anything she had ever experienced.

"So, Susan, what is your favorite body part?" Lunette dipped some white crab meat in a melted butter and garlic mixture, letting the herbed grease coat her fingers too. Carefully, she fed Larry whose mouth covered the offered food and fingers, holding the sweet tidbits. Her tongue cleaned the fingers and then sucked whatever might have been left.

Susan cleared her throat and took a moment to let the giddy feeling in her stomach settle. "Ahh, well...favorite body part..." she paused as she watched Larry dip a finger in the mixture and draw it across Lunette's lips, which Lunette then leaned over toward Larry. Larry's tongue traced the outline of Lunette's lips, tasting the garlic mixture, and then fluttered against the slightly parted lips, but not entering.

"Uh, huh, body part." Lunette reminded her as she drew away from the teasing tongue. Lunette tasted some of the food from her plate as she waited for Susan's answer.

In Susan's imagination, she was picturing putting the same sauce over Caitlin McKenzie's nipple and tasting it and then trying other body parts.

"Hmm," she cleared her throat and her mind from the images in order to stay present. "Well ...not any particular part really. I..." suddenly it dawned on Susan that her past relationships had always been to take care of her immediate need to release sexual tension, settling for whatever she could get in those brief encounters. Little time was spent in any sensual play, even with Junior, who liked to play games. It had been nothing she would call sensual...and if she really wanted to be truthful with herself, she had no interest in her partners outside of the mutual release. She felt like yelling 'Eureka' at the sudden realization of why her partners never brought out the sensuousness in her. *Duh, birdbrain. Jeeze! It took this long to figure out an amazingly simple...*

"You know, I don't think I've really explored that side of me...or anyone else's." She cleared her throat as she watched Larry's hand move under the table, sliding over Lunette's thigh and under the short skirt. Lunette sucked on a dripping piece of lobster in a suggestive way, groaning over it as if that alone was giving her pleasure. By the time desert had arrived Susan was ready to join the duo on their side of the bench.

While Lunette calmly ate her desert, Larry slid her tall frame under the table, removing one of Lunette's shoes, and starting at Lunette's toes, gave her a lip and tongue massage. It gave Susan an idea of what she had missed in her past of not going below the groin for stimulation. Larry stopped at Lunette's knee and then slid back in her seat.

Lunette slid under the table and showed Susan what it felt like, removing her left shoe and starting by sucking on her little toe. Because the table was see-through, Susan could see what Lunette was doing, realizing she had missed a very arousing bit of foreplay in her previous encounters

...until she thought of who she had been with and deciding there was no way she would have done this to any of them.

With Susan's senses fully engaged, Lunette could have simply run her hand over her legs and she would have shorted out, but instead Lunette stopped at her knee and looking up through the glass smiled at Susan.

Uh, oh. I'm in trouble here. Susan cleared her throat and took a deep breath.

Lunette moved back up to her seat and smiled sweetly at Susan.

"Shall we get down to business? Hmmm?" Larry asked.

Susan nodded. In the condition she was in, there was no way she was going back to her hotel room by herself.

Larry and Lunette drove her to a small house across the bridge. Looking around the neighborhood, Susan decided that it didn't matter which side of the bridge she was on, it was crowded. The house was in the middle of the hill, or so it looked like in the dark. The porch light was on, and a light over the drive way came on when their car pulled up. A shinny black Harley was parked against the garage.

The door was not locked, and the three of them trooped into the front room. The house interior had no knick-knacks or scattered family photos. There were three chairs, two padded and metal with leather cuffs on the arms and legs. A long couch with a variety of pillows was on the other side of the room. A thick glassed coffee table, with rings on the inside of the thick legs was in the center of the room, dividing the chairs and couch. She noted that they were the same type of rings on the chair's legs but did not have much more time to think about what the furniture implied.

Lunette moved behind Susan, and whispered, "Larry will undress you; you are to do only what I tell you. If there is anything you feel uncomfortable with, the word is Lunar."

Lunette stood behind Susan and removed her coat. Larry's large hands slowly moved down Susan's bare arms, while Lunette, moving to stand behind Larry, slowly undressed Larry from the latex shirt. Susan watched as Larry's breasts were exposed, looking larger than she had thought them to be. Her dark pebbled areolas surrounded taught nipples.

Larry's hands rose to unbutton Susan's blouse, slowly. Without removing it, she slid her hands under the loose blouse and cupped her breasts.

Lunette cupped Larry's breasts, her fingers pinched and teased them as Susan watched mesmerized, and nearly jumping when her nipples were treated the same. Her eyes blinked a few times as her nipple rings were tugged, sending a fire to her mons. A groan rumbled in her throat.

Lunette's hands moved down to Larry's stomach...Larry mirrored the movements on Susan's body causing Susan to shiver. Teasingly a finger was drawn across the sensitive skin below her navel, and then slid behind her, cupping her buttocks and squeezing a fresh liquid release down her legs.

Larry's hands slowly moved back up to the small of Susan's back where she felt the zipper to her skirt release some of the tension around her waist, making it loose enough to remove her lace blouse without tearing it. The texture of the blouse moving against her skin had her senses tingling and on hyper mode. The tall dark haired woman's lips touched her neck lightly and Susan's eyes closed at the exquisite feeling it evoked down to her toes.

"Keep your eyes open," Lunette ordered.

The caressing lips moved to suck on her pulse point, while the large hands slid back to her buttocks, moving under the skirt and grabbing her butt firmly. Larry leaned close to Susan's ear, and without touching her, she whispered, "I want to fill you with my dildo, making your insides hot."

Susan was surprised when her heart beat faster and her body shivered in anticipation. Larry's teeth grabbed some of the skin on Susan's neck, biting it. A deep groan came from Susan as she shuddered with want and was about to move her hands to reciprocate when Lunette restrained them, pulling them against her waist.

"You only do what I say you can do," Lunette reminded her. "Disobedience has its consequences," was the throaty laugh.

Larry's arms wrapped around Susan's waist and she was effortlessly lifted up so that her nipples were mouth level to Larry's protruding tongue, where she not only ran her tongue around her erect nipple, but sucked on each accompanied with bites. Holding her captive with one arm around her waist, Larry ran a finger along her slick and swollen neither lips. Susan cried out and laid her head on her hard shoulder, letting the shudder of want and need travel through her before she lifted her head. She wanted to wrap her legs around Larry's muscular waist but smaller hands on her thighs kept her legs dangling. Lunette moved behind Larry again. Susan could see over Larry as Lunette kissed and suckled Larry's buttocks, pressing her face between her crack while her hands were snapping straps on Larry. Larry merely held Susan, not doing anything at this point. When Lunette moved away from Larry, she slowly lowered Susan until Susan was aware of something pressed against her apex. Susan's legs automatically tried to wrap themselves around Larry, but Lunette again restrained her.

"You have disobeyed me. An infraction warrants a punishment."

While Larry held her against her a slap on her bottom took her by surprise, and then another. The low growl she felt vibrate in her throat surprised her, and she almost disobeyed again for another slap, which she found erotically stimulating.

Larry slid Susan's body down her, letting the tip of a dildo press against her wet lips, but not going in. A naked body pressed up against her back. "Soon enough, you will feel it, filling you, fucking your insides with enough friction it will light a bonfire," Lunette's voice whispered.

Lunette's hands roamed over her back and buttocks while administering slaps and pinches. Larry sucked on her breasts, and played with the nipple rings. Susan's body was engulfed in sexual arousal, something only her dreams hinted at. When she leaned into Larry, she could feel the shaft pushing against her, which had her moaning for penetration. Lunette moved the three of them backwards until Susan felt the table behind her. Larry turned her around and pushed her into a bent position over the glass table. Lunette sat on the table with legs spread moving toward Susan's face. Between her fingertips, she had some clear thin plastic saran wrap, carefully held so it did not tangle.

"Remember, when you don't want to do something, just say lunar," she whispered, pulling Susan's face toward her after laying the wrap carefully between her legs. Behind her Susan could feel Larry run the tip of the shaft the length of her sex teasing to enter. Susan groaned and would have pushed back into her but the large strong hands had a firm grip on her hips controlling her. Slowly Larry entered her, letting her get use to the thick dildo filling her, before starting to move in and out.

Susan could feel her insides squeezing and releasing from the pleasure and wanting to feel more, wanting to feel the heat movement would bring. She groaned as her hips moved on their own volition, matching the strokes along her slicked walls.

Lunette pulled Susan's face into her center. Susan tentatively ran her tongue up and down the swollen lips, getting use to the saran wrap and then the swollen lips they covered. She remembered fantasies of her own, on whose face was pressed between her legs, and how she would have

112

liked it done to her. Her teeth gently grabbed the nub of nerves between the swollen folds and flicked her tongue as she felt Larry slowly withdraw the shaft before thrusting in again. As Susan sucked on the swollen lips, she felt the quick and deep thrust of Larry and as she picked up speed, Susan sucked harder moving her lips to cover the swollen hard nub.

"Suck me harder!" Lunette groaned her instruction.

Susan's own brain focused on the penetration she was experiencing and it took a few moments for the command to register. A sharp slap on her butt reminded her, as Larry increased the rhythm and slaps. As Susan's excitement rose, so did Lunette's as she pressed Susan's head between her heated thighs.

It all ended too quickly to Susan's way of thinking, as Larry suddenly pulled out of her. Susan moaned at the empty feeling her throbbing walls felt at the abandonment. Lunette moved off the table, while Larry pulled off a condom and quickly replaced it with another. She then directed Susan to lie on the glass table on her back. There was a small box of saran rap precut squares near the table and Lunette laid one over Susan's bare mons. Her wetness held it in place. Lunette knelt above her in a sixty-nine position; with Larry standing behind Lunette, pushing the dildo into her. Lunette kept her buttocks up high for Larry's penetration and lowered her face between Susan's legs. Susan nearly leaped up when Lunette's mouth covered her soaked and swollen lips. Her eyes closed with pleasure as she expressed it with her hands that wandered over Lunette's moving legs that were following the thrusts above her from Larry's penetration. When she opened her eyes, she could see the shaft of the dildo sliding in and out of Lunette and it shot a hot fire of excitement to her belly and further down south.

For the entire night and into the early morning, Susan was introduced to a new type of play and found the erotic side of sex opened up a whole new world to her. Before the night ended, Lunette had strapped on a dildo that had two ends and both women fucked each other until Susan was too sore to go on. This was the first time she fucked a woman, an experience that she knew, she would be doing a lot more of. She also realized how erotic it was to have someone watch her and Lunette, as her imagination seemed to find ways to entice their watcher.

***

A pair of green eyes watched the three from twelve vantage points that the cameras gave her. Two were in the floor beneath the glassed coffee table giving a good view of the naked body pressed flat against the tabletop.

Black gloved fists opened and closed slowly, releasing some of the tension, but not all. Larry moved Susan back onto the table, this time holding her hands above her head while Lunette entered her with a dildo, lifting the agile woman's legs above her head for deep penetration...and to give cameras a good view of the dildo entering her shaved pubic area.

The voyeur's breathing became heavier.

White cheeks flattened on glass as each thrust pushed her harder into the glassed surface.

The voyeur's eyes moved to the camera that focused on Susan's face.

After three hours of show time, in a script the voyeur had written, it was now nearing the final part, and it was up to Susan to take the initiative of playing her part -- switching roles with Lunette as the aggressor. Would she do it or would she stay passive? The tall black-leathered woman leaned forward in her chair, waiting to see if her perception of the woman was correct. She nodded pleased, when Susan did as she anticipated she would. Her judge of character proved correct again. A smile appeared as her eyes stayed focused on the dark haired women's face whose head was thrown back and her eyes were closed as she neared her climax, riding Lunette hard. Susan's hips moved frantically against the wiggling Lunette, who was groaning out encouragements to her student.

Open your eyes, Susan Nikolas!

As the climax hit Susan, her eyes popped open and a cry of pleasure came out softly as she gave a few more stokes to the woman beneath her.

And who are you imaging you are fucking, Ms. Nikolas?

******

Queen's Lane

Chapter 11

Two weeks later

[So, how's our dove doing?]

"She's all right Hanna. Nice person, too, but ya gotta watch out for her. She's got a devilish streak in her. You remember that Dom manikin as you enter the Dom section? On her second day at the store while Tom was showing a customer a new set of leathers, Susan dressed herself up looking like the manikin and slapped him on his head with the damn riding crop...I mean...right between the legs! The customer liked the demo so much, she put a down-payment on the whole outfit!" Jack was laughing so hard at his recounting that he nearly dropped the phone.

[Yeah, yeah. So, she's going to be giving shows, huh? I hope your Tom can survive that shit.]

"She'll be okay and Tom can hold his own. Only, if you ever go there, be careful in the restrooms. This morning Tom said she dressed one of the male manikins up like a slave and strapped a dildo with cock ring on it and put it in the boy's room. Tom gave her back by putting one of the female manikins in girl's restroom tied up with a gag ball in her mouth and bound up in scarves. You know, with those two playing tricks, it's going to be real dangerous after a while."

[I'll be sure to keep that in mind and not visit the rest room next time I'm there. So, where is she staying these days?]

"Michael gave the okay for her to stay at his place until he gets back since she said she would take care of his pets. He's happy his kids are together. They were depressed being parted and being away from Michael. Have you found out who's following her around yet?"

[Uh huh. Hired help; he doesn't know much. While we checked the guy out that you spotted, we found a few others lurking about. There were three shifts watching her...paid in cash.]

"Wonder who is that interested in her? We'll make sure she doesn't go out with anyone we don't know. Hey, next time you see Mistress M tell her she especially likes that saddle she created."

Hanna started to giggle, something Jack found hard to image the tough looking woman doing.

[Uh huh. Caitlin already knows. She was up in the office when Tom was showing it to her. Now I know why she finds the woman so fascinating.]

"Oh, yeah. Tom said she was wearing this tight leather pant outfit and just hopped up onto the saddle, and tested the damn thing out. Her bod, so Tom says, was nice to watch as she balanced on the thing, teasing him like he was interested. Hell, I would have liked to seen that! According to Tom, what she did on that saddle had him blushing ...which I'm sure was her intention. When she finished, she told Tom it's a pretty neat toy and the creator must spend a lot of time with herself. You want to know why she thinks it was created by a woman?" He did not wait for a response...."because guys already have the motorcycle.]

Both laughed, wondering what Mistress M had thought to see her pigeon demonstrating the use of one of her creations in front of her.

"Well, I'll talk to you later."

[Okay. Caitlin sure does pick the odd ones to fall for.]

"I personally think she's doing better. This one's not married to a nut case, isn't hunting for someone to take care of her for life, knows how to manage a checkbook, and isn't stuck with lack of an imagination. I think Mistress M needs someone with a mischievous streak."

[I hear her father is homophobic. It's good she's outside of his influence. It will give her a chance to find out what she's all about.]

"I hope Susan Darlin' doesn't get too pissed when she finds out how the tables have been turned on her."

[She was warned two times not to be searching for Caitlin. If she still persists…she's open for turn-about. This is the weirdest turn-about ever, though. Well, keep an eye out for anyone that gets too aggressive with her.]

❈ ❈ ❈ ❈ ❈

Queen's Lane

Chapter 12

"I got to admit, since playing with you two I can admit to being all those things I've heard since a kid as being terrible, and honestly say…I like it." Susan smiled at the two women whom she had been meeting a few days a week for a month now.

"Well, you certainly have come a long way, kiddo," Lunette chuckled as she brought her whip up to Susan's bare butt cheek and slapped it.

This evening had been a good evening. She and Larry figured their training time was drawing to an end, and not just because Mistress M, whose judgment of people was nearly flawless, had said so, but because from their own experience they could feel the change. She was no vanilla princess anymore.

"So, how about we celebrate with a night at the *Erotica*?" Larry suggested. "Say tomorrow night? It will celebrate our last time together…a graduation present from us."

Susan took a deep breath and then let it out. "I guess this student is reluctant to say good bye …but, you're right. It's time to get out on my own now, huh?"

"It's time for you to go out and practice it with others. Just make sure you practice safe sex and have fun. That's what this is all about...erotic fun. Remember...if you get bad vibes from someone...get the hell out of there. That's why we have intuition ...use it." Lunette told her seriously.

"How about if we pick you up at your place, say about eleven-thirty in the evening?" Larry told her as she put her pants back on.

"Okay, sounds fine."

"Okay. Wear the red outfit with the heels. Hm? And the halter-top that lets your nipples show. Got to show off those nice rings. Right?"

Susan nodded. She had a mixture of feelings. She felt trepidation at stepping out on her own and also she felt excited at going to the *Erotica*, a club that she had heard mentioned a few times as very private and difficult to get into.

****

"Hey, girl! You drop one more thing and I'm going to have to flog you!" Tom yelled at Susan from the top of the ladder.

"So flog me and stop threatnin'," was Susan's tart retort as she picked up the leather apron again and handed it to Tom.

"So, girlfriend, what's got ya so damn nervous?" Tom asked curious as he clipped the apron on the overhead display.

"It's *Erotica* night."

"Isn't every night an erotic night? I mean, girlfriend, with all these toys surrounding you here, you can have it every night," Tom teased.

Susan laughed, blushing. "No, I mean, Lunette and Larry invited me to the *Erotica* tonight as a graduation present."

Tom's eyebrows rose. "Well, well, well. Not so vanilla anymore, huh. More like erotic chocolate." He grinned.

"It's kinda hard to be labeled vanilla when I'm selling this stuff, Tom."

"It's not the same. Doin' it or being a part of the scene is different than just talkin' it."

"Oh, yeah! That is definitely true." Susan started to laugh. "Now all I need is my lady love, huh?" she joked.

"Uh huh, for sure. While you're out there getting some real time experience you may just run into your Lady Love." Tom smiled at her watching the blush that covered her face. *Hm, I wonder who has you blushing that nice shade of red. Does she happen to be the devilish Mistress McKenzie, herself?*

*****

By ten thirty, Susan was dressed in her tight red rubber outfit. Her skirt curved over her buttocks with her butt bared, her red spiked heels that she felt uncomfortable in were strapped up over her calves, and the black mesh nylons were held in place with garters that hung from the short dress. As Lunette requested, the rubber bra that merely formed a cup around her breasts had a convenient hole in which her ringed nipples hung out. Nervously, Susan kept giving herself looks in the mirror thinking about how important it was to be invited to the club *Erotica,* and about how important first impressions were. That's what Jack had told her.

The door rang right on time. Opening the door eagerly, before her was Larry dressed in a black rubber tuxedo outfit. Susan knew of the surprises that were under the coat she was wearing over it. If a neighbor had a weak heart and happened to spot her uncovered, chances were he or she would go into cardiac arrest. Larry had a very nice body, and what she wore did her justice.

"Very nice," Lunette smiled from the back seat.

"Oh, yes. I see you are pretty tight there yourself, Mistress Lunette," Susan teased her as she slid in the back seat of the cab. Lunette was impatiently tapping a riding crop on her bare knee.

"She's in a rare mood, so we'll both have to be on our best behavior," Larry told her smiling. "Okay, John Henry, to the place of debasement and decadent behavior."

"Now that can be just about anywhere on a Wednesday night, Darlin'."

"The place for tonight is the *Erotica*. We're going to initiate our student here into the wild and woolie wonderful world of visions and fantasies."

"Ooooh, well, I must say…you three had better be at your best because I heard Mistress M is in town."

"Do say!" Lunette remarked dryly. *I wonder why. Can't be because we told her it's graduation night is it? I wonder if she'll present herself to the young blood, though; she still needs some polishin'. Well, it's going to be an interesting night.* Lunette glanced over at her partner Larry and caught her wink.

"So, who is Mistress M? Oohhh. Is that the same as the name on some of those toys in the Ole Leather Shop?"

"None other." Larry smirked. "But…I doubt we'll meet up with her. She moves around in a closed circle of friends."

"Why, is she stuck up or something?" Susan laughed at her joke.

Lunette and Larry joined her, though for different reasons.

"She has so many people that want to be her student, sub-dom or just to watch, that she likes to avoid it all. Most of them just want a free show, and that isn't going to happen."

Lunette shifted uneasily at the realization that Susan was the type that would turn it into her mission to learn about this 'Mistress M' just for the sake of curiosity of who was behind the name and fame. Mistress M did not like her subs taking it upon themselves of revealing anything about her without her say-so.

Their arrival at the club saved Lunette from any further curious questions from Susan as the people costumed for the night were already parading up the stairs.

"Oohh, wow. Look at that outfit! She actually had the nerve to walk down the street in it." Susan's eyes opened wide at the scantly clad Lemon Drop.

Larry looked at Susan and was about to say something when a motion from her partner stopped her. "Come on, let's get ID'd and see what we can get into."

****

The smell was the first thing that assaulted Susan's senses. Rubber, leather, sweat and sex, mixed with some other smells she did not recognize. The second thing was the various styles of dress or undress. If she were interested in buying more clothing for her nighttime wardrobe, this would be a good place to study the styles.

"She makes her own," Lunette nodded toward where Susan was looking.

"It's...different." Susan watched the small-breasted woman move past them, getting the quick up and down look that was more directed at what she was wearing than her attributes. "I like it though. Kind of shows off the body parts you want someone to pay attention to...no?"

"She's strictly a voyeur. However, she does designs for many of the women in here, including Lemon Drop, the woman you were admiring on the stairway. When someone asks her to design an outfit, she watches what her customer does, what she likes, and then designs an outfit that fits that customer."

"Ahh. Well..."

"All you need is a pair of chaps and a harness to lift your breasts to show off those nice looking rings," Larry told her grinning.

Susan looked at her and stuck her tongue out.

"Ahhh, ah. In here that means something." Lunette grabbed the playful tongue with her fingers, and then let it go.

"Let's get seats and watch the center stage for a bit," Larry suggested, eyeing her destination.

The night was entertaining for Susan. She had not realized sex could be so varied only limited by imagination, and that it could be even more erotic than what she had covered with Lunette and Larry, which she gathered was what they intended to show her.

Her initiation was into the art of voyeurism. It nearly drove her crazy. When the night or morning ended, she was too wired and horny to sleep when she got home. For two hours she worked out in the small gym the owner of the apartment she was sitting had setup in the third bedroom.

*****

Susan's eyes opened to the sun on her face. *Morning? Yeah, sun's shining through the blinds on the left side. Still morning.*

She stretched languidly, enjoying the feel of the silk sheets on her naked body. *What a night! It was definitely a good idea to hold off looking for Ms. Recluse for a bit. I got a feeling she is going to be one tough cookie to convince to let me take a bite out of.*

Susan giggled at the thought of just what part of her cookie body she would like to sink her teeth into. "Oh joy!

Guys, you certainly have inspired this student in the arts of yummy exploration."

She rolled out of bed and padded to the shower.

"Okay, today is my day off so shopping for food and hm. Maybe the guys want to go to the bar tonight. Uh, huh."

She was grateful that her new friends, Tom and Jack got her a job working where Tom worked, the Ole Leather Shop. She planned on putting her new education to use in her seduction of Ms. Caitlin McKenzie...once she located her.

"Oh, yeah. I need some maps of the coast, topographical. She's the type that would hide out in the woods...but, close to the ocean. Ugh! I think I worked out too hard last night. Masturbating is less strenuous." She turned slowly under the warm shower water, thinking of spending time in the Jacuzzi next.

She did overdo the workout on the bag last night. Her shoulders were hurting. She was going to have to join the club near by. They had kickboxing and some other interesting classes throughout the day. It certainly would make her lunches interesting.

*****

One week after leaving Lunette and Larry's tutelage, and scopein' out the local meat market, with Tom and Jack's encouragement, Susan accepted a date from a tall woman that had red highlights in her hair.

"So, what kind of place is this?" Susan asked nervously as the woman handed her coat and purse to the woman at the door, and then escorted Susan to one of the rooms.

"A suite of rooms to play in." Gayle turned to her before she opened the door. "If you want to stop the play, the word is hobo."

Susan nodded. She had already told Gayle she did not go in for anything that went around her neck. In fact, that was what got Gayle and her talking. Gayle was into past life exploration and thought since Susan could not think of what in this life would give her such fears, that it may be a hanging experience she had in a past life. That sounded like something she could pass up exploring.

Gayle opened the door and turned the light on which did little more than shine like a low watt bathroom night light would. Gayle took control of Susan immediately and it took a considerate amount of discipline from Susan not to react. She patiently waited as cuffs on her wrists and ankles buckled. As she stood quietly, Gayle's lips whispered a question in her ear if she minded being blindfolded.

Susan shook her head for no.

The dark leather mask covered her eyes. She was led to what she thought was near the bed. For a moment she thought the door had opened, because the air moved about her, but it could also have been from Gayle moving around her. While she stood, hands moved slowly over her body, removing her clothing, careful not to touch her skin that was bared. As with most of her partners she imagined it was Caitlin, and as usual it sent goose bumps along her arms, and a trembling of anticipation that was felt in the pit of her stomach and radiated out like a hot fire at the first touch. As the last of her clothing left her body, firm hands guided her to climb onto the bed, and then to lie on her back. Her wrists were pulled over her head and secured to each head post. Her legs were pulled apart and were bound to the foot posts so she was spread eagled on the bed. Her capturer made certain she could breathe and she was comfortable with the mask over her eyes. While she was deprived of sight, her other senses seemed to jump to hyper vigilance and all the other sounds in the room became important. The sounds were intriguing and Susan could feel herself squirm on the bed involuntarily as the footsteps approached her.

"Remember, when you want this to stop...just say hobo," the voice whispered so close to her ear she jumped.

Lips pressed against hers, gently at first, and then as Susan responded, they became more ardent. A tongue ran across her bottom lip, and then fluttered between her slightly parted lips, not entering the willing mouth that sought more of the other's thick muscle.

The lips moved down her jaw line, to her neck, and across her chest where they engulfed one of her ringed nipples. The sudden feel of cold on the other nipple brought a gasp from her parted lips. Susan felt a tongue swirl around her nipple pausing to suck hard then swirl again as the other nipple was titillated with cold. Her nipple rings tightened for different reasons, sending a fire of desire to her already wet center. Her hips rose from the bed sending a message to her capturer that she wanted more.

Then there was nothing...lips moved back to cover hers, as if to silence her or to swallow her moan as something dripped onto her stomach that was hot, yet the feeling left quickly. The lips left hers and she waited for the next sensation. A finger slowly stroked her neither lips, which were wet from her first image of Caitlin binding her wrists. Her body trembled from the stroke, and then it was gone. A burning sensation at the top of her breast quickly cooled...another on the other breast... moments passed before cold lips covered her nipple. A groan and tugs at her restraints were all Susan was able to do.

Something feathery, crossed her body ....which had Susan squirming from the sensation. Again, there were moments of no movement until a tug on a nipple ring had her body rising from the bed. The strain on her bonds creaked the headboard as she pulled at them from the sensation. She cried out something she was not sure of; her excitement mounting and her desire to feel the body of her tormentor against hers was driving her crazy. Her head turned sideways when the touch of what she guessed was ice, dragged across her clitoris.

Susan panted and struggled with her bonds, wanting to capture the hand that was between her legs as the cold cube slid inside of her hot center. Her legs and arms pulled at their bindings. Then it was out. Something touched her toes, light and then sucking. A mouth covered her big toe, sucking on it.

"Caitlin!" Susan called out without thinking, as all of her attention focused on the body part under a sensuous attack.

The sucking stopped but her body continued to hum, shaking her with a need to climax. Lips close to her ear brought her attention to the breath that was tickling her.

"You spoke without my permission, slave," the soft voice told her. "You shall be punished for that infraction."

Susan held her breath for a moment, trying to figure out what she might have said but remembering nothing but sensations.

Her wrists and ankles were unbound, and she followed the pull on her wrists. She felt the hands guide her to bend over, with her hands curled over a bar.

The first slap of a paddle on her bottom was to prepare the skin, and the second was just a bit harder. Susan's image of Caitlin delivering the punishment had her legs shaking with excitement. By the sixth blow, she could smell her excitement and another's and she was swaying as she struggled to remain bent over.

Hands moved over her prostrate form, feeling the heat on her reddened bottom and then moving between her legs where her lips were swollen and wet from her excitement.

Her legs were spread and she could feel a body crawl between her legs, then a mouth covered her swollen bud. One flick of the tongue brought her to a climax, surprising her and Gayle, her partner. The woman tried to continue stroking Susan's sex with her tongue but Susan's body was shaking and her legs started to give.

"Missssstresss, please. Let me...." she groaned.

Susan's legs collapsed and arms wrapped around her and carried her to the bed. Again, she was positioned and bound in a spread eagle position on the bed, but this time face down. Lips breathed close to her ear.

"You came without my permission, slave. For that, you shall be punished again."

For her mistake she was paddled while lying face down. A completely different feeling than when bending over. When finished Gayle turned her over and loosened her legs, drawing them up and then moving her hips.

"Ooohh," Susan groaned as she felt something solid slide inside her. Her hips rose to meet with Gayle's, and Gayle's hands pushed her hips back to the bed. Lips fastened on hers and teased her but did not enter what Susan offered as an inviting orifice.

Gayle's hips started slow, working more on Susan's frustration, controlling her until Susan thought she was going to toss the woman off, if she could. Instead, Susan wrapped her legs around the woman's waist pulling the moving hips closer to her and the rod deeper inside of her. Gayle growled in Susan's ear and she quickly dropped her legs.

"Please Mistress, faster!"

The rhythm increased and the force behind the penetration had her moving on the bed until a change in the positioning had the bed's support plants bending.

"Yesss. Harder!" she hissed as she could feel the fire on her insides build up.

Suddenly the motion stopped and before she could object, she felt the bed move as if Gayle was changing positions. She felt lips cover her labia and in a languid motion from a tongue that started near her anus swept to her clitoris, she lifted her body off the bed as lights flashed behind her eyes.

"Ohh, gawds!" Susan tried to bring her bound arms to trap the body that she thought was kneeling over her.

This was the first person she had been with that did not use saran wrap to cover her, and the feel of the roughness of the tongue over her sensitive folds was positively divine, especially since in her mind's eye it was Caitlin. She made up her mind then, that she would reserve that feeling to Caitlin only.

"Please...can I cum, Mistress?" she gulped out as the rush began. Her body did not wait to hear the permission that was given.

*****

Caitlin watched from the other side of the mirror as the tall woman blindfolded Susan. She rose from her chair and entered the room, directing the tall woman with hand signals to slowly undress Susan, using her mouth and hands to tease her, and then to tie her to the bed spread-eagled. Caitlin took over at this point using candle wax and ice cubes to arouse her and then fucking her with a dildo until she gave her permission to cum with a whispered yes at her plea for release. Hearing her name cried out when Susan climaxed the first time, was exhilarating, but to prevent her from the indiscretion again, Caitlin had to discipline her. The swats of the leather paddle on the reddening bottom were arousing to Caitlin and after she finished she crawled under Susan and pressed her mouth against the swollen lips whose bud broke against her face as soon as she pressed her tongue against the hardened nub. Again, her sweet captive uttered the forbidden name.

Caitlin was familiar with being in other people's fantasies, but for Susan to call out her name, not aware that she was sharing whom her fantasy was about ...that left her with uncertain feelings. She forced herself to lighten up, after all, she was behind Susan's education for a reason.

*****

Susan occasionally saw Gayle again. They waved through the crowds of people, but the emotions she experienced with Gayle had her avoiding her for another encounter, and instead she looked for others to fulfill her fantasies. Each woman she arranged dates with introduced her to another aspect of bondage with paddling being a central play and Susan being a submissive. Before each game began, she was sure to tell them collars were out. If she had known she had this fear while she was in therapy, she would have talked about it instead of beating around the bush about her dreams of Caitlin McKenzie.

Tuesday evening she had found another such type and rather than setting up a future date, Susan went with her to a motel room. She had her bag filled with condoms that could be used in place of a dental dan, should she run out, as well as for covering dildos. So far, she had no complaints over the use of protective shields.

"Do you come here often?" Susan asked as the woman closed the door behind her and removed her coat. For a moment, Susan wondered if maybe she was out with a hooker, though no money was spoken about.

Oh, yeah. Susan forgot the question as the woman stood before her looking every bit of something she wanted to have rubbing against her and stroked until she hurt. Tight pants slipped off, and her blouse followed quickly. Breasts glinting with nipple rings were erect and ready for Susan's hungry lips to suckle and tease. The woman also had a clit ring, which had ideas in Susan's head as what she could do.

Susan decided she would take control tonight as she watched the woman move to a dresser near the door and pulled out a two-sided dildo, rubbers and some lubricant. Susan went to the drawer.

"My toy box. Want to look? You like?" the woman offered.

Susan pulled out some soft leather cuffs for ankles and wrists. She slid her hand behind the woman's neck, as Lunette had showed her to do when she was going to take control, and pulled the woman's face to hers, "You mind if I lead?" she whispered softly into the red hair covering the white ear.

"Hm. No. I'm flexible."

"The word is red," Susan whispered and while she kissed the woman, her hands were fastening the cuffs around her wrists. When her prey was bound, she kissed her way down the naked body until she got to the ankles and buckled the cuffs around each ankle.

Susan led her to the bed and fastened the woman in a spread-eagled position - face down on the bed, taking time to make sure her captive was comfortable. Susan rubbed her hands together, thinking it was about time she put what she had learned to good use.

There were candles and matches, but no ice cubes in the small refrigerator in the corner of the room. There was fabric of different textures, which was just as good. Fastening the dildo to her, she straddled the buttocks and began her candle wax dripping, using her lips and tongue between drippings. She rubbed the fabric across her back and then in varying pressures she moved it to other parts of the body as she moved to sit beside her. Susan was experimenting how to tease and decided it was better not to be in contact with her victim's body all the time. Finally, it was Susan who could not stand it any longer and loosening the ankle straps, she hoisted the woman on her knees and slid the dildo into her wet vagina opening, and fucked her until she tired, enjoying the sight of the bright red dildo entering the reddened buttocks that she slapped as her excitement mounted.

Her lesson that night was, once a woman who is used to dominating is loosened, most likely she will take revenge, for Susan found herself flipped on her back, trussed up with gag, clothes clips over most of her body, and being fucked with a dildo larger than the one she had been using.

It was a nice encounter and both women seemed happy when they parted company, with neither exchanging names nor numbers.

*****

Six Months in the City

Wednesday morning, seated on the couch dressed only in her panties, Susan sighed happily while sipping her flavored coffee. About six months had passed since she had moved to San Francisco, and it was all like living in a dream, which was going to have to end soon. Pulling her calendar over to her, she looked over the day's list of what to do. It was her day off from the leather shop so she needed to get some chores done, like purchase cat and dog food.

Yep, her calendar noted that she either look for a place of her own or get the travel bug again. Shifting her position so her legs tucked under her, she sighed at the more comfortable position. Her twat was sore from the previous night's activities.

Turnabout is fair play, she giggled to herself as she remembered that just as she loosened the wrist restraints to her victim, she found herself expertly tossed onto her back and quickly tied up. That was the second time that had happened to her, but this time, she wanted it to happen. It was a delicious punishment to go from mistress to slave.

With a click, the large TV screen shut off, which had the morning news running and pulled out her notebook.

"All right...let's see what's going on here. Living in San Francisco is expensive and unless I'm on the waiting list with those in the know or influence, finding a place to rent in The City is not possible. Living in the Bay area can be a possibility, but..." she wanted to move on. She came primarily to Northern California hoping to run into Caitlin or someone that remembered her business, but she was running into a stone wall.

"I want to find Ms. Recluse. There is a boat registered to her at Drake's Bay. However, that record is a year old. Therefore, I'll just take a drive along the coast ...lookin' for her. Her vehicles are registered to a business where everyone is tight lipped." Susan looked at the cat, Minnie, as if explaining this to her. "You know Minnie, it's a good thing I stayed here a while. Had a lot to work out, and one of them is what am I going to do to get Ms. Recluse to come out of her shell and give me a chance to run my number on her. I got it all worked out here." She tapped her head with the eraser side of the pencil. "But, it won't work unless she wants to play. What d'ya think? Do I have a chance?" Minnie was purring so Susan took that for a yes.

Susan picked up her cell phone and dialed Sam. His phone was busy. She had been sending him E-mails from the leather shop's computer, though she could have done it from her laptop that sat unused in a corner. Her family's life went on without her. Jimmy was back in college getting an MBA in San Diego because Daddy had put his foot down after Susan was ousted, that he either ship up or ship out. It could be Daddy found out that Susan was doing most of Jimmy's office work to keep busy, though she felt he already knew that. It was just time for Jimmy to buckle down. Sam's business moved out of his condo into an office space where he had three full time workers employed. And Daddy was Daddy, always busy with business...though she made sure she kept him updated on her health by stopping at one of the remote offices Nikolas Corp had in the Bay area.

Susan tapped her teeth with the pencil. From her collection of maps that she had been accumulating, she pulled one out that had colorful tabs marking likely spots Caitlin McKenzie would live. It had to be where she had access to a dock. She grinned as she thought how she had scored a point in guessing that Caitlin sailed often enough to get calluses on her hands and the deep tan sailors do, like her father and Uncle Johas, who did the weekend fishing scene on her father's 21' cruiser.

Her occasional fantasy of Caitlin was becoming a daily fantasy now. Sometimes she imagined she saw someone like her standing at a corner waiting for someone, but the image would disappear when she blinked. That was the trouble with fantasies...they were not solid and that is what she wanted.

She sighed heavily as she thought of her sexual encounters that were fantasized encounters with Caitlin. It was driving her crazy to go home without really having Caitlin.

Caitlin I sure hope you know how to paddle as well as my one-night encounters, but if you don't...maybe you'll let me teach you. What are you like, bad girl?

"Gordon's Creek. What do you think Minnie?" she asked the black and white cat that had moved to look over her shoulder on the couch. The loud purring continued so she figured Minnie agreed.

"Okay. We're sticking to Plan A. I look at camping vans tomorrow. A van seems more practical than a car and then looking for a hotel or motel in a small town," she told Henry, the tiny Pomeranian that curled up on the chair across from the couch. She did not want to leave little Henry out of her conversations.

So, the idea she had been playing with was now going to be put into action. She wrote down the supplies she would need.

The idea of leaving soon had her restless. She decided she would visit the private club *Erotica* and play voyeur tonight.

It's going to drive me crazy to watch and not get any but...

The thought had her grinning.

Good discipline.

She did a speed dial on the phone; the original owner had Jack and Tom as number six. She waited until the recording stopped.

"Hi guys. It's me, Susan. I've decided to take that touring trip up the coast like we talked about, so tomorrow I'll be looking for a camping van. But, tonight, it's *Erotica* night. I'm going to do the voyeur scene. And yes, Jack. I had a rough night last night."

She grinned and hung up.

"Ahh. One more call to Daddy's corporate boss over here." She did not call him often; more like touching bases so her father knew she was all right. Another interesting side to her father that had her puzzled since he did not want to talk to her directly...after all she had humiliated him with the hearing, which he insisted on, and of course there were the pictures of her naked self sent over the Internet for the world to see.

"Hi, this is Susan Nikolas....yeah, that one. Is Mr. Stevens in?...Hm. Can I talk to his secretary?...Yes, I'll wait. Thank you."

While she waited, she noted her toenails needed clipping and repainting. She ran her hand over her mons to see if it needed a shave, she had shaved it two nights ago. She let her finger rest where the clit ring had once been. Tom's idea that it should be done for someone special had her picturing Caitlin. After all, she was the person who made her take off the first one, so she should be the one to replace it. Made perfect sense to her.

"Yes, Mrs. Marshall, this is…yeah, I'm still in San Francisco…I'm going to purchase a vehicle tomorrow and I don't want to be hassled with the usual stuff of having an out of town driver's license and ….right…right. I…what kind of vehicle? Well, I was going to look at a camping van …nothing too….right….right! Oh, where are they located?" Susan scribbled the name of the person to see and the address. "Oh…he would? Well, sure. No, no. That's quite all right. I can get there myself, no need to deliver it. Thank you so much, Mrs. Marshall. Good bye."

Susan sat back and tried to place the voice of Mrs. Marshall. *Erica Summers. Used to be Uncle Mark's secretary until she got married and transferred to San Francisco. Hm. What is his business? Come on, Susan, you have a very good memory. Something to do with fleet deals. I'll have to give the place a call and find out who owns them. Can't be having Daddy pay more for the vehicle than what it's worth.*

Hooking up the laptop Susan signed onto the Internet and looked up Roadteck vans. By noon, she had the one she wanted in mind, called the dealer Mrs. Marshall had given her and placed her order. Mr. Marshall took over the call and assured her he had it on the lot and would have it ready for her by tomorrow at ten.

Susan spent some time boxing up her few belongings, and then dropping off at the local corner market for dog and cat food and supplies for her new vehicle. She started her list with what she considered the most important items such as, a coffee maker, her favorite coffee, small creamers that were both powdered and what needed to be refrigerated, and lots of filters.

*****

As Susan was stepping out of the shower, she heard the phone ringing.

"Hello?" She used the towel to wipe the water that was dripping on the chair she was leaning over.

[Hi, Peaches. So it's *Erotica* night huh?] Tom's voice came over the phone.

"Yep. I've decided to go back again. Before I leave town, anyway. I'm ready to really enjoy the sights."

[Of the Coast or of the prime cuts at the *Erotica*?]

Susan laughed. "Both. I picked out and ordered a Roadteck over the Internet. I'll pick it up tomorrow at the dealer."

[When are you leaving?]

"I can stay a few more days if my leaving is going to put a crimp in the shop, but with the regular staff and the two new people you're training..."

[No, you won't be causing any problems leaving...except we'll miss ya...and your jokes.]

"I'll keep in touch and it's only for a few weeks, maybe less."

[I would feel better if you had a big bad dog with you.]

"I've had some experience with self-defense, and I've been reading the same stuff about women disappearing as you, maybe more. I got my laptop and will logon at regular intervals and give a diary of my travels. I'll be careful and paranoid."

[I wish I could say that makes me feel better,] Tom admitted.

"If it helps, I'll stop at three fortune tellers and see what they say. Would that make you feel better?"

["If one of them said your life was in danger, would you put this off until you get someone else to travel with you?]

"My life is always in danger...have you seen the way some of those tourists drive? They are so focused on looking for street names or their damn maps, they forget to look for the pedestrian or the people on the bikes...and they're going the wrong way on a one-way street!"

[Right. Hey, last night Ray told us you have him looking for something like a castle...with moat.]

"Hm. It was not a castle...I just like privacy. A place with a lot of land around it sounds just like what I want. I want to wander around in my house and backyard....naked if I want...without someone peering over a fence, tree or airplane. The City or the Bay area doesn't have enough space between one building and the other to fart without your neighbor knowing, and Russian Hill, as much as I love those homes, are not something I'm interested in investing at this time. I think the taxes alone would eat a substantial hole in my monthly allotment of living funds."

[You sound like a movie star.] Tom laughed. [What are you going to be wearing tonight?]

"Well, I haven't gotten to that part yet. Any suggestions?"

[The red leather harness with your breasts showing would really show those nipple rings of yours off nice...and those chaps with your white cheeks and pubie showing would have everyone watering at both mouths.]

"You think?" she laughed

Tom chuckled. [You have a nice time tonight. Stay safe and don't forget to give us a call when you get back, okay?]

"Okay. Jeeze, you sound like my brother. You'll have to meet him someday. Us small town people love to meet up with someone that can expand our horizons...in many ways."

*****

The *Erotica* as a private club, did not mean you had to have money to be a member, though it did help because anonymous was the key word, and those with money were more prone to be able to pay a blackmailer then those without it, so they were more likely to be preyed on. It helped that Susan's problem in her hometown was remembered. Her first visit was eye filling and educational. Her other visits had been with knowledgeable guests who were frequent visitors but not members. Tonight, she was ready to visit alone.

In this club, sex was at it's rawest with or without partners and with and without fetishes. Voyeurism was an art form here, behind peepholes or watching TV monitors, with or without company. Partners were shared, humiliated, slapped, banged and tied up in every imaginable way possible. Wednesday nights were woman's nights while Friday nights were mixed, and Saturday nights, men only.

Freshly shaved, toes and fingers freshly painted, and wearing her thin leather chaps with her buttocks and crotch showing, she chose the harness halter-top with her breasts, midriff and shoulders bared. The harness merely lifted her breasts from underneath while the leather straps crisscrossed her back. To complete her outfit, she had her now favorite long leather coat to keep her less exposed to the elements until she reached the club. From the window, she could see her cab arrive.

Her cab driver was John Henry who worked the late nights. Due in large part because of his intimate knowledge of The City, he made his best tips working nights. During his off-hours from educating the curious tourists, John Henry was a drag Queen with his character Shady Lady, giving stand-up comic versions of tourists seeking the livelier sights of The City.

"Where to, Baby Cakes?"

Susan had flashed him her outfit, before sliding in, knowing he loved the show.

"Ooohhh. You are just hot to trot, Missy."

"Thanks John Henry. The *Erotica*. So, how's the scene checkin' out?"

"Kinda cool for most but for you ...uhh uhhh. Sizzle, sizzle. I think you're too hot!"

"Well, we'll see. Last night's fun has me sittin' sideways and both cheeks are sensitive."

"Ohhhhh baby. I know those days! Don't you just love it!"

They both laughed.

*****

The club was not slow for the time. People were just arriving and getting their partners and themselves ready for their shows. She moved around looking at the center dais where a couple was doing a dominatrix thing, and in the corner a three-way with two others watching was warming up. She moved to the peepholes to see what was going on in the rooms. The rooms that were occupied had a green mark on them. Two were occupied. She moved to one of them and watched two women and Larry.

Ahhhh. She moved to get a better view of the women noting one of them was Lunette. Her bare bottom was being paddled while her mouth was working on Larry's nipples. Her breasts were hanging as she was on her hands and knees while the other woman was paddling her behind.

A groan came out of Susan's throat as she imagined the pleasure of the paddle and her face buried in...Caitlin's red mound. Breathing harder she watched as Larry positioned to lie on her back and the other woman straddled her dildo while drawing Lunette near so she could ...

Susan moved on to the next room where there was another threesome going on.

Now this is interesting. Damn, that dildo is too big to be fun!

Two women wore dildos. The one without the dildo was being fucked from behind while she was giving a

143

blowjob to the other. Susan shook her head thinking she would much rather feel the lips pressed against her cunt.

Susan watched the three women until she had to go sit down and give her shaking legs a break. The images were more to add to a growing collection of what she wanted to practice on Caitlin...if she could find her. She found a table near the center stage where a woman was putting on a show of fucking two others in all sorts of positions.

"Would you like a drink?"

Susan's brain froze for a moment before her mind started on the ponderous job of sorting out the reality of the voice from wistful thinking and dreams. Shaking her head to clear the image it conjured up, her eyes started to track up from the bright red stiletto heels, the long red leathered thighs with slits up the sides to the buttocks, hinting at a tattoo on the skin, past the strong large hands that held a leather crop, up the bare stomach ribbed with muscles, past the deep v cut halter top and finally to the tanned face of the dark red haired of her fantasies and dreams....Caitlin...without her long hair.

"No? May I join you?" A chair pulled out and Caitlin sat with her feet firmly planted on the floor, and the leather around the calf muscles stretching.

Susan nodded not being able to take her eyes off Caitlin who now wore her hair cut close to her skull. There was a fresh scar on her left side that ran from her scalp to her shoulder. Susan's heart pounded in fear for her, and then her eyes moved to her muscular shoulders that were bare, showing a scattering of freckles against a deep tan.

"Come here often?" Caitlin asked in a low voice that sent shivers skittering up Susan's spine.

It did not stop there, as goose bumps ran up her arms, the skin around her nipple rings tightened, a fire burned in her groin, and her neither lips became engorged with the desire to be touched by this dream person.

Caitlin's sharp eyes noted the changes in Susan's body, and her breath lengthened, as she watched in fascination at her effect on Susan.

Susan's eyes were still soaking in the image of Caitlin's body in detail to have heard the question clearly.

Caitlin leaned forward and whispered. "I give you permission to speak."

Susan blinked a few times and then sat up taller. "What do you mean, give me permission?" Her voice sounded distant to her ears, and as she shifted her weight, she flinched as her weight moved to her sore center.

Since Sharon's arrival to the club, Caitlin had watched her from the third floor; another feature of the club where voyeurs could watch voyeurs on the floor below.

Caitlin's eyebrow rose. "You hurt yourself?"

"I ...no."

Confused at how to respond since her wits were scattered, Susan collected her thoughts by facing the women on the center stage. Clearing her throat, she nodded to the one that was licking the dildo before taking it into her mouth.

"What is the excitement of giving a blowjob to a dildo? I don't get it."

Caitlin smiled. "Imagination and the proper stimulation, Ms. Nikolas, go a long way."

Susan glanced back at Caitlin and was caught up in her dark eyes, nearly diving into their pools of darkness to find the malachite she knew was there. "Well...I..." she looked back at the woman whose hips were thrusting the dildo into the other woman's mouth. Her mouth became dry as images of Caitlin wearing a dildo and she pleasuring the redhead with her mouth...feeling the muscled buttocks with her fingers...pulling her in closer. Susan nervously cleared her throat as she could feel the heated flush that suffused her face.

"Oooh. You've come a long way, Ms. Nikolas," Caitlin laughed in a seductive voice.

Susan blushed. "You know, I...could you call me Susan? Please?"

"Uh huh, since you asked nicely." Caitlin watched the red flush on the dark haired woman's face darken. "You still like to be fucked?"

Susan's heart stopped for a moment as her imagination moved to other images. She cleared her throat again. "I...yes, but I also like doing it." Her voice strengthened.

"So, when you strap it on and fuck the girls....what does it feel like, Susan?" the provocative voice asked.

Susan looked up into the dark eyes, not realizing that her own light blues were picking up the small light in the room and sending shivers down the tall woman's frame. Instead, she remembered a conversation they had almost a year ago.

Ahhh. We are playing. The thought sent a rush to her as she took a deep breath. "Do you mind?" she asked Caitlin nodding to a space near her.

Caitlin indicated where to place her chair.

She picked up her chair and placed it close to Caitlin so she would not have to yell over the drums beating out a primal beat that added to the atmosphere, and that sent vibrations through the metal rings in her exposed nipples.

Susan waited until Caitlin bent her head towards her. The muscles in Caitlin's shoulders shifted as her weight moved to her left arm.

"It feels very good," she husked into the shell shaped ear. Susan imagined her breath tickling the ear that was a hairsbreadth from her lips. "The feeling of penetrating a woman is as nice as being penetrated. It can be with a finger or a dildo, but I like to fill my women up, and a dildo does a nicer job of that...sliding in and out...feeling the woman buck against me...reddening her cheeks that I'm banging against with slaps...urging her to move faster. Sometimes..." Susan paused, watching the eye lashes flicker, "I like to tie them to a chair and sit in their lap when they are wearing a very long dildo. And then, sometimes, I just want to fuck her...hard...and fast...I delight in her cries of pleasure and her squirming to wrap her legs around me, to pull me in deeper." Susan's lips touched the skin of the woman whose breathing had deepened and whose hands were held in tight fists wrapped around the ridding crop on the table.

Caitlin straightened slowly, and motioned to a leathered bar slave. *My dear little whore, you are the one that is taken and screaming to be fucked, but your story will do.* "So, it's still a good fuck you are looking for...hm?" Her eyes raked the erect nipples and up to the muscles that were well defined on her shoulders, and then returned to the nipples whose tautness tempted her mouth to pucker around and her fingers to tweak.

Caitlin ordered herself a drink and a seven-up for Susan. Susan raised her eyebrows at the ordering of a nonalcoholic beverage for her.

"You don't need any more loosening up. You're doing just fine...but you will need something for a dry throat." *The seduction has begun, Ms. Nikolas and I'm the one that will be leading. Do you think you're up to it? If your nipples are any indication...I'd say yesss.*

Susan smiled back, finding Caitlin's smile doing all sorts of things to her stomach and further down south.

I can't believe this...my dream...my fantasies are coming true. She's here and she wants to play...with me! Oh joy, I owe Aphrodite an offering or two...I'll have to get a statue of her and surround it with bouquets of flowers or maybe something in leather.

Unable to stand the intensity of feelings she was getting from exchanging a long stare with Caitlin, she turned back to the group that moved to the center stage, hoping to gain control of her emotions. Though facing the center group she did not really see them, as her senses were focused on the person sitting so close to her she could swear she felt her body heat...and it was sizzling – or, was that her own body?

Caitlin looked very different with her buzz cut and the stiletto heels...and was that a tattoo on her legs? Susan struggled to get the giddy feelings she was experiencing in control. She wished it was an alcoholic drink Caitlin had ordered for her.

The server returned and set their drinks in front of them. Susan gratefully sipped her drink realizing her throat was dry.

"Ever get your ring replaced?" Caitlin asked as she sipped her drink. She wanted to keep Susan's senses tantalized, stimulated – and nervous.

"Not yet." Susan wanted to ask her if she had one but decided it would be more interesting to find out another way. Feeling a little surer of herself, she lifted an eyebrow and asked, "You offering to replace the one you took from me?"

Caitlin smirked. "The way I remember it...you gave it to me. However, if you want ...I'll get you a replacement," Caitlin purred the offer.

Susan felt her backside tighten at the answer. Her labium that was already humming seemed to move to numbness from the desire that was overloading her senses. Susan shifted her weight, squeezing her legs together desiring some release. It was difficult to smell any one individual's secretions since the place smelled of sex and other odors Susan had not been able to identify, but she was sure Caitlin could smell her because looking up at her she found a pink tongue was slowly being drawn across her bright red lips. Susan was not sure but she thought Caitlin nodded to her and this brought her to another level of arousal.

"So, do you come here often?" Susan asked in a hoarse voice. She cleared her throat and felt the red flush recede, somewhat.

Caitlin leaned toward Susan and with lips touching her ear and asked her, "Do you want to play?"

Susan shivered at the touch of lips and hot air that brushed against the outside of her ear. Swallowing, she nodded and fought the impulse to look away to lessen the intensity of the moment that had her heart beating so hard against her chest cavity she thought it would break a rib.

Caitlin tapped Susan on the arm and then gestured for her to stand up. Rising slowly, she felt Caitlin's hands on her leathered hips with one that slid seductively over her bare buttocks as she guided Susan to sit between her legs. Her bare back pressed against Caitlin's chest, which allowed her to feel the steady beat of Caitlin's heart.

Long leathered thighs pressed against the outside of Susan's. While squeezing them between hers, Caitlin rubbed her nose against Susan's ear, letting her hands slide slowly over the trembling thighs and then between her legs. Caitlin dipped her finger into Susan's wet center and wiggled her finger back and forth. Her teeth grabbed skin on Susan's neck causing Susan to push back into her and press her legs together to capture Caitlin's finger. The drums that were beating around them drowned out the groans from both women.

"That woman over there...tell me what you let her do to you," Caitlin whispered close to Susan's ear.

Susan moved her head jerkily to see whom Caitlin was looking at and spotted Larry with Lunette. She did not think Caitlin knew about her relationship with the two women but rather wanted her to tell a story – which at the moment she was finding difficult to come up with as her brain seemed to have shorted.

Susan swallowed and shuddered as she felt one set of Caitlin's fingers move up her bare arm, followed by lips that sucked and bit her arm in a wet trail up to her shoulders. The other remained between her legs, sliding slowly along slick swollen lips. Her nipples tightened around the unforgiving metal sending a different type of tingle to her neither lips, loosening a gush of hot liquid essence onto Caitlin's stroking fingers.

"Did you let her fuck you?" a seductive husky voice asked.

Susan's eyes watched as Caitlin moved her hand to pick up her iced drink, bringing the cold glass to touch Susan's nipple.

"Tell me," her low voice commanded.

"Uhh, oohh," Susan moaned letting the physical touches and the timbre of the voice consume her.

Susan's breathing deepened and her throat constricted as she strangled off another groan. She nodded mutely. Somehow, she could not bring up anything about being with another as she felt Caitlin's other finger tease her bare skin, moving so slowly to her breasts.

The pressure of the rings on her erect nipples was distracting her from coming up with anything clever to say, to say nothing of the finger coated with her wetness that lifted to her face, and tease her slightly parted lips. Susan opened her lips and Caitlin inserted her finger, playing with her tongue as Susan sucked on it, tasting herself. Caitlin removed her finger and after setting down her cold drink, she cupped Susan's breasts, one hand warm and the other chilled. Fingertips pinched and squeezed her hardened nipples.

Moaning louder Susan pressed her shaking body into Caitlin's, whimpering her need to Caitlin.

"What did it feel like...her filling you?"

Caitlin felt a different shiver against her. "How did her mouth feel touching your breasts, or on your sweet cunt after she fucked you?"

"Caitlin," Susan whispered in a voice deep with need.

Caitlin gave a tug on one of the nipple rings, and then pinched her nipple with a steady increase of pressure.

Susan wanted Caitlin's finger that was spreading her liquid over her swollen bud to enter her and end her fantasies – thus making them real.

Caitlin smiled from the steady pressure of Susan against her and the moans coming from the heated body that was shivering against hers. As she increased the pressure on her nipple, her prey groaned low in her throat, almost sounding like a growl, giving Caitlin pleasure in the expression.

"Caitlin..." Susan's soft voice begged. "Please...."

"Please, what?"

"I want you," she rasped.

"How much do you want me, whore?" Her voice purred in her prey's white shell shaped ear as she continued to play with the sensitized nipples with one hand and the other stroked her neither lips.

"Very much," she breathed.

"Will you beg me to fuck you?"

"I'm begging you, Caitlin. Please...." Susan twisted in the chair, moving her mouth to Caitlin's ear. "I want to feel you inside of me. I want you to take me however you want. Please, Caitlin, take me. Play with me, fuck me, just...take me please, Caitlin, now."

"You will do whatever I ask, whore?" the husky voice asked softly.

Susan shivered. "Yes."

"Will you be my whore...only mine?"

"Yes."

"Well, then, let's see if you can be with a mistress such as I. The first rule is that I give you pleasure and no one else – not even yourself, unless I say so. The second rule is that you do not cum without my permission."

Susan nodded. Caitlin stood up, pulling Susan with her. She guided Susan up a flight of stairs by way of pushing Susan ahead of her, and letting her hand rest on the bare bottom that was above her. At the top, Caitlin turned her around to face her, pressing her against the wall, kissing her on the lips hard, demanding entrance into her mouth and getting it. Strong hands kneaded her buttocks, and against her bare mons she could feel a leathered thigh press against her. Susan bucked against the press of leather against her sensitized lips trying to rub it for release. Caitlin's kiss was something Susan felt she could get lost in. However, breaking off the kiss abruptly Caitlin whispered in her ear. "Whenever you want me to stop, Susan, say the word Sodom."

Susan nodded leaning against the wall for support. Caitlin tugged on her hand, pulling her into one of three rooms lining the hall. She was pushed onto her knees before the door closed on a darkened room. The darkness was quickly broken when a flame to a match sparked.

"Keep your eyes to the ground, whore."

When Susan obeyed, making no sound, she felt a lash sting across her shoulders.

"You are to answer me, whore, with yes or no, Mistress."

"Yes, Mistress." The fire from the strap's lash slowly turned into a throb, which distracted her for a few moments as movements and sounds of a drawer opening came from her left.

"Come over here, whore."

"Yes, Mistress."

Susan was about to rise from her knees, however a flick of Caitlin's hand indicated she was to remain on her knees.

Once she was kneeling before Caitlin, she waited with her eyes focused on the tips of Caitlin's shoes.

"Who is your Mistress?" the voice asked softly.

"You are my Mistress," Susan responded.

"Are you prepared to prove it?"

"Yes, Mistress."

Caitlin moved so she was standing behind Susan.

"Give me your hand."

Susan hesitated, "Which hand, Mistress?"

"Right."

Caitlin buckled leather cuffs around each wrist and then her ankles. She felt Caitlin breath at the back of her neck and almost arched into the lips she imagined near.

A warm hand touched the back of her neck, causing chills to run through her body. Lips teased the skin at the nape of her neck, then caught up the skin, and gently squeezed. Susan's body shook with suppressed need and in her mind, she tried to be in the moment instead of thinking about finally being with the person she had been dreaming of since she heard her voice.

Caitlin's mouth moved along Susan's jaw line.

"Open your eyes, whore."

Susan's eyes popped open. Caitlin knelt in front of her. Caitlin's face neared Susan's and as she watched the blue eyes that showed wanton desire, her lips touched Susan's. At first in a teasing tasting way, and then roughly as she deepened the thrusts of her tongue into Susan's open and willing mouth.

Susan groaned and moved her cuffed arms to pull Caitlin into her. For but a moment, Susan experienced what it was like to have her bare breasts pressed against Caitlin's leathered ones; feeling her heart beat as strongly as hers, heated skin against hers. Tongues engaged in combat and when both stopped for air, Susan ran her lips down Caitlin's jaw line to her neck.

A hand strongly grabbed her jaw halting her progress, which Susan tried to loosen.

"Do not fight me, whore."

Susan was breathing heavily, and she had almost missed the words due to the loud sound of her pounding heart in her ears.

Caitlin rose to her feet.

"Undress me," she commanded.

Susan's hands eagerly reached for the leg in front of her. She eased the heel off one foot and then the other, letting her hands slide over the muscled calves as they slid to the heel of the shoe.

"May I raise, Mistress?" she asked softly.

"Yes."

Susan rose slowly, letting her hands slide up the leathered pant legs feeling the muscles twitch beneath her hands. She loosened the waistband of the pants, running her hands around the waistband until Caitlin's hands stopped her. Susan's hand wrapped around the waistband of the pants and began to slide the pants down, making it slow in order to drive Caitlin crazy as she was doing to her. A part of her mind was snickering at the payback she would reap on Caitlin for deliciously torturing her.

Susan lowered herself as the pants did, letting her breath tickle the goose-bumped skin as the pants slid to the ground. Susan was on her knees and before her, in the flickering candlelight, were two powerful legs with tattoos. One side a colorful phoenix and the other leg a dragon, starting at the knee up to her hips with their fired breath facing Caitlin's trimmed brown mons. Susan inhaled Caitlin's arousal and was leaning toward the apex between the muscled thighs when two hands held her still.

"Whore, you have not finished."

Susan rose, again, sliding her trembling hands up the warm torso. The leather bra was easy to detach but again Susan drew it out, running her fingers lightly and slowly to the clasp and then using the flat of her hands in a sweeping motion to slide the bra off. Her palms grazed the ringed nipples as she slowly moved her palms to the shoulders, and then down the arms to rid them of the leather bra straps. She moved her body close to Caitlin's so that both their erect nipples brushed. She dropped the bra on top of the red heap of leather, not taking her eyes off Caitlin's eyes that held hers captive.

"May," Susan's voice cracked, "I kiss you?" she whispered hoarsely.

Caitlin pointed to one of her bared breasts.

Susan leaned forward, her mouth and mind focused on possessing the nipple whose ring glinted in the flickering light. As her lips surrounded the puckered skin, both women moaned. Susan's tongue swirled around the dark nipple and then sucked until she could taste its juice.

Excited, Susan's hands cupped the breasts.

Her hands were quickly restrained.

"Did I say you could lay hands on me, whore?" Caitlin's voice was raspy, which encouraged Susan.

"No, Mistress," Susan stifled her disappointment as her mouth was set to feast on the dark brown erect nipples.

"You will be disciplined, so you know what my punishment is for displeasing me."

Susan was pulled up by the cuffs to the foot of the bed. Caitlin ran a chain through the cuff rings and then pulled so that Susan's arms were spread between the two posts and bent forward so that her face rested on the bed. There was movement behind her and more opening and closing of drawers. Susan anticipated a spank but was surprised when it was a lash that crossed her buttocks. It was the first time she had a lashing.

"Were you anticipating something else, whore?"

"No, Mistress."

The burning sensation turned into a steady throb, but Susan did not have time to think about it as another lash fell across her buttocks.

Caitlin gave her five lashes and then released her from the bedpost. Caitlin's mouth descended upon Susan's and both women let themselves get lost in the encounter, this time Susan resisted putting her arms around Caitlin to pull her closer.

"You are a fast learner, whore," Caitlin whispered. She grabbed the chain that still connected her wrist cuffs and led Susan to the side of the bed where Caitlin climbed onto the bed and reclined. She pointed at the small dildo she was now wearing. Caitlin already knew Susan did not like what she was going to ask her, but it was a test.

"Kiss it. Show your Master how much you will appreciate it when it takes you."

Susan crawled onto the bed still dressed, and wrapped her hands around the base of the dildo watching the green eyes close to mere slits at the pressure her grip put on it. Now, Susan felt in control.

Ahhhh. Double headed.

She leaned down to the tip of the dildo, running her tongue over the head then opening her mouth to just put the tip in, pushing on the dildo so it moved against Caitlin. Groans from the redhead told her she was doing it right. She continued to move more of the dildo length into her mouth, grateful it was small. Her hands rested on Caitlin's hips, feeling the woman's hips move to meet her downward movement. The feel of Caitlin's bare skin brought a small groan to Susan as she started to slide her hands behind the hips to get a better feel of her.

Jeeze! But this turns her on! Cum for me, Caitlin.

But Caitlin hissed a warning. "No hands." Her fingers wrapped around a dangling nipple ring on Susan and pulled on it.

"Yes, Mistress." she hissed as she wavered on the bed from the sharp pain that quickly turned to pleasure that burned to her core. Taking a deep breath, Susan pulled back and licked the surface of the dildo, giving it more moisture, and then ran her tongue in circles at the top, pushing harder on the end. Caitlin's hands moved behind her head and encouraged her to continue. Her hips rocked as Susan again took the shaft into her mouth and moved up and down the dildo, taking in more at each downward movement. The idea of what she was doing to the softly groaning Caitlin excited her and as Caitlin's hips began a steady motion,

Susan hummed as she slid her hands behind the moving hips and felt the muscled buttocks flex as they moved.

"No...hands...whore," a hoarse voice reminded her.

Susan ignored her and tightened her hold on the muscular buttocks groaning again as the image of what she was doing to the tall woman filled her imagination.

Caitlin grabbed Susan's hands and roughly pushed her on her back. "You have disobeyed me again, whore." the voice that whispered near Susan's ear was filled with suppressed passion. Susan dared not dare smile.

Caitlin did not want Susan to stop, but she committed an act of disobedience and that demanded discipline to be metered out. She pulled Susan off the bed toward the footboard where she again pulled the chain through the rings at each bedpost, spreading her arms like wings between the posts. Susan's face touched the foot of the bed.

Ahh. You were about ready to cum, my love! You think you're going to drive me crazy with not letting me cum – but two can play the game.

The first slap of the paddle was just a pat to warm the skin, but Susan trembled as her fantasies were coming true. The paddle over the whip marks earlier made added to Susan's sensitivity.

"What do you say to your mistress, whore?"

Another slap, harder this time, filled the room.

"Mistress...."

Another slap, and then another.

"Well?"

"I...I'm..." at that point her brain shorted and she forgot what her previous experiences had taught her to do in this role. Her entire focus was on the pleasure the paddling was giving her and most of all...by whom. Instead, she buried her face in the soft mattress and wrapped her fingers around the chain that held her wrists apart, trying to remain standing and not let the climax that was so close, to wash over her.

"Well, then...you shall need to be shown your place, whore."

After the sixth blow, Susan was groaning with pleasure and thrusting her buttocks toward the paddle. Caitlin stopped when her buttocks were red and hot to the touch.

"What do you say, whore?"

"Thank you, Mistress." Susan was grateful her brain was back in working order and she remembered what Shawna had taught her on some of the correct sub and dom behavior.

"Now, let's finish what you started...with no hands." Caitlin's hands pulled Susan into position with her hands securely wrapped around Susan's leathered waist, admiring the sight of the bared mons and breasts that dangled over her.

Caitlin lay on the bed and this time had Susan kneeling over her in a sixty-nine position, with her exposed clitoris over Caitlin's face and breasts dangling over her stomach. "Now, finish, my whore," she ordered in a soft husky voice.

As Susan once again wet the dildo, she could feel a finger run over her highly aroused backside that was tingling from the paddling. Groaning she increased her pressure on the dildo and her motions as Caitlin's hips once again moved to their own rhythm, with Susan trying to keep up.

Fingers that were exploring Susan's center, slid into her core, and along her throbbing walls, stroking her to the same rhythm as Caitlin's hips moved. Susan tried to continue working on Caitlin. But, as Caitlin's fingers found her G-spot, and began to rub it, Susan lost her concentration and gagged as she missed a stroke from the thrusting hips. A slap on her thigh had her struggling to concentrate on Caitlin when her own needs were moving to the forefront.

Three fingers entered her and began to take up the same rhythm as her mouth was over the slicked dildo that rubbed against Caitlin sensitive clitoris.

Susan could feel Caitlin cum, it was silent but her body spoke volumes as it lifted a few inches off the bed while the fingers that had been inside her became stilled. She wanted to impale herself on the fingers that were in her but the one hand on her hip kept her in place.

Caitlin's hands moved to Susan's leathered hips guiding her to change positions so she was facing her yet still kneeling over her. Caitlin fondled Susan's nipples watching the blue eyes filled with desire and the need to climax.

"Fuck me," she told Susan as she pinched her nipples hard.

Susan lowered her self on the dildo, remembering that Caitlin would also be feeling her thrusts. She braced her elbows alongside of Caitlin and started to work her hips.

"Look at me," Caitlin ordered. Her hands returned to Susan's breasts, kneading them and pulling at the rings that increased the lubrication on her inner walls as she slid the phallus in and out of her, groaning as another pinch on her nipple brought another shudder to her body.

Susan's watched Caitlin's dark irises where she became a drowning victim. Susan could feel Caitlin's desire and need to cum rise and she groaned as Caitlin's hips increased their tempo.

"Caitlin....I...am....need...cum."

"Wait, whore."

Caitlin's tempo increased and Susan eyes fluttered as she tried to hold the rising tide that threatened to break against Caitlin's imposed will.

"Mistress, please...may...I...cum?" she pleaded. "Icantholditanylonger!"

"You may cum." Another pull on a nipple ring had Susan roaring out a deep scream with Caitlin's name, as all her fantasized climaxes at the hands of Caitlin were realized at last.

Caitlin could feel Susan shudder on top of her as she collapsed on her sweat-covered skin. Caitlin's arms hugged her close, her own body trembling from the after math of her own climax. Her hands soothed the body on top of her holding off her own continued need to re-explore Susan's body. Caitlin moved her hands to remove the belt that held Susan's pants on, not letting the phallus that kept them connected move. She left the bra harness on, since it kept the breasts supported and left the nipples tantalizing displayed.

Hmmmm. Thinking of the erect nipples, Caitlin moved Susan's body so she had easy access to them.

Susan moaned when lips curled over her nipple, playing with the ring and then the tongue twirled its way to the other. Susan's hips moved against Caitlin's wanting to feel the friction from the shaft again. The lips moved close to Susan's ear, breathing near it and causing a shudder in her body.

"Remove the dildo, whore," was the whispered command.

Susan hesitated, not wanting to break the connection, and then slowly and reluctantly she lifted herself, letting out a small gasp from the emptying of her core. As she unstrapped the harness from around Caitlin her hands slowly wandered over the sensitive skin, following the base of the dildo and then sliding her fingers up the shaft into Caitlin. Susan moaned, feeling the moist throbbing walls. She pulled the dildo out with one hand and left her fingers in, finding her G-spot she stroked it until Caitlin cried out her name. Susan watched the woman of her dreams as she came, leaning down she kissed her mons, and laid her head near the tattooed phoenix, waiting for Caitlin to recover. A hand stroked her head gently, while Caitlin's other hand was gripping the bedding.

"Whore, give me a massage."

Susan nodded and was about to rise when Caitlin continued. "Without using your hands, until I say so."

Caitlin rolled onto her stomach. "Proceed."

Susan lay her body over Caitlin's, pausing a moment to relish the feel of her form fitting to Caitlin's and pressing her bare mons against her crack where her moisture trickled down to commingle with the dark red head's own juices. With her tongue and lips, she nuzzled the back of Caitlin's neck, sucking, biting, and licking the skin and delighting in the feel of the muscled body under her squirm at one particular hard suck. Susan wiggled her body down, leaving a trail of kisses and red marks where she sucked hard. She was marking Caitlin as hers – for this night, anyway. Her tongue put swirling wet marks down the spine and at the small of her back, Susan bit her gently. Caitlin groaned and spread her legs as Susan moved her face over her butt, kissing, licking and nipping her.

Caitlin pushed herself up into the body that fitted on top of her. Their skin combined was hot and sensitized so she could feel the hard nipples and rings as they pressed against her back. She willed her hands not to clutch the bedding as Susan's wetness trickled between her buttocks and down to her lips that were begging to be touched.

Not yet. Wait.

Susan spent a few moments behind the backs of the knees of the long legs, taking a long tongue swipe across the sensitive area before continuing downward. Susan switched positions so that while still sitting on Caitlin's buttocks, she was facing Caitlin's feet with her muscled thighs squeezed between her legs. Bending one of Caitlin's knees, she ran her tongue over the big toe that wiggled in her mouth. Groaning Susan took the toe in her mouth and sucked on it, running her tongue over its length and then moving to the next toe. With subtle pressure, she rubbed her dripping mons over Caitlin's butt, giving the majority of her attention to the toes, sucking, biting and tickling, using tongue, teeth and lips.

How long are you going to wait, Caitlin? What does it take for you to let me press my lips against your sweet thick pouty lips?

When Susan was finished with the other foot Caitlin rolled over for her to continue her administrations. When Susan reached her apex, where nestled in the dark red hairs was a tight bundle of nerves waiting for release, Caitlin's hands guided Susan to her needful center.

Ahhh. I'm going to make this count, Ms. Caitlin Ann McKenzie.

Susan used her thighs to push Caitlin's legs further apart as she buried her face in the center, smelling deeply Caitlin's scent. It somehow seemed familiar, as was her taste. Susan ran her tongue up and down the sensitive lips then buried her tongue in her opening, getting Caitlin to buck against her face. Susan returned her tongue to the outside finally wrapping her lips around the nub and gently tonguing it to a release. It answered her question about Caitlin...she wore no clit ring. Susan slid a finger inside of Caitlin while her tongue played with her. Strong thighs shook on either side of her face. Caitlin's hands gripped her head, encouraging her to deeper.

Caitlin was loud in her climax, calling out Susan's name, much to her pleasure. And when Caitlin recovered, she pulled Susan into her arms and held her. Both of them held on while the final tremors left them. Both were exhausted.

"You make a very skilled whore," Caitlin murmured in her ear.

"For you, anything," Susan hummed.

"Be careful what you give away in bed so willingly while still in the throes of passion," Caitlin murmured as she kissed the dark short hair.

****

Time was difficult to tell in the window-less rooms, but somewhere far off a ding could be heard. Susan was curled up in Caitlin's arms, whose breathing was so slow she

162

thought she was asleep. Susan nuzzled Caitlin's chest and let her tongue play with the nipple ring.

"Stop that. It's time to go."

"Sounded like a dinner bell to me." Susan continued her play for a few more minutes, without any resistance, and then a hand reached out and gave a hard tug to one of her nipple rings.

Caitlin disentangled herself from Susan and flicked a light on. They both picked up their things and all the toys they used they left in the center of the bed.

Susan delighted in Caitlin's hands that rested on her bare buttocks as they exited the room.

*****

"So, where are you staying?" Susan asked as she squinted outside at the early morning rain. She pulled her coat closer around her, grateful it was lined.

A cab pulled up and it was John Henry.

"Hey, John Henry," Susan greeted as she slid in. "Isn't your shift about over?"

She got a big smile in return.

"Well, looks like you bagged a full nighter this time, baby cakes," he winked at both women. His music was a Rosetti opera which he adjusted the volume before turning onto the busy street and headed in the direction of where Susan was living.

Susan smiled looking sideways at Caitlin who said nothing. "We can give you a lift to your place, or you can stay with me..." She told the tall woman who had pulled a black cap over her nearly shaved skull. Susan wanted to ask her about the scar, but there had not been an opening to ask.

"How about John Henry dropping you off at your place and then he'll leave me off somewhere?"

"Boy, you are mysterious, Mistress McKenzie," Susan whispered dramatically.

"Uh huh. It gives me privacy from my fanatical public," she whispered back.

Susan cleared her throat. "I...I'm sorry about the detective. I just wanted to see you again."

"Don't send someone else to find me. You're here now...when I want you...I'll see you."

Susan looked at the tall woman and sighed from the desire that still filled her. She turned her face to the outside. "**Will** I see you again?"

"Yes."

"When?" the question was so soft, Caitlin wondered if it was asked.

Caitlin studied the dark curly haired woman for a while. *You broke your rule again, Caitlin. So...should you tell her every night if she can take it or...when neither of you can stand the separation any longer?*

"I have some business here that's going to take one more day."

Susan looked at the woman. She could read nothing in the woman's face. Smiling, Susan pointed a finger at her.

"You owe me a ring."

Caitlin smiled. *Shit! That does it.*

"I certainly do. How about today, noon, we meet at La Machelle's for lunch. A ring maker right next-door also does the piercing.

"Okay." Susan was thinking of her list of things to do and how she was going to fit everything in. She had to have her things moved out and the place cleaned by tomorrow. The owner was returning in two days and Tom wanted to make sure everything was in order before his friend and boss returned.

She had already figured out what she was going to store in the van and what Jack said he would hang onto until she found her place. But now... now that she found the person she was going to go looking for....

"So...when your business is finished... where do you plan on going?"

"Home."

It was like pulling teeth without pliers.

The cab drew up in front of the apartment she was staying at.

"You look like you could do with a good nap before lunch," Caitlin remarked as Susan stepped out of the cab.

"Yeah.   But I got things to do.   You know... business."

"I'll see you at noon.   Be on time."

Susan nodded as the cab pulled away. Susan did not notice the person in the car that parked up the street sit up, nor did she notice that the cab paused at the top of the hill. Her thoughts were on Caitlin and how lucky she was that Caitlin found her.

Hot damn!   She found me!   I found her!   I need a statue of Aphrodite and lots of flowers to put around it!

* * * * *

Queen's Lane

Chapter 13

Showered and with fresh clothes that were more appropriate for the weather, Susan left the apartment for the Dinners down the street. She needed to eat breakfast hoping the fuel will give her more energy. When she was in her twenties living without much sleep was easy...in fact, even in her early thirties. Was it when she hit thirty-five that she decided she was not cut out for the forty-eight hour day?

She was sitting at a window booth which she liked because she could check out what was going on outside while waiting for her food. Her eyes followed one particular car that kept going around the block as if it were looking for a parking space but passing up the ones close to the Dinners' doors. By the time she had her meal in front of her the driver found a spot further up the street. The rain had stopped and clouds were giving way to more blue than gray sky.

Susan kept her eye on the driver, noting the occupant did not get out of the car. She was getting a bad feeling...the kind that she knew by now not to ignore. Pulling her cell phone out she dialed Sam. She sighed. His voice mail. She called Tom and Jack's number and was surprised she got Tom.

"Oh! Hi, ya Tom. Off today?"

[You didn't hear?]

"Hear what?"

[Someone torched the shop last night. Good thing the store has sprinklers or the place would have been lost.]

"Oh, shit." Susan's eyes went back to the car that was sitting up the street. *You are being paranoid, Little Bop. Get a grip. Take charge.*

[Yeah. Shit is right. Janey was able to rent the empty store across the way until the shop is cleaned up. So the store will be closed a few days as they dry off things, see what is salvageable and get what has been saved moved to the new location.]

Susan closed her eyes and hoped nothing was going to happen to Michael's apartment, the dog, cat...and the fish tank. "I'm real sorry. I...."

[Jeeze, Susan you're making it sound like you had something to do with it. It's not your fault, Susan.] It was said in a very firm voice.

Susan's eyes opened quickly and focused on the car up the street. The hairs on the back of her neck were standing up. It was so bizarre but...the feeling of danger was there and it never steered her wrong. She wanted a bodyguard, at least until she left town.

[So, have you checked out your van yet?]

"No, no. Ahh. Look Tom, do you know of a good bodyguard company? If not, that's okay. I can look one up in the yellow pages."

There was silence for a while.

[You afraid of traveling alone?] he asked cautiously.

"Yeah. I guess all your words of caution are finally taking effect." She laughed nervously. *I only need one for as long as I'm in town.*

She could hear movement in the background then a grunt.

"What are you doing, Tom. Playing with yourself?"

[Funny. Okay, you got a pencil and paper?]

She fumbled for a pen and pulled her napkin toward her. She was hoping the napkin manufactures were clever enough to remember that their napkins had to be tough for wiping as well as writing.

"Okay."

Tom gave her a name and number. [She should be awake by now.]

"Thanks."

She hung up and quickly dialed the number. Something she learned when having bodyguards around her for six months was that they were more skilled at figuring things like this out than her.

Damn, how am I going to fit the appointment to interview the bodyguard, pick up my van and meet with Caitlin. Caitlin is priority. Then, how was she going to explain to her bodyguard that she was going to get her clit pierced and not to do anything if she should cry out.

[Hanna here,] a deep voice filled with sleep answered.

"Hanna, this is Susan Nikolas. Tom Hudson recommended you to me."

[What did he recommend me for?] The voice sounded curious.

Susan pulled the cell away from her ear and regarded it suspiciously. It sounded so like Caitlin.

Susan cleared her throat and put the cell back to her ear. "As a bodyguard."

[Uh huh. You expectin' trouble?]

Susan laughed nervously. "I think it's already here. I don't plan on staying in town much longer, so I need someone to watch out for me for a few days, starting like right now. I'm kind of in a...I think I'm being stalked, and I need to finish some business here then sneak out before he knows I left. However, I'm not sure how to evade him until then. He keeps finding me." *Damn. How did he find out I moved to San Francisco? Small town news I guess.*

[All right. Where are you now?]

"The Dinners, it's a ...."

[I know where it is. Stay put. I'll be right over. I suppose you have a credit card or something just so I can get the bill rolling...business ethics and all that.]

"I understand perfectly. Bill the Nikolas Corporation. Here is the number of the card...." She rattled off the number and gave her a name to talk to, "Mrs. Erica Marshall and tell her I'll be picking up the van, well, you tell her when you think we can pick up the van today, but I've got an appointment at noon back here, and I'm not going to be late."

[Okay. Don't go anywhere!]

"I won't." She was too shaken to want to take off. For six months she had forgotten about her stalker. All she was concerned about was Jack's fear of her getting mugged if she walked the streets in the evenings around the bars. Her senses told her she was not over reacting right now, and if she was...better safe than sorry. She just found Caitlin and she did not want anything to spoil it.

Susan finished her breakfast by pushing her food around and finally catching the server's questioning look.

"Coffee, and yeah, I'm finished." Her eyes returned to the car frightened for a moment when she did not see the dark figure in the driver's seat. "Shit! Where did he go?" she mumbled.

"Now don't be getting up and flying out of here," Hanna's voice told her.

Susan turned to look behind her startled. Hanna was all lean muscle. She was tall, wore nondescript cloths, her auburn hair was pulled back into a ponytail, and her green eyes....Susan shook her head and blinked.

"You must be Hanna." Susan stuck her hand out and watched large hands bury hers in a warm clasp.

"You must be Susan Nikolas. Mrs. Marshall gave me a brief note on some trouble you had in your hometown. Is this person that's stalking you part of that?"

"I sure hope so. I would hate to think I'm starting some kind of a collection."

"Uh huh. So, he's up in that car, the dark blue Toyota Tercel?"

"Yeah. How did you know?"

"I checked before I came in the back way. It's the only car with someone sittin' low in the seat with the side mirror tilted at an odd angle.

"Oh."

"So, just what are your plans for today?"

"Well what do you recommend?"

"Tell me what you plan on doing today and I'll give you my input."

Susan looked at the woman peculiarly. Her tone of voice was so like Caitlin's.

"Okay. I was going to pick up a van for travelin' today. Then at noon have lunch with ahh...well, with a friend and depending how that goes, leave town either tonight or tomorrow."

"Where do you plan on travelin'?"

"Gordon's Creek is my first stop."

"Any particular reason?"

For a moment Susan's face turned red. "I'm lookin' for someone. It seemed to be a good place as any to start." *Damn, how the hell do I explain the person I'm having lunch with is the person I'm traveling to find...Shit! Caitlin, why don't you just tell me if you're available or where the hell you live...I'm not some stalker!* Although, she did wonder for a moment when looking for someone and stalking someone became the same thing. *How about when the person tells you in no uncertain terms...she does not want you to be looking for her.* For a moment she wondered if Caitlin had said just that and then decided it was not a thought she wished to pursue at the moment.

"You can do better if you just hire someone to look for that person. Who are you lookin' for?"

"I've tried that and...got a warning not to have anyone else look for her." Susan's face broke into a smile at what Caitlin had told her this morning. "I'm looking for a woman."

"So...you want to share the name? Maybe I can find her for you so you don't have to go off traipsing all over the place with a perp chasing ya." *Damn Caitlin Ann you have this woman going nuts for you. Why not just stop the game and take her back to your damn cave and introduce yourself? If it doesn't work out...it doesn't.*

Susan looked out the window for a moment. "Caitlin Ann McKenzie," she said softly. Through the reflection in the window she could see Hanna looking surprised.

"Ms. Nikolas, if Caitlin wants you to know where she is...she'll tell ya." *Hells bells she's even got her middle name.* If Hanna did not have to look innocent, she would have been hooting.

"You know her?!" Susan's suspicious brain put similarities of Hanna's demeanor and Caitlin's together and had a very interesting mix of feelings.

"Hell, the woman used to be the best bodyguard I ever did train." Hanna was laughing to herself at what she knew Caitlin would punch her good for saying.

"You trained her...I thought she owns or owned her own company?"

"Yep. Sorta retired after the last job. Likes the quiet life of a recluse. Let me give you some good advice...leave her be." *Like she's really going to listen to that stupid advice. They both like this stupid game of 'find the bear in her cave'.* "I mean, you chasing after her, she may think you were stalking her."

Susan bristled. "I am having lunch with her today."

"You are?"

"Yeah...and...we plan on...well...anyway."

"Well, then...ask her where she lives so you don't waste a trip up to Gordon's Creek."

"You know where she lives?!"

"Now did I say that?"

"Damn it Hanna. She's back in my life and intends on disappearing after today! She's driving me crazy!"

"Well, girl, I'll tell ya, you aren't the first that's been pantin' like a puppy dog and sniffin' like a hound hot on a trail for her." Hanna gave an inaudible sigh. Caitlin was so damn gun shy over intimate relationships that she had developed an elaborate game to see just how serious someone was interested in her and just what they were interested in her about. "When was the last time you saw her?" As if she did not know just by the goofy look on the woman's face. This was her employer, she reminded herself.

"Last night...I mean this morning."

"That's the reason you keep moving around on the bench?"

Susan's face turned bright red.

"All right. It's you life. You said you needed to get to the van place, right? So, let's get going. I have our transportation out back."

Her transportation was a hog, a shiny red Harley Davison with two helmets wrapped around the handlebars.

Hanna swung her legs over the monster and then pulled her helmet on. "Mount the thing, girl, and strap the helmet on. I don't have seat belts so hang on."

✝✝✝✝✝

The trip to the van sales office brought Susan face to face with Mr. Marshall, the manger of the place. They sold, besides Roadteck vans, BMWs and adjacent to that lot, Mercedes.

"You own these three lots?"

"Yep. So, you're the Nikolas' kid that got run out of town for doing what everyone else does. It's amazing they haven't moved into the 21st century. I won't deny I didn't look at the shots on the Internet. I hear there's a virus now in the pics. Good for you. Looked like you were out of it in some of them. You get that kid that did it yet?"

Susan's face turned red. "No. I'm working on it."

Hanna hid her own smile at remembering seeing them too since Caitlin had downloaded the pictures when she heard of them from one of the bodyguard's and did a trace to the source. *Damn woman was already stuck on her! Well, guess that goes to prove she's not dead to the vibes like we all thought. Wonder what kinda toys she'll be creatin' with this one around.*

Susan sat down to go over the price and paperwork, noting that she was not being overcharged.

"Just where do you plan on keeping this thing until you leave?" Hanna asked as both of them looked over the new van.

It was a 190-versatile Roadteck that had a double bed in back and two singles up front. The porta-potty area extended to a shower with privacy doors on both sides of the walkway acting as shower walls. Hanna noted the seating of four people comfortably up front, but guessed Susan was only interested in two people.

"Well, before Junior showed up, I was going to park it somewhere on the street."

Hanna pulled her cell out. She made arrangements for the van to be picked up and for it to be serviced and ready for her by afternoon.

"All right, Mr. Marshall, my associate Miles Guntry will be by. He's going to pick it up and get everything ready for Ms. Nikolas here. Ask him for his ID, will ya? He's too cocky for his own good," Hanna grumbled, then nodded to Susan to leave.

"Come on. When exactly did Caitlin say to meet her?"

"Noon." *Miles Guntry? That's the name of the guy who Caitlin borrowed the sport car from. Damn! How small can the world be?*

"She hates it when her dates are late," Hanna hummed as she kicked her hog into a throaty purr and with her passenger hanging on, headed back across the busy bay bridge.

They were five minutes late and Susan was curious what Caitlin was going to say when she noticed she had hired a previous colleague. She also wondered if Hanna was going to say anything to her about Susan looking for her.

Susan was disappointed when Caitlin gave no special indication at seeing Hanna. She wondered for a moment if Hanna was telling her the truth. Hanna merely dropped Susan off then told her she would be back. Susan was hoping she meant she was going to check out the apartment before she returned.

It took all of twenty minutes for Caitlin to give into her curiosity. They had their menus and a glass of water placed carefully before them.

"So...what are you doing with Hanna?"

"I hired her as my bodyguard. See anything you like?" Susan smirked. *Ha! She finally asked!*

"Why do you need a bodyguard?"

"I think Junior found me."

"Junior?"

"Yeah, remember the clit ring I gave you?"

"Cobley, Junior."

"Yeah. Interesting that he should show up today. I sure hope it's not some psychic thing tied up in clit rings, or I'll give them up entirely," she muttered as she laid down her menu with a soft thumb.

"When did you first see him?"

The waiter appeared with his pad.

"This morning while I was having breakfast. Yes, I'm ready to order. How about you?"

"Crab salad, glass of white house wine."

The waiter glanced at Susan expectantly.

"I'll have the house special with a glass of burgundy."

"So, how did you get Hanna's number?"

"Some friends recommended her to me. She said she trained you in the business, and you've sort of retired."

Caitlin sputtered, "**She** trained me! Like hell! And I didn't retire. I'm taking a vacation... indefinite!"

Susan laughed delighted in Caitlin's openness. "You know, now I know why she reminds me of you."

Caitlin looked at her suspiciously. "Why?"

"When people work together for a long time, they start sounding like each other. Just like with a married couple. If she hadn't told me she knew you, I would have thought it was such a weird coincidence. I've been having so many of those since I came to this city, you know?" For a few moments, Susan stared into the green eyes whose dark iris's seemed to expand as far as they could.

"What brought my name up?" *So, you think too many coincidences. That's good. You think.*

Oh, oh. "Ah. I told her I was having lunch with you."

"Uh huh."

"Where do you think she went anyway?"

"Mindin' her business," Caitlin returned cryptically.

"Oh. Well, I hope that is checking out the place I'm staying at. I don't want anyone getting hurt because of that nutcase."

*****

"Are you sure you want this on me?" Susan looked at the gold ring that had a small diamond on it.

"Yep. The diamond makes it easy to find you in the candlelight," Caitlin teased.

Susan looked up at woman she wanted to really settle down with. It must have shown in her eyes because Caitlin cupped her hand on her chin and kissed her gently on the lips.

"Let's get to know each other a little more before we start with that, huh?"

"Right. So, what are you going to do, just show up in my life whenever?" Her voice sounded shaky to her, as her stomach was doing some funny things from the kiss.

Caitlin smiled. "Maybe."

"All right ladies. Next."

*****

Now Susan was really sore. Sitting was uncomfortable and she had to remember not to wear tight pants for a while. It was not that the pain was unbearable…it was the distracting desire she felt from the throbbing lip as to why it was there.

Hanna was waiting on her bike outside of the Ring Shop. She grinned at Susan but quickly wiped it off at the glare Caitlin directed toward her.

"You two finished?" she asked with her eyes glinting with humor.

Caitlin ignored her and turned to Susan. "I have your cell number."

Susan nodded and hoped when she called, she would give her enough time to hightail it back into town, because she was determined to find out just where Caitlin lived.

"Hey! How did you get my cell number?" By the time she had turned around to finish her question Caitlin was nowhere in sight.

Susan pulled the helmet on and winched as she settled on the seat behind Hanna. There was no comfortable way to sit and the vibration from the bike that was picked up in the ring was not good for employee-employer relations.

"So what are you going to do now?" Hanna asked at the first red light, turning her helmeted head to study her rider. She was laughing inside about the squirming body behind her thinking how the vibration from the engine must be driving her passenger nuts...not to mention that it was also her employer and Caitlin's little whore, as she loved to call her lovers.

The sudden stopping motion, with her jeans pulling on the ring had Susan seeing stars.

"Well, I'm going to move the few boxes I've packed to Tom and Jack's place, and take two to the van. I sure as hell hope he doesn't do anything to the apartment I'm staying at. The owner has a dog and a cat and a big ole aquarium."

"1215 B street east, right?"

"How did you know?"

"Part of the business. I got someone watching the place. You'll be safe for a while."

"If you found me that easily it's a wonder he hasn't done anything before this."

"Well, my job is to protect you for as long as you are in The City, so don't worry. You're covered." *And Caitlin's been scarin' the bejeebes out of the others that have been hired to follow ya by the little dickhead, so ya need not worry, Honey. You're guardian angel is watchin' over ya. The fact that he's here means he can't hire any more people so he's got to do it himself.*

The two women entered the apartment from the back way. Hanna had cupped her hands and hoisted Susan over the fence and she followed with less ease. All Susan had left to pack were a few cloths she left hanging in the spare closet.

After Henry checked Hanna out he returned to his bed and pouted. Susan was thinking he was lonely for his owner. Minnie did not even put in an appearance.

Hanna made a phone call while Susan threw her long coat into the box of things she was going to take with her in the van: four boxes and two suitcases. She accumulated when she said she was not going to, but they were her play clothes and some toys and supplies for the van.

"What's all this?"

"Those two boxes will go over to Tom and Jack's, the friend that recommended you to me, and those two are what I'll take with me in the van. Warm clothing and stuff."

Right. Play stuff just in case I can talk Caitlin into playing house with me in the van. Provided she doesn't get pissed that I'm tracking her...but, I don't think so.

"Have you ever camped in a van?"

"No. I thought I would learn as I go."

Hanna nodded and then flipped open her cell phone as it rang. Without answering it she studied the number on the face and then returned the cell to her hip.

"Come on, let's get these boxes over the fence; our courier is here. And...we gotta get you familiar with operating that van before you get out on the road."

"Great!"

*****

Jack and Tom were not at home, so Susan left her boxes with Cindy, who was a friend of the two guys. She said they were helping with the burnt out shop.

"Tell them I'll keep in touch."

As she gingerly sat on the back of the motorcycle, because it was getting more uncomfortable, Hanna leaned back. "It's not smart to be leaving them messages about your whereabouts. You said this guy is an electronics whiz? He'll be monitoring their calls I'm sure."

"Well, I'll call you then, and you can let them know whatever you feel is safe. How's that? I'll keep a running tab with ya. Whenever I'm in town...it'll give you a steady income," Susan joked.

"I already got a steady income...but...every little bit helps."

They rode to the outside of San Francisco, over the bay bridge and past Oakland. Susan had not the slightest idea where they were.

The van, her van, was parked in a motor home and RV lot, where a young man had the hood up and was looking at it.

As Hanna pulled up, she revved the hog's engine a few times. The car that had her two boxes for the van pulled up alongside of her new RV.

The young kid with the same auburn hair and green eyes as Hanna turned around and grinned.

"You're too old to be drivin' that thing. When are you going to give it to me?"

"When my arthritis gets to be cripplin'."

"That's going to be too long. Hi, my name's Miles."

"Hi, I'm Susan," Susan shook his hand.

"What have we here, an AA meetin'?" Hanna grumbled.

Miles laughed. "I got the van fueled up and ready to go. Nice little home. Oh, and I have Miss Business like you ordered, Boss."

"Miss Business?"

"A dog," Hanna told her briskly. "G'wan. I got it covered here," she told Miles.

"Right. Have a nice trip." Miles got in the vehicle that had been carrying her boxes, humming a tune Susan barely recognized.

"As long as you go traipsing around the coast alone you need someone to keep a watch. Just make sure you bring her back soon. Come on. Let me introduce you to her."

"Are you sure you want me taking your dog with me? I mean, I may be gone for a long time."

"Hardly. Didn't Caitlin tell ya she'll be callin' ya?"

"Yeah. You think soon?"

"Give her a month."

"A month!"

"Okay, maybe a few weeks."

"Hanna! How do you know?"

"She comes into town every two weeks. She has business here. So, you're still determined to go lookin' for her?"

"Before she showed up last night, it was what I had originally planned on doing. I hadn't seen Caitlin for over a year. So I might as well continue with my original plan. It'll give me something to do until Junior gets tired or something. He's got a warrant out for his arrest, you know?"

"Your boredom is going to get you into trouble with Caitlin." Hanna shook her head. "And yeah, I know about the warrant. I already notified the police for ya. They told me you hadn't called them yet. You got somethin' against the police?"

Hanna slid the door open and a medium sized dog threw itself into her arms. Now Susan understood why Hanna had not opened the door right away.

"Hi, there Missy. Okay, let's get her to work. Stand there, Susan. Missy, work, protect." Hanna picked up Susan's hand and for the next twenty minutes got Missy and Susan used to each other.

After her training, while Hanna went to get a hose for her water tank and an electrical cord at the supply store, Susan put the supplies she brought away while talking to her new four-legged friend. When Hanna returned she showed her how to operate various goodies in the van and how to open and close valves for her stove, water tanks, toilet waste tank, how important it was to make sure the van was leveled before turning on things, and what was under the hood.

"You must have driven one of these things," Susan told her as she sat behind the wheel of her brand new home on wheels.

"Yeah. It's been awhile but things haven't changed much. Come-on. Follow me. I'll find a safe place for you for the night. Missy, don't be beggin' for table scraps," were Hanna's parting words.

****

Chapter 14

"Well, Missy, looks like this rest stop will be where we put up for the night. Damn, I am tired. Come on, let's both take a potty break."

It was well past midnight, and she had kept awake by talking to Missy. Hanna had insisted she take a nap before heading out. She had two hours, which was plenty. She was jut too wound up. It was more from the prospect of looking for Caitlin than running from whoever was following her.

After both Missy and she had returned from their bladder and sniff break, she put in her call to Hanna's voice mail, telling her where they were and that she was tired. She even got Missy to bark once in the phone so Hanna knew she was okay too. She also called her father's answering machine and let him know she was sight seeing along the coast.

After locking all the doors, she fell asleep quickly.

****

Morning was bleak. It was gray and promising to rain.

"Missy, I love this type of weather. You know why?"

Missy was more interested in the can of food she was preparing, but Susan pretended it was because she was a good conversationalist.

"Neither do I. I just like it."

Susan was proud of herself that she remembered how to turn everything on and turn it all off when she was ready to roll.

"You know Missy. This is kinda nice for one person …and a dog…but, it would be nicer with two people. Huh? You could trade places with Ms. McKenzie. You probably would like your own bed better, huh?"

Missy chose not to ride on the front seat so for the next few hours as Susan took her time driving along the coast, she would occasionally ask Missy how she was doing. She had two weeks to do nothing but avoid Junior if the police did not catch him, or until Caitlin called.

The rain came down in torrents and at noon, Susan found a RV place with all the conveniences of hook-ups. After connecting everything under the downpour, she was happily smelling and hearing the coffee drain into the small glass pot while she dried her hair, and reveled in the clean and dry cloths she had changed into. Her wet clothing was stringed across the small space that served as her potty and shower area where they could safely drip dry. Her refrigerator was nice and cold, and her cream did not curdle as it hit the Hawaiian-Hazelnut brew.

"Too bad you don't know how to use a toilet Missy…correction, since I don't have toilet seat covers, you can't use the toilet."

After she finished her cup of coffee, Susan put her leather coat on and took Missy out into the rain for her to do whatever she needed to do. After Missy walked around looking miserable in the rain and not doing her 'business' as Susan chose to call it, they both reentered to the comfort of a dry van. Once the excess moisture was toweled off Missy, Susan started to make her calls.

It was three calls: one to Jimmy who was between classes and would let their father know she was fine; left a message for Sam; and then, she left a message on Hanna's machine.

Susan looked out at the rain that was falling through the trees that surrounded her, wondering what was bothering her. It had nothing to do with Caitlin, she decided with certainty. The feeling was not what she had when she first rolled in and set up. It was a dark feeling that started about an hour ago.

"You know Missy. This is a real creepy feeling. Like, Junior's around. But, I know he can't know where we are." She sighed heavily and the poured herself the last of the coffee. "Sometimes paranoia stinks," she muttered.

After about thirty more minutes, the time it took to unhurriedly finish her second cup of coffee, she cursed and pulled on her coat. "Come on. You go take a leak and I'll pull up stakes."

In the rain, it was cold and windy, making twisting the hoses and attachments into their storage space nice and neatly difficult. She kept blowing on her cold fingers trying to get them to be more flexible.

Finally finished, she looked in the door where she had pulled it slightly ajar to let Missy find her way back in. She could see her wet tracks.

"Missy?" she called to be sure. A very wet dog peeked out at her. "Good girl. Wish you could wipe your feet though."

Susan slammed the door shut and walked around the van with a flashlight, giving a once over look, making sure everything was ready and locked securely from the outside.

She stepped into the driver's seat, and while the engine heated up, she removed her coat, draping it over the seat that Missy did not want to sit on. She flipped up the heat to hurry with the drying. In the poor lighting in the campsite, she pulled out carefully, maneuvering around this and that and barely finding the road that led to the exit of the park. It was late and the check out enclosed stall was closed. She dumped her papers in the small box on the outside of enclosure, just as she was told to do when she checked out, and started up the road. She paused for a moment, waiting for a two-trailer truck to slowly gather up speed to pass by her that was also pulling out onto the freeway. Turning slightly she could see a light come on and someone reading a map in his car.

"Oh, shit! How the hell...?" Susan did not wait; she pulled out using the side of the slow moving truck to block the person from seeing her.

"Damn it to hell, Missy. What's he using, tea leaves?"

"More likely listening in on your phone conversations."

"Yeeeeahhh!"

A long arm reached over and kept the steering wheel steady.

"Caitlin! You just about scared me into my next life!"

"Hm. And what are ya? Cat, bird, horse...?"

Caitlin moved the coat that was draped over the chair to the back. She slid in and put the seatbelt on.

"How long were you back there?"

"Not tellin'. Trade secret."

"Well it couldn't have been for long. Not many places to hide here. And your coat's wet."

"Good eye, Sherlock."

"What are you doing here? Not that I don't mind. Damn, Caitlin, I missed you." Susan was blinking tears away and finally for both their safety, Caitlin switched places with her.

Caitlin found another place for them to park for the night because Susan was crying for all sorts of reasons and both women were tired. Caitlin sat in one of the seats that had more room for two, pulling Susan in her lap and holding her until she stopped crying.

*****

Susan looked up from her completed task of pulling the double sized bed out, which had once been a dinning area. The windows had their covers snapped into place. She could see Caitlin sitting in the passenger seat with the small reading lamp shinning over her head. There was a map unfolded covering Caitlin's lap as she studied it. Susan was hoping it was not the one she had all the little colored flags marking docks.

Missy was curled up in the driver's seat sleeping.

So, Missy sits only in the driver's seat, huh?

Pulling her jeans off, Susan moved into the small closet that was both a toilet and shower stall, pushing aside her still wet clothes. Since the water tank did not hold enough water for a shower, Susan contented herself with a sponge bath, and then brushing her teeth in the sink an arms reach from the toilet.

Clad in panties and a T-shirt she looked around in the sudden darkness.

"Caitlin?" she whispered.

"Over here."

Susan guessed Caitlin was inspecting the bed and noticing it was not friendly to tall people. "How did you get there without me seeing you?" There was absolutely no way Caitlin could have gotten to the back without passing behind her, regardless of the fact that it was dark.

"Trade secret," Caitlin's voice sounded like she was smiling.

As they traded places, Susan's hand rose instinctively to touch the warm body that leaned into her, and Caitlin gave a brief kiss on her forehead.

"There's a handful of new toothbrushes and two different toothpastes in there," Susan told her softly while letting her hand slide down the warm body.

Caitlin nodded and slid by Susan, resuming her trip to the shower stall.

*****

"Do you realize that this is the first time I've ever slept with you...I mean sleep?"

"You have once before....in a sports car."

"That doesn't count."

"This won't count either if you keep talking till its time for us to get up."

"Oh, right. Good night, Caitlin."

Susan was having a hard time not touching Caitlin in intimate places and when she would, Caitlin would move her hands away.

"Go to sleep. If you can't I'll sleep up front and Missy can sleep with you."

Susan turned her back toward Caitlin, thinking that would make it easier. After about twenty minutes, she heard a distinct sigh and a soft curse. Caitlin's body pressed against hers and an arm draped over her waist, pulling her in close.

"Woman, you are a distraction," Caitlin breathed in her ear.

Susan's body automatically arched into her and a groan she tried to stifle leaked out. Fingers slid down her stomach over her shaved mons and to her lips, where the ring was pushing against her swelling labia, vibrating with need.

"God, you are so wet," Caitlin breathed in Susan's ear. "What were you thinking about that got you so wet, little whore?" Hands slid her panties down over her butt.

Susan shuddered and pressed against the hairs that were tickling her crack. "You, Mistress," she whispered.

A hand cupped Susan's sex, and a finger slowly stroked her. When she tried to control where the finger would go Caitlin gave her a warning growl.

"Don't move! Don't make a sound," she whispered the last command. Her lips nuzzled the back of Susan's neck while Susan moved a hand behind her to feel a muscled buttock cheek of Caitlin's as it undulated against her.

"Tell me, what were you imagining?" Caitlin whispered.

Susan tried to hold still, widening her legs as much as she could while Caitlin teased her with her mouth and fingers. Some sounds escaped Susan when a finger pulled her clit ring.

"I...was imagining you taking me...just like you are now." Susan groaned when a warm hand moved to her nipple and pinched it.

"You can do better than that," Caitlin growled.

"I...while I was brushing my teeth, I imagined you found the box of toys I have and you picked out the ones you liked. When I came to bed, you attached a nipple chain to my rings and had me...." Susan stopped to take a breath as Caitlin pulled one of the nipple rings, "sit on your face. Every time I told you I was about to cum...you would pull on the chain...until I begged you to let me cum." The last bit was rushed out. Her attention was sorely divided.

Caitlin leaned near the panting woman's ear, "You are not to cum until I tell you."

Caitlin's long fingers slid into Susan's slick entrance. Susan cried out with pleasure and tried to suck the fingers further into her. Her insides tightened around the long digits, reluctant to let them go as Caitlin stroked the warm slippery walls.

Caitlin leaned down to her ear again. "You are not being quiet. Turn over and put your face in the pillow."

Though the chances of a night audience in the pouring rain was not as great as Junior finding them, Caitlin was more interested in the continuation of the control game she had initiated at the beginning of their relationship. She was wondering how far she could push Susan and what she would do when she reached that point.

Susan rolled over, gripping the pillow.

"Don't forget to breathe," Caitlin purred in her ear.

Caitlin pulled her panties off and then laid her longer body over hers. Susan buried her face in the pillow and groaned at the same time, pushing her butt into Caitlin's stomach. Caitlin rubbed herself over white buttocks, smearing her juices and making the muscled globes slick. She slid a hand around the front of Susan between her legs. Susan spread her legs, allowing Caitlin easier access, while lifting her body up into Caitlin's. Caitlin's fingers gently tapped the ring that was wet from Susan's juices.

"Fuck me," she ordered as she presented two fingers at Susan's opening. Susan moved herself over the fingers and muffled the moan that shook her body as she slid over the long digits. They curled inside of her as she moved her body. Caitlin matched her thrusts as her wet pussy moved against her butt.

Susan could feel Caitlin's panting breath at the back of her neck and then lips pressed against her shoulder. Susan's nub of nerves was being touched by Caitlin's thumb each time she thrust down on the fingers, and her hips were getting more frantic as she could feel her climax approaching. Caitlin was resting some of her own weight on her elbow that was on one side of her, but Susan imagined she would be getting tired soon, just as she was from carrying some of Caitlin's weight.

"Caitlin, please, can I cum…?"

"Not yet!" Caitlin panted, as she undulated against her so hard that Susan was barely able to lift herself high enough to clear the fingers before swallowing them up again.

"Caitlin..." Susan begged. "Please..."

"Cum for me, now," she ordered as she continued to rub against Susan's wet buttocks, and moments later moaned her own release.

Susan turned under Caitlin, breathing heavily. She pulled her in close. Her lips closed over Caitlin's, concentrating on the taste of the toothpaste. She flickered her tongue against the slightly parted lips until they opened wider and she pushed her thick muscle through. Susan could hear a low growl rumble in her throat as her tongue fenced with Caitlin's and both women pressed against each other with hands touching and grasping, as if they had been parted for a long time.

*****

The sound of the rain beating against the small van almost drowned out Missy's whine to be let out. Caitlin was under Susan who had maneuvered the taller woman's body so she could comfortably run her hands over her when she wanted to reassure herself that Caitlin was really with her.

Caitlin prodded Susan, "Off."

"What if I say no?"

"You clean up."

"Oh." Susan lifted herself and looked around in the gray light for her clothes. Both women dressed as Missy continued her little dance. Caitlin unlocked the door, peered out, and then stepped out into the rain with Missy.

Susan reluctantly made up the bed and began her inspection of foods to begin preparing something warm for them to eat. *Eggs, cheese, hmmmm. I know I bought some mushrooms, yeah...*she put the ingredients in a bowl, and then realized she needed to turn on the gas.

Wait a minute. I gotta get this boat level before turning on anything.

After checking the levelers and raising the one side to its mark, Susan slipped on her raincoat. Stepping out in the rain, she looked around for Caitlin and Missy. She could not see either. The rain was not heavy, but it was enough to get wet in if she stood out in it long enough. She leaned down to turn the gas on, feeling the cold knob turn as she twisted the valve open. Turning her head slightly at the sound of a heavy footstep behind her, she could see an arm descending toward her. Moving to the side, she turned and raised her knee into the midsection of her assailant, and as she lost her balance, used the back of the van she fell into to give her enough support to kick the bent over figure in the head.

"Good kick." Caitlin and dog were at her side.

Caitlin hauled the body up and peered into the dazed bum's face. "Go on back to your camp and don't bother us again." She shoved the man forward. "Or you'll lose your valuables."

"Camp?"

"Yeah. There's only two of them. They have plenty to eat, and they're nice and dry," Caitlin told her just in case Susan might want details.

"So why was he over here?"

Caitlin looked at her disbelievingly. "You are alone, female, and have a warm dry place to bonk."

"And breakfast..." Susan stepped back into van. *Dah, Sherlock. You have got to be more careful!*

She finished the preparations for breakfast while Caitlin stared out the windows.

"No toast, but...we do have coffee."

Caitlin looked up at Susan and nodded. She shifted her weight and sat facing Susan who sat down, picking up her fork and waiting for the questions.

"So, tell me. How did he trace my calls?"

"Eavesdropping in on phone conversations is easy...you left voice mail with Hanna giving her your

locations. I told her not to use that for client contacts."
Caitlin thumbed her plate with her fork.

"How did he know I hired her?"

"Hanna told him."

"Why?"

"Stalk a stalker. Harass him as he harasses his victim." She took a bite out of her food and when she finished chewing, she added, "He must have access to a lot of cash."

"Cobley's Electronics credit card. His daddy owns a big electronics firm that does business in Mexico, a few hours across the border. Why didn't she just grab him until the police arrived?"

"She had him, but he's a little slicker than her and got away after she gave him her riot act. He's getting cash from someplace...maybe his daddy gave him one of his own cards. Where's your cell phone?" *He's not using any under his name or the cops would have nailed him by now.*

Susan leaned over to where she had stashed her purse and drew it out.

Caitlin pushed her cleaned dish aside and pulled out a small knife attached to her key ring. She slid open the case, poked around with the tip of the knife.

"I just got that one. My other one bit the dust. I was able to keep the same number."

"Where did you get it?" she asked.

"The store on 7th avenue. Why? You think they planted something in there? Caitlin, it came right out of the box and into my hands. This is not like the clit ring, is it?"

Caitlin had a small dot on the tip of the knife blade. She held it up for Susan to see. "Well, it must have left your presence for a moment sometime, because this is a signal device."

"Signal...well, why did my phone work? Wouldn't it interfere with the cell signal?"

"Have you been getting many calls?"

Susan laughed. "Strange as it seems, I don't have very talkative friends or relatives. I'm the one that usually does the calling."

"Uh huh. Come on. Clean up and let's get out of here."

"While I clean, what are you going to be doing?

"Looking around. If you see anything that looks suspicious...get out of here. I'll catch up with you. Okay?"

Susan resisted asking her how she would know where she was going but did not want to open up the conversation as to what all the flags marking spots on her map were about...as if Caitlin could not figure it out. Susan had the place cleaned up and the engine was warming up when Missy and Caitlin returned.

"Let's get out of here."

While Susan drove, Caitlin dried herself and the dog off.

*****

Chapter 15

"This place isn't even on the map, Caitlin," Susan grumbled as she pulled into a small one-pump building that she was not even sure anyone was at.

"Which map is that, Susan?"

Susan cleared her throat as the tone of voice told her maybe Caitlin was going to say something about the marks on the map after all.

"All of them."

Caitlin got out and pumped the gas, disappeared into the small office and came back out.

"Go up that road right there."

"Are you sure this van....all right, all right!" *Little Bop, don't question Caitlin when she's in a bad mood.*

The van creaked and sank into the soft mud but it kept moving on. There was a brief break in the soft dirt and the road branched off in two directions.

"Left."

They hit the soft dirt again, and there were plenty of trees and brush on both sides blocking Susan's view of where they were, if she took the time to look, but she was busy steering over a path not made for vehicles.

"Turn right here."

Susan did not bother to challenge Caitlin as she turned into a cleared space that was not even a path. Caitlin hopped out and started to guide Susan in parking the van.

She turned off the engine once Caitlin was satisfied.

"Come on."

"Do I need anything?"

"Nope. Leave everything including your cell."

Caitlin and a very happy dog were off through the woods. Susan followed, turning around to get her bearings and hoping she could find the van when she had to.

The path they ended up on led to a dock where a white Bayliner, about twenty feet, was rocking against it's slip. Missy appeared to be familiar with it because she ran up the dock and hopped into the boat. Caitlin stopped Susan from stepping aboard. Missy jumped back out onto the deck and barked.

"Good girl, Missy."

"Hey, that's pretty good. Does she look under beds too?"

"Have you ever been on a boat before?"

"Yeah. I know there are storage places under the beds."

While Caitlin warmed the engines up, Susan was sent to release the lines.

"Don't fall in. The water's cold in January."

"Ya don't have to tell me that, mother," Susan mumbled as her cold fingers struggled with the line. The boat shifted and she tossed the line into the boat, then grabbed the railing and hauled herself back in.

Caitlin did not waste time and as soon as Susan was standing solid on deck, she kicked the boat into high gear and headed out to the ocean. The small bay only had one small dock.

"Is this your boat?"

"Nope."

The tone of voice reminded Susan of her first trip with Caitlin. She refrained from any more questions and instead sat back and watched Caitlin fly the boat to only she knew where.

The abrupt stop had Susan falling off the couch she had settled down on to nap.

"Hey!" Susan struggled to get up, rubbing her sore hip where she fell off the couch. Climbing up to the deck she watched as Caitlin was tying the lines to another slip post.

"Let's go."

Missy was out and scampering along the wooden surface, disappearing into the darkness. Rain was falling lightly.

"Can I ask where we are?" Susan asked as she pulled her coat on.

"You can ask," Caitlin told her as she walked swiftly along the plank. She held the gate open for Susan then moved towards what could be a draped motorcycle.

"In the rain," Susan mumbled disgustedly.

"You have a helmet with visor. Consider yourself lucky."

"What for?"

"You have me blocking most of the weather and a visor to keep the water out of your face."

"Oh. What happens with Missy?"

"She rides up front." Caitlin pulled the cover off a black Harley and folded it up into one of the saddlebags in the back. She also pulled a small raincoat out for...Missy. At least some of her would be dry.

Susan looked at the black bike thinking of one she had been seeing on some of her dates parked near by. People around the Bay Area must like these vehicles.

"Poor thing. No helmet, visor or a Mistress to keep her warm."

Caitlin actually smiled as she slung her long legs over the machine and tipped it upright. She handed Susan her helmet and brought the machine to life. Missy dutifully jumped up on the gas tank and waited. Susan sat in her spot and wrapped her arms around Caitlin, rubbing her wet cheek against the wet leather coat.

*****

Chapter 16

Riding with Caitlin was not the same as with Hanna. It just felt different, and the way her clit ring was humming from the engine's vibration, Susan was surprised she was able to resist the impulse to dragged Caitlin off her bike and into some nearby bushes.

After about thirty minutes the engine was cut and they coasted along a bumpy road, deep into the forest that was dark, spooky, and dripping with the mist that was still falling. Susan was cold, though her hands had been tucked under Caitlin's coat just above her belt buckle, but occasional shudders shook her frame as she hugged the taller woman. She wondered how Missy could take it.

Caitlin nudged the engine back to life as they rolled into a shed whose door automatically opened at their approach. The engine was cutoff as they bounced over a ramp and into the dark storage space. Caitlin leaned back a little as she kicked the stand under the bike and dismounted, careful not to kick her passenger.

"So...I take it this is home." Susan dismounted undoing the helmet strap as she did. She did little dips with her legs trying to get her cold wet pants to change position against her almost numb legs. A small red light had turned on at their entrance, giving her an idea that the shed was made just for the bike.

Dark irises looked down into her blue. Caitlin gently pulled the helmet off Susan and ran one hand through the short curly hair, and then firmly pulled her head toward her with her hand behind her neck.

"Rule one, Susan. This is my castle." She leaned toward Susan's ear. "Do you accept that rule?" she whispered softly.

Susan felt the warm air of Caitlin's breath against her cold ear. Her heart beat faster and her mouth became dry at all the possibilities of what that implied.

"Yes," she whispered back. "Whatever you ask," she added hoarsely.

"Ask? I won't be asking," she returned matter-of-factly looking down at the blue eyes that looked up at her so trusting. *Let's see how you like my world, Ms. Nikolas.*

Caitlin set the helmet on the bike and turned, walking out of the shed with Susan following, wondering if she would be able to give Caitlin what she needed...and if Caitlin would be willing to give her what she needed. The shed door automatically closed behind them.

If Caitlin had not taken her hand and led her through the dark forest, she did not think she would have found the small cabin. In the dark, it blended in with the environment. After wiping her feet on the mat, Caitlin unlocked the door and stepped into the front room. Again, a small red light came on. Susan was wondering what the red lights indicated.

Standing back, Caitlin let Susan enter before closing and locking the door behind her. Caitlin flipped a small switch next to the door and walked into the kitchen. Susan looked around, taking in the Spartan environment, while rubbing her palms over her thighs trying to bring some warmth into her legs. The interior was composed of two rooms, with the kitchen tucked into a corner and separated by a counter. She figured the open door into a dark room was to a bathroom. The furniture consisted of a table with two chairs, a double bed, and a bookcase. Susan stepped closer to read the titles of the books.

Bondage for Beginners, by Mistress M. How to Live with a Dom, by Mistress M. How to Tie Up the Love of Your Life, by Mistress M. Jeez! She's the same person that designed some of the toys in the leather shop. I wonder if Caitlin knows her.

She slid out one of the books and turned to ask Caitlin if she could read the book when she realized she was alone. Susan stepped around the counter that separated the kitchen from the rest of the room and found Caitlin sitting with one leg dangling over an opening in the floor with the light from the opening shinning on her. Caitlin was removing her second boot. Missy was nowhere to be seen.

Susan tucked the paperback in her coat pocket, and sat next to Caitlin, following her example, and then followed Caitlin down the stairway that opened up into a room that gave the appearance of a miniature art gallery. Three walls were covered with paintings and erotic sculptures artfully arranged around the room. A circular couch sat in the center of the room for someone that wanted to study the works. Where a fourth wall would be was a circular stair, showing other rooms across from it on the same level they were on. As Caitlin stepped onto the deck the opening above Susan's head closed. Glancing up quickly she only saw a ceiling. Once she stepped off the stairs they folded up and became an interesting sculpture.

"Jeeze, what a hideaway!"

The area they were descending into was a large circular space, separated by partitions, and in the center of the area was a staircase that led to other levels. Susan hurried behind Caitlin who started down the spiraling stairway where she could see two more levels of living space. Dim white lights came on the second level as soon as Caitlin stepped on the stairs.

"Oh, wow!" Susan followed Caitlin into a black, white and red bedroom that looked like a huge playroom. One statue, a black shiny dominatrix, stood larger than life with her outstretched arms sporting rings and leather cuffs. The ankles and waist also had cuffs. In another area of the room, a chair stood with the appropriate bondage accoutrements and next to it was a glass case on the wall that held various styles of whips, paddles and some things Susan had never seen before. The bed had leather straps with rings attached on each of the four bedposts and above the head post, had something Susan could not even guess at what it was. Caitlin took Susan's shoes from her hands, and put them in a basket. She gestured to the tiled bathroom and Susan gathered it was an offer to clean up.

"A shower, boy do I feel I need it. I need to thaw out." She stepped into the tiled room seeing her image everywhere mirrored back at her. The mirrors magnified the light. Susan began undressing while looking over the elaborate bathing area.

So, which mirror is the shower behind?

She peered around one privacy partition and found a large tub with a lot of accessories for play and intimate cleaning, lined neatly along a rack. Susan could feel the heat between her legs increase with anticipation.

This is a playground. I wonder if she has a steady playmate.

That started some very unpleasant feelings so Susan closed those down with a sharp reminder to herself that they had no commitment...yet.

Caitlin entered the bathroom and undressed. This was Susan's first chance at really looking at her, and with the mirrors she was able to get a view of all angles, which she made sure she took time to study.

Gods, but you are so magnificent!

Caitlin had the body of a serious athlete, well balanced in the upper and lower regions without being bulky.

The lights from the bathroom revealed more color in the tattoos that begin at her knees and wound around her thighs. Susan breathed in slowly letting it out as a small trickle of liquid down her center reminded her that this was real and not a fantasy. It also gave her a good view of the scar and again she wondered what had happened.

Caitlin crooked her finger at Susan and pointed into a wall space that turned out to be a shower stall. As Susan stepped in she realized it was over six feet long with a cupped seat at the opposite end of where the showerhead was.

"Looks nice."

"It is." Caitlin turned the shower on and tested it for temperature.

Susan turned around as the pressure on her shoulder guided her to face Caitlin. She was handed a sponge and soap. Caitlin kissed her forehead. "Wash yourself, for me." She stepped back and sat on the curved seat at the other end of the shower. Her legs were parted. The phoenix and dragon where shadows on her thighs, and her carefully clipped pubic hairs were reddish brown.

Susan began, going slow and spending some time soaping her breasts and then her apex, gently playing with the clit ring. Closing her eyes from the hot jolt of pleasure a gentle tug gave her, she enjoyed the feel of Caitlin's eyes on her.

Well, you've been figuring out how to seduce this woman, Susan, and here you are. She's obviously a voyeur so give her a show she'll enjoy.

"Keep your eyes on me."

Her eyes popped open and she watched Caitlin's eyes, using them to guess at what Caitlin wanted to see.

After every part of her body had been cleaned, stroked and rinsed, Susan wondered what to do next.

"Now, clean me."

Caitlin turned on a knob near her and the small hose with a sprayer came on with the water from the shower turning off. She spread her legs further apart and waited.

Susan took the hand held showerhead from Caitlin and began her job, starting with her head that had about a third of an inch of hair giving a reddish tint to her scalp. This gave her a better view of the thin white scar that ran from her head down to her shoulder. She stood between the outstretched legs using one hand to spread the soap, until Caitlin reached up to hold the shower nozzle, allowing Susan to use both hands. However, the spray was directed between Susan's legs and the spray was hitting the ring tugging at her labium.

"Ahhh, may I have the hose back, Mistress?" Thankfully, Caitlin gave it back to her, letting a smile crease her lips. It was temping to lean down and kiss her.

Susan watched the green eyes close as the water and soap cascaded down the tanned face. Susan leaned forward near her ear, letting her eyes take in the nipple rings that glinted as she moved.

"May I kiss you, Mistress?" she whispered softly.

Caitlin titled her head up toward Susan. "Yes."

Lips pressed against lips as Susan stepped in closer between Caitlin's legs. She ran her tongue along the outside of Caitlin's lips, teasing to enter but not taking the plunge. Finally, she drew back.

"Thank you, Mistress."

"Get on your knees," Caitlin directed her after she finished soaping and rinsing her back.

Susan knelt between her legs on the rubber matting. Caitlin took the nozzle and wet Susan's hair, and then soaped it. Susan closed her eyes from the pleasure of feeling Caitlin's strong fingers scrubbing her scalp. As the water sprayed through her hair rinsing the soap down her face, a pair of lips closed on hers sucking her lower lip then releasing her.

"Stand up....Turn around...Bend over."

Susan followed each direction. As she leaned forward, the washcloth ran across her buttocks with the water nozzle following behind rinsing the soap off. She closed her eyes as the sensations that were a caress went over her body. Caitlin's hand tapped her leg to spread wider. The washcloth ran along her clitoris and her crack, the water nozzle following. As the water hit the clit ring Susan's breath caught and a small shake in her legs started.

"Spread your cheeks."

Susan reached behind her and pulled her cheeks apart so her anus opened wider. Water shot up her followed by a sponge and then some more water. Susan heard the water turn off behind her and the shower came back on. Lips kissed her buttocks, followed by a tongue, which ran around her anus opening. Susan let out a soft moan that she thought only she heard. Caitlin's face pressed between her cheeks followed by a small bite on one cheek. Susan jumped and let out a startled giggle.

"Wait here."

Caitlin left the shower for a moment then returned with a razor and gel. For a brief moment things stopped for Susan as she stared at the razor in Caitlin's hand. Caitlin caught the change in Susan's expression and handed her the razor.

The moment passed and Susan took the razor, smiling up at Caitlin. "I don't want to give you a beaver burn."

Caitlin smiled

While Susan spread her legs, Caitlin took charge of spreading the gel over her.

"Gods! If I knew how erotic this would feel for someone to help with my shaving..." Susan leaned forward and kissed Caitlin's forehead, "I would have asked you sooner," she whispered. Eyes met and time passed as each woman was deep in her own thoughts, yet along the same lines.

"Uh huh. I remember you already were shaving when we met." Caitlin finally broke the silence.

"Yeah." Susan cleared her throat, nervous. Whether it due to the present or a past experience, Caitlin was not certain.

Caitlin carefully inspected the shaved and rinsed skin between thighs and mons, letting her hands casually slide to the back of Susan's buttocks. Caitlin leaned forward and sucked on the pink freshly shaved skin twirling circles with her tongue until they came to her apex where she pushed Susan gently back, her mouth covering her lower lips. Susan sat on the seat spreading her legs wide and pulling Caitlin's face closer into her.

"Yessss, Mistress," Susan hissed softly as a tongue slid up and down the folds of her thickened lips and then around the ring that pierced the swollen flesh; Caitlin's ring.

"Oh, Caitlin!" Susan held Caitlin's head gently.

Caitlin continued her tongue massage feeling the thighs under her hands tightening as Susan neared her peak. Caitlin smiled wondering if Susan would remember to ask her permission to cum. If she didn't then the discipline would have to start over, if she did..."

"Cait..lin..." Susan struggled to slow the intense wave that was sweeping over her.

Caitlin took the hard nub of nerves in her mouth sucking on it then flicking her tongue against it.

"Mistress, I...please...can...I....cum?" she panted.

"Yesss." Caitlin lifted her face away from her lover's center long enough to see cerulean eyes staring at her with desire. It gave Caitlin a rush and she returned her lips to press against the ring that was bestowed on her squirming subject, realizing that she was forming a relationship deeper than the others she had dabbled with.

Susan's cry of release echoed in the bathroom sinking to a small keening sound as Caitlin refused to let go. Susan squirmed nearly from her grasp.

"Hey, come up for air," Susan panted pulling the face firmly from between her legs.

Caitlin laughed huskily and kissed one of the shaking thighs. To cover her uncertainty, she rose to her feet, then quickly rinsed off. "Are you hungry?" Caitlin asked as she stepped out of the shower, pulling Susan with her.

Susan nodded hoping Caitlin meant it in a sexual way. She did not want to stop.

Caitlin handed Susan a towel, which Susan used to dry off Caitlin's body. Caitlin did not object. She pulled Susan toward her, bringing their lips together. A tongue ran the length of Susan's slightly parted lips; flickered on the outside of them and then withdrew.

Susan groaned when Caitlin pulled away.

"Dry yourself," she commanded in a whisper.

Caitlin dressed in a large shirt, no underwear. The shirttails covered her buttocks and pubic area but the arch on the side of the shirt's bottom gave a good view of the sides of her tattooed legs. Susan wondered if she had the shirt tailored just for that effect.

"Rule two," Caitlin reached for the towel in Susan's hands. "I will be the only one to wear clothes until I say other wise."

She tossed the towel into the clothes hamper and took Susan's hand tugging her gently after her. Caitlin led the way back up to the first level where her kitchen was, looking like a gourmet's playground.

"Wow! I take it you like to cook."

Caitlin pointed to a chair for Susan to sit at. "Sometimes. Fish okay?" She realized that she was losing her command resolve with Susan and for two important reasons she could not. One was that she needed to first clear this stalking problem with Junior and the other…they needed to find out if they were compatible before she...there Caitlin stopped.

"Slide forward in the chair and spread your legs wider," Caitlin directed as she moved to the refrigerator.

Susan's bare skin on the rough fabric felt erotic against her sensitized skin and opening her legs wider gave her a weird sensation as the cool air that breezed against her hot lips did nothing for it's heat. The clit ring seemed to protrude out of her moist folds as her lips thickened. She could feel moisture trickle, tickling as it dripped down to her anus. Susan could smell her arousal as she watched Caitlin prepare a meal.

"Do you mind leftovers?"

"No."

"Good. Touch yourself."

Susan's hand went to her breast, kneading it and bringing the already erect nipple to a harder erection. Her other hand caressed her round stomach and slowly moved between her legs. Her breathing was deepening as she kept her eyes on Caitlin, who would pause now and then from her preparation of their meal and watch Susan, desire showing in the green eyes.

Caitlin set out two plates and spooned the cooked fish and rice on both plates. Caitlin leaned toward Susan as she placed a bowl of freshly prepared salad in the center of the table and kissed Susan.

Susan's head was thrown back and she was breathing, as she was almost ready to cum. Her eyes popped open to Caitlin's kiss.

"You are not to cum unless I say you can. That's a given."

Susan groaned and moved her hand away from her clitoris, just as she was going to relieve the build up. Caitlin leaned down and reached for the clit ring, holding it between two fingers, pulling on it slightly. "This is mine."

Susan grimaced and shuttered at the shock it sent to her aroused nerves.

"Eat your meal."

Susan was going to squeeze her legs together for some relief when Caitlin stopped her.

"Leave your legs spread."

If Susan was not so horny she would have giggled.

"Great," Susan mumbled. "You know, I could catch a cold with my legs wide open like this...Mistress."

Caitlin raised her eyes to look into amused blue ones.

When both women were finished, Caitlin nodded toward the plates. "Wash the dishes."

Caitlin watched as Susan moved, enjoying the movement of her back muscles and legs as weight was shifted from one leg to another. Unable to just sit and watch any longer, unusual for her, she stood behind Susan, uncertain. The heat that radiated from both their bodies had Caitlin's hands twitching. Caitlin leaned forward, resting against Susan's back, running her hands over her body and feeling the skin pebble under her palms.

"Gods...." Susan breathed deeply, pressing against the body that leaned into hers. "Mistress..." she exhaled. It made washing dishes difficult for her, though enjoyable. Caitlin's hands set fires wherever her hands caressed, and slapped. When she finished with the dishes, Susan turned in her arms.

"Caitlin, please. I want to taste you." She looked up into dark iris' that were filled with the lust she felt throbbing throughout her body.

Caitlin kissed her lips, while walking back to one of the chairs. Caitlin sat with her legs spread, pulling Susan's head so her face was inches from her apex.

"Mistress, may I?" Susan asked softly.

Caitlin did not trust her voice so instead she pulled Susan's face in closer so that it was buried between her thighs.

Susan ran her tongue on the outside, picking up Caitlin's wetness on her curled tongue. She rubbed her face in Caitlin's swollen lips before resuming running her tongue up and down the thicken lips. Caitlin came before Susan had much time to tease her. She could feel the hard nub quiver under the press of her tongue and then Caitlin cried out.

Strong hands gripped her head when she continued to suck on the lips, and pulled her away.

"Enough," Caitlin breathed heavily.

Susan stood up and wrapped her arms around Caitlin until she kissed her forehead and gently pushed her away.

Caitlin tugged on Susan's hand and showed her into the room next to the kitchen.

"This is the library. Make yourself comfortable. I need to check on some things."

A few hours later Susan looked up to see Caitlin watching her.

"You ready for bed?"

"Yeah." Susan's tired mind provided erotic images of what sleeping with Caitlin in her own bed would be like.

Caitlin led her back to her room, the level below the kitchen and library.

"Use the toilet now," Caitlin advised. She stepped to a dresser behind the tall dominatrix statue, her naked tattooed body blending into the shadows in an eerie way.

Susan breathed deeply, noticing the clean smell of a forest that circulated in the underground fortress. She was feeling a little off-balance and not really knowing why.

"May I take a quick shower...Mistress?"

"Yes."

Caitlin sighed to herself as she removed some leather items from the bureau drawer. The sounds from the tinkling bells on the wrist and ankle cuffs gave her pause as she thought about where she was going with all of this for the hundredth time. Maybe it was a mistake to bring her here...but she had brought others here...except, she was sure who was mistress and who was slave. With all her heart she wanted Susan to be okay with all of this. Caitlin snickered to herself. Who fell for whom? But she did not have a problem with that. She had a problem with bringing Susan here when she had other issues to deal with, and she was stacking the emotional cards on her side by bringing her to this environment and training her to be…to be what? A sub? A Dom? By her summation, Susan would be whatever she wanted her to be…some of the times…Was that what was worrying her…that Susan is not a controllable person? No. Caitlin knew enough about people and herself to know that that was one of the qualities she had picked up in her and obviously …it was something that attracted her to Susan. Susan was a switch.

Caitlin moved to the light knob, looking up at the night-lights as they dimmed to what she dialed. She did not know for how long she was standing mentally going over her method of testing the worthiness of a mate as opposed to others. She felt uncertain as to whether it was a matter of choice or rather an obtuse circumstance known as fate. Whatever it was, she was going to make sure Susan was sure she wanted to be with her before they became too involved.

"Hey." Susan's breath caught as she stepped out of the bathing room and peered into the darkened bedroom. Tiny sparklingly lights were on the arched ceiling, twinkling like real stars, and there was even a thin crescent moon putting off its own light in one corner with a faint line hinting at its complete circular shape.

"It's beautiful," Susan breathed.

"Thank you," a soft voice returned. "Come here, whore."

The voice was low and sensuous to Susan's ears, sending goose bumps moving up and down her arms. Susan tossed her towel into the laundry bag just inside the bathroom door without looking to see if it dropped in, and approached the shadowed figure that the lights from the overhead stars revealed little of. Standing before Caitlin, Susan tried to read the woman that stood naked before her. Her eyes took in the dark painted toe nails, the tattoos that started at her knees and up to her thighs, the round breasts with dark puckered skin around erect nipples whose gold and diamond nipple rings sparkled, and then past the elegant neck where a pulse was beating faster than that of a resting heart beat, and continued up to dark eyes that were not difficult to read.

Caitlin leaned toward Susan. "Turn around, whore." Caitlin's soft lips brushed Susan's ear.

A shiver skittered down Susan's spine, and while her heart beat faster with anticipation, she turned as was commanded. Her nipples pulled against the rings that were unyielding, aching to be touched, and her lips at her apex swelled from desire with her clit ring sending a burning sensation for the release of liquid from her core.

A warm hand that started at Susan's shoulder ran down her arm stopping at her wrist. Fingers curled around her hand, and then something that was soft and made small tinkling sounds wrapped around her wrist. Susan's eyes tracked to look at her right wrist while her left was treated to the same adornment. It was a soft black leather wrist cuff. The inside was padded, and the outside had small bells and a ring for attaching it to something. Hands seductively trailed down her legs, where ankle cuffs were also wrapped snuggly around her limbs. Caitlin rose behind her letting her hands slowly and suggestively slide up her thighs and then her arms. The heat from both of their bodies had beads of sweat breaking out along Susan's body. A mouth nuzzled the top of her ear, while Caitlin's hands cupped her shoulders, pulling her against her hot firm body.

"Rule number four…you go only where I tell you and when I tell you," the soft voice commanded.

"Yes…yes, Mistress." Susan's heart was beating loudly in her ears. Her eyes moved to the tall dark Dom statue and she gulped hoping she was going to be introduced to the dark lady.

"Get in bed." The soft breath tickled Susan's ear. "The left side."

Susan sat on the black silk sheet, liking the feel it had on her skin as she slid between the sheets.

"You know, if I turn out to be a restless sleeper...we may both go nuts with these...making all this racket, Mistress." She jingled one wrist for effect.

"Consider it behavior modification then... because I'm sure you don't want to keep waking yourself up."

You have got to be kidding! You expect me to just go quietly to sleep after all this? Not even a kiss?

Caitlin pulled covers over her. Leaning in close, Caitlin's lips touched her neck, moving to her ear, where a tongue traced the outline stopping at the lobe. Teeth gently grabbed the lobe and then Caitlin's tongue continued back up her ear. A wet curled tongue was stuck into Susan's ear causing her to shiver.

Yeow! That's new!

"Sweet erotic dreams." Caitlin's lips kissed her neck and then she leaned back, settling for the night.

"Same to you, Mistress." *And many more, you brat! You are going to drive us both to distraction if you keep playing and don't let me give you a lip clamp or something. Humph. Damn! I'm gonna have to turn the tables here. But tomorrow. I'm tired.*

However, sleep did not come easily to Susan. Looking up at the ceiling, she drowsily wondered what constellation she was looking at and then wondered what caused Caitlin to seek her home underground, away from the stars she seemed to like. Susan sighed.

Little Bop, you wanted to find out about Caitlin, and here you are...in her very own... fortress. How lucky can you be? Gawds! Who would have thought I would be here six months ago, or even a month ago?

Susan turned her head to study her bed partner and found dark shiny eyes watching her. Susan's mouth curled up into a smile, matching the one that was on Caitlin's face. Susan leaned toward Caitlin and whispered softly, "I could drown in the pools of your eyes...got a life jacket?

*****

Sometime in the night Susan's dreams became dark and sinister. It was along the same line that her nightmares took during the hearing. She had thought then that if she knew what it was that was causing her to run in this dream sequence, she would get over her fear of it. But she just never had the nerve to face it -- so she just ran. Now, she wanted to see what this fearful thing was about. But the more she pursued it through dark mazes, bright lights, and smoky places, the further it retreated in the shadowy unclear dreamscape, and that was frightening with its unseen terrors.

Soft words spoken to her in Caitlin's voice helped her find her way back to a safe place, above the maze that had her confused and feeling alone.

*****

Caitlin was still awake when Susan's breathing changed to a deeper breath of someone that was asleep. Sighing she looked up at the shadow of the dominatrix statue that was nearby. She wanted to strap Susan to her Dark Lady, and introduce Susan to another level of her world....but, later. By the expression on Susan's face, she knew Susan was open to the experience but that would have to be for another time when they had more time to play...and...when Junior was not a problem. She wanted no interruptions.

Careful not to wake Susan she rose to let Ms. Business out.

Well, Caitlin, so far she has not freaked out about being down here, and she's going along with the sub role, sort of...but, how long are you going to keep this Dom attitude? It can get rather tiring and you know once you let your guard down...she'll be in there. Okay, so, what's the next lesson...you wrote the books on this stuff...you've been setting up the training for others...but, oh, joy...she's not like the others. She's got this fascinating mixed energy, that...hmmm.

A big smile appeared on her lips as she remembered the night in the bar.

Oh, yeah...that is a night I will always remember. Alcohol or no, I'm sure that heat you were putting out, Ms. Nikolas would have still been there...And oohhh, baby, and when you removed that clit ring. Embarrassed or not...you knew just what you were doing to me, and you were not drunk. Yeah. I think you had all of my attention by then...and that was a long ride home that had my imagination driving at heavy rpms. But I'm glad we didn't do anything...with what you went through at home...I would have just told your father to shove it and taken you away.

Hmm.

That trial...something bugs the crap out of me about it...and not just because the focus was on Susan. Odd to put all the focus on the victim; which even the papers had labeled her as. Why, then did they hound her? Why not Cobley Senior or harp on Junior's recent past? I dug it up easily, so why not the papers? Does Senior own an interest in the papers? That's right...something to add to my list. I'll do a background on those two patriarchs. Why is there so much bad blood between them...and is that why her father refused to attend any of the court hearings, because Cobley, Senior was there for every one? Damn. Caitlin, you need to stop with the thinking or you won't get much sleep. In the morning...you'll have a plan.

An hour after Caitlin had settled into her own slumber, but before she sunk into a deep REM sleep, unfamiliar movements beside her awakened her. The smell of another's sweat and irregular breathing brought her to consciousness swiftly. By the soft lighting from the overhead replication of stars and a half moon, she could see Susan was not having a good dream. Not touching her, for fear of adding to the nightmare, she leaned over and whispered in her ear. She kept up her murmurings, watching for signs that Susan was working her way out of it. When the sleeping woman's breathing leveled off Caitlin lay back down.

Restlessly Susan cried out.

"It's all right, Susan. I'm here." Caitlin touched her shoulder gently establishing a connection, and then pulled her toward her.

Lantern light eyes flickered open. "What?" a sleepy voice asked. The bells jingled as she moved a hand to stroke the arm that was reaching out for her.

"You all right?" Susan asked in a thick sleepy voice.

"Yeah. Just wanted to make sure you were okay."

"Hm. Of course I am. I've got my own bodyguard, don't I?" Susan buried her face in her neck and kissed her. "I am so happy you found me," she confessed in a whisper. "I want this to work out." With that last confession Susan sank back into a deep slumber.

Caitlin stroked the bare shoulder near her and wished the same.

*****

Chapter 17

Caitlin felt lips pressed against the back of her neck, then a very wet tongue, and then lips again as they sucked on her skin. A shiver that ran up and down her spine settled in her stomach giving her a warm feeling that could easily turn into a hell of a bonfire if the lips continued doing what they were doing.

"Mistress Caitlin, if you don't give me permission to pee somewhere, we'll be changing the sheets here," Susan whispered in a dramatic stage whisper, letting her breath and then tongue caress the ear they were near.

Caitlin rolled over and looked at the grinning Susan whose expression quickly turned to a pout. "Mistress, may I...relieve myself?"

"Uh huh. Since you asked so nicely, whore, you have my permission to pee in the toilet." Something told Caitlin if she did not say exactly where, Susan's prankish nature would find somewhere to urinate that would be an inconvenience.

Susan pulled the covers off her, flinging them back, leaving Caitlin exposed to the cool air.

"Hey!" Caitlin objected hiding her grin. "Damn. You're going to bear some watching." Caitlin got up and put on another shirt with tails that covered her buttocks and pubic area, but arched over her hips. Normally, she wore nothing in her private habitat, but Susan's lessons needed to be continued, both subtly and not so subtly as to what her role as a sub entailed. Until their roles were established, Caitlin would be the only one wearing clothes, though....she had a feeling Susan wasn't going to be a demure sub, no more than she would be a strong Dom. Sighing she could not help the grin that creased her lips at the challenge of getting to know Susan and knowing that Susan felt the same about her. A little flutter in her stomach signaled that she did not mind the challenge at all. It was amazing how a night of sleep...in her own bed, did wonders for her take on one of the problems. She followed Susan into the bathroom, exchanging places on the toilet.

"I warmed it for you, Mistress." Susan leaned close to face her as if to kiss her but instead she whispered, expelling more air than needed, "May I brush my teeth, Mistress?"

Someone else's morning breath was not something Caitlin was in the habit of experiencing so she leaned away from Susan.

Oooh, yeah. I'm going to have to find something to keep her busy, or...treat her as an equal...Oh, no. Not yet. With us being down here and nothing to really distract her, I will have to suffer her endless questions about this place, my life, why do I live here...ooooh, no joy. She'll drive me nuts with those questions, and I gotta concentrate on getting this Junior stuff wrapped up. Naww. I think it's best to leave her as a sub for now! She still doesn't have that role down right. Yeah...as if ...Caitlin stifled the laugh she almost let out.

"There are some toothbrushes...wrapped in the drawer on the left side of the sink and toothpaste. You may brush your teeth with one of the brushes."

Caitlin completed her business watching Susan lean against the bathroom sink while brushing her teeth. The bells on the cuffs jingled as she moved. Her legs were spread slightly and the muscles of her legs and back were interesting to watch as she moved. Intentionally, Caitlin was sure, Susan bent over to pick up the dropped paper that had covered her toothbrush. Caitlin chuckled at the suggestion the bending over gave.

"May I take a shower, Mistress? It's part of my daily ritual. Morning and night, type of thing."

"Yes, whore, you may." *Ahhh, giving me some idea of what her needs will be. Very good. Hm. Well, maybe I'll just have to add a few of my own rituals to hers.*

Back in her room, she pulled on leather pants over her socked feet and picked up her shoes, just in case she needed to rush out while Ms. Business was out for her potty break and inspection.

Susan's morning shower was quick, and when she entered the bedroom, Caitlin was dressed in street clothes and holding her shoes. Susan hesitated a moment, feeling her heart beats increase. Worried, her eyes raised to Caitlin's.

"Time for Ms. Business to go out for a potty break," Caitlin crooked a finger at her and headed for the staircase. Caitlin quietly ran up and around the spiral staircase, knowing by the sound of the bells that Susan was following. Susan's momentarily look of uncertainty at her being dressed was not missed.

Was that because she thought I was going to leave her here alone...is she claustrophobic? If I have to leave for one reason or another before we find out what Junior is using to track her, I can't have her panicking here while I'm gone, nor can I take her with me.

On the first floor directly across the kitchen separated by the spiral staircase, was her security room where monitors, phones, PCs and just about all her electronic surveillance equipment were located.

It also had a large screen where she watched some of the films of Susan being trained. She was not sure just what Susan would say about the films or about the education she had given her without her knowledge, but in due time she would tell her. That was one of the things she did, arrange the training of subs and doms; matching the student up with couples or teachers that matched the student's temperament. It was a part of her that Susan would either accept or reject...and...Caitlin glanced at Susan...and then, Susan would have to decide what she was going to do about it.

Caitlin stood in front of the monitors that her cameras revealed of the surrounding wild life, in the trees, the sky above her forest, the shed and the cabin. No one appeared to be around. The heat from Susan's body that was close to hers was noticed, and it set little prickles of desire to her groin area, but her attention shifted to the type of tension around Susan that was not sexual, and it increased as they stepped into her security room.

"All right Ms. Business, attention! Up the stairs for potty time and scout."

The stairs uncurled from the sculpture they were in and the ceiling exit slid open. Missy happily took off up the stairs and out the pet door in the cabin. Both women watched on the monitor as Missy sniffed around and looked for a place to do her business.

"Aren't you afraid she may run off after some wild creature?" Susan asked quietly as she looked around the room. Something about the room reminded her of something … cameras? Oh, yeah...her nightmares of ....*nightmares? I don't have nightmares of cameras. What a dumb connection. I think I'm just nervous about being underground.*

"No, **she's** well trained."

The meaning of the message took a few moments to register with Susan. Turning toward Caitlin, she watched the tall woman's head turn toward her with a smirk. Susan stuck her tongue out at Caitlin.

"Is that a challenge, whore, or is that an offer?" Caitlin asked. An alarm had her turning back to the monitors. "There is a small area she can do her thing in. This is a wild life area... domesticated dogs have no business around here. They mark everything their bladder can water and to a creature from this area, it signals that it is another's territory. They live in a shrinking living space because we humans are not controlling our own population."

"Hm. Park Rangers don't allow domesticated dogs on a lot of the wilderness trails for that reason," Susan mentioned.

Caitlin nodded and turned her attention back to the monitors and Susan returned her thoughts back to the persistent bit of memory that was teasing her at the edges of her consciousness. It was being a real pest. Not so easily caught but leaving behind clues to its presence...like the cold feeling in the pit of her stomach. Her eyes moved restlessly along the monitors not sure where the increased anxiety was coming from.

Claustrophobia? "How safe is this place anyway? I mean what would happen if someone jammed your equipment? Or turned off your air? What would happen if there was a forest fire? How do you evacuate from this place?"

"All exits are marked, but this has enough air down here to not get me worried, and if there was a forest fire above us.... this would be the safest place to be. Are you worried about Junior?"

Junior? Yeah, it has to do with Junior. The cold knot in Susan's stomach tightened. He always managed to find her, or his spies. Then again, she was not really hiding. How many people knew Caitlin lived in the forest, underground? Would he find a way to smoke them out?

"Yeah."

Nervously and for warmth, she rubbed one hand over her arm to take some of the chill out of her, though most of it was coming from the pit of her stomach. The noise from the cuffs was annoying and she stopped. She let out a puff of exasperated air.

"What makes you think he would know about this place?"

"He keeps turning up when he shouldn't, doesn't he?" Susan began to pace, her nervousness escalating to near agitation as the bells jingled. *What the hell is happening with me? I feel like I'm getting a panic attack.*

"You're..." began Caitlin.

"It's not paranoia!" Susan turned toward Caitlin feeling some relief from the pressure that had been building up in her. "The fact is he keeps finding me!" The cold feeling in the pit of her stomach was threatening to turn into a nauseous gag. *Oh, shit! I hope she has a toilet or sink near by.*

"You're not giving me much credit or Hanna," Caitlin told her levelly. *Now what triggered this? Monitors? The woods? Does she know about the cameras in her apartment in Colina? It's not like I can tell her I checked her place out...damn, Caitlin. You will eventually, but now is not a good time. So, what is weirding her out?*

Caitlin's eyes searched the room again for what could being unnerving Susan. Maybe it was a combination of things. Caitlin watched her as she rubbed her arms again. She was not going to give Susan anything to cover herself...it was part of her sub training. Besides, her nipples were standing out and from Caitlin's experience; she knew how the rings in her nipples were providing a distraction from her fear. She glanced at the screen that monitored the life support of the underground hideaway. Giving a small inward sigh, she moved the mouse to select the temperature, clicking it up two degrees higher.

"You have every right to feel like you've been watched and monitored..." Caitlin started and then decided to leave it at that, for now. The monitor dinged her that a warm body was approaching the cabin.

Ms. Business had finished her duty and after lifting her nose and sniffing the air, she trotted back to the cabin.

As soon as she cleared the pet door, a panel slid down over the exit which a monitor showed as secured and the light went to red. The medium sized dog carefully clambered down the stairs with the ceiling sliding shut over her. When all four paws hit the floor with a thud, the ladder folded up into an entirely different shape of sculpture than what it had been the previous day. Susan studied it for a while distracted, but keeping her arms wrapped around herself. Missy obediently trotted to her designated area to lie down.

A smile creased Caitlin's face as she watched Susan's eyes flicker over the art piece looking puzzled. Turning back to the console, she logged onto her system for mail. Three were of immediate interest. She gestured to Susan to take a seat on a cloth-covered chair.

"Sit down and get comfortable. This shouldn't take long. This place is secured with a lot of exits, and backups to the life support. I no more want to be stuck in here than you. What kind of bodyguard would I be if I take shelter in a corner with no exit?" Susan's face was reflected in the monitor Caitlin was facing. Susan nodded at her back and had sat in the chair, looking uncomfortable, though not as she had been moments earlier.

Turning her attention to the memo that flashed on the screen she opened it up to read. Jackson, one of her employees sent a status report. He staffed the private pump near where they had left the van. He reported that John Cobley, Jr., had passed by and that their perp was using a model airplane with a camera to spy out the land. His small plane flew over the dock where they had escaped in the boat as if he knew exactly where they had headed and he had only been thirty minutes behind them. It was as if not only did he have a homing device planted on Susan, but he also had access to some kind of satellite that could keep track of her. That requires money and contacts, which was why Caitlin brought her here. Whatever device he was using to track

Susan with, it would not penetrate through the material that made up her underground home.

Damn. Aside from jewelry, where else could he have planted something to track her? Inside her? Sonofadickhead, could he have? Jeeze! That would mean he did it on their first night together... the night she doesn't remember anything.

"Susan, you said your first time with Junior, you don't remember. Do you think you were drugged?"

Susan looked up from the screen that showed the local squirrels playing tag. "Ha. I would like to think that...but I think I just drank too much and blacked out. Drinking and black outs run in my family. I've learned for me, three drinks is a good cutoff."

"So, you don't remember anything of your first time?" *So, when did you learn this, before the bar at Flagstaff, or after? Maybe the trial changed her drinking pattern.*

Susan was quiet for a few moments, looking down at her hands that were intertwined. She went over the same track she had gone over hundreds of times; sorting through her memories for any new information. It was the same thing the court and public hounded her for, for the duration of the hearing. Not even the hypnotist could drag anything up.

"Nope. But the morning after was hell to pay. I was sore everywhere with a hell of a headache to boot. The second time, which I remember well, we played games...warlord, slave, Viking or something or other...just a lot of role playing." For a moment she paused. Should she tell Caitlin that one in particular turned her on? "So I guessed it was pretty much the same thing for the first time."

Caitlin raised an eyebrow at the hesitation, but said nothing. "So following the first time you were with Junior you were sore...did you wake up with any bruises or just bad feelings?"

Susan looked uncomfortable and unconsciously she shifted her body and eyes, then looked back toward Caitlin but not at her.

"Hm. Sore as if I had been fucked...nothing unusual there. Bad feelings were more from the hangover and not remembering how the hell I got to..." she thought a moment longer. "We weren't in his apartment...the real big clue was there were no personal things of anyone's in the room except our clothes. When I had made a comment on that, he said it was...a playroom...which later I thought was odd because he didn't say it was his playroom. I didn't get a good view of the front room, nor did I see just where we were. I was feeling too rotten to care or even notice how long it took him to drive me to my car. He was talking so damn much I was just barely holding my own. I was pissed off that I went to bed with the nerd."

"Any bruises you couldn't explain?" *Now, that was a nervous twitch. How many times had they asked her that on the stand? Is that why she's uncomfortable?*

Susan shifted again. "Why do you keep asking?" She could feel her heart rate increase, like on the witness stand, and even then, she panicked, not understanding why she was feeling so anxious on talking about something she could not remember. It did not make things any better to have Cobley Senior staring at her for the entire hearing. Since the hearing was her father's idea, she resented that he was not there staring back at him.

"Is it something you are embarrassed to talk about?" *Talk to me, Susan. What is scaring you?*

"No."

"Susan, I saw the film clips he released on the Internet. Some of them were obviously makeovers, and some scenes I had found erotic...You've probably already figured out that I'm a voyeur, among other things." *Actually, Susan...I was turned on by you being shaved, though I would have wished to have been the one that did it.*

For a moment, Susan's face paled. "I'm....that bastard..." Her face went from pale to pasty and Caitlin grabbed a water bottle she usually had around her console. She moved over to Susan opening it and offering it to her.

She waited for Susan's color to return. "What's going on, Susan?" she asked gently. "How do you feel? Do you remember something?" She was getting more concerned as the pulse point on Susan's neck continued to beat rapidly. Her hands cupped Susan's elbows in case she needed support.

Susan pushed Caitlin back firmly, as if she needed air. "What's going on? How do I feel? Nothing and numb. You sound like my therapist or that damn hypnotist the court sent me to. I don't remember....I told them, and I'm telling you...." Susan's voice was not raised, but it was low and intense. Her breathing was heavy as if she had been running.

Susan started to pace in the small area, blue eyes showing near panic as she tried to come to grips with her unknown fear, frustrated that she could not articulate it or want to remember it.

"Susan?" Caitlin asked in a soft voice.

Susan shook her head.

"Susan, look at me," Caitlin's voice commanded. "Come here." Her voice dropped lower.

Caitlin turned the woman around and pulled her back to sit between her legs on the padded and comfortable chair. Caitlin wrapped her arms around the chilled skin and rocked her, not saying anything as Susan's cold hands hung onto the arms that were folded around her.

"I remember waking up...with ...I had some bruises...I....can we do something else, Caitlin? Please?"

Caitlin kissed her head and nodded against her. "Are you hungry?"

Caitlin felt Susan's rib cage expand then release. "Starving."

They both sat for a while more. Caitlin concentrated on warming the body that snuggled closer into her as if seeking something more than what she was getting. Caitlin waited her out, hoping she would verbalize it rather than have her guessing.

"I can make pancakes or French toast," Susan offered.

"Hm. I haven't had either in a while." *Ahhh, no Mistress may I. She doesn't want to play at the moment.*

Susan wiggled a little feeling the soft shirt against her backside. The warm body that pressed into her bare back had her visualizing in detail what body parts were touching hers, down to the strong thighs that were sandwiching her own. This was nicer than remembering unpleasant what ifs. Susan sighed and felt a tear roll down her cheeks.

Now what was that for?

Others quickly followed the one tear and a bewildered Susan wiped them away as fast as she could.

"I...don't know where this...these...are coming from." Her voice surprised her as it came out in sobs. A distant part of herself was confused about what was happening.

Caitlin leaned her mouth above Susan ear. "Have you given yourself a good cry lately? You've been under a lot of pressure for a long time." Caitlin was going to release one of her hands to stroke Susan's arm but Susan's grip tightened around her arms to keep them in place. "I'm not going anywhere, Susan...go ahead and let it out...it feels better. I'm here, for you. Just cry. That's it."

Susan's body was by then shaking with sobs, and Caitlin held on, rocking her when they lessened somewhat. Caitlin slid one of her arms under Susan's legs and arranged her so she was sitting on her lap. Carefully she turned the chair to face the console so she could find a box of tissues in one of the drawers.

"Gawds! I don't remember ever crying like that." Susan's head cradled comfortably on Caitlin's shoulder as they both idly listened to some soft music in the background. "What is that music?"

"Celtic. How do you feel?"

"A lot better." She patted the muscled arm that her face was near. "I got a nice comforter here. Are you hungry?"

"Uh huh. Still want to cook?"

"Yes, Mistress. What would you like?"

Ahhh. We are back to the game. "French toast with some cinnamon in the mixture, my lovely whore." She nuzzled the neck that arched as she moved her face against it.

"Right...lovely with puffy eyes and a stuffed-up nose. So, Mistress....Cinnamon, huh?" She titled her face to look up into the dark green eyes that were looking down at her smiling. "Isn't that one of Aphrodite's herbs from her magical belt?"

"Up." She gave a firm push to Susan. "I don't need any assistance in my libido area. My imagination is fertile enough."

"Yeah? Well, can your body keep up?" *Ooooh, and what are you going to do with that challenge, Mistress Caitlin?*

"A bit uppity again, are you, my whore?" Caitlin's voice lowered and Susan felt the beginnings of a tingle, the pleasant kind that promised more things to cum.

"Shall I bend over and wait for your punishment, Mistress Caitlin?" Susan asked in a mock demure tone, planting a seed but not expecting it to germinate right away.

"That's an idea." Caitlin grabbed her cuffed wrist and tugged. *But not when you expect it, my sweet whore.*

Susan was expecting Caitlin to take her over her knee and paddle her...or was hoping. But Caitlin led her around the staircase, directly across from the room they were just in, to the kitchen and showed her where everything was located.

"Come here, whore."

Caitlin pulled out a chain from her shirt pocket. Warm fingers that started at her neck, slowly slid down her chest to the tip of her right nipple, gently at first, flicking it, then, as it grew hard, Susan closed her eyes to control the feelings the nipple ring and Caitlin's fingers were causing. Weight tugged at her nipple rings. Looking down she found the chain dangled between her breasts, the ends attached to each ring. Caitlin smiled and gave a little tug on the chain, sending a burning feeling through her nipples and down to her clitoris.

"While you're cooking I need to take care of some business." She grinned and turned to leave the kitchen.

Most of what Caitlin said was missed and it took a few replays for her to hear it in its entirety. Susan took another deep breath as she watched the tall woman leave the kitchen area.

Whoa, Susan! That body and that woman... You're gonna ruin this game of hers if you run after her and jump her bones. I think from day one... yeah, she put a spell on me. I think I need to take some deep breaths here, but I sure can think about how I would like to strap her down and lick her everywhere till she begs for mercy. Hm. I hope she's not allergic to strawberry jam. Gawds, and just a few moments ago I was so damn cold and now...but, what a way to go.

Her eyes followed Caitlin as she walked around the staircase and over to the other side where her monitors lined one wall. Turning back to her work, she started to pull out the eggs, milk, cinnamon, whipped butter, honey, and whatever else she could find. She even found some walnuts.

*****

[Good morning to you, Caitlin.] Hanna's voice sounded irritated. [The perp was picked up last night and then escaped along with a few other prisoners sometime early this morning. Thank goodness they didn't put him in with the dangerous criminals.]

"So, you said you got a chance to speak with him. Were you able to get an idea of where he's got the device planted on her?"

[Nope. He's a bit too cocky, if you know what I mean. What does he think he has or knows, that he feels he is going to win this game? That's probably what's so damn irritating. Willy said he sees this as some kind of a game, this stalking thing.]

"Willy's back?"

[Uh huh. He's the one that questioned him. Thought he could intimidate the hell out of him. Not likely. Yeah, he got lucky and had a full load to bring back the same day he delivered. Damn lucky his partner was rested so he drove the majority of the way back. He asked if you want to take one week off and all of us take the bikes for a trip up the coast.]

"Maybe. Let's see where this goes. Have you found out where Junior has been staying and sent anyone to his place?"

[He's been stayin' in the van and various hotels when he started to stink. I sent Hal to their hometown. He knows some of the people and the place after working as her bodyguard for those six months. He made some friends when he was off duty. He thought he would work them for some info. Jenny is his partner on this one. The scenario is: she's his girlfriend, and since they are on vacation she wanted to see where he was working for six months. How's the pigeon doing in that den of yours?]

"She's fixin' breakfast. Where was Junior picked up?" Caitlin was watching the monitor, zooming the camera in to view Susan's nipples that were in full erection from the weight and swaying of the chain as she moved. Susan kept glancing her way, across the staircase. That look kept Caitlin distracted.

[Back at the RV place where she bought the van. They called the cops, but he had a police scanner in that rental car and heard the dispatch. They caught up with him on the bridge.]

"Did he find the van while he was up here?"

[Nope. Tracks were covered right behind you. The guys wanted me to thank you for finally bringing some action their way.]

"Well, it's not over since he got away again. Put everyone on tactical alert in that area. Keep in mind he can listen into the communication devices. Let's see how creative this class of wanna-bes is."

[Her father's agent, Howard, is calling frantically trying to locate her. It seems she checks in regularly with family members and no one has heard from her for two days.]

"Call her father directly and tell him what's going on. Maybe he can apply some pressure on someone he golfs with."

[What? Caitlin sometimes you speak in riddles. We have contacted his office. My guess is he would rather have Susan call and say she is all right. Ahh, which brings me to another twist in this sordid mess. Tom sent an E-mail to her brother Sam's address, but…I think there is a bug in his mail. WEB service came over to do maintenance on the PC at the store because it was running real slow. They found some curious cookie files that were hanging up the other programs. Bell called them markers, or something like sniffers, that he traced to a received E-mail that was supposedly from her brother Sam. I told them to pull out the hard drive and put in the backup they keep in the safe. We've got the drive in the shop with Miles and his dad lookin' it over. Hell, those two haven't played together since Miles whipped Willy in one of those weekend militia sorties.] Hanna started laughing with Caitlin chucking.

Willy, Hanna's husband, and a group of his old war buddies played commando tactics every six months with any of their interested offspring participating. Families were separated just to even out the odds so the same team would not always win. Willy was embarrassed when his son trapped him, unintentionally, while he was taking a wizz. It probably would not have helped the situation if Miles had told him that it was something Aunt Caitlin had taught him while she trained him to work for her protection firm.

"It doesn't hurt to be cautious. Your perp's got an electronics background, but not in WEB stuff. This isn't just about Susan and Junior. There is something bigger going on here. Things don't add up to a one-person operation. For one, whoever posted those WEB pictures of Susan, had to have been following her for some time to get the wide range of expressions. And, that scene of a male shaving her was not Junior. What we do know about the man in the picture, is he's all balls and not much stick, he's got a big gut, and from the white mark around his finger, he wears a large ring. I'll bet because of the ring's size it would have been recognizable and that's why it was removed."

[I can just picture what the police line up is going to be like...]

"Pass that onto Hal. Maybe he can remember anyone that wears an unusual ring on his finger and has a gut as big as an elephant."

[You think there's some kind of sex club going on or they were just doing a smear campaign on her?]

"Both are not new. Sex clubs are as old as men are. The use of the date-rape drug is big with government types, men with power problems, and the Hollywood group. In addition, imposing other peoples' faces onto bodies is done on the Internet all the time. Therefore, we may have other victims or...willing partners. I'm sure it's all tied into that first night Susan spent with Cobley Junior. I sure would like to know why Susan can't remember a certain night and why she is being stalked. So, let's dig deeper. We haven't done any checks on John Cobley, Sr. so start one on him and...check out her father, Mr. Nikolas too. That is another thing that's so damn odd. Cobley, Sr. was at all the court hearings according to the news. In the film clips, he was always staring at Susan. If his physique matched that person on the WEB, I would understand why and would be going down there myself to speak with him. Was he listening for something or just interested in intimidating the hell out of Susan....and that being the case...why the hell wasn't Mr. Nikolas there to give her some support if he was the one that insisted on the hearing? And, most importantly...why Susan? Have the team get tapes of the hearing. See if anyone can see what parts of the hearing had Senior sitting up and taking interest. Then I want to know...ASAP. Gotta go. Breakfast is ready."

Caitlin made a short side trip.

*****

Susan had the table set and was pouring coffee into a carafe she found when she heard Caitlin.

"Hi, you're just in time, Mistress." Susan put the pot back and set the carafe on the counter with the table setting.

Caitlin was studying her. She held up a small clip with two thin chains attached and glass balls on the ends. She beckoned for Susan to approach her. As Susan stood facing her, a mere hands width apart, she ran a hand down the white muscular side, over a taught butt and then in front of her, sliding down to her shaved mons. Caitlin leaned toward her, taking possession of her lips, her nose brushing against Susan's as she gently caressed her lower and then upper lip, feeling the body tremble against her hand.

Susan blinked a few times at the contact, letting the feeling of her sensitive skin telegraph all sorts of messages to her other body parts and then back to the brain, to confirm that she was definitely turned on. She groaned when Caitlin slid her tongue in her mouth, and felt the other woman's warm skin press up against her. Her own hands rose to touch the sides of her lover, pushing aside the loose shirt and touching the soft skin. Caitlin's lips moved down to her neck, leaving kisses as her head moved down her body. Susan closed her eyes and sighed. Her eyes popped open when she felt lips then a tongue on her stomach. The mouth traveled down to her mons, sucking gently on the bare skin above her apex. Susan's hands went out to hold onto Caitlin's shoulders as she shivered from the fire that shot straight to the heart of her desire. Susan could feel a trickle of her juices sucked up with busy lips.

"Gawds…Caitlin…Mistress," she whispered hoarsely.

Fingers gently parted the sensitive skin that was moist around her clit ring. The sudden tug that added a different kind of fire to her quivering thickened lips nearly distracted her from the new tickling sensation along her thighs. Breathing through her mouth, she looked down at what Caitlin was doing. She had attached a clip to her clit ring. Susan blinked a few times at the weight and sensation she was not accustomed to. Her hands moved to Caitlin's head wanting her to continue, but Caitlin was rising to her feet.

"Hm. Smells good. It looks good, too."

Susan was standing alone near the sink, rocking on her bare feet from the sudden loss of contact. When she was able to focus again, Caitlin was smiling at her from her chair.

"I've never had chopped walnuts on my French toast. Tastes good."

"Uh, huh." Susan let out some air then walked gingerly to her seat.

"Standing is more comfortable," Caitlin told her as she sipped her coffee.

Breakfast was quiet in the verbal area, but between the tickling of the dangling balls between her legs and the added weight on her clit ring Susan's body was more focused on the sensations of her lower extremities than on what her upper extremities tasted.

Susan finally reached under the table to scratch her leg where the balls were dangling.

"Leave your hands above the table," Caitlin quietly instructed.

Mistress Caitlin, you are driving me crazy here and if you don't do something about my frustrated libido, I'll be doing something to yours. "Finished with your plate, Mistress?" Susan asked a bit too sweetly.

"Yes, whore. Breakfast was very nice."

Caitlin pushed her plate towards Susan, distracted with trying to figure out what could be so terrifying to Susan when the subject was even broached on the night she could not remember.

Drugs, threats, brainwashing ...hypnosis? What is it? She didn't like the hypnotist experience. That's odd because they usually work on getting the client to feel they are in a safe environment before they even began the induction.

Susan bent to remove sponge and dish soap from the cupboard under the sink where they were stored following use. Caitlin did not like clutter, she noticed. Even her cooking pans hung inside a cabinet. Movement to her left had her turning her head to the side where tattooed legs stood. Caitlin's hand rested on her shoulder, keeping her in a bent position. She stood behind Susan, pulling her buttocks against her prickly pubic hairs. Hands slid slowly over her bent body, heating her skin to a pink flush with excitement.

Caitlin moved Susan's cuffed wrists to the counter where she curled her fingers over Susan's so that both sets of hands gripped the sink edge.

Susan could feel the warmth of Caitlin's body as it covered hers, her hard nipples pressing against her back. Hands moved along her side grazing her dangling breasts that were erect from the effect of the swinging chain. A warm arm curled around her waist while Caitlin's other hand gave a tug on the chain. Susan's knees almost buckled from the fire that shot from her nipples directly to her clitoris.

"Oooh, gawds...." Susan breathed heavily trying to keep her shaking knees from collapsing.

Lips and hands continued to run along her body, teasing her sensitized skin.

"Mistress, you...ooohh. I...."

"Shush, whore," Caitlin whispered in her ear.

Something started to push gently against her lower lips, not wanting entrance just letting her know that it was there. Susan groaned as the head pushed against the clip and she automatically pressed against it, feeling the tip slide in.

Is that what it feels like? Yesssss. Jeeze, now I know why she wears long tails on her shirts. What a nice surprise.

"Now did I say you were ready, whore?"

Suddenly the pressure from the clip was gone and Susan could feel a finger at her entrance feeling her readiness. Resisting the urge to push to impale herself against the finger, she gripped the sink harder.

"I think, my excited whore, that you are being too uppity. I did not say you were ready. What you need is a reminder who is Mistress. Wait here." Caitlin pulled the chain attached to her nipples to keep her distracted.

Susan hung onto the sink, feeling her heartbeat through her body as the chain swung from her nipples. The air stirred around her, signaling Caitlin's return.

"Prepare yourself, whore."

A palm caressed her pale cheeks on her bottom, and then a smack with a flat paddle, light as if to prepare her for more to come.

Oh, gawds. Yessss, Caitlin! Harder! Yessss.

Susan's groans caressed Caitlin's ears. She was familiar with Susan's preferences, knowing how much teasing she could take before her body erupted into a climax.

Susan was swaying from the lack of strength that were in her legs, as all her energy focused on what was between her legs. A finger slid along her thick wet swollen lips then slid into her slippery core. Her inner muscles tightened quickly around the finger, attempting to draw the finger in further.

"I think you are ready, whore." The voice near her ear whispered.

The rod slid in, with a moment of resistance. Her walls were well lubricated, and now throbbed joyously as its space was filled. Strong hands gripped her hips, pulling her against the muscled thighs with a satisfying sound, and for the deepest penetration possible.

Susan groaned and wiggled onto the shaft that was deep inside her. Her insides and outsides were throbbing with the desire to feel the heat from the friction of a moving dildo, which Caitlin did not deny her. Caitlin began slowly and then increased her grinding moves as Susan moved along with her. Sounds from the jingling of the bells on her cuffs, and two women's pantings intermingled with groans were all the conversation that was heard for a while. Caitlin reached around Susan and while her hips continued beating against Susan's white buttocks her fingers stroked Susan's nub of nerves, pulling on her clit ring to change the type of sensations and then returning to stroke her clitoris until Susan was shuddering against her.

"Mistress... please....may I cum?"

"Yess."

A slap on her bottom along with the increase of friction on her inside walls gave her the final push over into the realm where everything focused on just the rising pleasure, and then the explosion. The roaring in her ears and lights behind her eyes overwhelmed her senses, spreading to her limbs, which became boneless in the aftermath. Susan had cried out Caitlin's name before she sagged against the sink counter.

Caitlin held onto her as she wavered, almost falling. When Susan's breath was nearly back to normal, Caitlin slowly withdrew the dildo from her slick insides.

"I just wanted to show my appreciation for breakfast," Caitlin whispered, nipping her on her butt before letting Susan straighten up.

■■
*****

"Clean yourself, everywhere. Everything is here. I will be on the third floor down." She leaned next to Susan, as if to smell the scent of sex on her. "Do not shave yourself...that is my job." Leaning back, she nodded to Susan. "When you are done, whore, present yourself for inspection."

With that, Caitlin left.

Okay. What did Tom tell me about subs and preparations...hmmm. Susan was looking along the wall near the toilet at the supplies and was getting a good idea of what was in store for her.

An hour later Caitlin could hear the jingle of the cuffs. She smiled and continued with her lay-ups. Finished she rested the bar in its support and rested a moment. She could feel the blue eyes she was smitten with travel over her naked and sweating form. With an effort, she curbed the smile that threatened to work its way onto her lips as she imagined what Susan was seeing as her legs straddled the towel-covered bench she was lying on. She used a corner of the damp towel to wipe sweat from her face. Sitting up, Caitlin studied the athletic body of Susan's with her imagination supplying her with images of them practicing some forms of self-defense with nothing on and the film rolling.

"I thought you would like to keep up your work-out regime," she offered.

Susan nodded, moving away from the figure she would much rather watch, letting her eyes travel around the equipment in the room. "Well, this is going to be a first."

"What's that?"

"Working out in a gym naked. You know, there used to be worries about people not wiping the equipment from their sweat and picking up something unpleasant. Now there are rumors specifically about women who can and do get all sorts of diseases from each other's fluids that they leave on the equipment. Do you think it's just another one of those male myths?"

"Hm. Before I believe in a study, I would like to see just what questions were asked **and** what answers were used for making the conclusion. All studies have built in prejudices."

Caitlin hid the grin that wanted to come out. "For that matter, men secrete fluids too while working out...so maybe someone will get impregnated when sitting on a bench some guy just left all wet."

Susan turned around from the weight rack she was studying to make a face at her joke. "All right...then I better clean anything I sit on so you don't pick up any pheromones from me."

"You may remove your cuffs. There is a towel over there that you can use to clean the equipment if you drip." A smile curled at the edges of Caitlin's lips as she went back to her own workout.

For the next hour, while Caitlin continued her work out with sweat dripping from her naked form, Susan was able to work off some of the physical energy she was building up from watching. She was surprised that she did not knock herself out from running into overhead equipment while stealing looks at Caitlin as she moved under the stress of weights.

Susan sat up from the bench she was studiously working a set on and looked for the hundredth time over at Caitlin. Her eyes traveled down the sweaty deltoid, bicep, past the corded lower arm to the wrist, and then to the hands that were gripped around a weight, lifting it to slide onto the bar. In well-practiced motions the weight was locked into place and then she moved to the other side of the bar, repeating the process to balance the weights. Green eyes lifted to hers.

"Can you spot for me?"

Oohh. Not a command but a question? This must be a neutral corner...for the moment. Susan nodded her head and quickly laid the weights down she was carrying to her workout space, and then moved to stand behind the weight bench. She looked down into Caitlin's eyes as she made ready to lift the weights.

Oh, joy. This is going to be distracting. Two thoughts echoed.

Caitlin finished her workout first, signaled when she stepped into the shower stall, which Susan took as a cue that her own workout should end. She had gone longer than she normally did, wanting to watch Caitlin and now watching her silhouette though the shower door had her thinking.

"May I enter, Mistress?"

The door opened. Susan stepped in, looking up at lips that were descending to hers. Susan let the soft lips tease hers open, parting them slightly to invite a deeper kiss. Susan rested her hands on Caitlin's hips for balance as she was turned so that the water was hitting her back. Caitlin leaned into her as she turned a knob. Suddenly the water went from the shower nozzle to an overhead sprinkler.

Hmmm. Dial a warm rain shower. "Hmmm," she purred her pleasure.

Hands moved to her shoulder, applying pressure. Susan moved down Caitlin's body, but not before stopping to suck on her breast, licking up water before hungrily filling her mouth with an erect nipple. Her tongue pulled on the nipple ring when Caitlin increased the pressure for her to continue her downward movement.

So, you always want to control do you? Hm. I'll get you yet, Mistress Caitlin McKenzie. Since you are finally letting me touch you, I will make sure you remember this.

Susan sank to her knees and pressed her face between the tattooed thighs, her tongue searching for a certain treasure between the dark red hairs.

Oh, gawds, this is the way to end a work out.

Hands gripped her shoulders tightly as she swirled her tongue around swollen lips and then back to Caitlin's hardened nub. Susan moved her hands behind muscled buttocks, digging her fingers in the tight muscles and drawing Caitlin closer to her. Sucking on each swollen fold Susan drew as much moisture as she could from Caitlin's shaking body, then again swirled her tongue roughly over her sex, before returning to the hard bundle of nerves. She did not play long before Caitlin shivered to a climax, letting out a small cry.

"Susan!" She gently pushed Susan's face away from her apex, where Susan continued to suck the lips that were slick with her essence.

"Hmmmm." Susan withdrew, kissing Caitlin on each inner thigh. *Boy, were you ready for me. So, you weren't just concentrating on your workout, huh, Mistress Caitlin?*

Caitlin leaned down to kiss Susan gently on her lips, pulling her up to her feet. Her hands pushed Susan against the wall turning the gentle kiss into a harder devouring lip encounter. Hands moved down her thighs and roughly entered her wet vagina. Susan lifted one leg wrapping it around Caitlin's waist, pulling her in closer as she fucked Caitlin's fingers that were rubbing her inner walls.

"Mistressss!"

"Cum for me, whore."

She hissed her climax as she felt the fingers once more plunged deep into her cavity. She wrapped both legs around Caitlin's waist and held on as the waves of her ecstasy rolled over her. Caitlin hugged her close and took possession of her lips as Susan again experienced a smaller shudder.

*****

"Caitlin?" Susan turned to her as she finished drying herself off after their shower.

"Hmm."

"Can I ask you a question…. personal?"

"You can ask." Caitlin gathered her towel and Susan's and along with some others from the hamper, and padded into another small area that had a washing machine and dryer.

"Oh…" Susan nodded to herself. *So, she doesn't have someone come in and clean. Well that's one question I don't have to ask.*

"I…I was wondering if …or …"

A soft bell interrupted her question. Both women let out a small breath of relief.

"Can you hold that thought?"

"Uh huh, yeah."

Damn, of all the times for an interruption. Well, it will give me time to rehearse this. Oh, right, like I can just say: Mistress Caitlin, how about if we switch roles tonight. I'll tie you up and drive you simply wet and limpy with my tongue and all my body parts, before I say you can cum. What d'ya say? It's not as if either of us has anything else planned …or do you?

242

Caitlin picked up a small phone in the room. *Why am I getting so nervous about what she's going to ask?* "Yeah?" After listening for a while, she hung up. *Well...I guess we'll both have to wait until later for her question.*

"I'm going to be out for a while. The book you picked up from the bookcase in the cabin is in your coat pocket still. The coat is in the closet in the bedroom we slept in. If you would rather another...I have two libraries with the larger one on the second level, directly across our bedroom. The only thing I ask of you is that you don't leave here. Junior can't get a trace on you as long as you are down here. If for any reason you do need to leave," she lifted the phone, "press these two buttons together..." She demonstrated, "and all the exits will light up." She left off that it would also set off an alarm in the security office, Hanna's beeper, and Caitlin's beeper. "If you feel frightened about being here, in the play room there is a program that has all sorts of places you can visit in the sensor-around-sound. Okay? The computer program is user friendly."

Susan nodded her head.

Caitlin quickly left her and ran up to the first level where she had a wardrobe for what she would need. A snap of her fingers brought Ms. Business excitedly to her side. Sensing adventure she was dancing around.

Caitlin looked up after pulling on the thick socks she wore with her heavy biker boots. Susan was watching her. *Oh oh, I didn't even hear her and those bells. I'm letting myself relax too much here.*

"You look....pretty impressive in those." Susan commented as Caitlin stood up.

Caitlin grinned. She was dressed in black leather pants, a black turtleneck sweater pulled over a Kevlar vest, and a leather coat padded for motorcyclists. She had a knitted cap over her head to replace the thickness of the hair she once had. She had not replaced her helmet with a smaller one believing her hair would grow in soon enough.

Her heavy boots, which she would put on in the cabin, would complete the outfit.

"That's the intention...to impress...with fear, hopefully."

"Whoa, big bad mama!" Susan giggled and then put on a solemn face. "It would have me forgetting to grab my baseball bat because I would be too busy figuring out how to get the hell out of Dodge." *More like how to jump on your bones, milady.*

Caitlin put a finger on her lips...which she quickly traded with her lips.

"I should not be gone more than eight hours...if I am, I will ring you. How's that?"

"I...hmmm. If you kiss like that for every time you leave....I can't wait to find out what you do for chasers. Okay. I guess that means I can pick up the phone should it ring while you're gone? I'll be all right."

"You might want to call home. Let them know you are okay...but try to leave off where you are for now and keep the call down to under three minutes...it's not traceable. I have a scrambler on this line...but limiting the time will cut down on someone from trying."

Susan gave her a hug and was grateful when Caitlin did not resist but hugged her back. She stepped back and picked up her boots. Susan followed her to the art gallery and waited until the stockinged feet disappeared into the ceiling before letting a big sigh out. The ceiling exit closed and the stairs moved into a new sculptured shape.

"Where the hell does she get these gadgets?"

Not wanting to think about where Caitlin was going or of being alone in the underground fortress Susan gave her brain a break and moved around the room admiring the art. She reengaged her brain when she paused to study one of the sculptures in the round that had, or so it seemed, fifty different figures of early Greeks or Romans demonstrating the Kama Sutra. The title of the piece, *The Kama Sutra of the Divine*, had her curious about the artist's models.

Jeeze, how the hell can...where is the rest of this person's body? Oh...yeah...gawds!

Susan circled the sculpture a few more times to trace intimately intertwined bodies and looking for the other part of the person. A penis, or was it a dildo, was sticking out of the sculpture in a rather vulnerable place. Susan resisted the impulse to touch it, because her mother had taught all her children to leave their hands in their pockets if they could not resist touching things in the store that were fragile or toys that were not theirs. She put her hands behind her back and moved to the other sculptures, which also were erotica inspired.

As Susan was studying another sculpture from the other side of the room, her eyes returned to the Kama Sutra sculpture.

Hey!

Looking at it from this angle, she could see that the whole area around that particular sculpture had a slightly different coloring...or was it from the lighting?

Susan walked back to the sculpture and looked around it carefully then moved to other areas around the gallery to study it.

"Hm. A booby-trap maybe. Would she do that?" Susan started to giggle. "I would. I would have a little pecker or a breast sticking out to tempt people to touch, and then have something happen to remind them what their mother's should have taught them when they were kids...don't touch...unless invited. Whoooo, Mistress Caitlin McKenzie. You are so devilish." *Hmmm. Did you booby-trap that big dom statue in your room? I just wonder what it can do...but I think I will ask on that one, before finding myself strapped upside down for eight hours.* Susan's giggles were faithfully recorded as she decided to make a closer inspection of her underground home, knowing that Caitlin had cameras in all the rooms.

"Hm. I should put on a show for her in her play room." She sighed. "Naaahhh. I would rather watch her face if I do play with her toys. Hm. Now, that is a way to get her ovaries all tied up in over production of hormones. Well, I might as well check to see where all these exits are before I may have to use them."

*****

Caitlin rolled her bike down the forest path, looking around her and above her with Ms. Business balancing on the seat with her nose in the air, testing for another human as her mistress had ordered her to do.

Once they were past a certain point, Caitlin turned on the engine and listened for a moment to the exhaust pipes, which were music to her ears. She avoided the loud roar in the forest and waited until she cleared it before she increased her speed, mindful of Ms. Business who was safely leaning against her.

Caitlin slowed to cruise at the appointed coffee shop as she spotted Hanna with Willy and Miles. Caitlin grinned at the family gathering, knowing Hanna missed her other two children that moved to other parts of the country with their spouses. Family bike-outs were a tradition since that was how Hanna and Willy met.

Nodding to them, she made a wide turn then headed up to a cleared parking lot. The air was chilly and promised more rain, but Caitlin liked the rain, though not riding on a bike in it. During the rainy season, she liked to stay in the cabin rather than her underground home, which had originally been a design for a very important customer who chose to go above ground instead. His wife objected strongly at the idea of living without windows. It did not matter since both security designs came from her firm. It also gave her a chance to see if it was possible to put together such a large project without gaining attention and with as little disturbance to the environment as possible.

Hanna's bike coasted to a stop next to Caitlin's and Ms. Business made an easy leap to her owner's bike when she gave the signal. Hanna rubbed the dog affectionately.

{So...you want to draw him out, do ya?} Hanna signed to her younger sister. {Well, ya got your wish.}

"Hmm." Caitlin agreed verbally. She could hear the buzzing that was like a bee. Caitlin leaned over and scratched Ms. Business's head. Nodding to Hanna she wheeled her bike smoothly around and headed up the coast to where a group from the security school was in training and was begging to get some real practice in. Caitlin's security firm trained people that wanted to go into the business and one of her training classes involved protecting out in the wilderness areas, like cabins or boats. This group would be graduating soon and were eager to get something with meat to put on their resumes.

Caitlin drove fast, both because she usually did and because she did not want Susan left alone too long. There was nothing she could get into that would compromise Caitlin, as things like that were stored in locked places, but she worried Susan may get claustrophobic. Living underground for a length of time was not for many people.

Whoever was following could probably guess she was heading back up to the lone gas pump where Junior had lost their trail the first time. Caitlin could not hear if she was being followed, but the small device she had strapped to her wrist was flashing red so she did have something trained on her. Caitlin increased her speed as the curling road straightened out.

After an hour Caitlin turned her bike into the side road that went by the small gas station. She made a U-turn and waited patiently. A white van turned into the side road and slowed down as it passed the closed gas station about fifteen minutes later. All four tires were punctured as it rolled onto the path Caitlin had guided Susan to follow the previous day.

Two bulldozers moved out from their camouflaged hiding and dumped a concrete barricade the vehicle would not be able to plow through in front and behind the van, pinning it between the blocks nicely. Caitlin waited for the camo dressed figures to secure the van and passenger.

This is too simple. Either Junior is actin' on his own or whoever he's representing is not that hip in this business.

Tape was slapped over his mouth, a hood covered his head and his wrists were bound in front of him. The doors on his van were pulled opened and the team carefully inspected the van as if it had a bomb.

"Hey, look at the inside of this!" One of the voices called quietly to the pack leader.

It was set up with electronic monitoring gear, something a covert group would run around with, a porta-potty, lots of water and packages of snacks. The van was neat and orderly, but then, there was not much room for messiness.

"Boss, this does not look like some kid stalking an ex girlfriend. This smells of something a lot more complicated. Huh?" The pack leader asked softly. "And a porta-potty? This is for parking and doing some heavy surveillance work by a team of one."

"Hm. This stalker has access to lots of money. Look at some of the husbands we found spying on their own wives and mistresses, for christsakes. But, I think you may be right about this not just being a case of some kid stalking a woman." Caitlin was worried about the money invested in the tech toys that the van had.

"I want ya to send a few more people out to back up Hal and Jenny. Check in with Hanna, before you pick your team. She may have some news from Hal."

He grunted a response. He glanced at her quickly watching the unreadable face until green eyes turned back to him. She nodded and they both walked to their van where Junior was being prep'd.

"All right, let's get this show going. I don't have all day," she told one of the guards softly. He nodded and gave her room to climb into the van. She was the one that would create a world for Junior's drugged mind and ask questions. The problem with any so-called truth serum was that its effects were not consistent with everyone and it did not give up the 'truth' as it may imply. However, Caitlin was just interested in what type of stories he would give her when she got him in a talkative mood, which the drug did do. Especially when she started a story along the lines she was guessing were close to what he was involved in.

After two hours of recording, Caitlin was weary of Junior and his stories. She was too tired to decide what was factual over fantasy.

Caitlin climbed out of the back of the van, looking around. "Send me a transcript of the story. While you guys try to figure out what's real and what is brag, I'll work on it at my place with Susan...if she's willing."

The masked face of the pack leader nodded. "Do we notify our..."

"Gregory at the Bureau? Yeah. But go the anonymous tip route. This one is a bit sticky. It's so close to the border...we may have more than U.S. citizens involved. Something as wild as this may also have other law enforcement agencies working it too."

Caitlin wheeled her cycle back onto the road and headed back for home, letting the conversation with Junior roll around in her mind.

Where in that sick world of yours is the truth? Are you the avenging angel sent by daddy's private club to bring Susan back? If so, why? You said you didn't know, but there has to be a reason. Did they give some sort of autosuggestion to Susan to forget her participation in some kind of boy's night out, and they are afraid it will wear off? Hm. Well, it's one thing we haven't tried with her, though she did mention she had met with the local hypnotist. Hmmm. Now that is interesting. Not many small towns have a hypnotist. Is he working both sides?

*****

Chapter 18

After inspecting her new home closer and counting the exits, and then studying the computer in the playroom, Susan decided she would rather read for a while. Curled up on the couch in a room located between the kitchen and smaller library, she enjoyed the fake fireplace. When she had first sat on the leathered couch, her bare skin stuck to the upholstery as she shifted around so she had taken the biggest towel she could find and laid it over the cushions. Her first book was a Mistress M book on how to live with a dom. Some of the stuff had her laughing, for it had been written, she guessed, tongue in cheek.

Time passed slowly when she could not see the passage of time, so after finishing one book, she visited the larger library and found another book to entertain her until she drifted off to sleep, listening to the fireplace crackle as if it had a real fire going.

*****

Caitlin entered the console room, tossing her leather jacket over the back of a chair and dropping her boots next to it. She pulled off the turtleneck sweater and tiredly she looked over the monitors that were keeping an eye on the place while she was gone. She unfastened the Kevlar vest and laid it over her sweater then pulled off the brief T-shirt. She stood in front of the monitors with only her leather pants and socks on. She located Susan curled up on a couch in the living room. She appeared to be sleeping. Two books were on the floor near the couch slip. Pulling a keyboard out, Caitlin typed in the command to display all the alarm messages for the last twenty-four hours. As she waited for the logsmsg command to finish listing the alarms she watched Susan's breasts rise and fall in a peaceful repose. The replica of a fireplace put out real heat and by the small beads of sweat on Susan's forehead and bottom lip, it was more than what she needed. Caitlin leaned over to another keyboard and checked out the thermal settings, then adjusted them. She had forgotten her last visitor liked it hot.

Caitlin returned her attention to the alarm log. A small low frequency sensor had picked up a trace. Frowning, she moved her chair to the front of that monitor. Quickly she typed in another command for narrowing her search. The search went back to the previous day and started to list the same type of alarms up until two minutes ago.

*Why didn't the alarm board go off? Ahh, I set it for a higher frequency. Well, I'll just have to change that. So, whatever it is, it goes off intermittently. It has to be implanted somewhere on her body because her belongings are all in an enclosed closet. I guess this calls for a close inspection of tiny scars or anything with a slight bump on her body...yeah. But it's going to have to be somewhere that she can't reach or would notice. Or, maybe she notices it but...*Caitlin sighed heavily. She was so darn suspicious…which was what gave her the edge over some of her competitors in the bodyguard business, but made her a real pain to work with.

Caitlin had stepped into the shower and was cleaning up when she heard the door open. Glancing around she found Susan standing in the shower.

Caitlin. smiled. "Got something planned, whore?" Her voice dropped into a seductive purr.

Susan grinned. "Yes, Mistress. It seems I have been neglecting you and wish to make it up right away."

I know I didn't write this in any of my books. This is going to be interesting.

"And...how do you intend on doing that, whore?" Caitlin moved behind Susan wondering if she was going to be able to stay awake for whatever Susan had planned.

"A complete body massage, Mistress. Since you are tired, I thought something low key would be in order."

Caitlin stood behind Susan noting her stillness as she stood waiting. The spray cast a cloud of moisture over her. Caitlin ran a hand over Susan's shoulders collecting the tiny jewels that were on her fine body hairs. Susan's shoulders rose as if she were taking a deep breath.

Susan tilted her head to look up into the green eyes that were partially open as they followed the fingertips that left a trail of goose bumps behind. Those same green eyes tracked to blue and came closer as Caitlin leaned in to take possession of lips that were slightly parted, waiting for her. They spent a long moment exploring each others lips then mouth interiors, breaking when one of them had to come up for air.

Caitlin lifted Susan, carrying her into the bedroom to deposit her on the bed where the cuffs and anklets Susan had discarded were lying. She pushed them aside and straddled Susan's hips slowly lowering her lips to Susan's taught nipples while sitting on her thighs.

"Oh, gawds!" Susan breathed when Caitlin's mouth sucked her nipple, with her tongue tugging on the nipple ring, sending a burning fire straight to her clitoris and with it a copious release of juices that covered her engorged labium petals. Hungry lips moved to the other nipple, giving it the same attention, before leaving a trail of small bites on her neck. Susan moved her hands, sliding down strong shoulders, enjoying the movement of the muscles under the soft skin, down to the small of her back to cup the tight buttocks. She groaned from the feel of the flexing muscles that moved with each thrust against her, sensitive to the dark red hairs from her mons rubbing against her. Susan pictured Caitlin's body moving against her, her muscles standing out as they strained pressing against. More warm liquid flowed down her legs, and onto the sheets.

"Mistress....I'm...."

"No," Caitlin groaned, "not yet."

Susan groaned in urgency.

"Yesss, now!" Caitlin hissed as she felt her own release just another thrust away, excited from Susan's groans. Susan's own cry of pleasure came a few more moments later.

Susan's hands tightened around the muscular butt and tilted Caitlin sideways.

"A massage, Mistress?" Susan purred as she rolled an unresisting Caitlin onto her back with Susan's legs on either side of her hips. Susan did not think she would be able to convince Caitlin to relax if she were given the chance to recover.

Caitlin let a small sigh out as the heat continued to pound between her legs. Susan lifted herself off Caitlin so she could get something in the nightstand's drawer.

"I see you've been exploring." Caitlin's hands slid over the body that shifted on her.

"Yes, Mistress." Susan carefully closed Caitlin's eyes with her fingertip. "You're tired. Just relax. You don't have to do a thing."

Susan wiggled a little, and Caitlin opened her eyes. Susan was sitting back on her thighs, pouring oil in her hands.

"Mistress, close your eyes and relax." Susan leaned forward and kissed the dark green eyes shut.

Caitlin breathed in deeply the scent from the oil as strong hands started to smear warm substance on her chest, moving smoothly around her shoulders, and then around her breasts, gently. Caitlin's tired mind recognized a pattern. Fingers firmly dug into the muscles around her neck that were sore from tension, squeezing and then releasing. A groan escaped her parted lips. The weight on her thighs shifted and a warm tickling breath near her ears sent a ripple of desire through her tired body.

"Relax....just let go....sleep," the tickling breath coaxed near her ear, and that is just what she did. A nap, her tired brain thought, was just what she needed.

*****

Caitlin's nose twitched at the smell of ...roasted lamb...baked bread....she breathed in deep to catch the other smells...a green eye opened suddenly...then another. Blue eyes were watching her from one of the more comfortable chairs. A book was propped up against knees that were dangling over an arm of the chair.

A slow smile formed on Caitlin's lips as they both studied each other letting the silence exist comfortably between them.

Then Caitlin cleared her throat...nervously. *What the hell am I all of a sudden so damn nervous about?*

"I hope you don't mind that I took over your kitchen, Mistress. I can't tell the time down here and since I was getting hungry I thought you might be too...especially since your belly has been growling at me." Susan raised an eyebrow at Caitlin with that bit of information and then went on. "I found a prepared chunk of meat sitting in the refrigerator so I guessed that that was for our next meal."

"Yeah, the lamb. You guessed right, it was intended to be for tonight."

"Ah, lamb. Can't remember having lamb for a long time. *Don't you dare say all meat looks the same to you, Susan. That would be giving the wrong message, and for sure...she is not like anyone else.* I hope I got the settings right."

"Hm," Caitlin hummed. Sliding out of bed Caitlin padded over to Susan's seated form, kissing her on the forehead. Her breasts hung temptingly close to Susan's resting hands with the diamonds in the nipple rings sparkling from the reflection of light from the reading lamp. "Thank you. Let me take care of business and then we'll go check it out."

In the kitchen the smells were stronger. After Caitlin checked what was baking she settled at the counter with Susan who offered her a loaf of freshly baked bread. She pulled a chunk off, passing the other half to Susan. Chewing thoughtfully, she leaned back in the chair while she regarded Susan who was chewing on her bit of the same loaf. The coffee machine sputtered with life in the background.

Caitlin had slipped on another long tailed shirt after getting up, while Susan's naked form was left open to Caitlin's sight.

"I had a chance to speak with Junior," Caitlin began, watching Susan's face for clues on how she was going to react to the discussion she was opening up.

"Ah."

Well, the subject of Junior doesn't make her nervous. That eliminates one thing.

Caitlin got up from the table and began pulling out mugs for them and filling them with coffee. Caitlin's eyes returned to Susan who was resting her chin in her hand with her elbow resting on the table. Her cuffs jingled as she moved.

"Must have been an interesting bit of news. Like what you would read in a newspaper, huh?" Susan finally gave into the need to nudge her hesitant lover...*lover? Would she call herself that?*

"Oh, yeah, sex, drugs and rock-in-roll." Caitlin gave her a small smile and then sipped her coffee. She carefully put her mug down on the bar. "He rambled a bit, but...I would like to..."

"What kind of story did he tell you?" Susan interrupted with mixed feelings. She could feel her pulse quicken with anxiety. Why? Was she afraid Junior may have told her something about their first time together, of which she would have no way to refute, or was it because she could not remember anything and did not want to? As her heart pounded she could see Caitlin's body shift, as if waiting. What could Junior possibly have told her that would make Caitlin hesitate to tell her?

Caitlin watched Susan's body change from relaxed to tense with her pulse point on her neck quickening. It confirmed her suspicions that it was more than a natural fear Susan was experiencing. Susan was not uncomfortable about sex or about talking on the subject so it had to be something more.

"I would like to...use hypnosis on you.... but..." Caitlin put a hand up as she watched Susan rise from her chair with her facial expressions showing a myriad of emotions. *What's going through her mind?*

"But..." a soft voice choked out.

"First, I want to show you something... about me."

A ding sounded and Caitlin rose from her chair and peered into the oven at the thermometer that was in the roast. "Uh huh. Not taking chances I see." She indicated the thermometer.

Susan took a deep breath, and then shook her head, clearing her throat. *What does Caitlin's life have to do with this Junior mess?* "I don't do much oven stuff or even stove cooking so...no." A weak smile moved her face. "I...we're lucky you got back in time to make sure the settings were right. You're even luckier that the lamb was already stuffed and tied up there. Do you like all your meat tied up like that?" She asked, finally letting the smile move into her eyes. "I noticed there were other types of meats wrapped up in strings in the refrigerator."

Caitlin pulled the dish out and set it out on the counter. "Just the tasty kind." She leaned against the counter and studied Susan. *How do I prepare her?*

"How do you know what's going to be tasty. I mean...one choice of meat from another...bet they all look alike...even the plucked birds except one is bigger than the other."

Caitlin smiled. *I know she's speaking in metaphor...so...where are we going with this?* "You're right. It's a....hmmm...sort of feeling about this choice of meat over that one...smell, color, sometimes just a feeling."

"Ah. Like a psychic thing?"

Caitlin grinned. "Yeah. Sometimes it works and sometimes it doesn't."

"That simple? And if it doesn't?"

"I pick out what I believe is the right choice of meat, prepare it with the right ingredients to bring out it's best flavor..." she stopped and watched the grin on Susan's face, now relaxed. Caitlin enjoyed the mirth that was playing around her eyes. "and...if all the preparations prove to not make the first bite tasty...."

"Into the trash?" Susan asked.

Caitlin shook her head. "Don't want to waste...I just look for someone that would appreciate it more."

"I see." Susan watched her as Caitlin nodded then turned back to finish her meal preparation. *So, how much of that was metaphor for your choice of women, Mistress Caitlin McKenzie? And, if you don't find me worth keeping...who do you plan on palming me off on?*

Thoughtfully Susan reviewed her own awakening into the sensual world that Caitlin seemed to live in. She had been lucky....the people she had been with had not hurt her, nor had she picked up any diseases, feeling thankful all the women she had been with practiced safe sex. And if the various subjects of the books from Caitlin's library were any indication about the complexity of this woman, she would have some real interesting learning experiences ahead of her. It ranged from BDSM to spiritual sex. Susan laughed to herself. *Oooohhhh, but the religious establishment would not like that. They want to control everything, especially sex, climax and birthing. What the common healthy woman can enjoy. So, Mistress McKenzie you believe in sensuality being another link to universal oneness...or whatever...or do you just read about it to know what's knocking around in some people's minds?*

"As I mentioned a while ago, after dinner, I have something to show you," Caitlin told her as she mixed up a salad.

Susan slid off her seat and set the counter with plates, glasses and eating utensils. She found linen, placemats and napkin holders in the form of animals. She chose a lion for Caitlin and an elephant for herself, sliding the napkins into the round ceramic holder and then sitting herself back in her tall chair, waiting for Caitlin to finish what she had to say.

Susan held her breath for a moment. "And then?" she encouraged.

"Then you can decide where we go from here."

Susan watched Caitlin's body language, feeling that there was a lot more being said.

So, you want us to have a future, but it's dependant on how I see you? Wow.

If Susan had not already been sitting, she would have had to sit down to let that revelation do all its nice things to her. Susan looked down at her hands for moment to get a handle on the happiness that was nearly bubbling out into a yell of hurrah or something that was loud to show how she felt about hearing that bit of news.

When she looked back up, Caitlin was finishing off the last of her vegetables not seeming to know how that comment affected her. A sudden shyness crept up into Susan's composure as she realized all the energy she expended to catch this woman, no longer was needed. Or was it? Now what?

She's doesn't like a boring sub or slave, one who is predictable. I know she doesn't. So, Susan you are going to have to get a grip on yourself and get rid of the wimpy feeling you got creeping up in your limbs from hearing she likes you enough to...to give you the choice of where this relationship will go. Gawds! I feel like a puppy that is greeting her mistress as soon as she gets home. Piddling all over the place, tail waggling and butt with it. How disgusting! The images she conjured up and threat of a giggle helped her get a handle on her feelings. She was sure a piddling dog was not what Caitlin had in mind for a companion ...*lover*...*spouse*... *life mate. Whatever!*

After dinner, both women cleaned the kitchen and then with a bottle of green tea and two wine glasses headed for Caitlin's movie room. Caitlin decided that if she was going to show Susan a part of her voyeur side and that she was behind Susan's lessons in expanding her knowledge of sensuous sex, then it would be in the voyeur's atmosphere, and not some small monitor in her security room.

Susan took a seat in one of the chairs, pouring the golden chilled tea into two glasses that Caitlin held. "Hey, not just green tea but with plum juice and ginseng. Is this an aphrodisiac drink?" Susan studied the green bottle and its contents.

Caitlin laughed as she took her seat next to Susan. "Actually, I first bought it because it said green tea and I liked the bottle. Now I buy it because it tastes good." Caitlin sighed and distractedly took the glass Susan handed her.

"To a good movie." Susan saluted her. "Got popcorn?"

Caitlin cleared her throat and looked annoyed at Susan.

"It's my way of handling my nerves. Shit, Caitlin. Can't you just tell me what you're preparing me for?"

"Me...for a lot of different reasons."

"Oh." Susan watched her for a moment. "Well, you certainly have a lot of talents and interests...if your library is any reflection of your tastes...and this place."

There was a moment of silence. "I'm going to show you some films, it's part of who I am and... well..."

The first film was started.

Caitlin showed her three films. One was a film where she was the star, and was doing a dom routine on a man and then on a woman...it was from over ten years ago when she first got the idea to teach with tapes because too many wanna-be doms were bothering her for lessons. The people in the first tape were also people Susan would recognize. The second tape was of Susan with Lunette and Larry and the third....was of her blindfolded with Caitlin.

Susan closed her eyes and listened to herself as she came, calling out Caitlin's name.

So...my feelings were ...right. A smile curled her lips as she heard slaps from the paddle. Opening her eyes she watched Caitlin disciplining her for speaking without her permission...calling out her name, which she had not realized she had done.

I was right...it was her. A small flutter within her had her blinking the tears away, realizing that she had not been alone and that Caitlin **had** been nearby.

There was silence when the last tape finished. Caitlin had watched Susan's face through the showings, and by Susan's pulse beat on her neck and the smell of her arousal, Caitlin was sure she would get no objection if the action was moved into the present, but right now was not appropriate.

She needed to stay focused, for she was about to ask Susan to trust her...but not as a lover. If Susan asked her to do the same thing, she did not know if she would and therefore, she needed to make sure Susan knew more about her than what she had. Before the tapes were shown, she knew Susan would say yes...she saw the happiness in Susan's face when she gave her control of the relationship. Susan at that point would have agreed to anything before thinking it through. It gave her a giddy feeling to have that much power over someone... and that's what was so peculiar...as a dom she had many who willingly gave that power to her, and yet this was not the same. She really had feelings for Susan...since she the first time she had heard her voice. Amazing how this attraction game worked. She understood now why some people would travel across great spans of land and water just from hearing a voice.

Susan's small laugh had Caitlin rising an eyebrow, waiting. She was good at that.

"It is erotic to see myself being made love to...by you..." A small tear ran down her cheek. "I was so lonely and thought that if I imagined you were the one that was there it would help...and it did. I guess that goes to show you that if you wish hard enough for someone or something...it comes true."

Caitlin brushed the tears from her cheeks and waited for more. Susan seemed to be getting ready to ask something. Her hand rested easily on Susan's shoulder, feeling the tenseness then relaxation.

"How long?"

"After our first conversation I wanted to know who you were. I did a background check on you."

Wow. Talk about first impressions. "Why?" Susan took a deep breath and added, "and what did you find?" *I don't think I've ever had a background check. I guess if I was to work for the FBI or something...except...thanks to*

Junior...that ain't gonna happen. Good thing I don't wanna work for them.

Caitlin's hand dropped to her side, but Susan's hand reached out for her hand, intertwining her fingers and taking comfort that Caitlin's warm fingers wrapped around hers.

Caitlin thought back to why she did the background. Was it a control issue? Could she get away with just telling Susan she did it all because she liked her voice...was it just her voice? It had to be more. Her attitude? She was just curious. Plain and simple. *Don't lie to yourself now, Caitlin. You remember how you were smiling when you didn't give her the information she wanted. You got hooked on the voice and the attitude and started your game of control right then. Baiting the trap and just waiting for a certain fish to nibble. You knew she would take the bait. You are lucky as hell that she didn't turn out to be too young to play, but that's why you did the background. You had to know.* "Partly business. Your brother bought a horse from the farm, and then disappeared...and partly because I was just curious." She gave Susan a crooked smile. "What I found was just the usual sort of stuff...where you were born, went to school, work record...your age...nothing really personal deep or dirty."

"Until Junior."

Caitlin nodded. "He...talked about a men's club that his father is the president of."

Susan's face suddenly became deathly pale.

"Hey, are you...hold on..." She guided Susan to a chair. Caitlin fingers pushed acupressure points along Susan's arm and then her legs. "Breathe deeper, and let the air out counting to ten...Susan, breathe."

"I'm all right...Caitlin, I'm all right. Okay." She patted Caitlin embarrassed after she was able to collect herself. Things seemed to be moving too fast and in different directions. Embarrassment turned into anger. "Sonofagoddamndickhead."

"What's wrong?"

"I don't damn well know, but it's really ticking me off. Every time you ask me something about that place or mention things that should not be scaring the hell out of me...I ...what's happening, Caitlin? What...what did Junior do to me? I don't even know what you're asking about, so why am I scared?"

Caitlin shook her head. "I can only make a guess and then ask questions and see if anything comes up besides your fear."

"You're not going to tell me something like this may be a cult thing, are you? Please don't be running that bizarre line by me."

"I won't. I don't think it's a cult...just a bizarre men's club." Caitlin looked down at her hands that were holding Susan's cold ones.

"How about if we...relax in the Jacuzzi for a while?"

"What?" Susan started to laugh. "Actually, that sounds good. A whole lot better than talking about this business. I'm getting chills, feeling like I'm in twilight zone." Susan cocked her head to the side. "Hm. You know, I just remembered something really odd."

They both stood up and Caitlin took one of Susan's cold hands and led the way to the stairs.

"What's that?"

"It was a conversation I overheard at the party I first met Junior at. The conversation was between one of the out of town guys that came with Junior, and Johnny, a friend of mine. Junior was hanging with these four guys...they gave most of us women the creeps so none of us wanted to talk to them." She giggled a bit, more from nerves than amusement. "Johnny is gay but goes out with me and a few other women that know him, just so he can be cool. If Daddy knows his top salesman is gay, he won't be getting any more promotions. Believe me when I say, Daddy is so damn paranoid about everything...I'm surprised he doesn't have fetishes and luck charms all over the place." She paused as they continued down the stairs to the floor that had the workout room.

"Holy Mary, mother of....jeez! How did you get a pool down here? Wow! A waterfall too! Oooohh. This is great! I didn't see this when I was looking around. Was it turned off?"

"About the party?" Caitlin nudged.

"Oh, yeah. Well, Johnny was looking uncomfortable so I went to go rescue him. I overheard one of the guys talking about the Men's Night Out. It's a bar in nearby Tanner. Looks skuzzy on the outside and has topless dancing. A NOT place for Johnny." She pursed her lips. "Anyway, I teased Johnny about that and he gave me this real scared look and said that was not what they were referring to and they were crazy SOB's."

"And?"

"That's all he said. I was pretty lightheaded about that time...I can't remember too much about the party after that, or how I ended up with Junior. Damn!"

Susan looked at the Jacuzzi they were standing near. "Is this always warm?"

"Yeah, this place runs on solar cells, and micro chip technology that's soon to hit the U.S. if the government would stop running interference for the polluting energy companies. Hop in."

The leather pants and socks she had not removed since she had arrived back were discarded and she joined Susan in the bubbling pool.

"This is great. You know that looks so tempting to slide right down into the pool," Susan told her.

Caitlin grinned. "My very thought."

"Really!? That's what it's for, then? Wow. That is so cool!"

"Cool? I thought that went out in the seventies or something. But yeah, it's a slide but it gives a fast ride and an abrupt drop.

Susan was already moving toward the edge looking over. *Wow. Heights. Hm.*

"Hey." Susan looked up at Caitlin as she slid a comforting arm around her waist.

Susan reached out to cup the side of Caitlin's cheek. "I...can't thank you enough for teaching me about you, Caitlin. I...it seems so bizarre for me to say that when you had your ..."

"Employees," Caitlin supplied.

"Employees, show me the ropes I...it just makes me...I'm glad I had a chance to see if all of that stuff was for me." She took a deep breath. "It would have just about killed me...if after we started dating...and I couldn't be...or do a lot of that stuff." Susan stroked the strong face for a moment. "So...?"

Caitlin leaned closer and kissed her briefly on the lips. "Don't be giving yourself entirely to me. We're still at the beginning stage..." *Shit, who am I kidding?* Her face broke out into a grin and Susan tugged at her ear.

"Yeah, right. More like the ending of the introductory part, **dear**. So, Sherlock, just what is it that you're relaxing me for....oh, right. You said hypnosis." Susan shuddered. "I keep thinking of that creep the courts sent me to. If my attorney hadn't insisted he be there, I would have insisted on one of my bodyguards to be there."

Susan looked down the chute into the pool and pushed herself off, holding back the scream she wanted to let out. A splash next to her as she was coming up from the bottom of the pool had her reaching out and touching skin.

Both women came up laughing. For a while, they both swam and used the chute a few more times, before Caitlin continued the conversation.

"Why were you uncomfortable about the hypnosis? Was there something about the induction?"

"What's an induction?"

"It's a method of talking you into relaxing, your body, thoughts ..."

Susan shook her head at what she was saying. "He had me sit on this folding chair; damn thing was too uncomfortable to relax. I couldn't get hypnotized. He had this annoying clearing of his throat that developed all of a sudden. I think my lawyer made him nervous."

"Or, maybe he didn't want you hypnotized. Is he the only hypno-therapist in town?"

Susan pulled herself out of the water and took the towel Caitlin handed her from the enclosed closet.

"He's not a therapist. He uses hypnosis for weight loss, stop smoking stuff and whatever other annoying habits you may want to get rid of."

"Why did the court recommend him?"

"Let's see...I think it was Colby, Sr. who made some damn snippy remark that made it to the newspapers and Daddy's lawyer...errr...my lawyer, demanded something...couldn't remember exactly what...it was a circus, and I wasn't a willing participant. I was just trying to get by one day at a time." She looked over at Caitlin remembering that she thought about Caitlin a lot during those times and when she heard about that she was going to be hypnotized, she was frightened they would learn about her fantasies of Caitlin. At the time she still was having a problem acknowledging what that implied about herself.

"So...you want to try your hand at it too?" She tried to keep her voice steady but she could feel her heart quicken at the thought.

"Come here." Caitlin opened her arms and Susan stepped into them, hugging her tightly. "How can you be cold in this heat? Listen to me." Caitlin's voice changed.

She gently ran her hands over Susan's arm. "You are safe here with me."

Susan slid her arms around Caitlin's waist, pulling her closer into her. "I believe you." She looked up and Caitlin kissed her waiting lips.

"You are safe with me." Caitlin told her again. She moved her hands seductively down Susan's body. Susan sighed and buried her face between Caitlin's breasts. She sucked on the side of one of the freckled globes, not able to resist the temptation.

"I know I'm safe with you," she repeated. "So...about this hypnosis thing...when do you want to start?" She kissed the other tanned globe, sucking gently on the skin beaded with water drops.

"When you feel you're ready." Caitlin bit back a giggle as roaming fingers and tongue had her skin jumping with tingles.

"Well, I'm tired...relaxed....and horny. I think somewhere in there is the right mood. Wouldn't you say so?"

"Hmm. Tired and relaxed, yes. Horny is not where it's at." She kissed the tip of Susan's nose. "Come on."

"Right," Susan returned, squeezing the hand that tugged her along.

Caitlin led Susan into the large library deciding that the atmosphere was better suited and the chair was comfortable. She pulled out two blankets and draped one over the chair and the other on the couch she was going to sit on.

"Sit in the chair, Susan." She sat cross-legged on the couch and waited until Susan settled in the chair. "Get comfortable....take a nice deep breath...close your eyes and let your breath out...and begin to relax...." Caitlin spoke slowly and clearly, beginning the induction, watching Susan's body to let her know what to focus on to relax and how deep she was relaxing; counting her further down, modulating her voice and slowing it to reflect a slowed and relaxed pace.

"...deeper....deeper, relaxed. Now... imagine a place that is special, peaceful and very safe." Caitlin watched the face relax. "Yes, you can feel the peacefulness and safeness all around you. This place is where you will always be safe, Susan. This is **your** safe place where **no** harm can come to you, where you can come **anytime** for strength, renewal and peace."

Caitlin then asked Susan to describe her safe place to further impress its atmosphere on her senses. Then she moved her on...."And these positive and peaceful feelings will remain with you, growing stronger and stronger as you continue to relax deeper and deeper. If at anytime, Susan, you feel you need to come back to consciousness, you will easily and effortlessly come awake, feeling refreshed and awake. Now...you will relax further ....deeper....deeper relaxed. You are safe as you move deeper, deeper, down, down...down." Caitlin's voice grew softer and slower.

"Okay, Susan. I'm going to ask you to remember something that happened over a year ago....it started with a party...where you met Junior....do you know what I'm referring to?

Susan's head barely moved.

Caitlin thought it would be safer to start at the night of the party where she first met Junior and then into what she and Junior did that night that had her mons shaved. She patiently worked with Susan's fear of remembering parts of that night and morning, giving her time to collect her self, and moving her to her safe place when the memories were too frightening. After two hours Caitlin decided it was enough for the first try and started to wake her, counting her back up and watching Susan's face relax as the pressure to remember left.

Susan's eyes fluttered open then her head turned to look at Caitlin. Taking a shuttering deep breath, she let it out explosively.

"Wow." For a few moments she was still, closing her eyes and then opening them again. "It's like watching a scary movie but knowing I can wake up or walk out if it gets too scary. Thanks, Caitlin. I…realize now, that it was scarier not knowing what had happened. And, that garden I visited….it was…really a nice touch. I did feel safe. It was so different from…from what I was going through."

"Do you want to talk about any of the scary parts?" Caitlin leaned over and pressed her lips against Susan's forehead. Susan pushed the blanket cover back and reached up to pull Caitlin closer.

"Come here," Caitlin whispered, pulling Susan up and holding her. Arms wrapped around Caitlin and held her tight and after a long moment had passed Susan let some of the pressure go.

"Not right now, if you don't mind. I'd like to…sort of digest it."

"Okay. You were very brave to have remembered as much as you did. I think the drug they had given you, Rohypnol, had you unconscious for a long time. Roofies is the street name. Depending on what else they mixed with it, you could have ended up in the hospital. I think they then used some hypnosis to put fear into you of trying to recall anything you may have witnessed in your drugged state." She kissed Susan on the top of her head. "I'm going to check my mail and then work out on some routines. Want to join me?"

"Sure. I like watching you pump iron." Susan smiled. "And I sure could use a bit of a work out myself."

"I'm not lifting weights this time. But…I could use a partner…sparing. "

*****

Chapter 19

That night Susan woke up screaming and Caitlin rocked her back to sleep, though it was not into a restful sleep. Caitlin ended up finding a tape that had a quiet mountain stream with soft music playing in the background, hoping it would distract Susan's sleeping self somewhat.

Caitlin woke before Susan and she studied her strained face before leaning down and whispering in her ear something she had recently read.

Borne on a soft breeze came your scent
I breathed in deeply leather, sweat and sex

Caitlin's lips barely touched the bare ear, as she breathed in deeply Susan's scent.

Visions of your pink bottom bent low
My hands gripped the paddle for another blow

Caitlin's hand slid down the side of Susan until her hand rested on her buttock. Her palm cupped her cheek, squeezing it for effect.

Moans, cries and groans from my victim
Encourage me to enter her rectum

"Hey," a hoarse voice interrupted her. "Are you making that part up?" Susan rolled over and blinked up into dark eyes.

Caitlin shifted her position on the bed. "Maybe...maybe not."

"Thanks for watching over me last night, or when we were sleeping. What time is it?"

"Daytime."

"Well, Mistress, how about a bath or shower and then breakfast? I noticed the other day, that you have some fixings for an omelet."

"Do you like to cook, my whore?"

"Not normally...but, it's something to do as opposed to...what...? *besides jump your bones, my devilish Ms. McKenzie.*

"Hmm. Well...maybe I can come up with something besides cooking to occupy you."

In the shower Caitlin started their day off by having Susan clean her, starting with a washcloth and then with her tongue. Susan made sure it was an erotic experience that excited both of them, until she got to Caitlin's ears and decided to experiment by sticking her tongue in her ear.

Caitlin moved so quickly Susan was startled when she found herself lying on her back in the shower and Caitlin lying on top of her. In fact, Susan decided that if she wanted to get a rise out of Caitlin in the future...this was her ticket...

"Ohhh." Susan groaned as Caitlin bit her nipple and pushed down hard on Susan's fingers that had slid inside her inner core. Susan's thumb rubbed against Caitlin's nub of nerves. The trembling and tightening of the muscles around her fingers let Susan know Caitlin was nearing her climax.

"Fuck me hard, Mistress" Susan whispered, groaning again as Caitlin dropped the nipple she had in her mouth and cried out Susan's name as she hit her peak.

There was a pause before Caitlin started to move. Her lips worked their way to Susan's bare mons and sucked the prickly skin, not bringing relief to Susan as she moved on the water slicked shower floor.

"Wait here," Caitlin told her.

Susan was hoping she would not be long. She closed her eyes and let the water from the warm shower erotically massage her body.

"Kneel on this mat," Caitlin threw a thick rubber mat on the tile.

Susan did as she was told, with hands guiding her to bend over and rest on all fours.

Hands roughly caressed her buttocks, slapping one cheek and then another. Susan groaned and waited for more.

Caitlin spread her buttocks wide and rubbed the area around her anus opening. A finger slipped in just as a hand slapped her butt cheek again. It slipped in so easily Susan wondered if Caitlin had a lubricant on her fingers.

"Ohh, please. Mistress, yess."

The finger in her anus twirled around, and then it was gone. Again her buttocks were slapped and as the water beat against Susan's back, she felt something slide in both her vagina and anus.

Susan's immediate need was to feel the friction along her inner vagina walls and Caitlin's thighs beating against her buttocks, not realizing at first that both her orifices were filled.

Caitlin started slowly moving in circles and then as she picked up momentum from Susan's groans her thighs beat hard against Susan's butt. She lifted her face up to feel the water and it's gradual temperature change, and also the erotic feeling of Susan's buttocks against her groin as she pulled her into her with each thrust.

Susan could feel the warm water beat on her and the beating against her buttocks. It was exciting as palms slapped each cheek and she pushed harder and faster against the thighs that pounded against her. Panting she focused on the sensations she was getting from the dual dildo. Caitlin reached around her hip and using her fingers stroked her nub of nerves until Susan cried, begging for a release.

"Yes, you may cum, whore."

Susan's scream echoed in the shower as she pushed just as hard against Caitlin's thighs as Caitlin pushed into her. As Susan collapsed Caitlin withdrew the dildo, turning her gently, she laid on top of Susan. Susan's lips locked onto Caitlin's burying her tongue as deep as she could into her mouth. Susan's body was still humming and she wanted more of Caitlin.

Caitlin removed the dildo harness and pulled Susan to her feet and without drying off, Caitlin sat in the chair and pointed for Susan to kneel between her legs.

"Mistress, may I touch you?"

Caitlin nodded. Susan ran her hands over her tattooed thighs, between her legs and parting her thick swollen lips, proceeded to massage them with her lips and tongue. She drew Caitlin's climax out until Caitlin held her head, pushing her face away from her sensitive center and then rewarding the gifted tongue and lips with her own mouth.

Caitlin groaned at tasting herself on Susan's lips. She stood up pulling Susan to the bed without breaking their kiss.

"Mistress, more." She whispered as Caitlin's lips and teeth covered her nipple while the other played with her nipple ring. Susan's body arched as Caitlin tugged on the nipple ring.

"More what, whore?" Caitlin asked sucking the breast into her mouth.

Susan groaned and pressed her body into as much of Caitlin's as she could.

Caitlin grabbed Susan's hands that had grabbed her buttocks and were pulling them into her as much as she could. "You are forgetting your place, whore."

"I…only want to please you, Mistress."

"You, my pretty whore, please me." Caitlin breathed deeply. "Follow me." Caitlin let Susan go and pulled her behind her as she walked into the playroom next door to her bedroom.

She pointed to a saddle and Susan remembered her demonstration in the Ole Leather Shop that she had given Tom to tease him.

"Give me a show I'll be thinking about for the rest of the day."

Caitlin sat in the chair nearby with her legs spread apart, and watched as Susan mounted the saddle. When Susan settled into the saddle, the machine began to move slowly in a rocking movement. The pommel was like an English saddle's, something Susan could rub against if she had a mind to. Susan gave Caitlin a more erotic version of what she had teased Tom about, undulating on the rocking saddle, moving from one end to the other. After performing some erotic calisthenics on the saddle and teasing her watcher with brushing both sets of her lips against the pommel, she finally lifted herself onto her knees and balancing on the moving machine, she lowered herself onto the rounded pommel, undulating against it with more purpose.

Caitlin mounted the saddle and sitting behind her, quickly slid her hands along Susan's legs, her fingers slid inside of her, while pulling her closer to her.

Susan's eyes closed momentarily, as she rocked against the fingers that were curled inside of her. Caitlin found her G-spot and stroked her with each forward motion. A small groan escaped her.

"Fuck me, whore," Caitlin's voice whispered in her ear. "Show me how you can ride it."

"Mistressss."

Susan's arms were tired but she wrapped them around the woman behind her, pulling her in closer. She lay back, feeling breasts pressed into her back and a heart pounding against her skin as wild as her own. Caitlin's fingers rubbed her walls, starting the release of the energy that had been building up in her lower belly. Leaning forward again, Susan moved over the fingers, pushing against the pommel for additional stimulation.

This time Susan cried Caitlin's name loudly, and then collapsed against Caitlin who cradled her until Susan could recover.

While Caitlin cleaned the equipment, Susan left for the kitchen to fix the promised omelets.

Susan was pouring coffee when Caitlin dressed in a long sleeved shirt and what Susan thought were shorts, slid into her chair at the dinning table. By her expression, Susan guessed something had happened that Caitlin was not happy about.

"What to share what the frown's for?" Susan asked as she poured Caitlin a cup.

"We're going to have to move this Junior business along into a higher gear."

"Hmm. How?"

"You're going home for a visit."

Chapter 20

Susan's head was resting against the window of the Discovery II Range Rover that Caitlin was driving through some very boring farmland along highway 5 in California. The last Susan remembered was watching a small rainsquall approach them from the North while in the front of them was a blue sky with no clouds. Not stifling her yawn, she let out a small squeak when it ended.

Caitlin looked over toward her amused. "Ah, awake at last."

"You are not much of a conversationalist in a car," Susan pointed out. "So, unless you want me to sing to myself to stay awake..."

Caitlin laughed. "No, thank you. I heard you sing."

"Where are we?"

"Two hours before we get off this paved road and use some of the dirt roads."

"Why all this clandestine stuff? As soon as I hit town they are going to recognize me and all this is for what?"

"Actually, we are first going to Narbone, the town that you found yourself in when you woke up the first time."

"Narbone? How...are you sure?"

"Uh huh. Before Hal disappeared, he traced the men's club as having their private parties there. They have this religious hall near by that's owned by the group that bought out the apartment complex you rented from."

"Hal...Lingstom? Hal Lingstom?" Susan asked unbelievably.

"Uh huh. He works for my agency."

"I figured that out! But, you didn't tell me he disappeared!"

"He volunteered to go down with another one of my employees and check out some things in your small town...like why you were singled out to be a victim of this group."

"When was this?"

"Just recently. One day he finds out about the apartment and the next day he's gone."

"Jeeze. He must have pushed some buttons hard if that place is so secret and up to no good."

"Yeah. That was stupid, unless he thought it was necessary. Hal isn't stupid...so it must have been necessary."

"How come you're telling me this now, instead of before we started this trip?"

"I needed to think...and you were tired. If you knew, you would be worrying about what was going to happen during the entire way here, not sleeping at all."

Susan let out a small curse. Already she was feeling anxiety at the thought of going to Narbone. Where had she heard the name Narbone? It was strange that she could not remember having ever been there, yet...it was only an hour from her hometown. That she knew. Why did she believe she had never been to Narbone before?

"You think they brain washed me or something to not remembering having been to Narbone before? You, know...I don't think I have ever been there. Daddy always refers to it as little Mexico, though I don't think it's any less or more of Hispanics than any other town that close to the border, including Colina."

"Hmm. What did he mean by little Mexico?"

"I don't know. Carlsbad or El Sidron have nice stores, nice people and most of my friends preferred those two towns over Narbone."

"So, other than this time with Junior, you have never been to Narbone?"

"I don't even remember visiting it with Junior, though, wherever we were, it wasn't familiar...but now, after so long...I may not even recognize anything."

"You don't have to. I just want to make sure Hal isn't around. He was supposed to rendezvous with Jenny but he didn't. Some of the others that were there as reinforcements said Jenny was being stalked before they made their presence known. They were posing as bikers, which is how Jenny and Hal arrived in your hometown."

"Oh joy. It probably had half of the citizens calling the cops that the Hells Angles had invaded," Susan was laughing. "While the other half must have been rushing out for their autographs."

"Oh?"

"It's a boring town with absolutely nothing going on."

"Not since your trial anyway."

Susan nodded. "Yeah, and I don't want to do that again. I wish Daddy tried another way to vent his anger at Cobley, Sr. I got a distinct feeling they have history, but Daddy won't even discuss it. You'd think it was one of those fraternity things, you know. Like the brotherhood of the police force."

"Yeah. That's a good guess." Caitlin stole another glance toward Susan. "How are you doing with this trip?"

Susan had not realized that she was sitting up straighter with her hands gripping the arm rests. Releasing her grip, she flexed her hands and shifted her weight, and then pulled at the seat belt fretfully. Finally, she responded, "I don't know. Maybe there is something in this hypnosis thing."

"There are a lot of ways to get a person to do or not do something without them being aware of it. Hypnosis is one way, mixed with drugs. I think there have been a number of movie thrillers and books using the concept. There's also been a recent case where a woman has accused the government as using her..."

"I heard of that! A few years ago. She said she was used as a prostitute for one of the government agencies...the FBI....as their sex slave! Good god! You don't think...!!!?"

"Hey, take it easy!" Caitlin answered alarmed at Susan's response. Caitlin glanced at her quickly as she took an off ramp to one of the side roads. "I don't know, but, we tipped off the FBI about something going on around here and according to our insider, it was moved on so slowly he thought maybe somebody was protecting somebody. If it were an FBI stakeout, he would have known it, but it was just a great reluctance to investigate it."

"Like the Mexican mafia or somebody's drug cartel is at stake here?"

"Why do you say that?"

"Nothing is as simple as just one operation running at a time. If this is something big...and it has my father nervous...I mean, I could not for the life of me figure out why he insists on having our main headquarters in a small backwater town. Most of the cities around there are Spanish with the exception of a small handful, and they go way back to when there was that white rule attitude."

"Do you think your father is involved with the Mexican mafia?"

"If he is, I wouldn't know. His business meetings are not in Mexico but in the eastern states...buying out companies...or in the midlands. I think he was discussing with Uncle Mack the idea of moving the operation to another state where the taxes were low but they have been discussing that for the last four years."

"Maybe this trial of yours had made up their minds. According to rumor your father is looking for a new home base in Ohio or Kansas."

"Gawds. I hope not in Kansas. The winds there will be giving people not normally suffering from allergies a bad case of it. And Ohio is too cold for Daddy. I think San Francisco or Florida. Besides the boat slip in San Diego, the company owns a slip in the Bay area and two somewhere on the Florida coast." Susan looked toward Caitlin smiling. "It's part of the family heritage to have a boat even if it's a dingy and remains in the backyard acting as a child's toy. Going out on the boat to fish to Daddy is like golf to some people...except, Daddy golfs too...but he sees that as part of business."

Susan leaned back in her chair, to think.

"So, do you share the family boat heritage?"

"No, not really. If I dream of escaping it's to the forest with occasional camp outs along the beach. We use to do that -- camp along the beach when we were younger."

Caitlin nodded as she took another turn off that was along a dirt road.

"Where are we going?"

"To meet with some people, I hope."

Susan sat up straighter fifteen minutes later as Caitlin took another fork in the road further into the side of a dirt hill. As they turned a corner an RV with motorcycles parked around it came into view.

"This is our mobile headquarters," Caitlin explained as they pulled up.

Caitlin slid out and was walking rapidly toward the RV with Susan scrambling to follow.

The door came open and a large man that Susan would have readily pegged for a rough biker gave Caitlin a big bear hug before letting her pass by him.

Caitlin turned around and took Susan's hand to pull her into the RV.

"Susan, this bear of a man is my brother-in-law, Willy Webster. Hanna's husband. Willy, this is Susan Nikolas. That's Mikey in the shirt that's too small for him, Georgia Peach sitting next to him, Jenny who came down here with Hal, Denny ...Tom, McCallum, and Tanner. Everyone this is Susan. All right, what have we got so far and who do you have posted as guards?"

McCallum started to give his report. Susan guessed he had been in charge until Caitlin arrived.

"We thought to wait until dark. If they do anything, it will be then. Meanwhile, we got a few posted in Narbone and Colina to keep an eye out for any unusual movement...including law enforcement."

Caitlin nodded and spoke to Susan who looked puzzled. "FBI presence."

Caitlin and her crew were standing around a cabinet that had seven small monitors recording scenes around the meeting hall that was suspected of being where the group they were interested in met on Wednesday nights.

"Tom, can you get the camera for this screen to swing a little to the left?"

"What's that?" Several voices at the same time chorused.

"An effigy," Susan supplied.

Everyone looked at her.

"Once a year there is a parade in Colina where people pick a character that best represents an unwanted part of themselves and burn it in a big bonfire. It's a twisted version of Lenten season only it's done on the last day of February so as not to take away from the Madre Gras. It started as a joke about five years ago in a bar, and the merchants found they could make money on it so it's been going on as a big bash. We're actually getting college students from all over that have effigies of some of their professors. They must have forgotten to read the fine print of just what Merd Cuppa is all about. Last year was real memorable for me...there were a few effigies of me, a handful of Junior, and a couple of his father and then the more normal ones of public figures that really made some mistakes in the year."

"Merd Cuppa?"

"Yeah. It was something else but the local Catholic Church objected so it was changed to Merd and Cuppa. What can I say? I wasn't part of the organizing committee. It's supposed to bring in tourists. Colina is a dying city with nothing much to offer. A lot of the big sweatshops and polluting manufacturing plants are over the border where they pay pennies a week for labor, if they pay them anything at all. And they can dump toxins directly in the back of the buildings and not take any protective measures both with the people or the environment. I tell you, the morality of this country is on a decline when anyone can create something and not take the responsibility for its impact on others including the environment."

"So, when does this celebration start?" Caitlin asked, redirecting the group's focus.

"The night before the last day of February the drinking starts."

"Willy, do you think you can get your group in place before it gets dark? I don't want to leave Hal in a position where we get there too late."

"We can leave right now."

"Okay. Go ahead. Susan and I will be heading toward Colina to see what we can shake up there with her presence."

As the other got up to leave, Caitlin held Willy back.

"Willy, what are you doing here?" she asked in a low concerned voice.

"Helpin' out. I know, I know. I said I wasn't going to do this stuff anymore 'cause it gives Hanna grief...but she sent me out here to make sure you don't do something stupid."

"I'm not going to do anything stupid!" Caitlin seethed.

"I know, but I wanted a little excitement in my life and watching Hanna pace and make noises that are not always translatable for a lady's ears is not where I want to be."

"Well, it's nice to have you. Just remember..."

"NO guns," He told her.

"Right."

After the riders roared off Susan who was waiting in the car for Caitlin watched the speck on the hill for a while, realizing it was someone watching them. She leaned over to the glove compartment and pulled out binoculars.

As she was focusing on the figure she could see they were smoking and they had a rifle cradled in their arm.

"What are you looking at?" Caitlin asked her casually as she slid into the driver's seat.

"That guy up on the hill top."

"It's one of our spotters."

"Caitlin, why do you guys need guns?"

"We aren't using guns. Darts or stunners, but no guns."

"Well, someone forgot to tell that guy up there that."

Caitlin reached for the binoculars Susan held out for her. She studied the figure on the hill that was pacing instead of making himself inconspicuous to anyone with binoculars.

"He's not one of ours." Caitlin told her softly, and then slid back out of the vehicle. A few minutes later she was back in the SUV belting herself in.

"He's a new hire that's about to be fired. I'll let Hanna handle it. That's her job now. Meanwhile, we're moving this camp. He's probably been spotted if this gang sticks to their usual behavior."

"Gang? Where are we going?"

"To talk to your father."

Susan held on to the seat as the SUV was driven as if it were a race car over a dirt road marked with holes and rocks that would worry most car tires and their undercarriage, to say nothing of whoever dared to follow too close. She wasn't quite sure which she feared most, showing up with Caitlin on her father's doorstep, or Caitlin's version of a wild ride.

"Why do you need to see my father?" Susan wished she had not asked that the moment she said it.

"You tell me." Caitlin answered as she swerved around a big pothole and surprisingly the SUV held it's ground, or all four tires seemed to remain close to the ground.

"You think he knows what this group is all about?"

"I do. And so do you. Unless you have a small device in your body somewhere, Junior always knew where you were. You always called home and gave them a location of where you were and when you didn't, Junior did not know where you were. That means either your family has their phones tapped, or someone in your family is giving them your location. Which I hope means, they only mean to keep track of you and not hurt you."

"My dad is not out to hurt me!"

"Good to hear."

"Nor is anyone else in my family. Caitlin, I'm from a small town that sees San Diego as the big city. Nothing happens except this perverted men's club and even then -- we don't know if it really exists. It could be from my imagination -- memories are emotion dependant. Easy to forget, embellish or create."

"So, you are upset with me because I am saying your father belongs to this group or are you upset because..."

"Caitlin, this is about a psycho who is stalking me...about a night I don't remember...and **maybe** about my father who is paranoid about scandal and would rather I stay out of town and live off my trust and income from the company rather than show up. Caitlin, I don't think we should be showing up all of a sudden on his door step and..."

"Have you talked to him since your trial?"

"No," Susan admitted.

"So, who do you call when you are saying you're calling your dad?"

"His secretary. John Howard, Sr."

"Why?"

"Cause Daddy is usually busy and...he's pissed at me for this mess."

"Did he say that to you?"

"Well...no, Mr. Howard...well, I think I just got the idea that he did from Mr. Howard always contacting me. But, I also talked to my brother Sam and cousin Saline."

"And they say your father is angry with you?"

"Well, they don't really talk about it. They just say that Daddy wants me to call in and let him know I'm still out there."

"Are you the only wandering child he has?"

Susan looked up at her. "No, Jimmy is away at college in San Diego. And Sam says he has been moving more of his business into the L.A. area so he's been flying up that way often to look for some office space. But I think he's going to settle in Long Beach. He found someone interesting that owns a condo on Second Street. And then, there are my two sisters, who I don't think my father talks to because he always uses them as an example as to why he will not make me a permanent employee on the company payroll."

"Why is that?"

"I'll get married, pregnant and put my family before the business."

"I guess he doesn't know about your interests."

"Nope." She sighed. "But, it's only a matter of time. It doesn't matter any more. I don't live here, I don't work for the business...nor want to any more."

"What do you want to do when you grow up?" Caitlin asked as she turned onto a road that would take them into a more affluent neighborhood in Colina.

"I'm still thinking about that."

"Looks like your father has company," Caitlin commented as she passed a house that had cars parked along it's curved drive way.

"How did you know he lived here? Never mind...dumb question. I never knew Daddy threw parties at his house."

Caitlin glanced at the lawns that had warning signs that the houses had alarms.

"Are there a lot of problems around here?"

"Yeah. We're close to the border and every once and a while, we get a real nut case with a gun...unfortunately, it's not someone from over the border but from here that wants to shoot all people with brown skin."

"Maybe the maid didn't squeeze his juice right."

Susan nodded absently, and then looked at Caitlin suddenly. "Was that a funny?"

"Not unless you want it to be. Who lives here?"

"Mrs. Oliver. Park in her driveway. We'll go and talk to her. She used to let me park here when I would want to visit with Jimmy without parking in Dad's driveway. He has this thing about us kids blocking his driveway. Honestly, Daddy had a lot of weird rules. If he beat us or did something really terrible to us, I would say it's just part of his character. But, some of these rules of his are odd."

"Don't you have a backyard to park in?"

"It's too far to walk from there to the front of the house. Daddy has these guard dogs that we are not to pet or play with that would make you pee in your pants if you met them face to face."

"So, Jimmy remained living with your father?"

"Yeah, for a while. He is the heir apparent so Daddy wanted to make sure he got up on time, to work on time, and dressed right."

"Until he moved away to college."

"Well, he did have a small apartment he took his girlfriends too."

"What about Sam?"

"Oh, no. Sam is gay and had no intention of hiding in a closet. He is really campy when he's relaxed. Daddy knew what he was all about since he was old enough to put one hand on his hip, as Daddy says. Sam moved out when he turned eighteen. Out of the five of us, Sam's got the most brains. At fifteen he had a small business going with our older cousins covering for him. What he's good at is starting businesses. He gets it going and then sells it."

The third ring brought Mrs. Oliver to the door. She had a shawl over her shoulders and a book in her hand.

"Little Bop! Where have you been? Do come in and bring your friend in with you. I was just about to pour myself some tea. Would you care for some?"

"Sure Mrs. Oliver. How have you been? This is my friend, Caitlin." Susan gave her a big hug, which the woman returned with as much enthusiasm.

Mrs. Oliver gave Caitlin a once over look and nodded with a smile.

She gestured to the spacious living room. "Gawn'in and I'll bring the tea."

"Little Bop?" Caitlin asked Susan in a low voice.

"A nickname my family calls me. I use to dance a lot when I was a little tike, if you want to know." Susan would rather give her the reason for the nickname than let Mrs. Oliver. Mrs. Oliver would give the whole embarrassing story and probably bring out the pictures too.

Caitlin walked around the room, not seeming to miss anything. She stopped at the bookcase and scanned the paperbacks that were stuffed every which way on shelves that seemed to be designated for paperbacks and then moved onto the hardback books. As she nosed around the titles, she could see Susan discreetly laying one of the pictures on a table face down behind the others. Caitlin grinned to herself. She already saw the picture. The toddler with all the birthday cake on her naked body must be Susan, she guessed.

So, Mrs. Oliver must be something more than a neighbor if she has baby pictures of Susan.

The three sat down for tea and with Caitlin prompting, Mrs. Oliver told funny stories of Susan's childhood. Caitlin noted that there was not much told about her siblings nor about her parents. All the stories were about Mrs. Oliver taking care of the infant Susan. Mrs. Oliver was her nanny before she married Mr. Oliver. The late Mr. Oliver lived in the house she was now living in with his aging mother. The aging mother passed away five years after they married and on the first anniversary date of her death, Mr. Oliver did not come home. Caitlin was surprised when Mrs. Oliver did not seem to mind, but she did have access to his assets and his lawyer so she lived quite well off and was able to pursue her own business interests, which was operating a nanny service.

"A nanny service?" Caitlin asked unbelievingly.

"It's what I know and it keeps me from getting bored. Would you like some more tea? No?"

"Mrs. Oliver, we're here to see Daddy, but he seems to have guests."

"Yes. They arrived about twenty minutes before you did. I thought it rather odd since one of them is Junior's father."

"Colby, Sr.?" Susan asked worriedly.

"Oh, don't fret child. They go back a long way, until they had a fight about a business they owned with the rest of the men in there."

Caitlin leaned forward. "Mrs. Oliver, this nanny business…your employees probably hear a lot of things that aren't for public ears. Am I right?"

Mrs. Oliver laughed. She wiggled her finger at Caitlin. "I read about you. About three years back you ran an agency that protected the rich and famous. The woman you were to protect staged her own hit while it was her husband that was the real target."

Caitlin nodded. "That wasn't in very many news papers."

Mrs. Oliver smiled. "I have my sources. My girls do hear things. Since they are only known to speak Spanish, they hear a lot."

"FBI."

Mrs. Oliver smiled again, nodding. "Very good." Then she frowned.

"You're an FBI agent?" Susan asked unbelievingly.

"Oh, no! Little Bop, can you see me with a gun or running their courses?"

"No, I can't."

"She's an informant. She's their cover for this operation."

She nodded. "My husband, he worked for these men that your father tried to sever ties with after he married your momma. He was very strict with you and your brothers and sisters because he did not want these people to use it as an excuse to pull him back in the organization, by addicting any of ya to their drugs or getting involved in their business. Your grandfather had a very good business going and your father concentrated on that. They wanted to either punish your father for something, or to let him know they still could pull his chain, so they chose you."

"Just what organization is this?"

"A gang. They call themselves the Band of Five, but it has grown. They traffic drugs, women, illegals, anything that a buyer wants from across the border."

"So, why are they meeting with Susan's father?"

"They are going to try and talk her father into not moving his business out of town. There are not many profitable businesses here, and he has one of the bigger ones. If he moves his headquarters, it will only be a matter of time before he moves two of the manufacturing and storage facilities too."

"The town is dried up anyway," Susan told her.

"Yes. They lost a lot of businesses over the border, which they own so that is not the problem. They need a legitimate business here to give reason why this town should stay solvent and they don't want to put their money in one so they're trying to twist your father's arm."

"That's why they let him do his thing and break with them."

"Yes. They needed a business the Feds would not be looking into."

"Well, how did the Feds get interested in the first place?" Susan asked what Caitlin wanted to know too.

"Junior was a bit too free with his mouth when he was in prison. So someone was sent out to check it out. They approached me and showed me that not only did my husband work for this group, but chances are they were responsible for his disappearance. By then, I was over Howard. Came to realize that life was more fun without him around, but when they asked me to do them a favor – oh, boy!"

"I bet you jumped at it!" Susan laughed. She turned to Caitlin, "She was one hell of a nanny. She gave me my first riding lessons at three years. We went hiking and back packing when I was five. We did all sorts of crazy things my parents did not know about. When I reached seven, she was no longer my nanny, but I would come up here and visit and we would sometimes sneak off somewhere."

"Her father is such a bore. Her mother was no better. Both were interested in their business and just as long as someone was with the kids that was fine with them."

"So, each kid had their own nanny?"

Susan shook her head. "No. My father's first wife stayed home. His second wife, my mother, was his secretary and she knew the business. So it was Sam and myself that had a nanny. Mother died in a car crash. We think she committed suicide because she had inoperable cancer. Daddy never recovered."

"She was feisty, like you Susan. Wild and sometimes reckless. You have your father's sister's looks, but your character, mannerisms and voice are just like hers. I'm sure it really drove your father crazy to hear you talk, and look at you, and not see your mother."

Susan nodded. "Yeah, he's told me a few times, I sound just like her."

"So, why are you back when you finally got away?" Mrs. Oliver asked curious.

"Do you remember the tall big blond guy that was acting as my bodyguard?"

"Oh, yes. He visited your father yesterday. He just about woke up the dead with them pipes on his motorcycle."

Caitlin frowned. *Why would he make himself obvious?*

"When I looked out the window from my bedroom window, your father was standing in the front lawn watching him drive away and slapping the paper on his leg…"

"Oh, boy. He must have been angry."

"Uh, huh. About two hours later the first of those cars pulled up. Been there a long time. Then today they all arrived again…early."

"Are you still in contact with the Feds?" Caitlin asked cautiously.

"Nope. Too dangerous. I keep one of these phone line detectors by my phone and it goes off every time I lift my phone. Got one of these UV devices to check the place out for bugs too." She lifted a voice scrambler from her pocket. "And I got one of these voice scramblers."

Caitlin lifted a brow. "You certainly are prepared."

Mrs. Oliver waved her hand. "It's just routine. I've read up on all this stuff and what to expect. Why, right now, they probably have someone scanning my place and noticed that you two are here."

"Why do you stay here if you have to protect yourself this way?"

"I'm not protecting myself...just being aware."

"Well, if they have noted our arrival, I think we need to get going," Caitlin told the woman, rising from her seat.

Suddenly Caitlin pitched forward, while Susan rose quickly to her feet to assist and she also suffered the same fate. Both collapsed unconscious onto the carpet, knocking over the remains of their drinks.

*****

Queen's Lane

Chapter 21

Caitlin woke with a nauseous stomach and a headache. It was the side effect of whatever was in her drink – she was sure of that. Her hands were bound behind her and by the bite it was nylon. She was propped against a wall. Someone kneeled close to her.

"She's awake."

Caitlin rolled and lifted her legs that were also bound together kicking the person in the chest and getting the satisfaction of hearing a familiar laugh congratulate her.

"Caitlin, you are one hell of a person to wake up." Agent Kenneth Allen leaned down toward her with a taser gun. "Don't think about it."

"What the hell are you doing?" Caitlin demanded angrily.

"Restraining you before you interfere with an official operation."

"Anything you're involved in gets people killed – most notably the hostages and other innocent bystanders, asshole!"

Ken looked over at his partner who was rubbing his chest. "She's just upset because she can't see her girlfriend get all trussed up. We'll take pictures."

Caitlin knew any further display would only give Ken pleasure, which she had no intention of doing. "This is

not an official operation or you two would not be here."
Caitlin suddenly grew fearful.

"Sure it is. We set up this sting and you just happened to supply the bait we've been looking for. For a while there, we thought we would have to get a look-alike."

The older woman, Mrs. Oliver, was standing on the stairs. She had entered the room unnoticed by any of the occupants.

"What are you going to do with her?" She asked indicating Caitlin.

"Leave her here. It's soundproof. We'll nab the gang and let you know when to let her go. Why don't you go on back upstairs? We need to give her a sedative to make sure she doesn't go anywhere, and she can get – violent."

"If she's a good guy, why are you doing this to her?" Mrs. Oliver asked.

"Because she also gets in the way. She's a civilian that is sticking her nose into official business. I told you before; if she gets involved your friend will get hurt."

Caitlin didn't dare say anything worried that Mrs. Oliver would get hurt and all for naught. Mrs. Oliver nodded and went back up stairs.

"You lied to her. You don't give a damn about her 'friend'." She eyed the needle that Ken was preparing for her. Suddenly he sank to his feet and without thinking, Caitlin rolled and blocked Andy's response. She felt his body fall across her.

Mrs. Oliver was quickly at her side with a sharp knife.

"I knew I made a mistake when these two showed up instead of my usual contact." She was shaking her white head.

Caitlin rubbed her freed wrists. "How long have I been out?"

"About thirty minutes. They had me hand over Susan to her father. Her father had me watching out for her.

He knew she would come here before she went home – to test out the atmosphere."

"Just who are you working for, just so I know when to duck?"

"Susan, right now. Her father doesn't know how close Susan and I are. It was for her protection. He has this fear of his kids not loving him so anyone they become attached to – he makes life difficult for them."

"By his behavior with his other kids and with Susan, I find that one hard to believe."

"He is rather clumsy on how to express his feelings for his kids...but if he were an ogre, he wouldn't keep track of them. He got himself involved with these childhood friends that were no good and tried to keep his kids out of it."

Caitlin bound the two agents up with nylon strips and removed the taser gun each agent had. "Since when are these standard issue?" she muttered angrily. She left them with their guns but removed the ammunition clips.

"Do you know where they have her?" Caitlin asked as she dug her cell phone out of Ken's pocket. It was on vibrate and it was vibrating.

"Caitlin," she answered briskly.

[Where the hell have you been?]

"Tied up. Where's Susan?"

[They moved her into the church basement.]

"That does not sound good. Is there a tunnel or something below the church that leads to that building?"

[We'll need a copter to give it a sweep and even then, people will have to be moving in it.]

"How long will that take? Never mind. Her father handed her over."

[No. He put up a fight. Got knocked out. He's in the church too. Should we bust in?]

"Do you see any agents anywhere around there?"

[Hell yes! They stick out like a sore thumb.]

"Where are they?"

[Around the church.]

"Fan out. They have to have another exit and have probably already left. I'll meet you at..."

"The Babot's. That's the brother-in-law of Colby. He put up the money for his business."

"Did you hear that?"

There was some talking in the background. [Yeah. We got the hound with us. We'll find it. Hey, the guy with the rifle at the top. FBI. Neutralized our guy.]

"Any casualties?"

[Just an FBI agent that will think twice about doing something like that again.]

"See ya at the Babots." She hung up.

"Come on. I'll take ya there, but you're gonna have ta stand out less."

"Gotta a hat?"

*****

"This place has enough alarms to make one wonder just what he's trying to protect," Caitlin whispered.

"Word has it, he's the treasurer of the church and the boy's club." Mrs. Oliver led her down what in some communities would be called an alley, but this one was well manicured and looked nothing like the alleys in the City. She wondered if the people here also had their trashcans washed each week.

"Hold it." Caitlin knelt next to a bush that was placed in a good position to have an intruder alert implanted within it. Her UV alarm was lit up. "We go past this and it will register our movement."

Caitlin turned around grabbing Mrs. Oliver and pushing her behind her. Before them was a large mixed breed dog, female. Female dogs had a different method of guarding property. They had the habit of attacking first and then maybe barking, meaning they were quiet hunters.

"Seantie, sit!" Mrs. Oliver ordered. However the dog was not watching her, Caitlin's hand moved and the dog stood poised, her eyes fastened on hers. Finally the dog lay down and remained still, eyes still on Caitlin.

"I think we have an answer to how we can get past these sound sensors."

*****

Caitlin and Mrs. Oliver were looking at the backdoor of a building that had cameras looking out over the back area. Satisfied that everyone on the Feds team thought that was where the action would be, she and Mrs. Oliver headed for a small storage shop for the Colby electronics store.

Caitlin's team had the door opened and spread out to make sure any monitoring equipment was not attached to an alarm or camera that they had not already dismantled.

"Found it!" whispered one of the men. One of the others quickly opened the floor panel and the team quickly moved down the staircase. Caitlin handed Mrs. Oliver an extra set of night goggles. One that should have been for Susan.

Mrs. Oliver raised her dart gun getting ready, as the two men worked on opening the door. Silently it opened. It was to a cellar. In single file the five members of Caitlin's team quickly moved down the staircase, spreading out into the room. Quietly they located a group of men arguing loudly, while another found Susan unconscious, being watched over by another in a side room who was playing solitaire, occasionally yelling at the others to keep it down.

Mikey quietly moved over to Caitlin, and signed her what he had discovered. Caitlin followed him, moving in stops and starts to make sure there were no alarms they would set off.

Before them was an underground vault, and it was opened. While Mikey guarded from outside, Caitlin took a quick inspection of just what was in the vault. Tapes. They were alphabetically arranged. By the titles it was of people. She moved down the row and found four with Susan's name. The dates did not make sense. Caitlin removed the four, stuffing them in her vest.

Caitlin pulled Mikey close and signed that the contents of the vault needed to be burned. Mikey nodded and moved into the room to figure out how to by pass the halon alarm. Meanwhile, Caitlin did a visual check with her other members. She knew if they stayed too long, their chances of getting out undetected would lessen.

Willy's big frame slid into view.

Damn! Trouble if he left his post. Caitlin looked at the others again and made sure that Mrs. Oliver was okay.

Willy signed that there were some people upstairs. The team quickly found places to hide, though there were not many.

Caitlin looked in on Mikey who was closing the alarm panel. He looked up and gave her the thumbs up. She signed they had company. He nodded and continued to work on setting a situation up for a fire to occur.

"Melvin!" An angry voice shouted and two men, one a very large man with a big belly, and heavy ring on his finger barreled into the room. The voices that had been arguing stopped.

"We're over here. The asshole isn't listening to reason. Dip shit!"

"Goddamhellalmighty, Nic! We got your goddam daughter! We're not asking ya to do anything illegal!" The large man bellowed.

"Siddown!"

The scraping of furniture and men grumbling could be heard, which Caitlin was not really interested in. Mikey slid next to her.

"Ready," he whispered close to her ear.

Caitlin nodded and gave the high sign to the rest. The guard watching Susan had moved over to listen to the others, and soon the men were arguing, with one man sitting in a chair gagged and bound shaking his head stubbornly. Susan was lifted and hefted onto a shoulder while the others watched to make sure they were not seen.

The team started to move out, with the reluctant Mrs. Oliver being dragged back. She was aiming to shoot one of the men.

They were back in Caitlin's vehicle and the others on their cycles within an hour.

"Where's the trailer?"

"Rolling."

"Mrs. Oliver, do you mind coming along with us? It's going to be hot in Colina for a bit. The Feds and their quarry will be shootin' at each other for a while. Could I interest you in a short vacation on a…" Caitlin's mouth turned up in a grin, "horse ranch…say up in the mountains, surrounded by a forest?"

"Wellll, that's original. Better'n some safe house in the city surrounded by a bunch of FBI agents with no sense of humor. Can I pet the horses? My bones feel too old to be ridin' 'em."

"Better yet, my mother will give you a tour, if you want one. You can even sleep in my bedroom."

"Who's gonna sleep in your bedroom," Susan mumbled, holding her head.

"Mrs. Oliver. How's your head?"

"Got any aspirins? Where are we?" Susan gulped the pills down from a canteen Georgia Peach handed her.

"On our way home. We're gonna take the long way and drop Mrs. Oliver off with my mother."

Georgia started to laugh, "Oh, gawds! I gotta be there to see this."

"She'll be all right. It was my mother's idea to get involved in this mess in the first place. She'll love to hear the details and how she was right."

"You're right there." Georgia nodded. She looked out the window at the lights in front of them. "Isn't that our home base?"

"Yeah. Get on the radio…a frequency we know the Feds aren't going to use, and tell them we'll meet them at Ridge Road. Great place to grab breakfast."

"What time is it?"

"Midnight. You've been out a while."

"Mrs. Oliver, is your business going to be all right with you out of town for a while?" Susan asked her concerned.

"I'll give Marcia a call at our next stop. She's been wanting me to take a vacation for months…since I forced her to take one. She's my business partner."

"Marcia Hernandez?"

"Yep. She went to collage, that junior one, got herself a degree in business and helped me get my business all set up. Hell, I hate the paper work. So, I gave her a partnership since she's doing the boring stuff."

"That's really nice. She always wanted to be her own boss." Susan yawned. "She always sold more chocolate bars then me."

*****

"Susan, wake up." A hand gently rocked her to wakefulness. She blinked her eyes at the early morning and burred at the cold. Snow was covering the fences they were driving by. Caitlin turned the Rover under an archway with Queen's Lane written under it.

"Doc Walker is your mother?" *Hell, I should have known. Now I know where Caitlin gets the attitude.*

"Yeah. Tried to get me to be a veterinarian too but I decided to follow in my daddy's footsteps. Sticking my hands up horses'...."she paused. "Ahh, having patients bigger than me was not my dream. Hanna wasn't interested either. We brainwashed our baby sister, Tendra into thinking that's what she wanted to be when she grew up."

"Nice job. Is she one?"

"Yeah."

As they pulled up Susan saw a familiar figure waiting for them on the porch, Tothito.

"Good morning, Tothito. Walker doin' chores?

"'Mornin' Caitlin, Georgia, Ms. Nikolas. Yes. You want to help her out? She's down two. I'll show your guests to their rooms."

"I'll help out," Susan offered.

"Me too." Georgia slid out of the car and stretched her legs.

Caitlin glanced at Susan doubtfully. "Ever take care of horses?"

"No. But I've seen how it's done. Ya throw out a handful of hay and...make sure they got water."

Caitlin grinned. "Hmm. Come along then, volunteer. Mrs. Oliver, this is Tothito, and she'll show you where it's nice and warm and if you want...there's clean towels, warm water for a bath or shower and then a soft bed."

"Sounds nice to me. I'll see ya later, Little Bop. Don't be kiddin' the tall one now." She turned to Caitlin, "She knows more than that, Caitlin." She told her in a loud conspiring whisper.

"Do tell," Caitlin drawled.

*****

Two hours later Susan could understand why Caitlin would rather not work on a horse ranch on a daily basis. She had mucked enough stalls that she was beginning to think the smell was stuck in her pores. Her consolation was when Doc Walker told her that this was the first time she had not heard a cuss word from Caitlin about feeding and mucking stalls. And all this time Caitlin was acting as if this was nothing. There was to be a pay back in this.

Breakfast was what she dreamed working farms or ranches should serve. Mrs. Oliver and Doc Walker got along fine...unfortunately for Susan and Caitlin, because they swapped baby stories of them. Even Tiffie got some stories told about her as she demanded to tell some stories of her own.

That night, as Caitlin and Susan were getting ready for bed Susan decided to find out just what Caitlin had planned for their future.

"So..." Susan began as she pulled on the large T-shirt Caitlin handed her.

Caitlin turned to her waiting expectantly.

"So..." Caitlin repeated. She held a hand out to Susan and drew her into her arms. "What are your plans?" Caitlin asked her.

Susan laughed in her shirt. "Funny you should ask." She looked up into the green eyes and ran a finger lightly over the scar she wanted to ask Caitlin about. There were a lot of things she wanted to ask Caitlin about. Instead...

"I will give my entire self to you, Caitlin ....but you need to know that this is a commitment I'm making here. I'm giving you my fears, nightmares, fantasies and dreams. What I need is a commitment from you. I'm not going to give myself to someone without getting something in return." *Has she already guessed that whether she makes a commitment to me or not...I will still give myself to her?*

Caitlin leaned close to Susan with her lips near Susan's ear. "When I first brought you to Queen's Lane...I was thinking about getting to know you better."

"Ah. And?"

"How about if we see how we do without the external pressure of imminent danger?"

"Caitlin, I'm not turned onto you or love you as I do because of an adrenaline rush of...of...fear...because some nut is stalking me." Susan stepped back from Caitlin not sure of herself with Caitlin anymore.

"Susan," a quiet voice called her back.

She looked at Caitlin's face and could see the concern.

"I'm sure about your feelings for me..." she started.

"You don't...." Susan interrupted fearing what Caitlin was going to tell her.

"I have feelings for you that I haven't felt for anyone for a long time...so long that I want to be sure. I want to be sure about me and that I'm not interested in you because of the excitement of a mystery that was around you when I met you."

Susan took a deep breath and then let it out. *Why was it so easy to let her run my life until now? I know what we have is real.* Susan nodded, suddenly flashing on her own life before she had met Caitlin. "I can understand you wanting to slow down. I'll..."

"Living together, we can find out if we're compatible...if you don't mind," Caitlin offered, knowing that Susan was off balance and frightened that she was going to abandon her. "We can then get an idea of whether you can stand how I prefer to live. Maybe you would want some changes, and maybe I can't make them and maybe I can." Her lips curled up as Susan's eyes shined with unshed tears.

"I would love to live with you. Where?"

"Well, I kinda move around, but my place in the forest is my primary residence. We can take trips to the city when you need to socialize."

"Okay," Susan breathed in and then pulled Caitlin's face down to her lips. "Hmm. Too bad we don't have..."

But she did not get a chance to say any more as Caitlin pulled her over to the bed.

*****

Chapter 22

Susan rolled over and flopped her hand on the space behind her. Cold and no Caitlin. She lifted her head and could hear Tiffie's little voice shouting her happiness at receiving something.

Floopie? Must be a rag doll or something. Gawds, I feel tired still.

Susan rolled out of bed and rushed into the shower over the cold floorboards and tiled floor in the bathing room. She was enjoying the hot water when she heard the shower curtain part. She blinked her eyes open and could see Caitlin leaning in to kiss her on her butt.

"Ohhh. Baby, baby. Bite me," she cooed teasingly. And Caitlin did.

A thumping on the bathroom door reminded them they were not alone.

"Hey! When can I use the potty?" Mrs. Oliver shouted through the door.

"Damn! Walker must have put her next door," Caitlin grumbled.

*****

"So, Caitlin...you gonna tell us what the phone call was about or are ya gonna make me hold your breakfast until ya tell us?" Walker asked and then looked directly at her.

"It was Mikey. He stayed behind to see what happened. FBI in DC got word about a big sting operation just outside of San Diego going down, and it was being handled by some field agents who did not file any papers on it. That got the locals on site, and from what I understand, a bad bust turned out to be a big bust for the bureau. They got a few 'wild cards' in their group and some important leaders in a smugglers' ring."

"Smugglers?" Susan asked hoarsely. "What...did they smuggle?"

Caitlin leaned over to her and gripped her hand. "Drugs, Susan. Just drugs. The sex club was used to keep members in line through blackmail and intimidation and others that they wanted to influence," she told her in a soft voice so Tiffie would not hear.

Susan looked up into Caitlin's eyes and knew she was lying. Caitlin's eyes moved to where Tiffie was trying to scoop her bowl of cheerios with a spoon.

"Okay, for now," Susan told her just as softly, but in a firm voice, though she knew that Caitlin would not hold something like that back from her, or would she? Or more importantly, did she want to know? The mood change was so sudden that Susan felt overwhelmed and then her stomach felt nauseated.

"Come on. Let's have a talk," Caitlin told her, taking her cold hand and pulling her to follow her.

Susan was not aware of where she was being taken, only that she was very cold and numb. When she did start to notice what was going on, they were sitting on a couch in a room she did not recognize and Caitlin had her cradled in her arms.

Susan's expanse of ribcage clued Caitlin that she was back with her.

"Hey, hon."

Susan pressed against her chest and leaned her head back. Caitlin's lips reached around and kissed her gently.

"Caitlin...what happened? All I can remember was that we were at Mrs. Oliver's and then...waking up on our way here."

"Mrs. Oliver slipped us a mickey. She was being squeezed by those FBI agents and your father and decided to give you up to the safer of the two, your father. After all, she still had the ace in the hole..."

"You?"

Caitlin squeezed her. "Yeah. So, you were handed over to your father who was worried about you and did not trust the men that have been blackmailing him for years. He thought you would be safer in his house. However, they grabbed you and him, getting past his alarms. Kidnapping and murdering is not the type of pressure they would put on your father because...it would not work."

Susan nodded. "It would only make him dig further in and stick to whatever it is they are trying to get him to stop. Reverse psychology doesn't work either...I've tried it."

"When we rescued you, we found a vault full of tapes with dates and names on them."

Susan turned around in Caitlin's lap, and then both women moved around to get comfortable in new positions.

"I removed the ones on you...I haven't looked at them yet, but I will tell you, I don't think they are any worse that what was posted of you on the Internet."

Susan snorted in disgust. "You said not all of it looked real, more like staged."

"Yes. The reason I say that is because what they showed on the Internet was you getting shaved and ringed. The rest was pasted together."

Susan shook and started to cry. "Gawds, I'm...."

Caitlin rocked her for a while until she felt her trembling lessen.

"So...what do you think is on those tapes?" Susan asked.

"I don't know for sure, but probably surveillance tapes. I could look at them first and then we can both see them or I can just..."

"No. No. I want to see them." She was quiet thinking about it. "Together."

"All right."

"I...need to see if some of these fears are from something that they did."

Caitlin hugged her tight. "You are such a strong person, Susan. When do you want to see them?"

"Now."

*****

No one but Caitlin and Susan were in Doc's office as they watched on her computer the CDs of their monitoring her and other family members. However it was mostly of her. Both women laughed at some of the stuff because it reminded them of home movies. It was not until a year ago, when Susan first went out with Junior that the taping took on a serious look. Susan was unmistakably unconscious and the men posturing her for pictures did not bother to cut themselves out of the pictures. Three of the men had sex with her. For now, Susan rationally compared it with the men she had sex with when she drank herself into a stupor. When the last tape finished, the two women sat in the dark in silence.

"You know, Caitlin? I'm sure I'm in shock right now and maybe tomorrow I will flip out...but the nightmares I have been having had me thinking some really scary scenes had taken place. These guys make me pissed off and wanting to take a shotgun full of buckshot to them. You're gonna have to keep guns away from me for a while," she joked. Or, she was hoping she was joking. Then she just started to cry.

Caitlin rocked her letting her work through the different levels of denial and anger until she finished it with tears.

Caitlin kissed her wet forehead. "When we get home, we're going to play on the slide and swim until we're tired, and then sit down to one of Willie's infamous Sheppard pies. And...if you are real nice to me, I'll give you a massage you won't forget."

Susan looked deep in her dark eyes and smiled happily. "I don't know how I got so lucky to find you. My biggest fear is that something will ruin our relationship."

"Hm. How many relationships have you been in?" Caitlin teased, knowing she had not been in any.

"None until now. Is this normal?"

"Live in the moment. Whatever happens, we'll handle it."

"Together."

"Yes. Together," Caitlin agreed.

End

About the Author

Irene Christie (pen name) was born in January 1948 in Hollywood, California and raised in Southern California. For the unusual at the time, the author studied acupressure, Tai Chi, ChiGun, Korean Karate, and Yoga. She graduated with a doctorate in psychology and after about six years of working as a counselor, decided it was not the type of career she wanted. Instead, she returned to writing.

I. Christie has visited a few places outside the United States of America, (France, Haiti, Canada, and most recently the XenaCruise).

The author is a lover of all animals, believing that all things are sacred though admittedly having a hard time putting it in practice for some creatures, i.e. fleas and cockroaches. Cats, birds and whatever the cats drag in, reside with the author.

Christie is a voracious reader; loves most types of music, (yep, including Blue Grass). Once an avid hiker, camper, biker, jogger and visitor to the local gym, nowadays she visits the gym a few days a week, stays off bikes for self preservation, and camps where there is the luxury of flush toilets, a shower and electricity when finished with a hike (that would be in an RV or hotel).

Along with writing, the author also is an artist in beadwork, embroidery, woodcarving, chalk, and pencil. However, writing has become a comfortable obsession, leaving the other tools to gather dust.

The author prefers to live near the beach where the smell of ocean spray is heavy in the early morning and night air. The author lived near the foothills for seven years and happily moved back to a beach city. The author's dream place to live is Bellingham, Washington, where the rolling hills and houses make for a wonderful walk and pleasing for the eyes, and where the bay is just below one's sight.

NOTE: This is I. Christie's first published book but certainly will not be the last. Watch the D2D website for future offerings.

We would like to invite you to read an excerpt from one of our favorites and a best seller :

Mavis Applewater's

PWP: Plot? What Plot?
Book I

A Baker's Dozen

Book II in this series will be released from D2D in 2004. The sections included here are not in the same order as they appear in the book and do not necessarily include all scenes with these characters.

Excerpt from PWP – Book I

SING FOR ME

PART ONE

Audrey looked around the lounge, wondering if it would be a bad thing if she simply bolted right then. "A blind date," she muttered in embarrassment as she ran her fingers nervously through her short blonde hair. She scanned the crowd carefully, looking for the woman she had agreed to meet. It was her friend Martha's idea. *'Okay, Martha described her as average height which would make her taller than me. She said she has brown eyes and hair. She also said that she had a great personality. I'm regretting this already.'* Audrey mentally reviewed the information that Martha had provided her with. In the back of the room she spotted a woman who seemed to match the description.

"She's cute," Audrey noted as the stranger looked up at her hopefully. Audrey made her way towards the back of the lounge. As she passed the baby grand piano she smiled, hoping that someone would be playing that evening. She

1

always found music soothing.

"Dee?" Audrey inquired shyly.

"Yes, I am," the woman responded eagerly.

"It's nice to meet you," Audrey said brightly as she offered her hand to the woman. She noted with some regret that Dee didn't stand and shake her hand. She just sat there with her hands folded in her lap. Audrey wrote it off to nerves as she took a seat beside the woman.

The waiter approached them. Audrey noted the young man seemed uncomfortable as he stopped at their booth. "Pinot Grigio," she ordered quickly and turned towards her date who was staring at the table. "Would you like something, Dee?" she inquired softly, noticing that Dee didn't have a drink in front of her.

"No," the brunette snapped.

Audrey's green eyes grew wide in surprise before she turned back to the waiter. "Just the glass of wine of me." The waiter nodded in understanding. The first alarm bell went off in Audrey's mind; she took a deep breath and mentally willed the waiter to hurry back with her drink. "So how long have you known Martha?" Audrey inquired in hopes of getting the conversation started.

"Why?" the brunette inquired in a fearful tone.

"Just curious," Audrey stammered as the second alarm went off in her head. "She said a lot of nice things about you," Audrey continued in a very slow and careful tone. *Too bad I'm going to have to kill her when I see her at the office tomorrow.'* Audrey smiled as the murderous thoughts ran through her mind.

"Really?" Dee responded, genuinely surprised at what Audrey had said.

"Yes, she did," Audrey continued in the same careful tone of voice. The waiter approached and placed Audrey's glass down. "Are you certain you don't want something to drink?"

"No," the woman snapped once again.

"Okay," Audrey stammered once again as the waiter made a mad dash away from the table.

"You can't be too careful," Dee began in a soft tone. "I saw this thing on the X-Files about contaminated water," she explained.

Audrey simply nodded her head as she saw the sincerity in the woman's eyes. "So what do you do for a living?" Audrey inquired, hoping that she could just polish off her glass of wine and get the hell out of there.

"Why?" Dee inquired suspiciously.

"Just making conversation," Audrey retorted quickly.

"That's what *they* all say," Dee responded sincerely.

"They?" Audrey blinked in surprise. *'Go ahead. You know you want to ask her,'* Audrey thought in an amused tone. "Who are they?"

"You know," Dee whispered. "Martha really said nice things about me?" she inquired, shifting gears rather quickly.

"Yes, she did," Audrey confirmed. *'Only she left out the part about you being a big wacko,'* she thought wryly as she continued to plan Martha's untimely demise.

"That's sweet of her. She's very nice. She didn't even blame me for the fire," Dee continued absently.

"Fire?" Audrey choked on her wine.

"Uh huh." Dee nodded. "They won't let me play with matches anymore," she added in a distracted tone.

"Or sharp objects," Audrey muttered under her breath as she rubbed her now throbbing temple.

"That too," Dee agreed as her eyes seemed to glaze over. "Who did you say sent you?"

"Martha," Audrey replied carefully as she moved

slightly away from the troubled woman. *'I just don't understand why Martha would fix me up with this girl. I know she said she was a bit eccentric, but this chick needs to be medicated.'*

"Who's Martha?" the woman snarled.

"Check please," Audrey called out quickly, hoping the waiter could hear her.

Dee began to ramble incoherently as Audrey looked around the room, searching for the waiter. The music filtered through the air. Audrey smiled at the sweet melody coming from the piano. "Who is that?" she choked out as she spied the vision of beauty seated at the piano.

"I hate this damn music," Dee growled.

"Probably interferes with the voices in your head," Audrey muttered as she searched for the waiter, her eyes never leaving the raven-haired beauty seated at the keyboard.

"No, that's not it," Dee stated in a flat tone. "I have to go," she said abruptly as she jumped up and stormed off.

The waiter finally approached and smiled at her meekly. "I'm sorry," he apologized. "But your companion scared me." Audrey looked the six-foot-three muscular man up and down.

"Coward," she growled.

"I don't mean to offend you or your friend," he quickly apologized once again.

"Blind date," Audrey confessed.

"Girlfriend, who would do that to you?" he asked in a light tone.

"A soon-to-be-deceased ex-friend." Audrey laughed as she watched all traces of masculinity vanish from his demeanor. "I'll just take the check now," she added in a pleading tone.

"Nonsense," he scoffed. "It's on me and the next one

too."

"I don't know." Audrey hesitated as her emerald eyes once again drifted back towards the piano player.

"I'll bring it to you at the bar by the piano," he suggested smugly.

"Oh well, if you insist," Audrey responded with a playful smile.

Audrey passed by the baby grand piano and found herself mesmerized by the brightest, bluest eyes she had ever seen. She almost tripped over the vacant stool at the bar near the piano. She blushed as she finally managed to sit in the chair. "Here you are," the waiter informed her as he placed a fresh glass of wine in front of her. "I'm Steve," he introduced himself.

"Audrey," she responded as she shook his hand.

"That's my partner, Kenny." He pointed to the bartender. "And she is Camille." He pointed to the goddess at the piano. "She's single after a nasty breakup a year and a half ago. Doesn't date the customers or anyone else lately. Tip her enough and she'll play anything you want. And girl, you have just got to hear her sing."

"I just love a family restaurant." Audrey chuckled as she settled back and listened to Camille play one soothing melody after another.

As the evening wore on Audrey felt herself becoming lost in the music and Camille's electrifying good looks. She tried to work up enough courage to slip money into the large glass snifter on top of Camille's piano. Each time she considered it, her palms would begin to sweat. Every once in awhile Camille looked over at her. Each time they shared a brief smile and Audrey was certain that her heart would explode.

She glanced at her watch and was shocked to realize how late it was. Reluctantly she left the bar and hailed a cab.

She was smiling as she crawled into bed. She didn't know if it was the wine or the Gershwin or Camille's overwhelming beauty, but she felt wonderful.

PART TWO

Audrey arrived at the office in a delightful mood the next morning, which surprised her since she'd had very little sleep the night before. She plunked herself down in the chair in Martha's cubicle and waited for her arrival. The tiny older woman screamed in surprised when she found Audrey in her cubicle with her feet propped up on her desk. "Hello, Martha," Audrey offered in a droll tone.

"Oh no," Martha gasped before swallowing in fear. "I called Dee last night and asked her how it went. She said you never showed up."

"Oh, I showed up all right." Audrey glared at her. "I'm not certain which of Dee's personalities showed up."

"She must be off her meds again." Martha grimaced.

"Her meds?" Audrey choked out.

"I'm sorry," Martha apologized quickly. "Dee is a very nice girl. It's just if she doesn't take her meds she has a few problems."

"Problems?" Audrey choked out once again. "Look, I don't mean to belittle Dee's obvious psychological afflictions, but why in the name of all that is sacred would you fix me up with her?"

"She's my niece," Martha explained tearfully. "And she's a good person. I thought she was doing better and she needed to get out and socialize."

"So me being the only lesbian that you know, you thought that I could take her out." Audrey nodded in understanding. "You should have told me."

"What did she do?" Martha inquired fearfully.

Audrey related in detail what had occurred on her date from hell. Martha simply rubbed her temple wearily. "I'd better let her mother know that she's pocketing her drugs again," Martha said in a tired voice. "I'm sorry about last night," Martha apologized again.

"Tell you what old pal of mine . . . ," Audrey taunted her as she finally got out of her chair, " . . . you can make it up to me by joining me for a drink later tonight."

"What gives?" Martha prodded.

"I'll tell you tonight." Audrey shrugged nonchalantly. "Just meet me at Vinnie's at eight o'clock."

"Eight o'clock?" Martha grumbled. "Why not just after work?"

"You owe me," Audrey asserted as she left the cubicle.

That night Audrey found herself sitting once again at the bar by the piano. "Well, hello again," Kenny greeted her. "I just knew you couldn't stay away from me," he teased. "Or is it Stevie that's caught your eye?"

"How did you ever guess?" Audrey played along.

"Okay, I'm here," Martha huffed as she sat down next to Audrey.

"I see your taste is improving." Steve laughed as he approached the ladies.

"Steve, this is my friend Martha whose life I've decided to spare," Audrey explained quickly. "And the grinning boy behind the bar is Kenny."

8

"You are bad woman." Steve wagged his finger at Martha.

"So now I know why I'm here." Martha groaned, looking at Audrey for the first time. "Nice dress," she exclaimed, taking in the short black beaded number Audrey was wearing.

"Thank you." Audrey blushed. "Pinot Grigio," she ordered quickly from Kenny.

"Stoli Raz and Sprite," Martha ordered. "As I was saying, am I here so you and your new friends can torture me?"

"No, sweets," Kenny interrupted them as he delivered their drinks. "That's why you're here," he continued as he pointed across room.

Audrey blushed as she watched her friend's eyes roam across the room. "Wow, she's gorgeous," Martha gasped loudly. Audrey looked across the room as Camille took her spot at the piano.

"I know." Audrey sighed deeply.

"Okay, so explain to me what you need me for?" Martha said before taking a sip of her cocktail.

"I couldn't show up here two nights in a row and just sit here by myself," Audrey explained, her eyes never leaving Camille's body. "She'll think I'm some kind of stalker."

"Imagine that." Martha laughed. "God Audrey, you should see yourself. You're drooling."

"I am not," Audrey snarled as she glared at Martha.

Audrey was about to protest her innocence further when the most beautiful voice she had ever heard began to sing. Audrey turned in amazement as her jaw dropped. For the first time in years, Audrey found herself rendered speechless.

"I love this song," Martha murmured. "Sam and I danced to it at our wedding."

Audrey was so mesmerized by the ballad Camille was belting out that she didn't realize she was gripping Martha's arm tightly. "Okay, let go of my arm," Martha protested as she pried Audrey's hand off.

"She is amazing," Audrey whimpered as she turned towards Martha. "How am I ever going to meet her?"

"You haven't spoken to her yet?" Martha grilled her.

"No, what would I say?" Audrey balked.

"I don't know . . . how about hello?" Martha suggested.

"And then what?" Audrey asked in a panic.

"Oh boy, you have got it bad." Martha chuckled. "Okay, try this. See those little breaks she takes between songs when people go up, put money in her tip jar, and request a song? You could do that."

"What would I request?" Audrey contemplated Martha's suggestion.

"You're pathetic," Martha groaned.

"I am not," Audrey snarled. "I just don't want to request something she doesn't know or like."

"Are you going to request Feelings?" Martha interjected.

"No." Audrey rolled her eyes in disgust.

"Okay. Well, you heard what she played last night; why not pick something from that?" Martha egged her on as she opened her purse. She removed a five-dollar bill from her wallet and thrust it into Audrey's hand. "Go on," her friend pushed. "And don't just request a song; try to talk to her."

"I don't know about that." Audrey blushed. "It's going to take all the courage I have just to walk over there."

"Okay, but I should tell you that she keeps looking

10

over here," Martha chimed in. "Go. She just finished a
song."

Audrey braced herself and climbed off her stool; her
legs wobbled slightly as she stood. Somehow the petite
blonde managed to make her way across the few feet to the
piano. "Hi there," the singer's sultry voice purred.

"Hi," Audrey answered in a dreamy tone.

"Did you have a request?" Camille asked as she
played around on the keyboard.

"No . . . I mean yes," Audrey stuttered as she
blushed.

"Well, what would you like?" Camille encouraged
her, blue eyes twinkling up at Audrey.

"I have no idea," Audrey confessed with a light
laugh.

"I don't think I know that one." Camille laughed
along with her. "I'll tell you what. I'll play something just
for you. That is if your friend won't take offense?" Camille
hesitated as she nodded towards Martha.

"Martha is just a friend," Audrey explained quickly.

"Good to know," Camille responded with a dazzling
smile. "And you are?"

"Audrey," the blonde said with a slight blush.

"You are absolutely adorable," Camille said softly as
her fingers continued to glide across the keys. Audrey
simply blushed harder as she found herself unable to speak.
"How about this?" Camille said softly as she began to play
the soft melody. "What I'll do . . . ," Camille crooned softly.

Audrey's heart pounded wildly as she debated
whether she should remain by the piano or return to her seat
at the bar. She finally convinced herself to move but her feet
refused to cooperate. Camille's electric blue eyes never
broke contact with Audrey's sparkling green ones. With

each note Audrey sunk deeper into Camille's electrifying gaze. As Camille finished the ballad, Audrey was certain that she was going to melt on the spot. "Thank you," Audrey whispered shyly.

"Any time," Camille replied softly as she took a sip of water.

Audrey blushed once again as she finally willed her body to move. Finding her way back to Martha, she sat down with a heavy sigh. "Now that was interesting," Martha teased her.

"Shut up," Audrey scolded her as she watched Camille play the piano. Her long fingers stroked each key tenderly. Audrey bit her lip as she watched those fingers work their magic. She couldn't help but wonder what those fingers would feel like stroking her skin.

She sighed deeply, totally lost in her thoughts when Martha's chuckle snapped her back to reality. "I'm sorry," she apologized in a dreamy tone. "So tell me about your niece Dee. Is she going to be all right?"

"I hope so," Martha responded in a heavy tone. "She wasn't always like this. I honestly thought she was getting better. When she was a kid she was outgoing and loved life. Then she started to change. At first we just thought it was the stress of starting college. You just never think that someone close to you could suffer from a mental illness. We finally got her help. It seemed to take forever to find the right meds for her."

"A guy I knew in college went through something similar. The meds they had him on seemed to suck the life out of him," Audrey offered compassionately.

"Dee went through a lot of that," Martha explained. "This time was different; she seemed to be responding well."

"So now she goes back on her medication? And she'll be okay?" Audrey said hopefully.

"It's not that simple," Martha continued. "It's not like taking an antibiotic. She'll need to be sent back to the hospital so she can be monitored."

"I'm sorry, Martha," Audrey said tenderly.

"Well, it's a long road. I just wish I could understand why she stopped taking her meds." Martha sighed deeply. "So what are you going to do about tall, dark, and lovely over there?" Martha taunted her as she nodded towards Camille.

"Well I . . . Uhm . . I don't know," Audrey stammered.

"What do you mean you don't know?" Martha scoffed. "She seems to be very interested."

"You think so?" Audrey blushed.

"Are you blind?" Martha gasped. "Ask her out."

"Now?" Audrey stuttered as a sudden panic rushed through her.

"No, not now," Martha chastised her. "Maybe when she takes a break or after she finishes for the night."

"I don't know." Audrey hesitated.

"Look, you didn't come all the way down here just to stare at the girl," Martha pointed out. "Whatever you're going to do, you should do it soon. A woman like that isn't going to be available forever. She is single, isn't she?"

"According to Steve she is," Audrey informed her eager friend.

"Then go for it," Martha instructed her firmly. "The worst thing that will happen is she'll turn you down. But at least you'll have tried."

Audrey pondered her friend's advice as they sat back and listened to the rest of Camille's set. The evening wore on as Audrey's mind tried to conjure up just the right words to ask Camille out. Before she realized it, Martha was yawning. "Why don't you go," Audrey offered as she glanced at her watch, realizing that it was indeed very late.

"Goodnight," Martha agreed readily as she grabbed her coat. "Let me know what happens," she said as she hugged Audrey.

Audrey listened to Camille for another twenty minutes, trying to bolster her courage. She clapped politely as Camille finished for the evening and began to gather her belongings. Audrey chewed on her bottom lip nervously. "You better hurry," Kenny addressed her. "Camille usually just packs up and leaves right away."

Audrey could feel her heart beating wildly as she tried to will herself to stand up and walk over to Camille. She was just about to stand when she noticed the dark-haired woman approaching the bar. "Well, that's a first," Kenny said from behind her. Audrey watched the woman's graceful movements as she crossed the room.

"Kenny, can I have a glass of white zinfandel?" Camille requested as she turned towards Audrey. "And whatever the lady would like," she offered with a sweet smile.

"Thank you," Audrey responded with a smile of her own as she pushed her wine glass over.

They remained there just staring at one another as Kenny filled their order. "You're very talented," Audrey finally managed to say.

"Thank you," Camille answered. The rich timber of her voice sent shivers up and down Audrey's spine.

"You just seem to melt into your music," Audrey continued, hoping to work up the courage to ask this beautiful woman out.

"I love music. During the day I teach music at Warner Junior High," Camille explained as she slid some money over to Kenny who pushed it away. Camille curled her lip and glared at Kenny. The bartender simply stuck his tongue out at the musician. "So what do you do?" Camille inquired.

"I'm an accountant," Audrey answered with a shrug.

"Really?" Camille responded in a surprised tone. "Sorry, you just don't look like an accountant."

"I don't?" Audrey toyed with her.

"Well . . . uhm . . ." Camille blushed slightly as she tried to explain herself. "It's just that you don't look like the type to stay locked up in an office all day long pouring over numbers. You're in such great shape."

"Thank you." Audrey laughed lightly. "It's true. That part of my profession sucks but it has its up side as well. Like a steady paycheck." Camille raised her glass in agreement. "Would I be out of line if I offered to buy you another drink?"

"Not at all," Camille agreed.

"Last call, ladies," Kenny informed them.

"Perfect timing," Camille responded. "Another round, Kenny."

As Camille engaged in a friendly banter with the bartender, Audrey took the opportunity to allow her eyes to roam over Camille's body. Audrey absently licked her lips in appreciation. There was something about Camille's long legs and firm body that caused her body to tingle all over. As Camille turned back towards to her, Audrey quickly averted her gaze.

As Camille went to offer Kenny money, Audrey reached out quickly and grasped her hand. The warmth of Camille's touch made her tremble slightly. "This one's on me," Audrey said softly, her face flushing slightly as she spoke.

"Right," Camille responded smoothly. "You are so beautiful," Camille added, her blue eyes burning brightly.

Audrey looked away shyly as she paid for the drinks. "Sorry, I'm not usually this forward," Camille apologized. Once again Audrey could feel her body respond to the sound of Camille's voice. This time her stomach clenched slightly and her nipples inexplicably hardened. "Normally I'm really quite shy," Camille continued.

"You're shy?" Audrey blinked in surprise. "Why on earth would you be shy? I mean you are . . ." Audrey's mind raced to come up with the perfect word to describe the goddess that stood before her. ". . . breathtaking," Audrey concluded as Camille smiled shyly in response.

Audrey realized that she was still holding Camille's hand when she felt the taller woman's thumb lightly brush the back of her hand. "You know it's getting late," Audrey noted as Camille frowned slightly. "One of us better ask the other out or for a phone number or something before they throw us out of here," Audrey teased slightly, regretting that their time together was coming to an end. "Camille, would you like to go out with me sometime?"

"Yes," a husky voice responded.

"When?" Audrey pressed, feeling the fire building inside of her.

"Now," Camille confessed as her body leaned slightly closer to Audrey's quivering form.

PART THREE

"It's late. What did you have in mind?" Audrey's mind was spinning as she spoke. Her smaller body leaned slightly closer to Camilla's. Neither woman made a move to leave; they simply sat there holding hands as they sipped their wine. Audrey couldn't understand the intense attraction and desire she was feeling with every fiber of her being. She also didn't care. She simply didn't want the moment to end. She would follow it wherever it led her.

They finished their wine and finally released one another's hands. Audrey went to grab her coat from the barstool to find Camille holding it out for her. She smiled as she allowed Camille to help her on with her wool coat. She felt the warmth of the musician's hands even through the heavy material. Her body instantly missed Camille's touch as she put on her own coat and gathered up her bag filled with sheet music. Camille offered her hand once again. Audrey couldn't resist placing her hand in Camille's larger one and letting her lead her out of the bar.

Audrey wrapped her coat around her tightly. "Cold?" Camille asked in concern.

"A little," Audrey reluctantly admitted. Camille instantly wrapped her arms around her small body. "This is nice," Audrey murmured as she leaned into Camille's body, taking in the scent of the taller woman's perfume.

"Where would you like to go?" Camille asked as she nuzzled Audrey's sensitive neck.

"Anywhere," Audrey squeaked out as she stifled the moan that threatened to escape.

Camille stepped away from her slightly while keeping one arm wrapped around Audrey's waist. "I don't live too far from here," Camille said shyly, unable to look Audrey in the eye. "Would you like to come over for coffee?"

"Yes," Audrey answered before she could stop herself. She knew in her heart that neither of them wanted coffee. Yet there was something about this woman that was driving her senses into complete overload. She was helpless to stop what was happening between them. And she doubted that she would if she could.

As they walked in silence their bodies brushed together and they shared innocent touches that served to stoke the fire that was steadily building within Audrey's soul. The blonde could feel both hers and Camille's breathing becoming ragged and she knew it wasn't from the brisk stroll.

They entered Camille's apartment and the musician offered to take Audrey's coat. The blonde handed it over along with her thanks. As Camille hung up their garments, Audrey did a quick scan of the tiny apartment. She smiled as she noted that the space was far too small for more than one person. The thought of not being interrupted by any pesky roommates was very appealing at that moment.

Her eyes drifted across the room to find Camille standing nervously behind the sofa. She could see a tiny kitchen illuminated behind the taller woman. "So coffee?" Camille inquired In a shaky tone. Audrey could feel the heat from Camille's body as she shook her head in a negative response.

"Do you want coffee?" Audrey inquired carefully as she crossed the room to stand in front of the other woman.

"No," Camille confessed in a husky tone.

"Good," Audrey responded in a sultry tone as she reached up and laced her fingers through Camille's raven hair. Audrey was now standing so close to the tall musician that she could feel their hearts beating in unison. Through half open eyes she watched as Camille's face drew closer to her own; she could feel Camille's breath on her skin.

Their lips met shyly, brushing tenderly against each other. The feeling of Camille's warm inviting lips washed away any fear or hesitation from Audrey. The accountant wrapped her arms around Camille's body and drew her even closer to her. She reclaimed the musician's lips eagerly, tasting them fully.

Camille's hands roamed along her body feeling every inch of her. Audrey began to suck and nibble on Camille's bottom lip. Audrey felt Camille's lips parting slowly, inviting her in for exploration; it was an invitation that Audrey eagerly accepted. The blonde's tongue slipped gently into Camille's mouth, exploring the delightful warmth she discovered there. As Camille's tongue greeted her own, they began a fiery duel for control.

Audrey was so lost in the sweet taste of Camille's mouth she didn't realize that she was pulling the taller woman's black blazer off her body. It wasn't until Camille's hands left her body to assist her in removing the jacket that she realized she'd been undressing the woman.

The realization did nothing to defuse her actions. Audrey needed to touch this woman and nothing was going

19

to dampen her desire, not even the nagging thought that they were moving to quickly. She moaned into Camille's mouth as she felt the musician's hands work their way up under the hem of her dress. Camille's strong hands cupped her firm backside.

The musician's touch sent a jolt through Audrey's body. The small blonde thrust her body into Camille's. Audrey was groping Camille with wild abandonment as she tugged her white silk top out of her black slacks. "Wait," Camille panted as they emerged from the kiss. Audrey was gasping for air as she laid her head against Camille's heaving chest. "This is happening too fast," Camille choked out.

"I know," Audrey panted in agreement as the two women continued to cling to one another.

They stood there in silence as their hearts raced uncontrollably. Audrey's hands still rested on the small of Camille's back which was exposed since the blonde pulled her shirt out of her pants. Camille's hands were still tucked up under Audrey's dress resting comfortably on the blonde's firm backside. Audrey listened to the rapid beating of Camille's heart, knowing that she didn't want to release this woman.

Audrey looked up to find Camille's crystal blue eyes smiling down at her. All they had to do was let go of one another and calm down. The look in Camille's eyes and the feel of her hot breath on Audrey's skin made it impossible for the tiny accountant to do that. Camille leaned in, Audrey leaned up, and once again they found themselves locked in a fiery kiss.

Hands continued to roam and explore as Camille massaged Audrey's cheeks. Audrey's hands felt their way up Camille's back and unclasped her bra. She felt the brunette's skin respond to her touch as she allowed her fingers to drift along her exposed back.

Once again they broke away from the passionate kiss to breathe. Audrey began to kiss Camille's neck as the taller woman moaned in pleasure. "Audrey, we really need to slow down," Camille pleaded as their bodies seemed to melt together.

"Okay," Audrey whimpered as she lowered her hands, feeling as much of the taller woman's body as she could before she released her. Audrey felt as strange sense of loss as they stepped away from each other. "I don't think I've ever been kissed like that," Audrey said in a breathy tone.

"Neither have I," Camille replied hoarsely as her eyes drifted over Audrey's body. "It's a good thing we stopped."

"Why is that?" Audrey wondered aloud as her eyes drank in Camille's flushed features. Her emerald eyes drifted down to Camille's full breasts that strained against her top.

"At this moment I haven't a clue," Camille confessed as she offered her hand to Audrey.

It was all the encouragement Audrey needed; she took Camille by the hand, giving it a gentle squeeze as she accepted it. She stepped in closer to Camille who seemed to hesitate. "I know what I'm feeling," Audrey admitted before placing a tender kiss on Camille's neck. "And I can feel what you are feeling," she added before placing another kiss slightly lower on Camille's body. "And I don't usually have sex on the first date, much less before the first date," Audrey continued as she began to kiss her way lower and lower, moving the material of Camille's top so she could taste more of her skin.

Camille's resolve melted away and the taller woman arched her body against Audrey as she ran her fingers through short blonde hair. "I want you," Camille growled out. Audrey looked up with pleading eyes. "I'm yours," she offered herself willingly.

Camille captured Audrey's lips fiercely and their tongues engaged in another sensual duel. Audrey felt herself being led. She was unaware as to where Camille was guiding her until her back pressed against the wall.

Audrey was on fire as she pulled Camille's blouse up and off her body. Just as quickly she removed Camille's bra without bothering to even look at the garment. Audrey was speechless as she drank in the sight of Camille's half naked body. She felt Camille's hands move across her thighs and back up under the hem of her short dress.

With one hand Audrey clasped Camille's strong back and with the other she lifted one of her firm full breasts to her eager mouth. She felt Camille grinding against her as she suckled the taller woman's nipple. Her wetness grew as she teased it. Camille's hands pulled down her pantyhose and underwear. Audrey was certain that she was going to pass out from the pleasure of Camille's hands caressing exposed skin freely.

Audrey slipped her thigh between Camille's legs and the two began to sway together in a sensual rhythm. Audrey continued to suckle Camille's nipple as her hands found their way to the zipper on Camille's slacks. As Camille's fingers drifted closer to Audrey's wetness, the blonde undid her pants and pulled them down her body.

They pressed their desire into one another's body, each seeking to pleasure the other. Camille arched against Audrey once again. The movement granted Audrey the opportunity she desperately needed. Her mouth released Camille's breast and her hands eagerly explored the taller woman's body. She felt Camille's exploration growing bolder as well.

Through their loose clothing, they felt their way to one another's passion. Each woman moaned in ecstasy as their fingers dipped into each other's wetness. Any clothing in the way was pulled up or down. Audrey couldn't believe this was happening as she began to tease Camille's throbbing clit. Her body arched against the wall as Camille's fingers mirrored her own.

Fingers pressing against openings and mouths tasted hungrily. They opened themselves to the other as their thighs parted. Eager fingers entered as their tongues resumed their dance. Each moaned into the other's mouth as their fingers plunged in and out.

Screaming out in pleasure, they climaxed in unison. Audrey clung to Camille who had collapsed against her. Finally their breathing calmed slightly. Camille placed a tender kiss on Audrey's lips before stepping away. The blonde leaned against the wall as she watched Camille remove the clothing that was now pooled around her ankles. With a sly smile she knelt before Audrey.

The blonde looked down as Camille kissed her thighs before removing her shoes, pantyhose and underwear. Camille began to place lingering kisses on the inside of Audrey's still trembling thighs. "Spend the night with me," Camille murmured against her skin.

"Yes," Audrey moaned in response.

Camille rose to stand before her. The woman was tall and seemed even taller as she stood before her naked. Once again Audrey accepted the musician's hand. Camille led her to the bedroom where she stood behind her and began to kiss the back of her neck. "I know we rushed things," Camille said softly as she continued to kiss her.

"This is either going to be a great one night stand or a sweet memory to look back on in our golden years," Audrey murmured in agreement as Camille slowly unzipped her dress.

"I can't wait to find out which," Camille whispered

hotly in her ear as she began to lower Audrey's dress off her shoulders.

Camille slowly removed the rest of Audrey's clothing, kissing her newly exposed skin along the way. Audrey felt as if she was being worshipped as Camille lowered her slowly onto the bed. Camille climbed on top of the smaller woman; they moaned as their bodies met for first time free from all barriers. They kissed deeply as their hands caressed each other's body.

Camille's long hair tickled Audrey's skin as the musician kissed her way down her body. She tingled with each brush of Camille's lips. She felt her lover nestle herself between her thighs. Audrey wrapped her legs around Camille's shoulders as the taller woman raised her backside. Camille's breath caressed the inside of Audrey's thighs before Camille tasted her lover for the first time.

Audrey gripped the bed covers beneath her as Camille slowly feasted upon her. Camille held the blonde tightly as her tongue explored all that she had to offer. Each time Audrey felt herself nearing the edge, Camille would slow her movements. "Please," Audrey finally whimpered in hungry desperation. Camille responded by capturing Audrey's throbbing clit in her mouth. Audrey felt her world spinning out of control as Camille sucked her clit greedily into her mouth.

With each flicker of Camille's talented tongue, Audrey felt the waves of ecstasy rush through her. Camille entered her lover with two fingers sending Audrey immediately over the edge. Audrey felt Camille's mouth leave her as her fingers continued to pleasure her; her lover kissed her way up Audrey's body.

Audrey looked up to see the brilliant blue gaze that filled her with renewed desire. Audrey's hand felt its way down her lover's long body. Her fingers felt alive as they reached Camille's overwhelming passion. She teased Camille's clit and once again she entered her lover. They rode each other's hand as their fingers plunged in and out.

The room was filled with the sights and sounds of their passion. Camille screamed out Audrey's name as she climaxed against her. Audrey followed quickly and once again they were clinging to one another. Once they recovered they climbed under the covers and curled up in one another's embrace.

"So this doesn't count as a first date?" Camille asked as she ran her fingers through Audrey's hair.

"No." Audrey laughed.

"But I thought we agreed back at Vinnie's that this was going to be a date?" Camille teased her. "Oh no. The boys are going to pressure me to find out what happened."

"I'm going to get the same from Martha." Audrey yawned.

"Can I ask what you were doing there last night?" Camille inquired.

"I was on a blind date," Audrey informed her.

"Oh?" Camille said with a frown.

"Trust me. I took one look at you and she didn't stand a chance," Audrey supplied. "Besides, she was unstable."

"And I'm not?" Camille laughed.

"Not that unstable," Audrey informed her. "So where are we going on our first date?"

THE END

PART ONE

Maeve stared at the constant blips on the computer screen as she rubbed her tired blue eyes. "Could this job be anymore boring?" she muttered under her breath. She looked over to find her roommate and constant companion sound asleep on her bunk. She was thankful for the times when the energetic little blonde was sleeping. It wasn't that she didn't like Jan; it was just that the little blonde was a constant source of energy and chatter.

Maeve was a quiet somewhat-reserved woman and now, four months into her tour, she was ready to climb the walls. Spending eighteen months in the Arctic Circle, trapped in very close quarters with possibly the most talkative person that she had ever met, and watching weather patterns was not what she had in mind when she enlisted in the Navy. But then again, if she hadn't slept with one of her shipmates, she wouldn't be stuck in the middle of nowhere.

She had to admit that Jan's overflowing personality was not the entire problem.

The other part of her dilemma was that she found Jan extremely attractive. Jan was small in stature with brilliant green eyes and a fabulous body. And she looked good in uniform. There was something about the way the khaki uniform clung to Jan's well-toned body that Maeve found completely captivating. The whole package sent Maeve's libido into overdrive. As if seeing her in uniform wasn't hard enough, the heating system decided to act up so both women were forced to wear only T-shirts or tank tops and boxer shorts. Well, Maeve wore shorts while her sole companion opted for walking around in a tank top and her panties.

"Yup, I'm in hell," Maeve grumbled as she split her attention between watching her computer screen and the rise and fall of her roommate's chest.

The irony of the situation was not lost on Maeve. She was locked up in a tiny room with a woman who drove her up the wall, and despite the fact that they were located in one of coldest places on the planet, it was so hot in their quarters that Jan was running around half-naked. Oh, and add in the fact that they were in the military and she wasn't supposed ask her attractive companion which team she played for. "It's going to be a very long year," Maeve concluded as she noticed Jan's nipples straining against the light cotton material of her top.

Suddenly bright green eyes blinked open and Maeve quickly averted her gaze to the computer screen. "Good morning," Jan greeted her brightly.

"Must you be so cheerful in the morning?" Maeve grumbled. It never ceased to irritate the tall brunette that the little blonde was Captain Spunk first thing in the morning. Maeve was the opposite. She was unable to do anything but grunt until she had her first cup of coffee.

"Yes," Jan said with a cocky smirk. "Anything interesting happening there?" Jan inquired as she jumped off her cot and stretched her well-toned body.

Maeve's pulse quickened and she bit down on her bottom lip in order to suppress the groan that was threatening to escape from deep inside her. Her eyes focused momentarily on a tiny mole on the woman's firm abdomen. Many a night she had fanaticized about licking that mole. Maeve snapped her eyes shut and shook her head as her roommate shuffled past her. "We have a free night tonight. What do you want to do?" Jan inquired as she headed off towards the bathroom.

"How about we go roller blading?" Maeve suggested sarcastically as her companion chuckled.

Maeve continued staring at the computer screen while Jan showered. Going outdoors was out of the question so they were left with playing cards, checkers, or using the Monopoly game that was missing most of its pieces. That was the extent of the exciting options available to them. Jan emerged from the shower clad only in a towel. Maeve swallowed hard as she averted her gaze. A whole new set of options instantly raced through her mind. Normally she wouldn't get all hot and bothered by a fellow crewmember, but she'd been locked up with this woman for four months and her body was starting to take over her thinking.

"So any ideas about what to do tonight?" Jan questioned her teasingly.

"Uhm . . . ," Maeve stammered as her mind drifted towards some very interesting ideas. She quickly calmed her erratic breathing and focused on the question at hand. "Checkers, I guess," she threw out in a blasé manner.

"Oh joy," Jan teased as she tossed her towel off.

5

Maeve's jaw dropped as she drank in the sight of Jan's naked backside. Once again she forced herself to focus on the computer screen. "Well, I don't hear you coming up with any bright ideas, Blondie," Maeve scoffed as she fought the urge to take another peek at her companion's body. Jan ignored her comment as she finished putting on a clean tank top and panties. Both items of clothing were the standard navy blue and clung much too tightly to Jan's body.

Later that night Maeve was glaring at the checkerboard, wondering how she'd gotten herself so far behind in the game. Perhaps it was the half-naked woman sitting across the Formica table. "Ready to give up?" Jan teased her smugly.

"No," Maeve growled. "I'm just lulling you into a false sense of security."

"Right," Jan scoffed. "You know, if you're that confident that you can make a comeback, we could make it more interesting. Say, bet some of the weekly chores on the game?"

"Such as?" Maeve inquired; her interest was suddenly peeked.

"Dishes, laundry and cooking for a week," Jan challenged her.

"You're on," Maeve agreed, finally feeling more confident. She flashed a wicked gleam as she jumped two of Jan's black checkers and cackled with delight.

"Don't start getting cocky," Jan warned her as she moved one of her pieces.

Maeve licked her lips, catching a slight spark in her companion's eyes as the brunette made her move and took another black checker out of play. "Maybe we should play two out of three games?" Jan suggested hopefully.

"Not so confident anymore?" Maeve taunted her as

she folded her arms across her chest in a defiant manner.

"You're toast," Jan growled as she made her move and took one of Maeve's pieces off the board. "In fact, why don't we sweeten the pot a little? Add in cleaning the bathroom?"

Maeve was feeling confident, but she was still behind in the match. "Fuck you," she spat out, thinking that there was no way she was going to pull extra cleaning duties.

"Well, there's that," Jan responded in a breathy tone.

"What?" Maeve stammered. Her head jerked up and Jan wiggled her eyebrows at her suggestively.

"We could play for that," Jan explained defiantly.

"For what?" Maeve choked out, hoping that Jan wasn't suggesting what she thought she was.

"A fuck," Jan offered with a casual shrug.

Maeve's eyes widened in disbelief as her jaw hung open. "Are you serious?" she said haltingly.

"I'm sorry. I didn't mean to make you uncomfortable," Jan apologized. "It's just that we're going to be locked up here for a long time and . . . Look, if you're not into women, please forget I said anything. I don't want to lose my commission because I was mistaken."

"What? And give up my chance to have this palace all to myself?" Maeve said, teasing the flustered blonde. "Don't worry; I'm not going to bust you. Besides you weren't wrong. I'm definitely into women."

"So you want to up the ante?" Jan suggested eagerly.

"You mean play for sex?" Maeve asked in bewilderment.

"Why not?" Jan challenged her. "We're stuck here for a long time and getting to know myself is getting a little old. Of course, this assignment is supposed to be a punishment."

"What did you do?" Maeve challenged her. Then it occurred to her that maybe the naïve looking Lt. Commander had made the same mistake she had. "Or rather, Lt. Commander Christiansen, should I be inquiring as to who did you do?"

"The captain's daughter," Jan admitted grimly. Maeve winced at the admission.

"And you, Lt. Commander Ryan? Just what little transgression did you commit to land you this plush assignment?"

"Let's just say one of my shipmates had a very jealous girlfriend back in port," Maeve confessed. "Unfortunately she outranked me."

"Messing around with someone who belongs to someone with more bars on her collar than you do." Jan chuckled merrily. "Not bright."

"I didn't know," Maeve argued. "It seems that her girlfriend slipped her mind until after we messed around. Serves me right. I don't normally get involved with other military personal. But we were at sea for a very long time." Maeve's body tensed as she recalled the horrific scene when she discovered the truth about Tonya's home life.

"Speaking of lapses in judgment, just what were you thinking when you decided to bed the Captain's daughter?" Maeve noted as Jan blushed.

"I wasn't," Jan admitted shyly. "Unfortunately I let Jose Cuervo do my thinking for me."

"Oops." Maeve cringed as she realized that was pretty much how she'd decided a fling with Tonya was a good idea. It was one night of shore leave and a few too many cocktails. And Tonya looked so hot in her dress uniform. As if the hangover wasn't bad enough, now she was stuck in the middle of nowhere watching blips on a computer screen.

"Oops is right," Jan confirmed, "And before you say anything - yes, she was twenty-one, and no, I didn't know who Daddy was."

"Okay, so we're both stuck on this iceberg for the next year because we couldn't keep our pants on." Maeve sighed heavily.

"So back to my original question," Jan pressed on.

"Which was?" Maeve inquired in confusion. Sometimes it was so damn difficult to follow the energetic blonde's conversations.

"Our bet," Jan reminded her coyly.

"Right." Maeve nodded as she blushed.

"That's an attractive shade. Now you match your checkers," Jan teased her.

Maeve's anger rose as the blonde taunted her. She decided to give the mischievous little brat a taste of her own medicine. "All right," Maeve agreed in a firm challenging tone and Jan's eyes widened in surprise. The startled look on Jan's face confirmed Maeve's suspicion that her companion never expected her to accept the challenge.

"Huh?" Jan muttered in shock.

"In fact, let's make it really interesting," Maeve added thoughtfully as she decided to torture Jan even further. "The loser can only give and not receive."

"Excuse me?" Jan said in shock as the tips of her ears turned pink.

"You know, the winner gets off and the loser gets a cold shower," Maeve explained as her companion squirmed uncomfortably in her seat.

"Not even a late night visit from lefty?" Jan choked out as she wiggled her hand.

"Nada," Maeve said firmly, challenging her roommate with a cold stare.

She loved every moment of Jan's predicament as she

continued to stare at the nervous little blonde. Just when she was certain that Jan was about to back out, the blonde glared at her defiantly. "Deal," she responded dryly. Maeve's heart suddenly stopped beating and her lungs felt as if they were about to collapse. "What's the matter Ryan? Chicken?" Jan taunted

That did it. Maeve wasn't going to back down now even though she knew that she should. "Deal," she growled in response. "Whose turn is it?" she demanded hotly.

"I forget," Jan responded honestly. Maeve groaned in exasperation. Then she realized that this might be the out they both needed to save face. "Not a problem," Jan said in a hurried tone just as Maeve was about to suggest that they call the whole thing off. "We'll just start over. Instead of two out of three, we'll begin a fresh game." Maeve's stomach clenched as Jan leaned over the table, revealing her ample cleavage. "Winner takes all," Jan purred as her eyes once again challenged Maeve.

"Fine," Maeve agreed before she could stop herself.

The board was cleared and the game began. Maeve felt slightly confident as both women maintained an even score. Her confidence and concentration vanished as Jan started to run her fingers across one of her breasts. "What are you doing?" Maeve stammered as she watched the blonde's nimble fingers brush against a nipple. Through the thin material of Jan's tank top, she watched in fascination as the bud became erect.

"I'm just getting ready for when you lose," Jan responded in a husky tone as her hand drifted down across her abdomen. Maeve blinked her eyes rapidly as she watched the small hand drift down even further. As she watched the muscles of her companion's arm flex, she knew where the blonde's hand had come to rest.

"Pretty sure of yourself, aren't you?" Maeve spat out, trying to sound confident as she fought to control her breathing.

"I just want to be prepared for when you have to perform your duty, Lt. Commander Ryan," Jan responded confidently as she continued to stroke herself. "So how long will you have to refrain from sex?" Jan asked as her arm continued to flex and beads of sweat began to roll down her body.

"You will be celibate for one week," Maeve shot back as she made her move and took another one of Jan's pieces off the board.

"You poor baby," Jan said softly. "One whole week after four months of nothing. I feel sorry for you," Jan empathized as she jumped over two of Maeve's pieces and snatched them quickly off the board with an evil cackle. Maeve clenched her jaw as she realized she was now down by one checker but she still had no intention of losing. Of course, she wasn't certain that she wanted to win either.

Maeve stared at the red and black playing board in a desperate effort to find some move that would even the score. "So, Ryan, when was the last time you experienced a good round of high impact aerobics?" Jan questioned her slyly. Maeve's mind instantly flashed to a motel room. It was the night before she was to fly to the Arctic Circle. An attractive redhead had her legs wrapped around Maeve's body. The leather strap of the phallus pressed against her skin as she plunged in and out of her companion's wetness.

The redhead was begging for Maeve to take her harder as Maeve suckled her nipple. A sheen of sweat formed on Maeve's body as she encouraged her lover to come for her. The stranger dug her nails into Maeve's shoulder as she screamed out in ecstasy. Maeve stilled her movements as her lover clung to her. Once Maeve felt her lover's aftershocks cease, she slowly withdrew the phallus from her wetness. She removed the condom and tossed it into the wastebasket.

She quickly took the harness off and tossed it onto the nightstand. Then she ripped open the package of dental dams and climbed up the redhead's body. Her date protested about not being able to taste Maeve's passion, but the sailor was horny not stupid. She insisted they continue being safe as she straddled the redhead and clung to the headboard. With her face pressed against the wall, she allowed this stranger to drive her over the edge.

Maeve wasn't normally so casual about her encounters but she was facing eighteen months of celibacy. She'd known what she wanted when she walked into the bar that night in a neatly pressed dress uniform and the redhead was more than willing to give Maeve the send-off her body was craving.

"Happy thoughts?" Jan's voice interrupted her memories.

"I picked up a woman the night before I flew down here," Maeve finally responded as she shook off the memory. She didn't miss the concerned look in the blonde's eyes. "I was safe," Maeve added as Jan blew out a sigh of relief.

Maeve went to move her checker when her hand started to tremble. She suddenly realized that, because of the Navy's constant vigil regarding STDs, she and Jan could explore one another completely. Her blue eyes drifted over to her companion who was still pleasuring herself. Maeve's heart raced at the thought of being able to taste every inch of this woman and having her do the same.

"Are you going to make your move?" Jan inquired in a sultry tone.

Maeve hesitated as her mind wondered once again whether she wanted to win or lose. The image of Jan kissing her way down her body suddenly flashed through her mind. She wanted to win. She moved her checker and tried to focus on the match. Unfortunately, Jan's arm increased its rhythm and the scent of the blonde's arousal was invading her senses.

Maeve's game plan went straight into the gutter. She was flustered as she fought to keep herself in the match. She wanted to win, but watching Jan pleasure herself was far too distracting. Before she knew what had happened, her last checker was being swept off the board. Jan held the red checker up triumphantly as her eyes twinkled evilly at Maeve.

"If you want to back out, I'll understand," Jan offered graciously. Maeve held the smaller woman's gaze firmly. Jan stood slowly as she continued to clutch the red checker in her hand. "I always pay off my debts," Maeve reassured her as she stood. She could feel the dampness of her shorts pressing against her as she moved towards Jan. She heard the plastic checker hit the floor.

As the brunette neared Jan, she could feel the heat emanating off the smaller woman's body. "I do want a rematch," Maeve insisted as she clasped the blonde's hips firmly. "You didn't play fair."

"Oh, you can have a rematch," Jan agreed as she ran her hands along Maeve's broad shoulders. "Just not tonight. Because tonight you belong to me," she said softly as she pressed her body against Maeve's quivering form.

Maeve cupped the smaller woman's face with both of her hands. She licked her lips in anticipation as Jan leaned into her touch. "And just what is it you would like me to do for you?" Maeve inquired hotly. Jan moaned in response as Maeve ran her fingers through her short blonde locks.

Maeve suppressed her own moan as their nipples brushed. "Tell me how you want me," Maeve encouraged the blonde whose hands were roaming across Maeve's back.

"On your knees, sailor," Jan instructed her firmly as her hands slid up under Maeve's damp T-shirt. Maeve swayed as the blonde's fingertips caressed her skin.

The brunette's clit throbbed with desire as she sank to her knees. She lifted the hem of Jan's top and began to trail her tongue along the blonde's firm abdomen. Jan wrapped her fingers in Maeve's long raven hair as the brunette lifted her top higher. Maeve ran her tongue slowly across the blonde's mole. The deep moan her lover released fueled her desire. She began to suckle the beauty mark she'd been fanaticizing about for the past four months.

"Maeve," Jan gasped as she leaned her body into the taller woman's touch.

Maeve cupped her lover's firm backside as she kissed and tasted her way across Jan's taut stomach. She massaged firm cheeks as she drank in the taste of her lover's skin. Maeve fought against the urge to pleasure herself as she dipped her tongue into Jan's navel. Slowly she slipped her fingers beneath the elastic waistband of her lover's panties. Jan's hips thrust forward as Maeve's fingers drifted beneath the cotton.

Jan's center brushed against her cheek and she could feel and smell her lover's desire as her fingertips glided across her firm backside. "Maeve," Jan gasped once again as Maeve's fingers sank lower, tracing the rim of her beautiful ass. Jan was panting heavily as Maeve's tongue and lips continued to feast upon her stomach.

Maeve felt her lover's hands leave her and she looked up to watch Jan remove her top. She was mesmerized by the vision of Jan's half-naked body. Her hands quickly ran up the smaller woman's torso, up past her rib cage until she felt the weight of Jan's firm full breasts.

Maeve could feel Jan's thighs trembling against her as she brushed her thumbs across the blonde's erect nipples. Jan ran her fingers along Maeve's outstretched arms. The blonde left a trail of goose bumps along Maeve's dark skin as she ran her blunt nails slowly up and down. Maeve nuzzled Jan's abdomen as she rolled her rose-colored nipples between her fingers.

"Yes," Jan hissed, her hips once again thrust forward. As Maeve kissed her stomach she could feel her lover's clit pressing against her chin. The musky aroma filled her as she kissed her way down her lover's body. Jan was quivering from her touch as her hands ran slowly down her body. Maeve captured the elastic of Jan's panties with her teeth as the blonde's thighs parted.

With her teeth and her hands she slowly pulled Jan's underwear down her trembling body. "I need you so much," Jan whimpered as she opened herself to Maeve's touch. Jan placed her hands on Maeve's broad shoulders to steady herself as the brunette completely removed her underwear. Maeve sat back on her heels and admired Jan's body. The first time she'd seen the little blonde in her khaki uniform Maeve had silently prayed for this moment.

Jan smiled down at her as she brushed an errant lock of black hair from Maeve's brow. The look of pure desire in her eyes sent a jolt through Maeve's body. Jan stepped away and walked backwards towards her cot, beckoning Maeve to follow her.

Maeve quickly scrambled her long body up off the floor and moved over to Jan who was leaning back on her arms as she sat on the edge of her cot. Maeve's knees started to buckle as her eyes drifted up and down the petite blonde's naked body. "I want to see you?" Jan said in a soft questioning tone. Maeve simply nodded in agreement before stripping off her clothing.

Her eyes never left her lover as she tossed her clothing across their tiny quarters. "How may I service you?" Maeve asked as she stood completely naked before her lover, offering all of herself to this tiny woman.

"Kneel," Jan responded in a breathy tone. The gaze from emerald eyes burned into Maeve as the taller woman knelt before her lover. "Your mouth. I want to feel your mouth on my body."

"Where?" Maeve encouraged her.

"Everywhere," Jan responded in a hungry voice as she parted her legs.

Maeve leaned in and wrapped her arms around Jan's body as the blonde wrapped her legs around the brunette's waist. Maeve's body pulsated as their skin melted together and her lover's wet golden curls pressed into her abdomen. Maeve leaned closer, feeling her lover's breath caress her face. She brushed her lips against Jan's. Her own lips tingled from the contact as Jan pulled her even closer.

Greedily she drank in the taste of her lover's lips as she ran her tongue along Jan's bottom lip. Jan's lips parted, inviting her in. She dipped her tongue into the warmth of Jan's mouth as the blonde cupped one of her breasts. Maeve moaned as Jan's palm brushed against her aching nipple.

Jan's hips thrust urgently into Maeve's body. The brunette could feel her lover's wetness paint her skin as their tongues engaged in a sensual duel. Maeve's hands roamed down Jan's back until she was once again cupping her firm backside. Jan was panting with desire as Maeve pulled her body closer. The brunette guided her swaying hips to rock against her harder as she began to kiss her way down the blonde's neck.

Maeve circled Jan's nipple with her tongue while she continued to guide her lover's hips in a wild rhythm. She suckled Jan's nipple in her mouth as the blonde's body arched against her. She teased Jan's nipple with her teeth and her tongue while the blonde begged her for release. Maeve could feel her own desire pooling between her quivering thighs as she moved her mouth to Jan's other nipple and lavished it with the same attention.

Maeve continued to feast upon her lover's breasts while Jan clung to her tightly. Maeve didn't know where her body ended and Jan's began as they moved in perfect rhythm. Jan's thighs tightened around her body. Maeve savored the taste of Jan's skin as she kissed and licked her way further down the blonde's torso.

Jan's hands pressed insistently on Maeve's shoulders, urging the brunette to nestle her body between her legs. Maeve ran her tongue slowly along the inside of Jan's thigh. The taste of her lover's desire on her lips was pure ambrosia. Slowly she licked her lover's wetness from the inside of her trembling thighs before flickering her tongue across the swollen nub that was calling to her.

Jan clutched her shoulders tightly. Maeve pried her lover's hands off her so she could drape the blonde's legs over her shoulders. She drew her lover's wetness to her and dipped her tongue inside Jan's swollen nether lips. She slid her tongue over them slowly, drinking in her lover's passion. Jan's hips arched as she pressed Maeve's head closer to her.

Maeve flickered her tongue across Jan's throbbing clit as she buried herself in the blonde. She could hear Jan moaning as Maeve suckled her clit. The brunette fought to hold her lover steady as she feasted upon her, teasing her clit with her teeth and her tongue.

Maeve drank in all that Jan had to offer before gliding her tongue down the slick folds and pressed it against the opening of Jan's center. "Yes," Jan begged her. "Fuck me," she groaned hungrily. Maeve plunged her tongue deep inside the blonde's center. She could feel the walls capture the appendage. Maeve's thighs trembled as she began to plunge her tongue in and out of her lover.

She could feel the blonde nearing the edge and she quickly withdrew from the warmth of her center. Jan growled in frustration. Then as Maeve began to lick her clit once again the blonde cried out in passion. Maeve lost herself in pleasuring her lover as she fought against her own aching need.

Jan's body rocked wildly as Maeve swirled her tongue around her clit, driving the blonde insane with need. Maeve held Jan tightly; her body began to convulse as the waves of passion crashed over her. Maeve suckled Jan's clit back into the warmth of her mouth. The blonde exploded in ecstasy as Maeve continued to pleasure her.

The brunette took her lover deeper, unable to take herself away from the nectar. Jan exploded again as Maeve's tongue flickered wildly across her aching need. Maeve could feel her lover gasping for air as she tried to pull away. She suckled harder, driving her lover into oblivion one last time before Jan collapsed against her.

Maeve rested her head against Jan's stomach as the blonde trembled and tried to regain her ability to breath and speak. Maeve kissed her quivering body softly. "I need to warn you that I have no intention of losing the next match," Maeve cautioned her as she climbed up the blonde's body and wrapped her in her arms. Jan could only chuckle in response.

THE END

THE LIMO

PART ONE

Julia growled at everyone who had the misfortune to cross her path as she stormed out of Continental's Gate Seven at Logan Airport. The weather had caused so many troubles and delays that she found herself landing four hours later than she had expected. The architect was tired and fit to be tied. She searched around, fearful that her limo would not be waiting for her. The, for the first time since early that morning, Julia Bell actually smiled.

Standing just outside the gate area was a petite blonde clad in the standard black suit and cap required for limo drivers. Her emerald green eyes peeked out over a sign that had "Julia Bell" boldly printed on it. Julia sighed as she allowed herself to enjoy the view of the blonde's well-toned body. "Oh yeah! Things are definitely looking up," she muttered softly under her breath as she approached her driver.

She towered over the small blonde standing in front

of her. She felt as slight flush of excitement as she detected a light jasmine scent. "I'm Julia Bell," she informed the driver who was now looking intently up at her.

"Welcome to Boston, Ms. Bell," the blonde greeted her politely. "Do you have any other luggage?" she inquired as she relieved Julia of her carry-on bag.

"Just one," Julia responded as she handed her claim ticket to the attractive young woman.

"Allow me to get you situated in the car and then I'll fetch your bag."

"Very nice," Julia answered in a husky tone as she allowed her blue eyes to wander up and down the young driver's body.

The smaller woman blushed slightly as she escorted Julia towards the airport exit. Shouldering Julia's carry-on bag, she instantly snapped open an umbrella to shield her passenger from the rain. She ushered Julia over to the limo, opening the door for her before placing her bag in the trunk. She popped into the driver's seat with ease, started the car, and picked up the phone in front. Julia smiled as she watched the blonde in the rearview mirror. She picked up the receiver knowing it was her driver.

"I'll be right back, Ms. Bell. The bar is located inside the door just to your left."

"Hmm," Julia purred, thinking that this little blonde was just what she needed to relieve her tension. She opened the small refrigerator that served as the bar, and helped herself to a tumbler which she filled with ice. She then filled the glass with a generous amount of Disaronno. Sipping the sweet amber liquid, she allowed herself to ponder what her driver looked like out of uniform, and just what would it take to really find out.

A smile crept across her face as she watched her driver reenter the vehicle. She watched the smaller woman settle herself into the driver's seat. As the blonde buckled her seat belt, Julia picked up the receiver that would connect her with the adorable blonde.

"Yes, Ms. Bell?" the blonde answered in a pleasant professional tone.

"Julia," she offered seductively, deciding it was time to test the waters. "And what's your name?"

"Tamara," the perky blonde responded as she put the limo into drive.

"That's unusual," Julia continued, hoping she was reading the vibes correctly.

"Not to me," Tamara countered brightly.

"No, I suppose you're use to it." Julia chuckled lightly. "I was *excited* to see you waiting for me."

Julia watched as a pair of green eyes looked up in the rearview mirror. Julia's smile grew as she caught the slight spark in those eyes.

"How so?" Tamara inquired, her voice lowering slightly.

"Well, with all the delay's I was forced to endure today, I was afraid that you might stand me up," Julia teased, pushing her underlying meaning a little harder.

"Never," came the breathy reply.

"Good to know," Julia responded as she watched the woman in the rearview mirror. A slight charge ignited within her each time their eyes met. "You really brightened my day," Julia sighed as she started to remove the charcoal blazer of her Donna Karen suit. There was a slight pause in the conversation as Julia tried to decide what her next move should be, or even if she should continue. A part of her felt a little silly flirting with the young driver. A confused look crossed Tamara's delicate features as she hung up the receiver.

.

PART TWO

As the limo inched along in traffic, Julia made herself comfortable by slipping off her shoes and unbuttoning her blouse slightly. As she sipped her drink, her eyes never drifted from her driver's image. Her fingers absently stroked her neck as she studied the long golden blonde hair pulled neatly into a ponytail that was hanging out from under her black cap. She reached for the receiver once again. Stopping herself this time, she decided that she wanted a little more personal contact.

When Julia leaned forward, she noticed the pair of twinkling green eyes that seemed to be focus upon her cleavage. A cocky smirk graced Julia's face as she thanked her lucky stars for the rain and the backed up traffic. She rapped on the glass divider to catch Tamara's attention. With a gleam in her eyes, she motioned for Tamara to lower the divider.

Tamara traced her lips with the tip of her tongue as she complied with her passenger's request. Once the barrier was down, Julia settled back into her seat.

"You don't mind do you?" Julia inquired with a slight leer as she wondered if the alcohol was clouding her judgment.

"You're the boss," Tamara answered with a sly smile of her own.

"Interesting," Julia mused before refocusing her attention

5

back to the conversation. "I just thought this might be a little more personal. Using the phone seems a bit impersonal."

"I know what you mean," Tamara agreed. "Kind of like phone sex."

Julia ran her tongue across her teeth, knowing that the blonde was testing the waters. "Really?" Julia said, playing along.

"Well, not that I would know." Tamara blushed.

"That's an interesting shade of red you're sporting there," Julia offered as she arched her eyebrow.

"Do you always treat your drivers this way?" Tamara asked.

"Never," Julia purred as she settled deeper into the leather seat and sipped her drink.

The two stole glances at each other as Julia began to once again trace her fingers slowly down her neck. "You know, I was feeling very tense after I got off that plane," Julia offered absently as she allowed her fingers to feel their way further down past her neck, creating an electric trail towards her cleavage.

"Are you still feeling tense?" Tamara asked. Julia didn't miss the soft tone in her voice or the subtle innuendo.

"I'm starting to relax," Julia answered in a breathy tone, allowing her fingers to linger on the gentle swell of her breast. She watched carefully, trying to gauge the young blonde's reaction as her movements grew bolder.

"If there's anything I can do to assist you, just tell me," Tamara offered as the blush returned in full force.

"Anything?" Julia asked as her hand slipped under the folds of her blouse.

"Yes," Tamara responded in a breathy tone as her eyes darkened slightly. Julia moaned as the prospects presenting themselves tingled her senses. She lowered herself slightly in the seat and began to tug the hem of her blouse out of her skirt.

"Can you see me? Do you want to?" Julia boldly asked her

6

driver.

"Yes," came the response with an equal amount of bravado.

Julia licked her lips and began to slowly unbutton her blouse. She couldn't understand what was happening to her. She was certainly by no means a virgin, but this was certainly something she had never experienced before. As she freed the buttons of her silk blouse, she cautioned herself to take it slowly so the moment would last. Julia held the pair of darkening emerald green eyes locked in a fiery gaze.

Julia's fingers continued their heated journey towards her ample cleavage. The feel of skin mixed with the silk of her blouse served to stoke the fire that was burning inside of her. Tamara bit down on her bottom lip as Julia freed herself from the confines of the last button. Julia accepted the soft moan that escaped from the blonde as an invitation to continue.

Slowly she opened the blouse slightly to expose the white lacy bra that lay beneath. The coolness of the air conditioner gently kissed her skin. Julia freely caressed herself, working towards her breasts. She cupped the lacy material that was holding them captive. Her breathing increased slightly as she felt her nipples hardening from her own touch. She felt an added thrill as she watch the bead of sweat that had begun to form on the driver's upper lip.

Feeling slightly light-headed, Julia allowed two of her fingers to slip underneath the lacy garment. She felt her skin beginning to burn as she watched Tamara grip the steering wheel tighter. The sound of a blaring car horn broke the spell momentarily.

As Tamara snapped her attention back to what was happening on the road, Julia felt a need to continue her exploration. Trapping one of her nipples roughly between two fingers, she pinched and rolled the bud, feeling the dampness pooling between her legs. Tamara maneuvered the black limousine through the heavily congested traffic as Julia's eyes fluttered shut in an erotic haze.

7

"Perhaps we should pull off the road?" Julia suggested in a breathy voice as she pressed her thighs together tightly.

"I'm afraid it will take some time before we reach a place that would be *convenient,*" Tamara explained in a husky tone.

"I don't know if I can last that long," Julia choked out pinching her nipple harder as her opposite hand began to feel it's way down her abdomen.

"I don't know either," Tamara concluded.

"Are you touching yourself?" Julia inquired hotly her eyes opening slightly.

"No," Tamara panted as her eyes darted back and forth between the traffic on the road and the torrid activities of her passenger.

Julia allowed herself to drink in the flushed features of her driver. She opened her eyes a little wider as her hand slipped up under her skirt. She knew that she was frustrating Tamara who could do nothing to release her own pent up desire.

"Once you find us a place that is more *convenient,* would you like to join me in the back so you can have a better view?"

"Yes," Tamara responded as she swallowed hard. "I'll do anything you want."

"Oh God," was the only response Julia's overloaded mind could conjure up. Julia's other hand released her breast and then joined its mate. She hiked up her skirt as her thumbs slid under the waistband of her nylons. She tried to steady her racing heart by slowly lowering the confining garment past her firm thighs.

Her need grew as she removed her panty hose and tossed them on the floor. She slid deeper into the leather seat of the car and lifted her skirt higher now that she had freed herself from her nylon prison. Julia arched her hips slightly to give her driver a full view of panties that matched the bra.

8

She continued to watch Tamara. The sight of the beautiful woman clad in the black uniform further fueled her desires.

Unable to contain her passion any longer, she opened her thighs wider. Julia slipped one hand between her thighs as her other hand returned to massaging her breast. She heard the sharp gasp Tamara released as Julia began to grind her wetness against her palm.

With her fingers pressed against the damp lacy material, she shifted to ensure that Tamara had full view of her activities. She continued to tease herself, her pulse racing and her head swimming with desire. Her only thoughts were of what she wanted to do with her attractive driver. Her fingers were already coated with her own passion before she slipped them under the delicate elastic. Passing the lacy barrier she dipped them into overflowing wetness.

Julia was unaware of the traffic outside. Her thoughts were focused solely on the beautiful woman sitting in front of her. So consumed was she by the fire, she never felt the limo pulling off the road and coming to a halt. Julia didn't hear Tamara release her seatbelt as she entered herself. Her hips arched as she plunged into herself deeply. She began to thrust furiously, her hips beating a wild pace.

She was so lost in her excitement that she hadn't realized that she now held Tamara's undivided attention. She finally noticed Tamara adjusting the rearview mirror and unbuttoning her black blazer. She took herself harder, teasing her own clit as she heard the sound of a zipper being lowered. Through a lustful haze, she watched a blonde head fall back slightly as Tamara's arm matched her own passionate movements.

"Harder," Julia demanded.

The two continued, each entering themselves wildly. Bare skin rubbed against the leather interior of the limo as their wetness flowed freely. Julia watched as Tamara's shoulders trembled. She knew that Tamara was falling over the same edge. Grunting and gasping harshly, driver and passenger climaxed together. Julia melted into the leather as she felt the stirring building again. She needed more. She needed to touch the young woman and be touched in return. "I want you," Julia demanded. The driver simply nodded in response.

Julia removed her blouse and skirt as Tamara pulled her black trousers up and exited the limo. When she opened the back door, she found her passenger lounging across the backseat wearing nothing but her panties and a lustful gaze. Tamara climbed in quickly to join her. Julia sat up slightly to allow Tamara a better view of her breasts. She reached up and removed the black cap from the golden blonde hair and placed the cap on her own head with a smirk. She then reached over to the sweet freckled face before her and undid the tie that was holding the long blonde hair in place.

Julia ran her fingers through Tamara's golden hair as she leaned closer to the smaller woman to slip the black blazer down her shoulders. Green eyes followed her every movement as the garment was removed. Tamara reached up to remove her thin black tie when larger hands halted her movement. Julia took over and gently pulled the tie open from its knot.

"So beautiful," Julia admitted honestly as she slipped the tie from around the smaller woman's neck. Tamara tilted her head bashfully and averted her gaze. Julia tucked two fingers under her chin and lifted her gaze up until the blue and green clashed in a smoky haze.

The rain fell harder, beating a steady rhythm on the roof of the limo. The sound matched the beating of Julia's heart. She unbuttoned the white oxford shirt and opened it slowly to reveal Tamara's well-toned body. She slipped the cotton shirt off and dropped it on the floor with the other remnants. Julia trailed a path with the tips of her fingers down from Tamara's neck to cup her breasts.

She ran her palms over them; her body ignited further as she felt two nipples harden simultaneously from her touch. Her touch then drifted downward pausing briefly on the mole that was on the younger woman's firm abs. She felt Tamara's touch on her shoulders. She swallowed hard as she felt herself being drawn in. Instinctively their eyes locked as faces drew closer to allow soft sweet lips to brush together.

They melted into one another, their passion deepening as hands searched, driven by the need to touch. The kiss ended as sweetly as it began. Julia smiled as she watched Tamara remove her own bra. Julia leaned back and watched Tamara shed the rest of her clothing. The sight of the younger woman's naked body moving towards her caused Julia to whimper.

Tamara pressed her body against Julia's almost naked form. They kissed again, without gentleness or sweetness. This kiss was formed out of raw passion and desire. Julia's senses reeled as Tamara's hands roamed her body. Tamara's mouth broke free from the kiss and captured Julia's breast. Tasting and teasing with her teeth and tongue, the sensation caused Julia's body to arch in response. Tamara pressed against her tightly as she treated her other breast to the same attention.

Thighs opened as Tamara kissed her way down the taller woman's body. Her hands eagerly pulled down Julia's underwear, removing the last barrier between them. Julia's arousal was all consuming as she felt passionate kisses and little nips. Tamara's long blonde hair tickled her thighs. She needed this woman. Tamara didn't need to hear the words but Julia knew her eyes conveyed the message.

Tamara lowered herself as Julia opened her thighs. Tamara's tongue tasted the taller woman as Julia wrapped her long legs around Tamara's shoulders. Julia felt a rush as she felt Tamara's tongue enter her. Unaware of what she was doing, she arched her back and thrust her hips as her hands pressed Tamara into her wetness. Her body seemed to be begging and pleading for Tamara take all she had to offer. Tamara eagerly complied. Julia found herself screaming out wildly as she climaxed quickly.

Julia collapsed in a heap as Tamara rested her head on her thigh. Time passed as the two simply rested peacefully.

PART THREE

As Julia looked down at her naked body, she smiled as she drank in the vision of long blonde hair draped over her torso. A pair of emerald eyes twinkled up at her. Smiling, she offered her hand to the young driver who smiled in return as she lifted her body. Julia gathered Tamara into a tender embrace. Julia felt content as Tamara traced her nipple. The gentle musing renewed her desire. Julia kissed the top of Tamara's head sweetly.

Julia lifted her body slightly holding Tamara as she moved. Tamara lifted her eyes to meet Julia's lustful gaze with equal intensity. Julia leaned forward, drawn to Tamara's lips like a moth to a flame. Lips melted together; each parting to invite the other in for exploration. Tongues danced together as bodies pressed together tightly. Moaning deeply, Julia cupped Tamara's backside to pull the woman closer. Tamara opened herself as their passions ignited again. Grinding against one another, Tamara straddled Julia's lap as she pressed the taller woman into the leather seat.

Julia growled deeply as she tore her mouth away from Tamara. "Turn around," Julia instructed her firmly. Panting heavily, Tamara complied. Julia opened her thighs as Tamara shifted position. She engulfed the younger woman who was now sitting on her lap with her back to her. Julia cupped Tamara's breasts roughly as she nudged the blonde's thighs apart.

Julia thought she would explode when she felt Tamara's backside grinding into her wetness. "I want you," Julia hissed hotly in Tamara's ear. Tamara moaned deeply as her grinding increased; there was no misunderstanding the young woman's desire. Julia continued to tease one of Tamara's nipples. Arching her hips, she pressed her wetness deeper into Tamara's smooth flesh. Her other hand felt it's way down the front of Tamara's stomach which glistened with a thick sheen of sweat.

Her fingers teased the golden curls. Julia's grinding increased as she felt the dampness. Tamara opened herself further as Julia's strong fingers reached further down. Tamara's passionate wetness flowed freely as Julia's fingers spread to feel her lips. Her thumb grazed over Tamara's throbbing clit. She could feel the smaller woman shivering as she began to grind harder, almost bucking against Julia's wetness. Julia couldn't hold back any longer. She entered Tamara, plunging two fingers deeply inside of her.

Their actions became electric as their rhythmic movements exploded in a frenzy. Tamara was begging for Julia to take her harder as the older woman gasped out for her to climax. "That's it baby . . . ," Julia encouraged,". . . . I want to feel you explode." Julia felt the walls tighten around her fingers as she slid them in and out of Tamara. Her pace increased as Tamara arched back, her thighs trembling, as she cried out wildly in her climax. Julia's fingers remained deep inside of Tamara's center as she continued to grind against her.

Tamara climaxed repeatedly as Julia continued to pleasure her until Julia exploded against her firm backside. Collapsing once again, they remained in the same position as spasms danced through their bodies.

Once they managed to regain their ability to breath normally, the two dressed. Neither spoke to the other. Shyly they avoided eye contact. Julia sipped a bottle of water contentedly as Tamara drove her to the hotel. The limo pulled up in front of the Parker House. Julia remained seated until Tamara unloaded her luggage and opened the door for her.

Julia stepped out of the vehicle as Tamara held the door open. Turning to the smaller woman, she smiled broadly. "If you don't mind, I'd like to request you as my driver for the extent of my visit," Julia said hopefully.

Tamara smiled broadly and simply nodded her acceptance. "I'll see you in the morning then."

Julia's smile grew as she handed a tip to the smaller woman. Tamara's smile quickly vanished. Julia gave her a questioning look as Tamara's expression turned grim. The doorman opened the door and Julia walked into the hotel. It wasn't until she stepped into the lobby that she had realized what she had done.

Julia spun around quickly. Her heart sank when she found the black limo and Tamara were gone.

The next day she wasn't surprised when a different driver greeted her. The events normally wouldn't have caused Julia to think twice. Going against her distant nature, she found herself calling the car service only to find that Tamara had been terminated after refusing to drive Julia. Upset by the news, she spent her free time trying to convince Tamara's employer to take the young college student back. Her efforts were useless and she feared that she had revealed to much to the younger woman's ex-employer.

When she flew home she accepted that she would never see Tamara again. After all it was just one of those things. But over the next few years, she did find herself thinking about a certain green-eyed blonde.

THE END

Order These Great Books Directly From Limitless, Dare 2 Dream Publishing

The Amazon Queen by L M Townsend	20.00	
Define Destiny by J M Dragon	20.00	
Desert Hawk,revised by Katherine E. Standelll	18.00	
Golden Gate by Erin Jennifer Mar	18.00	
The Brass Ring By Mavis Applewater	18.00	
Haunting Shadows by J M Dragon	18.00	
Spirit Harvest by Trish Shields	15.00	
PWP: Plot? What Plot? by Mavis Applewater	18.00	
Up The River-out of print ...While supplies last... by Sam Ruskin	15.00	
Memories Kill By S. B. Zarben	20.00	
Fatal Impressions by Jeanne Foguth	12.00	
	Total	

South Carolina residents add 5% sales tax.
Domestic shipping is $3.50 per book

Watch for more and upcoming titles:

Visit our website at: **http://limitlessd2d.net**

Please mail your orders with a check or money order to:

Limitless, Dare 2 Dream Publishing
100 Pin Oak Ct.
Lexington, SC 29073

Please make checks or money orders payable to: Limitless.

I

Order More Great Books Directly From Limitless, Dare 2 Dream Publishing

Title	Price	Note
Daughters of Artemis by L M Townsend	18.00	
Connecting Hearts By Val Brown and MJ Walker	18.00	
Mysti: Mistress of Dreams By Sam Ruskin	18.00	
Family Connections By Val Brown & MJ Walker	18.00	Sequel to Connecting Hearts
A Thousand Shades of Feeling by Carolyn McBride	18.00	
The Amazon Nation By Carla Osborne	18.00	
Poetry from the Featherbed By pinfeather	18.00	
Encounters, Book I By Anne Azel	10.00	Printer Error
Encounters, Book II By Anne Azel	10.00	Printer Error
Return of the Warrior By Katherine E. Standell	20.00	Sequel to Desert Hawk
Deadly Rumors by Jeanne Foguth	10.00	
	Total	

South Carolina residents add 5% sales tax.
Domestic shipping is $3.50 per book

Watch for these and more upcoming titles:
Visit our website at: http://limitlessd2d.net
Please mail your orders with a check or money order to:

**Limitless, Dare 2 Dream Publishing
100 Pin Oak Ct.
Lexington, SC 29073**

Please make checks or money orders payable to: Limitless.

The Bite	Morning Coffee	Always Forever	While You Sleep	Claire
Mine	Bubblebath	Loved	Female Beauty	All For You

	Together	My Love
Mirror		By My Side
	Your Love	
Perfection	With You	Your Eyes
		Mmmmm
Think of You		

Unless otherwise specified the cards will come blank, with no printing inside. You may, however, request something be printed inside at no extra cost.

Personalizing the cards will be done upon request or you may choose to have a pre-determined text printed.

- Photo Cards are $5.00 each US funds or $4.00 each when purchased in lots of 10 or more. Shipping is $.75 per card within the continental US Shipping outside the United States will be determined on an individual basis so that we may charge you only the actual shipping cost. At Dare 2 Dream you will never be charged a handling fee.

- Post Cards are $3.50 each US funds or $3.00 each when purchased in lots of 10 or more. Shipping is $.50 per card within the continental US For shipping outside the United States, see photo cards.

- 8 X 10 Photos of the images are available in glossy or matte finish for $8.00 each US funds Shipping is $1.50 per print within the continental United States For shipping outside the United States, see photo cards.

South Carolina residents add 5% sales tax.

Learn more about the photographer and the Gallery de Souza

Visit our website at: http://limitlessd2d.net/index.html

Please mail your orders with a check or money order to:

Limitless Corporation, Dare 2 Dream Publications
100 Pin Oak Ct.
Lexington, SC 29073-7911

Please make checks or money orders payable to: Limitless.

Printed in the United States
16519LVS00002B/194